A si

Tich wriggled out from the front end and then we three made it one by one and crouched on the lee side of the Cruiser from the incredible venom of that Spandau. Frankly, I felt like weeping. So near and yet so far. There I was kneeling beside Morris as if in church. Smoke was choking us. Any moment we were going to brew. I could see orange flames in the radiator flanges. Not much longer before the ammo bins would catch and the whole thing go up in a roar, chucking debris high in the sky, and us with it. I saw a glitter on the distant hills, like a sword swung at sunset. Then a smashing sound. The Cruiser yawed towards us, with a screech. The shot had careened off the front plating somewhere. We were going to brew. Tanks did it in diverse ways. I'd seen one Mark III near Hamman-Lif go up, its turret wrenched off it like a champagne cork and tossed to the sands beyond. But to run for it in this enfilade fire meant certain death …

Also by Geoffrey Wagner in Sphere Books:

THE SANDS OF VALOUR

The Killing Time

GEOFFREY WAGNER

SPHERE BOOKS LIMITED
30-32 Gray's Inn Road, London WC1X 8JL

First published in Great Britain by
Sphere Books Ltd 1981

TRADE
MARK

Photoset in Plantin

Printed and bound in Great Britain by
Cox & Wyman Ltd, Reading

'Courage is not simply *one* of the virtues but the form of every virtue at the testing point, which means at the point of highest reality.'

C. S. Lewis

THIS BOOK IS DEDICATED TO
THE MEMORY OF MY FATHER-IN-LAW

General Langley Browning, CB, OBE, MC, Italian Croce di Guerra 1914 with Clasp, Two Medals – Northwest Frontier of India, American Legion of Merit, Degree of Commander, Knight Grand Cross of the Crown of Italy, Knight of the Grand Cross of Malta, Commander-in-Chief MMIA (Military Mission to the Italian Army) at the time this story took place, Irish gunner and good soldier.

Also to a host of other fine soldiers of the time like John Noakes, Colonel Simmons (who ran Sardinia single-handed when the author was himself ADC No. 1 District-Sicily to General Heydemann), General Clayton P. Kerr, last sighted in Scarsdale, N.Y., 'Toby' Bauman, Dick Southby, William Warren (to be, by coincidence, a near neighbour as Dean of the Columbia Law School), and many others, both American and English.

G.W.

1

That January it was cold in the valley and the mortar bursts broke clear on a ground frosted to iron. The shell fragments clanged and splintered. It was before the infantry had advanced the length of the Garigliano, before the first big storms had broken and turned the fallow Italian fields into lakes of mud. We in tanks could still move. Our crews did so with chapped hands and frozen ears though we all wore balaclavas of thick wool over our pinched faces. Some of us sported odd decorated scarves which we had bought, or flogged, from the bazaars of Africa. There was a thin frieze of figures in black on those barren hillsides. They moved mutely between broken houses and low cow barns and as we passed them there was not much love lost on either side.

The earth was dead. The Gustav Line was holding firm. So they said, though Divisional intelligence seemed to consist in those days of a lot of bullshit orders about how to blanco our webbing and the like. The Liri plain had not then been opened. This was no fighting ground for tanks. The Boche had built themselves positions we had come to expect of them, precision-sighted in the mountains, mathematically correct for killing, all the way to Rome. The banks of the rivers had been sewn with non-magnetic mines which, at that time, it was almost impossible to detect. You set off a mine walking a few yards from your tank. It had happened to one of our young ensigns only the other day. He was one of a new draft we had been sent. Fresh from the Training Battalion, and Brasso order at Esher, they had stared at us dishevelled monks aghast. We did look weird. Most of us hadn't washed in two weeks.

Those pencil mines we all dreaded. They burst knee-height and nearly always got you in the groin. At Bir-Hakeim I had heard it, and I had heard it at Hamman-Lif. Dust, powder smoke, a man on his back looking up with panic in his eyes – *Did it get me there, sir?* At Sousse I had returned to a tented hospital where many of our men had been taken and met a nurse from Surrey running with ecstatic eyes to an older woman in white – *Matron, Matron, Patterson's had an erection.* Patterson was lucky.

And we had heard, in the gun-hot gulf of our Cruisers, a voice on our sets telling us from Chequers that Italy was 'the soft underbelly of the Axis'. And we had heard that Lady Astor had referred to those of us privileged to be in the CMF, or Central Mediterranean Forces, as D-Day dodgers; our tracks rumbled into laager and a song used to go over our Tannoy mikes after that –

We're the D-Day Dodgers, out in Italy –
Always on the vino, always on the spree.
  8th-Army scroungers and their tanks,
  We live it up – among the Yanks.
We're just the D-Day Dodgers, way out in Italee.

My fellows would join in and I would join in and sometimes we'd sing it to 'Lili Marlene' and sometimes to another tune I didn't know at first but I soon caught. A bit like the Eton boating song, really. It was only later my driver Tich, an aged Dickensian imp out of Liverpool who had joined us at Wadi Maktilla, told me it was the 'Internationale'.

We landed at Salerno, a holiday with pay;
The Jerries brought the bands out to greet us on the way,
  Showed us the sights and gave us tea.
  We all sang songs, the beer was free,
To welcome D-Day Dodgers to sunny Italee.

So it was cold on those hills and on the plain where before the war they grew tobacco. A tough time, I suppose, grey, with thin rain mixed with snow. A white time to come, when in fact the infantry patrols would go forward in white clothing, like house painters. We took turns to sleep on our engines and shared the warmth of blankets heated that way. We did not sleep on the ground beneath our tanks. A crew had done that once, and once only, under a Matilda; they had woken up when it rained, a long way from their squadron, to find themselves slowly sinking into soft earth. Not one had escaped. An untidy death. It didn't do to think about it, really.

It was before Anzio, it was before the fall of Monte Cassino. Everyone was waiting for the big breach in the German defences. According to the pundits in the Palace of Caserta this would allow the tanks to swan out in the low country, north of the rivers. Bailey bridges would take us over. That was the theory. Our squadron had been up as far as Castelforte already, and we had also come back. The Boche had left radio transmitters in that god-forsaken village and our instruments could detect them. I had been party to a particularly unpleasant search of two houses there, really no more than cattle byres, with the Eyties living with their mules and goats about them, and the sooner I forget it the better. I've been having these headaches ever since Salerno. I slept with my crew in a wood there. Well away from the Mark V. Awoke in the night to hear someone muttering and thrusting in the brush about. German voices. We did nothing. Then the sputter of a motor-bike combination gunning off.

No, we who had fought in North Africa knew the story. We knew that the Boche held to the last moment. Then, if your determination bettered his (and it didn't always happen, my God), he drew back quickly. With agility, you could say, as at Salerno where they had even rehearsed the possible landing, Godammit! And so a new front would reform like jelly, or glue, except that it was twice as tough as either, being made of tempered German steel, the kind they forged thumbscrews out of, for the concentration camps, and put the maker's name on, too. And so the soft underbelly of the Axis would tighten a notch harder. We had invested Cassino village itself – Guards units were there in the cellars with their Signals platoons in troglodyte communication – but the heights were still well held. Two thousand tons of explosive had been hailed on those Germans, without particular effect. Most of it was mortar stuff, and nearly all of it had gone down the other side, to decimate a few unsuspecting and hungry cattle. Lean cows rested on their backs with their feet straight in the air.

The thing was, we who had been through North Africa had been in a sort of way *displaced*. We knew the jerry. I won't say that knowledge was affection; but it was kind of communication. Otherwise, there were just the wogs. Jerry was systematic. If he decided to draw back, he did so, quickly. No stigma attached. I admired that. Well, our job would be to engage, read that decision, try to cut off his retreat. Sometimes it succeeded, sometimes it didn't. It depended on the ammo coming up. Six-pounder rounds got the precedence but couldn't do much unless you got close. In Africa, in the so-called Benghazi Stakes, swanning hither and thither in the blue, we had been individuals. Usually the squadron was our largest unit. Any order over Brigade level we viewed with a certain scepticism. The wog called our enemy the Chleuh. We adopted the name.

Meanwhile, none of us had forgotten Salerno. What a fucking finish to a so-called amphibious landing! First, we had been detailed to land on the tiny island of Pantellaria, the first such attempt by the Allies in the war. A piece of cake, they said. We rehearsed it on Cape Bon. I saw the maps. The Chleuh could have held it till kingdom come, so far as any tank commander could see. One short beach and that was all. But the Chleuh had pulled out leaving an Eytie Commandant who had insisted on taking his ceremonial sword into captivity. Brigade had agreed. So it was those days.

But Salerno had been a killing ground. Disgustingly unorganized, anarchic, tanks brewed without order, men maimed, dying in absurd postures, totally undignified, horrible. I had myself received a completely unexpected and unasked-for fragment of mortar fire just under the right knee. Only a morsel, yet hot and hurtful. An axe stroke in the forest.

They had taken me back to a C.C.S., or Casualty Clearing Station, put on a field dressing, and later I'd learnt that nothing was broken. The stuff kept on rotting out, in calluses, thereafter. I even grew attached to the wound. But my loader was killed – *and on the ground, too.* That was the fuck of it. The ultimate indignity. Like Tom Norcombe, shot squatting, while he shat. The rest of the crew had been lucky. We knew each other. That's all I can say. That's all anyone can say. And we know the Hun. A ridiculously methodical animal, but in his way not unlikable.

Two weeks later I was sitting on a bank of what had been grass chatting with a young officer in the Oxs and Bucks. We had been sent up to cover his advance. He was in battledress but pleasantly nomad, like ourselves, with a tatty ginger beard and under it a scarf that reminded me more of the Burlington Arcade than the blistered heel of Italy. He was waiting to ... go in.

I remember his languid ease, as we talked in undertones. He had come from Shropshire, hunted the fox, saw the ground ahead of us (pluming distantly with dark smoke) just as we did. Cut and run. Cover. He was a young man, but he liked killing things. He explained to me a theory by which (he said) when he went to Saint Peter's Gate all the grouse and hare and mallard and teal he had shot on the wet Shropshire wolds would advance, not to demand his death, but to intercede for him; he had saved them, by sudden shot, from lingering starvation in painful old age, from the tooth of the ferret and vixen ... It was then we saw the Hampdens returning from their mission, placid whales in a grey sky.

Inside them, we reminisced, would be navigators and pilots and turret gunners who would be sitting in Manetta's or one of the other black-market bars in Naples in a few hours' time, their RAF blue well-ironed. We felt no envy. They were poor bastards, too. So were the Boche.

My new-found friend pointed out to me a distant hillock from which at six a.m. each morning a German infantry man mortared them. Come rain, come shine. Inevitable as daylight and night. So, he had duly reported to the Gunners in rear and the position had been strafed.

The next morning, precisely at six a.m., a new German soldier with a new mortar had slipped into the hole where his predecessor had been buried forever, and had recommenced his bombardment. He, in turn, had been swept off the face of the earth by the high explosive of His Majesty's Central Mediterranean Forces.

But four days later another soldier had appeared in the dawn, patient in his helmet, and had placed his mortar near where the corpse of the other was still lying. Some order had gone out, it was plain. Since it had not been countermanded, it would be followed. That man was one with us. He too was killed. It was very like the screens of anti-tank guns Rommel had deployed in the desert. He never made a forward movement of his tanks without them and towards the end, when he was in full retreat, those unprotected trailers had hindered rather than helped him. But one knew the mentality. Rex Davidson's was of the same order.

Those anti-tank guns! What guns! A G3 Intelligence type had told us (information not to be transmitted to our men, of course, all of whom were fully in possession of it) that the Chleuh had known about Salerno weeks in advance. Hence they had even had time for tactical exercises on the landing ground. Our tanks had been hit rolling off the transports, the infantry as they ploughed out the LCI's on the beach. The Boche eighty-eights had as always been dug in well-nigh impregnably, hitting us right left and centre. There is nothing so demoralizing as being hit by an invisible enemy. Anyone in tanks knows that.

After Africa what could we say? We hated this assignment from the start, somehow. I have to be honest about that. Something came apart in us. There just wasn't the same camaraderie. And all those foreign units about. Why, you could even pick up Polish on your set. A terrible confusion reigned from the first day we landed, dead men of diverse types lying all over. In the confusion we had buried anything dead. Overhead the few Spitfires we could see, short of fuel, always seemed to be biting their own tails.

Partly thanks to all this, and a hopeless mess-up on the net (to which the inconsolable shape of my new loader-operator beneath me gave witness), our squadron was chiefly communicating via the melodramatic signals of hand from Rex's turret, its aerial twice shot away. He it was who led us southwards (if that was indeed the direction), out of the town itself, southwards out of chaos, and this had once more saved us. Rex Davidson, ex-Malayan rubber planter, rugger player, vagabond, Argentine polo player, had grown something instinctive inside him about tanks. Our present specimen was the Cruiser Mark V, fan-cooled, but Rex had graduated out of the little sardine cans of the Western Desert, the rickety A6's and A10's, with their pea-shooter guns and water-supplied radiators. Supplied, that is, when a Messerschmidt didn't decide to take a run down the convoy bringing up the flimsy *Safiyha* cans and puncture them to bits. Rex used to maintain that no one was a desert rat unless he'd drunk a pint of tea made with radiator water. And in some of that char you could have stood a spoon.

A rough assignment, indeed. Within an hour of embarkation I saw six of our tanks brewed on that Salerno beach. All very precise, as a matter of fact. Something we again understood. A man I had been at school with leapt goggled from his turret and writhed in the ground as if stricken with electric shock. Two had followed him. Then a genie's wand had drawn black smoke from the dying tank's depths and it had silently brewed. Thirty yards away another of ours had burst grotesquely, in a roar that made us duck; I saw the entire turret wrenched off and then, clinging to my mates, heard the clanging of debris as a giant beat upon our iron sides. When I looked up, the Corp who delivered our mail was turning silently in circles in pools of burning oil.

No doubt about it, the eighty-eight was our mortal enemy in those days. It had been so for some time. Rex himself was a 'four-year man'. That is, he was an original. He had been sent out in our Second Battalion before the war. A Cairo Cavalry type. There were few of those left in the Regiment by now, nor in the Brigade. Not so many in the Eighth Army itself, either. He was a D-Day dodger now, all right.

My gunner, clear of the breech recoil, hunched into his scope, sang it. My loader, checking the board bins with absent, abstinent fingers, joined in:

Naples and Cassino were taken in our stride,
We didn't go to fight there – we went there for the ride.
   Rapido and Sangro were simply names,
   We only went to look for dames –
The artful D-Day Dodgers, way out in Italee.

It was Rex who had shown me my first eighty-eight after I had joined in that draft which went round the Cape to Port Teufig. A yelping of locked tracks at the gouret and Rex had waved us down. The wreck of an old A6 was there, its glass vision blocks shattered as by spiteful schoolkids (bed looting, maybe?) – then the practical, guileless shape of the German gun pointing insanely at the sky, as though to challenge God Himself. A soulless metal lance wrenched off its carriage, now a stricken anvil. Impotent. Ghastly. It was so excessively made for death.

Rex had let us new men look at it, let it sink into our hearts, and then had explained that this admirable weapon had originated as an anti-aircraft arm. The story was that a Boche ack-ack battery had been close to overrun near Arras, or Verdun (the locations varied), in 1940 and not knowing what to do had simply tipped up the monstrosity horizontally, against the few French tanks attacking them. The successful result had been reported with celerity to Berlin. I remember asking Rex why our War House hadn't done the same thing, with our rapid-firing anti-aircraft Bofors, but he had simply shrugged expressively with those sloping shoulders of his, and given a shake of his great leonine head, in the tousled hair of which a filthy beret lay somewhat embedded. I believe we all felt secure in a sense that Whitehall didn't understand. And wouldn't understand.

In short, the story that follows is that of a man of my own race and my own country whom I met in artificial circumstances (if war can be said to be unusual among humans) in a white-calcined escarpment in the south of Libya. I had never met him before and I only knew him for a short time, but you will have to judge of the influence of his actions upon me. I suppose I was a typical young officer of the time, callow, eager, increasingly afraid at every new Thor-like hammer on the side of my tank or the splitting of sky about it. In short, I was a young animal. Just out of Oxford I had heard the declaration of war over the (then illegal) radio in a small T-type MG sportster owned by a Chinese Davis Cup tennis player of the time called Kho Sin Kee who had just roundly defeated me at Eastbourne. The sirens had sounded hours later, but nothing much had come over. I didn't understand the reasons for the war. Rex taught me everything.

At that time he was a Captain in command of the Recce Group. God knows what age he was. Probably far too old to join up, if he had had to. But in the Droghedas promotion came slowly. It was not particularly desired. We had a saying, 'The higher a monkey climbs, the more you see of his backside.' It was a fact. There was a tradition that we always addressed Majors by their first names in the mess, you didn't call them *Sir* as in 'charlie' outfits. Thus I addressed whiskery old Boer War veterans as 'Bones' and 'Wally' and the like. They seemed to tolerate it. Rex liked the reconnaisance group since it had such liberty of action. We could swan all over the place, right into the blue, laager here and there, and then off to his call the next morning. Clean days all, until the killing.

He was squatting over a tattered map in a wadi when I first saw him, wearing a pair of threadbare corduroy pants and an old cricket cardigan. I remember noting that its faded colours were those of the *I Zingari*, which club being translated is *The Wanderers.* He was one. He seemed entirely united with the gunners and loaders and drivers who crouched about him, consulting them rather than giving orders. That was what I noticed first, for the informality in forward troops was always impressive to those of us who had come out from bashing parade grounds in spit-'an'-polish units.

It was a virile, energetic profile, teak-tanned like those around, but with a great predatory hawklike nose and thick unwaxed moustaches of the darkest brown. I had heard about him since he had just added a Bar to his Military Cross, quite an achievement in our lot. Also he had a reputation (back in Cairo, back in the Gezira) of knowing many languages and many women, and directly I saw him I felt that his head, though distinctly original, had something human in it. I saluted, and he grinned. A leer, more than anything. As if to say: *who the devil are you, invading my solitude?* Campbell, Stirling and the others were of the same order.

The story had it that, in difficulty, mortal difficulty, near Bir Berraneb, he had had not one tank, but two shot from under him, all his crew killed and himself hit in the head. Bleeding profusely, and heavily under fire, he had run to and requisitioned a scout car for support. It hadn't been able to start. But a Bren-gun carrier, driven by a Glaswegian Scot, had, and the two of them had scoured the almost snow-white desert for succour until they had run into another regiment that had refused to help. Rex simply thundered on the side of a Honey (as it had been at the time) with the butt of an old Lee-Enfield and signalled peremptorily to it to follow. A whole squadron had turned off to assist him.

Apparently he had always had this authoritarian air, had been born with majesty, as it were. You felt it to look at him, rapscallion though he appeared. Allure. There were stories that he had even met Churchill during one of the latter's brief visits to Egypt and rather alarmed the official entourage with his independence. He looked like a tyke of perhaps sixty who ought to have been pruning rose-beds in Kent. But somehow you didn't see him in a city. Churchill's comment to a young officer in Alex – 'I'll find some sand for those desert boots of yours, m'boy' – was said to have been Rex's, originally. I wouldn't have doubted it. A strange personality. In the war and of the war. When I first met him I didn't know how much I had coming to me of both.

So I remember he made me a kind of ironic bow as I saluted, stamping. His batman was in the process of extending to him a soup-spoon of oil, which Rex swallowed through his horse-hair moustaches like some baby. I learnt shortly thereafter that the man suffered from haemorrhoids, badly, and that each time a Quartermaster Store came up he provisioned himself with numerous cans of mineral oil. These he carried, along with the tools, in the bins on the tank's flank, under some protective tracking. The scalding metal heated that oil, but Rex rarely failed to drink it – nor share it with another, similarly afflicted. And if the chemical supply failed, why then a dose of engine oil didn't hurt either, filtered through holed cans full of clear Libyan stones.

So he nodded and beckoned and drew me to the map and gave me our bearings and the task for the morrow. He squatted painfully, awkwardly for such a big man, a pair of bandaged pince-nez lodged on that bony nose, in a way that somehow diminished him. The men listened to him like a Buddha.

What follows is the history of this person under whom I served and whom I got to know as a *good soldier*.

Thinking it over, it is a sad story but, after all, I am not sure. All the pieces are by no means in place yet in my mind. The headaches started, and then those jerks in my sleep. Muscular fatigue, the MO said. Perhaps I'm still too close to everything Rex signified. That's what they tell me, at least. And still they encourage me to write. Every morning this empty lined page staring me in the face. It's like a desolation, really. What's wrong? All I've been is a junior tank commander, Cruiser Mark V's, Rolls Royce engines, driver in front, gunner, loader/operator beside me. People to kill outside. This is what I was licensed by my country to do.

But I am worried. The winter is coming on again. This is no dream. (And yet they want to know my dreams!) I have a feeling of losing some sense of existence. When Rex is there, it's all right. For that reason I keep this notebook to myself, in the cold and the north, and try to reconstitute as clearly as possible – and it isn't easy – these scratches in the mike on my ear, the customary bleak crackle of the set cutting in, and the men waiting for me below, their heads in black berets, on an icy morning of January 1944, in Italy, the tank itself covered with netting and branches and brush entwined in the netting.

'Hel-lo ABSALOM, SPIRAL calling. You are to return to FST figures six-seven-oh-three. Open. Force of enemy reporting moving westwards north of Castelforte. Avoid all contact. Over.'

I had just become twenty-two years old and I didn't want to die.

2

'Driver! Advance!'

The familiar rattle of the tracks on stony soil sent a shudder up my spine. Once more we were going forward.

'Turret down behind that ridge. Loader, both guns. All the ammo ready.'

Once more I was busy with the old orders. Tossing in their seats beneath me the two men moved automatically, the loader giving his gun-ready tap to his comrade. I lifted my binoculars. They seemed charged with memories. How much heat and death had washed across their lenses? But these were different ways, and other mountains. I was less sure here, than under that brazen bowl of African sky to which we had grown accustomed. To my left I saw Rex's tank bucketing forward to get hull down, saw him adjust the other headphones over his beretless, shaggy head. I picked mine up, too.

'Hel-lo, ROUNDER. Hel-lo, ROUNDER. HECTOR calling, HECTOR calling. Am in range of enemy column estimate figures two-oh transport moving northwards very soft-skinned . . .'

It sounded so simple the calm way Rex said it. He might have been in some club, instead of in that tank of his he called the Ironmaster. And the voice came back equally slowly, almost over-deliberate, from another lazily rocking armchair on the scarp. I knew it for that of Jumbo Richely, our commanding officer.

'Hallo, HECTOR. ROUNDER answering. Maintain your position. Maintain your position. All tanks to return to FST figures six-seven-oh-three. On my order. Off to you.'

'. . . am well in range of moving figures seven zero zero to immediate front. Repeat column enemy transport . . .'

Rex's interruption plucked at my ears and I tensed. Only I, in my tank, was hearing him. Gunner and loader waited patiently in the vicinity of my shins. In the driver's seat forward of us all huddled Tich, who had been a somewhat unsuccessful jockey in peacetime. We picked small men for his spot. In many ways he was the most important person on board. We all relied on the driver. And Tich, tiny, bent and fair-haired, had been with us since Kasserine. I did not want my excitement to communicate as I dropped the wireless mike and picked up my Tannoy.

'Driver! Hull down behind that bank ahead.'

The tank rumbled forward. I put on the other set.

'. . . estimate figures two-oh vehicles lightly protected,' Rex was going on.

Then Jumbo's voice: 'Hel-lo, HECTOR. Hel-lo, HECTOR. What is this you are saying? Why are you not conforming? Now hello, all stations HECTOR. You will return on bearing figures one fo-uh degrees. One fo-uh. A and B squadrons will maintain normal positions ahead of me. Avoid all contact, enemy forces reported. Conserve your ammunition. Over.'

There was the usual buzzing and bleeping, that indefinable hum of a set sending, then Rex's voice in exasperation: 'But, sir, I've got . . . they're on a plate . . .'

'Well hello, HECTOR THREE. You have heard our orders. Out.'

On a plate, indeed. I could see them now, using the periscope almost buried in ferns and brush. We were elevated in a short ravine, what we had called in Africa a wadi. Looking down northwards we dominated the fields and the plain. Two sad white roads trickled through this arid country. There were some tumble-down farms, a few cypresses straight as sentinels and then the next line of hills held by the Hun. For some time it had been tacitly admitted that this ground was theirs. As far as I was concerned, they could keep it. A Boche convoy was moving slowly across the northern end of that frosted plain, escorted by no more than a couple of Mark III's. It was indeed a heaven-sent piece of cake. Scout car in front, then a line of gun-carriers. I could even spot men unsuspectingly riding the roofs of some of the cabs. The ground was dotted with those peculiarly Italian hayricks, squat and round.

Looking along the ridge I could just see Rex's shaggy head over the forest of fern with which they had camouflaged his turret. He seemed to be beating the air angrily. Then he ripped off his head-set and I knew what he was going to do. We had been put on a new frequency two days before, and it was weakish. I spoke into my Tannoy.

'Gunner! Get ready!'

The man in the leather jerkin to my left beneath me moved instinctively in his seat, gluing his eye to the rubber ring of the scope sight. He knew now. He saw. No one in my troop had to be told. It was a good feeling. The gunner's name was Morris and he was by far the finest shot I'd ever had.

Each man had his own task, not only about the tank, but outside it. To Tich was delegated not merely the maintenance of the engines but also the preparation of our meals. He had in fact just been brewing breakfast on a primus when the order to mount had come. Squatting on groundsheets in the lee of our tank we had sipped scalding tea out of one half of our mess tins, greasy M. & V. (meat and veg) in the other. By a bit of luck that day we'd been blessed with a loaf of the excellent black bread jerry carried.

'Shit!' said Whitey as he heard the crackle of the set.

'You only have to start a brew, sir, and it's bound to 'appen.' Tich slopped his tea down like a dog.

'Where the hell's Morris?' I asked. Already the other tanks were revving up around us.

'I think he took the spade, sir.'

'Well, start up,' I told Tich. 'That'll fetch him.'

It always did. Poor Morris came at the double, carrying his spade, doing up his trousers and grinning awkwardly.

'You wouldn't want me to 'ave an 'orrible accident in the turret, now would you, sir?' he grinned at me.

'Come on, quick!'

There was the clatter of mess-tins as we packed up, the thunderous roar of the engines as Tich pressed his button in front. Familiar sounds, all. We clambered onto them and dropped in one by one. First Morris, then Whitey, then me. Whitey's first job was to stack the spare rounds ready, check the belt feeding into the Beza.

By this time I never had to tell these men what to do. Under Rex's leadership we had become a single organism, a precision instrument. Above all, it was a manner of not becoming afraid. A protection, if you will. We were all busy, in a sense, helping each other. There was always plenty to do when starting off on a swan like this. Each one of us shared with the others. Each command I gave was an extension of my nervous system, brain, belly, eyes, ears, lips.

And so I didn't even have to ask Rex's intentions. I simply followed them. There had been an intricate system of flags in the old cavalry days. These had been carried into tank warfare, when sets had gone on the blink in the western desert. But Rex had superseded even these with hand signals and, following such, we slipped over the lip of the scarp diagonally, making for the cover of the haystacks, so as to surprise and cut off the convoy ahead. My two other tanks followed me. Officially, a Recce Group had twelve tracked vehicles, but we had made the crossing with only seven and then Salerno had cut us down to four.

'Driver! Advance! Slowly as you go.' We didn't want to chuck up any dust.

'Trust old Captain D.,' said Morris without looking up from his eyepiece, but he said it with a grin.

I saw Rex's plan perfectly. We would slip down the hill to the cover of the ricks. They were made for open order. We would each keep one rick to the right, protection from the guns there might be on the mountain line eastwards. From this cover we would take the convoy. It was perfectly logical, so long as the Mark III's didn't see us first. It was getting back that worried me. Rex was a crazy bastard. But, dammit, the prey was too good to let it escape. It was some time since we'd had a chance like this, always pulling back and hunching hull down and creeping along cold lanes.

'Christ!' called Morris as we pitched forward, and his grin widened greedily.

I was abreast of Rex's tank now. It was charged like some camel. I could see all the absurd paraphernalia he ported around with him, including those cans of mineral oil. We plunged toward the hayricks. In the thin sun they carried a hirsute cover of greyish frost, each with a long stake driven through the centre. They appeared abandoned, forgotten, and I wondered what poor farmer owned them here, his beasts byred in his bedroom, no doubt. But they brought back England to me, and wet fields, and rough shooting, and plover's eggs for tea around a warm fire after.

Still, something in me had divorced myself from that and I looked across at Rex's huge head – on which he had for some reason put his beret – with what I know now was affection. His moustache bristled disdainfully. He had some regal air, appeared to be breathing deeply. You could not call any of us superstitious men but none of us denied the inward warning of the desert. I lived in this now.

A third tank aligned itself in the roughly arrowhead formation we had assumed and I saw the tanned face, dark eyes, and large ears of Edwardson. He had joined at the end of the desert fighting, just in time in fact to glean the Africa Star, the good old ham-'n'-eggs as we called the medal from its colour. Rex didn't trouble to wear his. Edwardson had lost his tank at Salerno, together with his loader, but he and the other two had virtually commandeered a Brigade headquarters tank whose gun had never been fired, driven it forward through the wood behind the beach and there, with the gunner loading himself, had taken two PZ KW IV's with it. There had been all hell to pay when he'd taken it back but our commanding officer had interceded and the thing was currently referred to Division. We hoped perpetually. He was a tall young man, thin and very correct, who had been training to be a pianist at the Royal College of Music in London before the war. Since that episode at Salerno I thought a certain sadness had crept into his eyes and he was quieter than ever. He gave me a rueful grin as I caught his eyes and then he pointed to his head and then to Rex's. I agreed.

The latter was in full form. His blue eyes seemed to shoot a last glance forward; then he tore off his beret and in a large gesture signalled to us to 'attack and follow' – in the old cavalry signal. Almost I felt I heard a *Tally-ho!*

But I was busy with business now. We were coming down from the crest at greater speed and would be spotted any moment, bouncing in the shell-holes and troughs of what must once have been a wheat-field. I slowed Tich a trifle. The convoy was moving away from us towards an old bridge. Sunlight caught the river. There was a coating of snow on those hills to our right, the ones that worried me, but I could see nothing glinting in the hard light. Fortunately the soil was chalky. We couldn't afford to be mired in mud on our retreat here. I reached my haystack first, halted with it guarding my right, and lost no time.

'Gunner! Two-pounder. Traverse right.'

Slowly the turret swung.

'More. Steady ... *on*! Nine-five-zero yards. Enemy transport. *Fire*!'

I had no more to say. Morris was me. He knew what to do. For a second I saw his dirt-encrusted fingers closing on his handgrip like a man squeezing a rotten apple in which was lodged a wasp. Then with a clang the breech retched back smoking at the explosion, yet before it had so much as reached the end of its run-out or recoil, Whitey had slid in the next round and with the mass of metal banging up again my loader gave the gunner the ritual, almost absent-minded 'gun ready' tap. The case of the old round smoked on the flooring.

'Fire again!'

Mine were the first two shots and both had scored. Morris' first had toppled a truck which lay on its side, already flaming. The second pumped wrenchingly into its engine.

But soon Rex and Edwardson were banging away and, as always when hit by tanks, the Hun column began running amok. The transport broke up wildly. Those who hadn't reached the bridge fanned out in the fields either side of the river banks for safety, lurching and bumping along. To my right now Rex's tank was bucketing like a pram in a panic as its gunner got off shots.

'Keep on with the two-pounder,' I yelled down. 'That gun-limber just behind ...'

Two spiders lay twitching in the oil slick by the first toppled truck. Others were scampering to be picked up by the dispersing vehicles. I had seen Morris' fingers slip to the Beza but we never liked machine-gunning personnel. Besides, if we could put out of action some of the heavy stuff on those transports ...

'Gunnner! Left a little ... little more. Two-pounder ...'

Then I heard it. The first time you heard that evil whiplash in the air overhead it struck sickness in your soul. They said you got used to it. I never had. Each time it sounded a little bit closer. Another rent in the air over those frozen fields told us only one thing. Eighty-eights. The Chleuh in the mountains to our right had reacted as quickly as they always did to our attack and had drawn them up on limbers. Young men from Hamburg or Frankfurt or Düsseldorf were looking at us from under forage caps with considerable attention, their crosswires closing. The hayrick beside me gave a sudden jump.

'Driver! Close down!' I called. But he didn't get my order.

I stared over at Rex. It had been imprudent, perhaps foolish, but carried out with his usual flair. The hayricks (one smoking) had given us cover and we wouldn't have to reverse to get out. We'd simply scatter and go hell for leather for the ridge. We had fallen like panthers on our prey. Half the convoy lay shattered and smoking. It was enough, surely enough. But Rex did not turn.

'Give 'em all you've got,' I shouted at Morris and this time he opened up with the Beza. A dry crackle and the spiders bounded. I hated it with all my heart. And I heard the next whipcrack of affronted air with animal fear. They were after us, all right. The shadowless squat shape of one of the Mark III's – the one not hit – nosed out to engage us frontally.

Edwardson had taken the one prowling at the rear of the column. I saw the flash of my gun, the breech beneath me bounding back releasing smoke and Whitey slipping another round in with such precision the gun slammed closed before even the 'gun ready' tap. Morris fired. I saw the slight curve of the shell and then the flash as it embedded just between turret and hull. Ordinarily, the Boche racked spare tracking there, but perhaps this small screen of Panzers hadn't bothered. Anyway, the tank brewed instantly. It was a perfect hit. I saw the commander leap out, counted two, three ... but the third figure tumbled back in the smoke, and the fourth never made it at all.

At this Rex, whose gunner had just set the tarp of a truck on fire, waved as if to say, Well done. Then he gave another wave which meant, Let's get to hell out of here.

But I waited. I had gone over the scarp first, Rex last. He was due to go before me now, Edwardson after him. His tank did not move. I heard a squeal of tracking and saw that Rex's gun was clearly aimed at the last, still untouched truck in the convoy. He had the Tannoy to his lips. But the gun didn't fire.

I remember wondering if something had stalled in his buggy. But there was his heavy head intently fixed on his evident target, while his right hand beat regularly on the turret's side with an old Italian rifle bolt he had taken to carrying about with him since Benghazi. I picked up my glasses. I saw a whole group of Boche running like hell from the tail-end of the truck, and scampering and jumping almost joyfully at their heels a tiny white fox-terrier, its scut up. One part fox-terrier, let's say, the rest Eytie mongrel. The dog was running hell for leather not wanting to be left behind. And I remembered how our fellows, too, developed affections – almost needs – for pets in the blue. Tich had kept a rabbit he had got somewhere in a port bin. It had shared our char and duff regularly thereafter till some desert cur had flushed it at night, in laager, under the stars and the moon. Tich had been inconsolable for weeks after that.

So I was watching the convoy break up like a brood of new

nuns at sight of Don Juan and wondering whether we ought to put some tracer into those oil spills to fire them and, suddenly hearing the higher rate of fire overhead which meant a Spandau or two I thought, My God, it was the waiting that did it.

Rex was waiting.

I remembered once, near Sidi Rezegh, after an engagement which had probably resembled those old naval battles of yore, actually running beside a Boche truck for about a hundred yards with my guns trained right on it. And I had seen – I had inspected – the face of the officer sitting in the cab right by the terrified driver. The face of a business-man of about forty, rather badly shaven, his grey hair close under his forage cap. And I was saying to myself, Christ I have to kill this guy. I have to riddle him with lead. We literally looked into each other's eyes in a manner I shall never forget, in a kind of mortal fraternity, I guess, then he took out his Luger and actually aimed it at our tank, holding the butt in both hands. I said 'Zero zero,' then 'Gunner! *Fire*!' thickly, and the gunner gave him both guns.

But why the hell was Rex waiting any further?

The truth was, he wasn't. Without closing down he had screeched around and was now making diagonally, giving as little vulnerable backside to the eighty-eights on the hills to our right, up back to the protection of our gulley. Edwardson had already begun to follow, manoeuvring clumsily around. The convoy lay in shambles on the bridge or about it. And at that moment Morris tapped my leg.

'Turret jammed, sir!'

I ducked full into the hull, my heart pounding, and tried a twist to the traversing layer. It wasn't that the turret had jammed, he simply wasn't getting any power from the engines. The engines had died. I yelled down to Tich through the desultory thuds going on in the air above us and he called back, 'It's the starter, sir,' but he must have shorted the switch or something because suddenly we plunged, rocking.

'Driver! Close down!' I repeated, as we ground round.

This time I heard the slam of the forward plate as Tich shut himself in. No driver liked doing that in Africa. The heat was fierce. But it was necessary for his own safety now, and ours. Tich put her to it. We began ploughing up those undulations the colour of dirty linen. Rex was way ahead by now, Edwardson too, their drivers zig-zagging to the crest not only to put off range for those gunners on the hills but to keep the thin armour at our tails at least in maximum ricochet.

I had no time to reflect further since a splash of light ahead told me that Edwardson's cruiser had been hit. It was still crabbing along to the ridge, however, and there seemed to have been no penetration. Rex vanished over the top where doubtless he would settle hull down and return fire. Edwardson was nearly there. We ourselves still had a hundred yards to go. I could see Whitey stowing shells away like fury but I wasn't risking traversing to engage some Hun I couldn't see, all I was praying was that we wouldn't break a track on this chalk and limestones hillside before making it. At that moment I heard an almost light patter on one side of the tank, a ripple that increased in fury as if we had been beaten with a giant's flail. For a second it didn't worry me, then I felt the whole animal falter and tremble. Cordite smoke filled our nostrils. My heart held.

'Driver! Full speed!'

Tich did not answer at first and the tank continued to stutter forward, as if the driver were rowing her over the ground, in gulps. Then we puttered upwards appallingly slowly.

'It's the bogie, sir,' I heard him call, wrestling with the levers.

Nothing attracts Boche fire like a stalled tank. There was pain in my throat at each flaying lash of the air above us. The eighty-eights were closing range, bracketing, as we stumbled grimly upwards. I banged down the turret flaps above my head, crouching braced on my calves against something or other as I tried to peer through the periscope. For an instant as I turned it, all I could see was another unharmed Mark III in the valley, its sprocket wheels bobbing towards us. I grabbed the Tannoy and yelled.

'For God's sake, speed up, driver!'

But we continued slowly, like a somnambulist. Maybe three miles an hour. Fire was stabbing and whistling over us from both sides now; it seemed only moments before we would be brewed like this. Whitey and Morris looked at me cautiously, sharing my fear, knowing it.

They asked no more than that I should do my duty by them.

Should we abandon tank and run for it?

Then it all happened at once.

Tich's voice came through quite clearly in my phones: 'Something stuck, sir. I can't get her out of first.'

'Try running downhill with it,' I suggested. We might just work up enough compression that way.

'No, sir, it's no good. I can't change forward at all.'

'Driver,' I said, as calmly as I could after another split of air outside, 'if you can't change forward, try shifting into reverse. We can go a damn sight faster backwards than this.'

And so it was done. I saw Tich's bony back bow forward. The tank stopped dead for a ghastly moment. It screwed round as he held to the right-hand track-locking lever. We turned. In the pause to do so I saw Rex's tank nosing inquisitively forward on the crest above us. Spandau fire was spraying all around but backing up the hill like this would at least keep our delicate engines from some of it. Then I couldn't see anything anymore. The periscope shattered in my face. We had sixty yards to go.

Tich had the tank waltzing backwards now, straight up the slope, and like the excellent trooper he was he knew enough to vary speed and direction slightly to put off Boche range.

'Judas Priest!' Whitey fanned his face.

We were all close to one another at that moment, the tank closed down and hot with powder-shot. Our dirty and ill-shaven faces could not conceal much of our emotions. These men had been through hard times with me; they had cheerfully supported hunger in the desert, excessive heat, the hammering of a determined enemy. I wondered what it was that made them hold firm. Whitey, in particular, resolutely showed disgust rather than fear. As we sat with our knees touching, waiting for it to end, I felt their courage converted into patience. It touched me, physically. But I read something else in their eyes before I properly sensed it myself.

When you're penetrated you either know nothing about it or everything about it. Boche shot had been known to cut clean through a turret, before its occupants could take proper account of what had happened. Equally, small-arms fire, entering the same, can ricochet on the slanting sides and kill all inside, even sieve their bodies several times.

So I knew something was wrong at once by their eyes. Then I sucked in smoke. We'd been hit, where I did not know, somewhere in the rear housing. The tank had stopped, dead. We were maybe forty yards from the crest. But we were going to brew. A dead tank was a sitting duck. Flames sucked in through the vents killed within seconds.

'Doesn't answer, sir,' Tich shouted. I could hear him uselessly stabbing at the starter. There was the high-pitched whine of the overhead cams, but that was all. Spandau fire was rattling all around us.

'She's brewing, sir.' Whitey. The newest.

It was enough. I made my decision. I flung open the turret flaps. Dark smoke was already pouring from our aft engine.

'Jump!' I shouted.

Tich wriggled out from the front end and then we three made it one by one and crouched on the lee side of the Cruiser from the incredible venom of that Spandau. Frankly, I felt like weeping. So near and yet so far. There I was kneeling beside Morris as if in church. I could see a sore on his calm hand on the earth. Smoke was choking us. Any moment we were going to brew. I could see orange flames in the radiator flanges. Not much longer before the ammo bins would catch and the whole thing go up in a roar, chucking debris high in the sky, and us with it. I saw a glitter on the distant hills, like a sword swung at sunset. Then a smashing sound. The Cruiser yawed towards us, with a screech. The shot had careened off the front plating somewhere. We were going to brew. Tanks did it in diverse ways. I'd seen one Mark III near Hamman-Lif go up, its turret wrenched off it like a champagne cork and tossed to the sands beyond. But to run for it in this enfilade fire meant certain death.

Whitey said: 'Don't worry, sir. Replenishment will find us another one.'

'Never was no good in second anyhow.' I saw Tich crouching beside me.

Fuck you, Rex, I was thinking, clinging to anger as a way out of terror, you got us into this, you bastard.

Then Morris shouted – 'Look, sir!'

He pointed to the rise. There, like a lumbering mastodon, a creature from other extinct ages, Rex's swathed and dented Ironmaster was coming down the ridge towards us.

'Idiot!' I yelled uselessly.

I could see the suicidal nature of the move. Riding fast down that slope the tank was exposed in all of its length, as if from above, and on top of it all the blighter hadn't even closed down his flaps. There he reared, with shaggy head and bloodshot eyes, beating away with that old rifle-boat as if egging on some old nag in a country point-to-point.

'Cor Blimey, it's the Captain!' cried Tich.

I waved Rex back. He was a perfect target even for that undamaged Panzer on the plain. We would all buy it, like this.

'Get back, you fool!' I bawled, though I knew he couldn't possibly have heard me in the din. Our own tank was burning thickly now, oily smoke reeling up the incline and perhaps providing a sort of screen which Rex was cleverly using. He rocked to a stop some ten yards to the lee of ours. In the smoke billows I saw him beckon.

'Okay, Tich,' I shouted, 'get cracking!'

He went first, the most valuable, the most trained, of us all. Tich did not hesitate. He grabbed a roll of bedding off the plating, undid a bin, took out a mess-tin, and ran for it. He jumped aboard Rex's tank and disappeared in the turret.

Morris went next, stumbling through the smoke as in a dream, and then he too was somehow or other swallowed up in that cloudy hull. Looking back at it, through the fierce whanging of light-arms lead, I saw in a break in the oil smoke that Rex had actually got out and was lounging on the gun, watching.

'Get back inside, Rex, you madman,' I shouted.

My mouth filled with smoke. I coughed once and turned to the loader-operator kneeling beside me.

'Okay, Whitey old man. It's your turn now. Your kit's with mine in front, isn't it? I'll have a shot at getting it off, don't worry. Run like Harry Blinders.'

I tapped him and he went. Then, doubling to the front of the fast brewing wreck, I tore at the corded bundle there, hearing the air crackle about me. I wrenched the great lump free, humped it on a shoulder, and pounded back through the reek. For a few moments I seemed to be marking time, making no ground, a man under water. Then I was alongside the Cruiser, which hands helped me scale.

'Driver! Full speed ahead,' I heard Rex roaring, and thought I heard some chuckle in his voice. I clung to the flaps. The old chariot lurched full tilt at the rise. A burst of m-g fire sawed strongly at the runner wheels low down and I flinched.

'You bloody ass, Rex!' I gasped, holding to my exasperation with the man as we lay over the turret together. 'Do you know what they happen to have out there?'

'Some high explosive, I'd say. Gunner, traverse a few degrees. On!'

The air glittered behind us.

'Get in your turret, Rex,' I said through my teeth to him. 'You know officers are valuable.'

The Chleuh were, indeed, picking us off in those days.

'Not', he came back – and, by God, I could see that he was smiling, 'the impression you gave out there just then.'

We gripped to the plunging tank. In the turret he had emptied to rescue us sat my two men, Morris and Whitey. But there was room for one more inside and as senior officer I wanted him to be there.

But then there was an unearthly kind of whooshing, a sort of enormous premonitory hushed rushing in the air, at the same time a fantastic grinding of tortured metal, followed by the explosion, a flat bang. The tank I had fought since Cap Bon went up in a roaring plume of smoke. With a final plunge we topped to safety over the ridge.

'Nice job, Cap'n.' Whitey grinned up from the cabin.

I got down first, my eyes congealed and running. Now it was over the imagination got to work. It was then you felt the fear. My legs were like lasagne.

'Thanks, Rex,' I said vaguely.

But when I looked up I saw him cursing on the sand shields. Strapped on the forward bins the thin cans of his blessed mineral oil had been perforated and the stuff was spewing out in runnels.

Edwardson was running anxiously up. When he saw us all safe he said, 'We'd better rejoin, don't you think, sir?'

'Cup of char first, sir,' Tich was suggesting.

'I could use a scotch,' Morris was saying shakily. 'Bloody thought we'd had it, then.'

'Make that a double, mate.' Rex's driver had come up. Smoke was still floating over us, though more peacefully now.

'We'll get you another bus, Geoff,' I heard Rex saying, above me. 'Meanwhile, you're welcome aboard ours. Such as it is.'

'Real good swan, sir.' Whitey was staring at the man a trifle unbelievingly.

I was still shaking. Tich was saying something to me – 'Good idea to reverse, sir. Else we'd have been hearing reveille tomorrow at St. Peter's. I still wouldn't say no to some char, sir, would you?'

I weakly shook my head. How he could methodically set about a brew at this point beat me, but Tich did so. While the men assisted – we had 'borrowed' some of those meth briquettes from the Americans – I looked over at Rex. He was trying to salvage what he could of his haemorrhoid oil.

'How the hell do you think you're going to explain this to Jumbo?' I asked him.

'Take Sergeant Smithers' tank,' he said without looking up. 'I want to watch Edwardson. There's something wrong ...'

He was standing in that characteristic pose in which I shall always remember him, feet planted apart, head cocked to one side, dreaming. His old cardigan with the colours of the *I Zingari* cricket club still vaguely discernible on its filthy collar was buttoned high. His throat was bare. Spikes of wiry hair from his chest stuck up. In one hand he played with a necklace of Greek worry-beads, *kombolai.* It was a habit that calmed him and I rarely saw him without it. They were of pale amber, with a green tassel.

'We took the convoy,' he said absently. 'What more do you want, Geoff? Look to your men. If they need anything, my troop will see to them.'

I saw him heave himself up, rather tiredly, on the sand shield, and I saw him stagger a second, grimacing. The right leg of his cord trousers was stained with blood at the calf.

'You were hit, Rex?' I asked him.

'It was when I got down to help that driver of yours get in.'

'Serious?'

'Not in the slightest.'

'All the same, you ought to see the MO. He can't be more than twelve miles back. I can take over for you.'

He touched his moustaches, smiled ironically, climbed in his turret without a word. I realised he would have some difficulty in explaining it away. Still, I was worried. I watched him put on his beret, then his head-set on top of it; then I made for Sergeant Smithers and his half-empty Cruiser. I would ride back on it.

We swanned back over the hills, following for the most part the railway line. My throat felt like an unswept factory chimney. Dozens of women and children lined these tracks, begging and scrambling for handouts from any passing troops there might be. There were chalkings on the station walls we passed, L'ARMATA ROSSA next to a tattered *Usate SuperFaust* ad. The faces of these people were sharp in the still low sun. Pale children begged urgently, their thin predatory fingers ready to clutch at the packs and pockets of passing soldiers. In Naples it was said that one saw boys with stumps for right hands. These *scugnizzi* had had their hands or fingers chopped off when scrounging once too often over the back of passing transport and pickups. All the women had sores on their bare legs. Troops were brought slowly up from the south in cattle-wagons; the locomotive engines ran on wood. These people were here to beg, and beg hard.

Once, in low fields, we passed an American prisoner-of-war camp full of German prisoners making towards a tent for their evening meal; they looked happy, well fed, warm, and were singing strongly:

Die Fahne hoch,
Die Reihen fest geschlossen . . .

For them it was over.

I picked up my headphones and put down the Tannoy. The frequency had shifted a bit and for a moment we only got foreign-sounding voices. They could have been Welsh. It was used in such regiments for putting off the Boche (one battalion had had a pile of Polish pamphlets dropped on them, as a result). Then Rex's calm voice.

'Hel-lo, ROUNDER. HECTOR calling . . .'

Jumbo's voice imperious: '. . . so what happened there, Three? Orders were to conform. I completely lost contact with you for a while there. Over.'

'. . . well sorry, sir, my set seemed to go U.S. for a bit. My operator's been working on it. We're moving on proper bearings now. Sorry about that. Over.'

There was silence, then our commander answered gravely:

'Hel-lo, HECTOR. Well, that is very odd. Afraid your set might have been hit or something. Try to maintain contact.

All squadrons now conforming. Off to you.'

And Rex again, gravely, only mildly apologetic:

'... ah, one of my tanks developed engine fire, sir. Yes, crew did best to extinguish but there was nothing for it but to abandon ...'

3

It rained that night in our bivvy. There was mud in our char as there was mud in our hearts, at the news of more men in our unit killed. A bricklayer from Stoke-on-Trent had bought it that morning, it seemed, and a fine lad we had always called Lofty. There had been sand in our mess tins, too, in the desert.

Moreover, this bivvy reminded me of a similar ruined building we had dossed down in, near Mersa Matruh, with the Khamseen howling in at unexpected angles. Anyway, we made do. The place nearby now was called 'Three Balls Junction' and there was a church a few miles away still standing. Sergeant Smithers had gone back to report or 'take the can'. Tell Rex's story, get me up a new tank. But, as always, the Recce blokes were left well forward, by themselves. As I have said, Rex had given up promotion for this liberty. By the time we left Bizerta he was surely one of the senior Captains on active duty in the Eighth Army. He liked it that way.

Most of these old farm houses were deserted. The peasants had scattered in the fighting and were only just beginning cautiously to come back. We saw them doing so, now and then; coming down the roads carrying chairs, some large swinging mirror, the top half of a dressing table originally bought with pride and love. Occasionally our Mobile Canteens helped them out, with cans of bully and *carameli* for the kids. The US Texas Division were fighting hard down towards Eboli and their 'compo' or K rations were much in demand, particularly since they were apparently 'expendable'. An American soldier could get one of these packets, break it open for candy, and toss away the rest. 'Three Balls' had now been cleared of mines and the German corpses had sunk into mud. But the winter promised to be the foulest ever and the Eighth was surely stalemated for another sea of mud. The rain came down in torrents here. Jerry had been chased to the Volturno, crossed and destroyed the bridges, giving all hell to the Oxs and Bucks in hot pursuit. The 167th Brigade had gone in to take Bare-Bottom Hill near Roccamonfina and Monte Camino and then the push was on to get across the 'soft underbelly' of the raging Garigliano, with Monte Castellucio behind it. An RE's nightmare. How could any engineer even think of those rivers at that time, the Garig (which became the Rapido north of Cassino) icy cold and in spate with every crossing carefully enfiladed, and more such rivers beyond. All the approaches and banks heavily 'S'-mined, or with the Teller that sprang up and unleashed hundreds of ball bearings at waist height. The Chleuh were ingenious miners, even if it could be said that we had invented the tank.

Rome, Highway 6, ahead.

Rex seemed unconcerned about his wound. Admittedly it was only superficial, yet a spent round of Ye Beste Essen had lodged in his calf, and was beginning to hurt. His leg was stiffening. I urged him to get it out in case of gangrene but of course I could never mention this on regimental wavelength, as so often we were. Already I felt that our commanding officer, Jumbo ('The Elephant') Richely, had taken our story of radio breakdown and brew-up with a considerable grain of salt. It but remained for someone in the upper echelons to twig and find Rex's antics dispensable.

Bivvying had been easy in the desert. You rolled up in a sleeping bag beside your tank or slung some tarp out on the tracks and slept under it, always hoping that no one in the vicinity was intending to maintain your engines during. The night sky was so great, so beautiful, so sumptuous. There were no night bombers in that sky, no irritation of engines worrying the texture of darkness above. Stretched on our backs, we looked up into that soft African obscurity lit now and then by toffee-apples as we called them, tracer shells sent up simply to indicate positions.

It was different here. In wet trenches, or tarps slung out beside our tanks over camouflage nets, we heard the shells whizzing over in all directions. Then there was the air traffic and the steady poom-poom of the ack-ack Bofors chasing the planes with the searchlights grasshoppering the night sky above. There had been heavy fighting around 'Three Balls'. Shattered farm buildings and a lot of German dead about still, which we were making the prisoners we'd taken get out of the mud and bury. A communal cookhouse of sorts had been set up in one of these broken buildings and there we would breakfast in the dark the next day at 4 a.m. on biscuits and weak tea with a bit of bully. We always had to be ready to move off by 4.30 a.m. and we'd just heard on the set that the Chleuh were sending down reinforcements of the 90th. Light and some new Panzer Grenadiers.

About seven, that same night I'd brewed, we ate in the cookhouse. The water-truck had just been up and the char was hot and good. The stuff we got from the river below only made you feel thirstier than ever after five minutes. Whitey was drying out our blankets on the softly whirring engines. Morris was setting the bivvy beside Smithers' tank and I was insisting Rex sleep dossed down on the engines themselves. He was limping badly now. I told him he ought to get fixed up. There was a house down the road which was occupied by peasants who had come back; I had helped an old woman there dig the dried peas she had stored in a gourd out of the ground only a few days before. There was a granddaughter called Maddelena with a beautiful eager face. They might have some local brandy left.

So we set off in the rain down the bullock track, having delegated squadron command to Edwardson and told him where we were going. A light moon scudded through clouds and what with the searchlights weaving it wasn't too dark. We didn't stumble much. Once we passed a peasant walking by himself through the mud at the side of the road, barefoot and less dressed than a scarecrow at home. He had a frayed straw hat on his head, was hugging himself with his hands, and in general looked more miserable than I had ever seen any wog. In fact, he looked as if he had just stepped off some desert island.

Rex growled a friendly *'Buona sere, signore'* at him but the man didn't answer. He seemed to be weeping.

We went on, Rex's limp becoming more and more pronounced with every step, passing a small cart with the oxen dead in the shafts and a bad smell coming from them. Or maybe it was from the jerry on the embankment nearby. He was sitting straight up as if at a bloody tea party with the whole of one side of his face squashed in. Streaks of fire lit up in great red glares in the sky overhead. Then a couple of women in black bombazine with children passed by, equally barefoot. They stopped and asked us if we had anything to eat. Rex fished some toffees out of one pocket for the bambinos and I gave them some chocolate I'd found by the side of the road in an American K-ration packet. They blessed us and went on, refugees returning to their burnt ricks, slain cattle and poultry. Then one of the children, a girl with inky hair and huge eyes in the night, came running back and asked me if, please, I had any soap. But I hadn't. And I wished I had, more than anything. We were in sight of the house now. It looked dead.

'A filthy war,' Rex was muttering to himself slightly ahead of me.

'Tell me,' I asked him, 'when you came down to get us on the hill today I saw you had the hawser ready. Did you really intend to tow us back then?'

'If possible. But you brewed.'

'Yes, we brewed. We all but had it, that time.'

'Still in one piece, though, aren't you?'

'Just about, I guess.'

He gave a strange sardonic laugh.

'To be as near to death as that is to feel alive,' he said.

But I came back quickly, 'Stow the philosophy, Rex. The whole thing was crazy and you know it. But I do owe you thanks.'

'You'd have done the same for me.'

Swearing to myself, I realised it was the truth. Where was this tyrant leading me? I wanted to get back to blighty whole.

'Think there'll be trouble?' I asked him. A tank was a tank, after all. It cost several thousand pounds. But Rex's reply was indiscernible and unprintable.

We had come to the house. There was a layer of iced mud across the fields in front of it. We began to cross them carefully, choosing the way we had gone before. These fields could still be full of mines and, whenever he had time, the jerry left a booby-trap or two about. You could thoughtlessly pick up an apparently abandoned haversack or steel helmet and find yourself as full of holes as a Swiss cheese. A dog growled at the entrance, where light leaked under blankets.

It was a huge old dog, with a lot of mastiff in it, that had guarded the place faithfully throughout. Apparently some jerries had come up one night to rob the place but the dog had kept them at bay, so they'd put a few bullets through it. But the dog wouldn't die and they had gone away. The old mutt staggered towards us in the dark, wagging its tail, for Rex never failed to give it some army biscuit when he came. He did so now, and the mastiff whined gratefully. Then we pushed aside the blackout blanket and went in. A toothless hag of seventy stood inside the threshold, holding up a kerosene lamp. She immediately asked if we'd brought anything to eat and then the usual questions from such people as to whether they could work for us, her granddaughter and she could do our washing.

Rex shook his head sadly and spoke to her in Italian. I knew that he spoke it fluently but always forgot that he could handle provincial dialects, some of which were pretty hard for a city Italian to understand. I got about one word of three out of their conversation.

The old woman began to break down, so we patted her back and gave her some cigarettes, common barter in those days. She cheered a little at that and led the way in. The total extent of the loss some of these refugees met on returning – all their goods gone – often completely overcame them. I know one of our tanks, at least, had stopped and the commander run into a house from which such wailing was coming that he thought a woman was being killed there.

Her lamp illumined a pair of pretty, frightened goats and a sad-eyed calf, the skin stretched tight about its bones. In the next chamber were chickens. Then one by one we went down a ladder into a large, poorly lit room lined with straw which was formerly the cellar of this barn. The family were living there now. As we descended I had my hand on my .45, covering Rex and our exit. Though we were known here, it was always best. You could never be too careful in those days. And I had seen in one dim-lit corner, by a hanging stretch of burlap, a meagre little peasant kneeling on the floor with his hands up apparently praying. Then I saw he had a peg-leg. The old-fashioned kind, a wooden stump which strapped above the knee.

As he made no movement when we came in and just simply continued muttering away, I was going to get a better look at him; but the old woman saw my glance and told me he was deaf. He remained on his knees there throughout our visit. I took it as one more sample of the fear the Chleuh had instilled in these people against our coming. We were going to rape the women and kill all the men, they had told these paisanos. Unfortunately, a Moroccan contingent of Ghoums the Free French had brought over hadn't helped to dispel the image much. Nor had the Gurkhas.

Rex treated the old girl with his usual great courtesy to women. He gave her a box of matches, then sat down heavily in the straw. I didn't like the look of him. His face had paled.

'My friend's wounded,' I said. 'We don't want to go to the dressing station. Have you any brandy? We need a disinfectant. Marc. Eau-de-vie. Anything.'

The woman stood holding the box of matches to her withered chest like a treasure. I was afraid she was on the edge of tears again. I can't take women crying.

'Spirits,' I said. '*Liquore*. Anything.'

Her lips seemed softly to form the words – 'We are all going to be killed.'

'*Non sta bene*. He's not well,' I said, gripping her arm. The bone felt hollow in my hand.

I suppose she thought it the old vino hunt. A couple of foreign soldiers would come in, sit around politely, smiling out phrases like 'La guerra no good' and 'Benito finito' and the like. What they were really after was some of the red ink the peasant kept stored in the cellar.

I showed the old lady Rex's leg. The wound badly needed cleaning out. He was looking very tired. The old man was still muttering ominously in a corner. I didn't like him somehow.

Suddenly a far curtain was pushed aside and I reached for my revolver. But it was only Maddelena, with a basin of those eternal peas she had been shelling in one hand. She set down the basin and came forward, radiantly and shyly smiling.

I suppose she was perhaps twelve, with a perfect oval face and high forehead. She wore the usual black frock, clog sandals, and had fair hair tied in plaits with blue ribbon either side of her face. She was so unobtrusively dainty and frail, yet always so shyly eager and cheerful with all that she reminded me of the kind of girl you met in Russian novels. Tolstoy's Natasha.

She greeted us effusively, then hung on her grand-mother's arm, comforting her and straightening the little kerchief on the old woman's grey locks. A whole life and soul seemed to have come into the room with Maddelena.

She said: 'We have something. Don't worry.'

'Please get it,' I said.

'It isn't very good, but it's strong.'

'Please get it.'

She scampered off like a bird and came back from behind the curtain with a dusty, anonymous bottle, half full.

'It's strong all right,' I said. 'Lie back now, Rex. This is going to hurt you more than it does me.'

'Give me some of that rotgut, Geoff.'

He took several thirsty pulls from the bottle, then opened his mouth wide in a vast sigh.

'Mixture of gun oil and Strega,' I suggested.

He shook his head. 'Local pear brandy. Excellent.'

'I'm glad you think so,' I said. 'On your tummy, please.'

'Don't worry. My blood coagulates excellently. What's left of it.'

He turned on his face. I took up his trouser leg. The old woman started to cry. Maddelena hugged her, turning away her face.

'Water,' I said. 'And let's have that lamp, would you.'

I took out my knife, a sort of Malay *kris* I had bought in Tunis, curved for swift entry, and I exposed the flame of the kerosene lamp and passed the blade through it.

'Relax,' I told Rex. It was my first attempt at surgery and I hated to hurt him.

But the bullet, a Spandau round I could see, was fortunately close to the surface. I didn't have to dig. I disinfected the laceration with the rotgut and then kept on washing it with the icy water Maddelena brought me. Rex twisted once, that was all.

'Painful?'

'Not too bad.'

'Over in a mo',' I told him.

'Any inflammation?'

'No.'

He was worried about gangrene. It came fast in the desert, but not here.

'It's quite clean, Rex. I'll be finished in a sec'.'

He groaned as I got out the bullet.

'That Edwardson,' he panted. 'He worries me.'

'Why?'

'He . . . he . . .' He panted again as I painted the wound with more marc brandy.

'He doesn't seem to . . . feel fear.'

'In that case, you don't have anything to worry about me,' I told him. 'I was practically pissing in my pants just now. There you are, old boy. Best Essen lead.'

He stuffed the round in his pocket as some sort of souvenir, I guess, as I took out my field dressing from the front pocket of my battledress trousers and bound the wound tightly for him. Then he sat up straight, his eyes closed.

'Merciful heaven,' he said, still breathing harshly. 'You'd make a lousy bones man, Geoff.' He passed a calloused hand across his forehead. 'Give me a fag.' I lit and passed him a cigarette. 'And please ask the kid ... have they got any olive oil?'

I grinned and put it to the hag. A canister for my squadron leader's piles. Not a request she heard every day, I'd wager. I'd send a man over with some bully – *carne*, which it wasn't – first thing in the morning. These people were beginning to trust us. Maddelena's eyes were swimming. (*'O grazie, grazie ...'*) If only they had onions, or tomatoes. It was the lack of fresh vegetables that irked us. Canned stuff, mostly bilge, was all we'd eaten for so long we had developed an extraordinary craving for almost anything grown in the ground. I had seen men tearing raw onions to bits with their teeth in North Africa – when they could barter for them, from the odd wog.

Rex was sweating and I wanted him to rest. And I couldn't keep from feeling there was something wrong here. After all, he could spend the night on a palliasse here, with these people; the old biddy and the chap on his knees still praying. Maddelena would look after him. I would take over the Recce Group. Each tank knew what to do. We'd get him in the morning.

But he wouldn't listen to this idea. Under his greying hair his face had ruddied a little. He had become more assured. He put the bottle to his chapped lips again and took a throaty swallow.

'Getting old, Geoff,' he said, laying hands on the muscles of his chest.

'I really am sorry if I hurt you,' I said.

'You didn't, much. But I'm beginning to get it now. The nerves are waking up. Nothing like a good peasant cognac for that. It'll be over soon.'

'Want to eat something?'

'No.'

'Well, I hate to see you drinking alone.'

I took the bottle and slugged from it again. It seemed to burn a hole in my stomach. I choked and coughed. What was this sudden sense of insecurity I had? I lit a cigarette.

'The ears of the enemy are everywhere,' Rex said softly, in a sleepy chuckle.

'What do you mean?'

I glanced around the room. Maddelena had sat her granny down in what looked like the rickety imitation of a Papal chair, the only one in the room, doubtless a treasured possession. The girl looked so frail but I had once taken a bundle off her head in the fields and it was as much as I could carry. She yearned to go to school.

Then I heard the mastiff growling.

'Someone there,' I said quickly, unclipping the holster of my .45.

'Probably,' said Rex, without seeming interest. His eyes were closed.

'Go and see who it is,' I told the crone.

She started towards the ladder, still softly weeping. The man kneeling and praying increased his tempo. Maddelena flew to me.

But already we could hear steps upstairs. The dog had let someone pass. It still could be a jerry, though, an escaped prisoner who had been to the farm once already.

'Rex,' I hissed, but he made no move. His mouth lay in a contented smile.

'That marc really hit me, Geoff.'

The steps were getting closer. I saw the old woman look up the ladder, begin to back down.

'Veng', ' hissed the girl at my side and in a second I was behind the curtain at the far end of the room, with my .45 cocked and Maddelena close behind me. I could feel her breathing on my neck in the darkness there. I could feel her body quivering next to me in the thin stuff; her breasts pressed liquid on my back, their horn-like shapes shuddering

on the rough stuff of my battledress blouse. Never had I felt so close to a woman somehow, as then, with Maddelena's pure and humble self close behind me in the dark, a quivering, fawn-like thing of purest beauty and youth.

Then her hand gripped my right shoulder as the feet began coming down the ladder. Directly I saw the issue boots, caked inches deep in Three Balls mud, then the buckled battledress gaiters, I relaxed with a sigh. Sergeant Smithers came into sight, huge and black-headed under his greasy beret. He came unarmed into the room and, taking no notice of anyone except the recumbent Rex, he stamped his feet and saluted.

'Cap'n Davidson, sir.'

'Yes, Sarn't Smithers?'

Rex sat up. It might have been some exchange in an orderly room.

'Just 'eard the news on the BBC, sir.'

Smithers had been a window-cleaner in Hull in civvy street.

'What news?'

'We got it on the set just now, sir. There's been a landing at Anzio, just south of Rome.' His open face split in a grin. 'Soon be over now, sir.'

'Think so, Sergeant?'

'Yes, sir. Sure as eggs are eggs. Jerry will clear off now, sir.'

'Well, thank you. We'll be back shortly. Fall out.'

Sergeant Smithers saluted, turned smartly to his right, and ascended the ladder in military order. We felt proud of him.

For a moment Maddelena clung to me. I looked into her gazelle-like eyes. She so yearned, she yearned. Her whole trembling body was a yearning, an offering, it would have been so easy to take advantage of her. And in not doing so, I knew that someone would, sooner rather than later. Probably some American, with a fat billfold of AMGOT notes. I only hoped it wouldn't be one with a wife and family in New Jersey or Denver. I tore myself from her terrified embrace and went back in the room, holstering my pistol.

Rex had put his hand into some inner pocket and taken out an object I had seen before, usually after moments of crisis. It was a battered black notebook, a sort of personal log of the day, scored over with scribblings and doodles worthy of any schoolkid's copybook. He'd put down what had happened, then add some bull I never understood like *The world consists of the facts of the case* or (another one) *Whatever we can say a thing is, it is not,* or some such tommyrot. The last time I'd seen his black book was after Salerno and the time before that near a beaten-earth drome in the desert. We'd been sent to defend it vastly under strength and watched some sixty Mark III's slowly advancing upon us. For some incredible reason I shall never fathom, the whole force then passed southwards of us without even firing a shot. So for me personally Rex's notebook had something ominous about it. I didn't like it. Page after page was sown with these runic utterances which came to his mind and seemed to me to make no sense at all. I saw him prop himself on the straw against the wall now with a mixture of emotions. He took the notebook between his hard hands and wrote slowly, as if with difficulty. I looked over one shoulder.

21 Jan
recce beyond the Lancashires Depot. That's how I still like war to be. Alone. Organised a sortie. Brewed a convoy. Geoff's tank brewed on returning. Bad show, that. Slight laceration in leg. Extracted by Geoff in old house near Three Balls. Flushed another fifth-column type there.

I was trying to get what he meant by the last when something he was writing underneath attracted my attention. His pen was an old kind, with a valve filler, and it scratched a lot in the silence.

No longer are we possessed by our possessions, but are now free to go out and possess the whole world. St. Francis of Assisi.

Then a blank.

Then: *The world is the nature of what exists.*

I was watching him closely because I knew he was going to do something. Surely enough, he did. He passed into action, quite calmly and logically. He stood up, took out his revolver, a .38 in his case which was light enough to be carried in a pocket rather than holstered, and checked its breech. Everyone in the room froze, myself included. Rex walked quickly past the praying man, pulled aside another curtain there, and pumped four shells into a small transmitting set he uncovered. The reports filled the room. Outside, the dog barked furiously.

'Let's go, Geoff,' was all he said.

He strode towards the ladder, limping less already. I started to follow him. I was holding the can of olive oil Maddelena had unearthed for him when she caught at my arm.

'You'll come back, won't you?' she said.

I nodded, yes. I said I would, but I never did. And that made me sorry, too. The old man was still praying like fury on his knees.

In the upstairs byre I started, 'How in hell ... ?'

Rex waved my question down.

'Just a second-rate signals post. Probably the Boche barely thought it worth while. Couldn't send far with that lot. But there must have been someone who came in to do it. I spotted the rod aerial stapled into an outer wall, under some vines, as we came in. Wasn't there before.'

'Are you going to turn him in?'

Rex shrugged. 'Suppose we should. MP and the rest. Frankly, I don't like to get mixed up in that sort of thing. I'm a soldier. Don't care for those little games.'

'The old man was a spy, you mean?'

'Who knows? Perhaps Jerry just paid him for hiding the post, so's they could use it from time to time.'

'You saw the aerial,' I said, thinking, 'but that wasn't enough, Rex. How in bloody hell did you know there was a transmitter there?'

'You get the feel of it.' He shrugged apologetically again.

'Nothing to it really. After all these years, there's a sort of sixth sense. I knew. Extrrrr-aordinary!'

He rolled his r's with relish.

'I don't understand you,' I said. 'I don't understand you at all.' We passed out into the dark and Rex fussed up the mutt who obediently rolled on his back for a scratch from those horny fingers. 'I don't understand, either, why you held your fire on that truck this afternoon. Why you didn't brew it. What happened, in Christ's name? I saw your gunner traverse right on those men.'

We began walking back again through the thin rain, under the stars. The dog threw us a last affectionate whine. I hoped it got enough to eat. It probably didn't.

Rex shrugged uncomfortably this time.

'Didn't you see that terrier?' he asked with a grin. 'A little lame-footed cur running right behind them?'

'Well?'

'There was this poor devil of some fox-terrier or other they'd picked up with them. Going hell for leather. You wouldn't have wanted me to take him too, would you?'

'And let a dozen Boches, all of whom can fight again, escape?' I tscked in the dark.

We plodded on in silence, our boots sticking. As we walked I noticed something I never had before. Rex's worry-beads were phosphorescent. They shone in the night! I remarked on it to him but he only mumbled back. He was still shaking and sweating a bit, I think, and I was worried about that wound. I was no doctor, nor ever hoped to be.

I drew him into song, to distract him and ease our return, under the strife-ridden sky.

Naples and Cassino were taken in our stride,
We didn't go to fight there – we went there for the ride.

Suddenly he stopped. I stopped, too.

The body was lying along a bony ridge ahead of us, as outlined by a suddenly rising Very light to our right. The gun was pointed right at us and in that illuminated moment we both ducked as one.

The corpse was that of an American, we found. He had been hit cleanly, in the back. No one had troubled to take his rifle from him, let alone bury him. Rex and I continued on our way. Alone, under the stars, we seemed to wander astray.

4

But Jerry didn't clear off just yet. By no means at all.

General Alexander's landing of a force of some fifty thousand south of Rome had begun as a complete success. Then bogged down.

Cassino – not the village itself, but the heights above it called Monastery Hill – seemed to have been accepted by higher command by this time as almost impregnable. The monastery rose sheer on the rock-face and made a natural position from which to dominate all about, notably the Liri Valley and the road to Rome. Thousands of tons of bombs had been dropped on it by now and wave after wave of infantry hurled against it, most perishing on the mine-fields of the approaches. By a tragic irony, perhaps typical of the war of that time, the Sussex had charged and gallantly won Point 593 which (with another position called Massa Albaneta) actually overlooked Monastery Hill. For a brief spell they were in position to fire down at the Boche in the monastery from above. But a flare had gone up and the officer in command of the Sussex had interpreted this as his battalion's previously arranged signal to withdraw. In fact, it had been an accidental Boche firing, it seemed.

No one who had been near it called Cassino a monastery any more.

We in the Droghedas had as our objective the crossing of the Garigliano river, now in full spate, and connecting in a network with the Liri, Rapido, and Melfa rivers, under the Matesi mountains. Never had the underbelly of the Axis looked less 'soft', or more muddy. The Garigliano was over a hundred yards wide in those days and what bridgeheads the 56th. Division were able to establish were quickly driven back into the boiling river. We badly needed anti-tank guns the other side, to hold off the quickly thrusting counter-attacks of German armour.

Sappers toiled in the icy water all day. Meanwhile, the enthusiasm about Anzio had receded. The Chleuh was holding off our landing there now, with his usual mobility of action, and it was said the place had become a killing ground. I was growing more and more depressed, waiting to go over that desolate river in which, by this time, so many men had already died. My hands shook in the morning. I had headaches more and more. We watched the peasants evacuating their buildings, carrying their sacks of flour and, when they were lucky, the odd sausage or two. I thought sadly of Maddelena and wondered how she was.

Finally, we got across, rattling in single file over a new Bailey bridge. Then, advanced strongly without much opposition to the heights of Monte Nata and Furlito, to our right (always we sought elevation). The mud seemed thicker this side. Everywhere we saw transport axle-deep in the gooey stuff and more than once were called upon to tow out some half-buried 20-CWT.

For the most part we kept to the farm tracks ourselves, moving from village to village. When the sun came up high on some frosty day, we'd laager down and eat biscuits and bully in some deserted, brokendown square, and count our lucky stars that we'd come through. There had been some bloody battles in these parts, but for once they had not had our number on. None of us knew much about the situation, really. We all dreaded being sent to Anzio. If any of the Regiment were to go, it would doubtless be the Recce Group. Jumbo Richely had taken a dim view of Rex's last escapade, wanted to get shot of him, I could see. As the saying went, Rex's ballocks were on a line. You couldn't do here what we'd done in the desert.

So our lot was to reconnoitre the terrain, pressing further and further northwards, drawing fire, then scuttling back, waiting for the big attack to be mounted when Cassino would be taken and we could all pour through and link up with

Anzio and take Rome. That was the idea. A lot of the time we guarded 'B' Echelon convoys coming up with ammo and provisions, just like those Panzers we had engaged with earlier. In general, it was our job to look dangerous and menacing. The front-line infantry, poor bastards, were worse off than we were. They lived in mud, the constant rain flooding their foxholes and dugouts and making life miserable for them. At least we could keep the odd flask of rum in our bins and more than once we solaced some of those foot soldiers with a tot. Unburied corpses, shattered equipment, pillaged rations, these lay all over the shop. I hadn't washed for two weeks and my socks were glutinous in my boots. But above all there was this premonition that next time would be it; and the feeling was never stronger than when we used to tune in to the BBC at night and hear those mellifluous accents from Portland Place telling us we had made a 'strategic withdrawal' here or there. We were a point on the map. Hill 82. The day I heard the woman screaming was a dark day, indeed. Perhaps it was a turning point. It happened like this.

'Hallo, hallo, all stations NATHAN ...'

Our code names were changing almost daily now, to the point of some confusion. God knows why so many of them were Biblical. Someone in Signals had been reading out of the front of the book, I supposed. But we were going in, I thought once more, sucking my breath and hoping I was looking calm, even if I'd never felt less so.

'... have identified force of enemy tanks moving towards friends sitting ridge figures oh-five-seven-three north. Advancing rapidly south-west. Will intercept.' Then Jumbo's voice more emphatic. 'Will intercept and destroy. Hullo, all stations NATHAN. Conform to me in present formation. Over.'

'BENJAMIN Two, ack and off to you,' I said after I had heard Rex's voice rather wearily acknowledge the order. We were for it again.

Then Edwardson: '... Okay, off.' Very curtly. His voice sounded funny.

'Scrub the brew,' I shouted to Tich who was fighting the inevitable primus under a tree. He cursed and came running.

'Two answering. Do positively identify three Mark IV's. Probably Ninetieth Light. Off.'

Under the rain we plunged diagonally down the hillside. Dawn was not far past and a gnawing line bisected hill and sky ahead. Visibility was bad, but worse for them than us this time, I calculated. They would be firing with what light there was in their eyes. The usual leap of animal excitement flooded through me as I balanced half out of the turret, my binoculars bouncing on my clavicles, and saw the great sweep of our Cruisers coasting abreast downwards. Like a string of three-quarters in rugger, really. There was courage in company.

My phones were full of a lot of crackling and whistling and I glanced across at Rex's head poking from his turret. We had breakfasted together on soya links and my tongue felt like a button-stick. As Rex had put it briefly, eating his, 'Remarkable how they perfect the taste of Olde Sawduste, isn't it?'

I switched to the other mike.

'Driver, slow a little ... Cannon, traverse right ...'

We were going into action. Then the sky split overhead. Something tore at the air and every bone in my face seemed to ache. Correction: we *were* in action. One of those blighters – I could not tell which – had seen us and sent up a welcome, as we advanced. Actually, a damn close call.

'Gunner! What do you see?'

Another wild tearing filled the air.

'Definitely 'ostile, sir!'

I'll say. But I couldn't get a target in this smeary marsh mist which was occluding the Panzers. They were flashing at us and slinging lead and it was clear it was to be something of a head-on battle.

Whitey gave me the other mike. Shot was cracking about but Rex's voice was profoundly leisurely, almost lugubrious, really. He was in his element.

'Hear me, Two and Three. Suggest you take what you can

and keep moving up and down ... well now, move a bit and use your judgement to withdraw up the hills, right of GERSHOM. Off.'

It was hard to hear. I strained. Static was splintering into my brains till I took over the Tannoy. I had seen something and so, I knew, had Morris.

'Cannon, traverse right ... on! Tank stopped eleven o'clock dark patch. Hit him! Hit him till he bloody brews! Fire!'

I forgot protocol in my excitement, an excitement that subdued sheer fear. The Mark IV had stopped. Or, Jesus Christ, was it a Tiger? It was the moment to get him whichever it was. Morris squeezed his trigger. The two-pounder flamed, making its usual pull on the chassis of the tank. The breech whipped back. I had forgotten to look away – a cardinal rule if you wanted to follow your shot – but yet I saw its strangely slow, unearthly lope, then lost it, heard the evil snapping of m-g fire somewhere, with tracers flailing all over the shop. The whole line was firing now and I couldn't see our shots. The air stank of carbide.

'Gunner, fire again! Brew that bastard!'

It was a real mêlée. There was great pressure in my throat. It was not good to fight like this. Also, we were doing so far too close to Edwardson's tank, and yet his head didn't seem to be ducking. Back in the blue I'd always been told that at certain rare moments in the desert you could, with crosswires on your target, and the correct refraction and lighting, actually see for a second or so the shot that put you out. Men swore to have done so. It was a kind of complicity with the enemy, I suppose. Or God. Then I saw our Panzer clawing slowly round, crippled. It had the shiny paintwork of a new arrival and I felt doubly pleased to have taken it.

'Down fifty!' I yelled to Morris. '*Fi-yerr*!'

The old bus thumped again.

As the air split to the flame of our shot I cried out despite myself, 'Shot! Keep on him till he brews!'

Our target was starting to do so. I glanced to my left. That crazy fool Rex was out of his turret altogether, standing behind the cupola in some dreamy stillness, head in hands as if attentive to some inner advice, watching me whistle shot over Edwardson's still unmoving head.

'Stick on him, Morris!' I cried, abandoning procedure. 'Give him all you've got! *Hit him*!'

They were getting out. A small, scholarly looking figure appeared on the cupola of the Tiger and toppled off, his clothing ablaze. He began rolling himself frantically on the soil. The crew began to follow.

'Gunner! Thirty-seven! Tracer low in the back as she turns. Fire!'

I held my breath, watching for the apricot rods to lash across that Italian hillside and stream into the Panzer. But nothing happened. I looked down. Whitey was feeding the Beza belt forward properly and I felt myself that I had ... *conquered sensation.* Then our tracer poured into the light armouring of the tank as it turned and its gas tanks jetted orange flames and black smoke almost instantly. But there were the spider figures running.

'Gunner!' I called. 'Thirty-seven! Men by tank. Fire!'

Nothing happened. I was panting. Morris' face was turned back up to me, not so much questioning as perhaps trying to understand. And I understood him all too well. I did something I had never done before. I swung a kick at his backside.

'*Fire I said blast you!*' I cried.

It was horrible. My gunner's head bent obediently to the scope and he put a burst into the still frantically rolling figure and it stopped rolling. An act of mercy, perhaps. But he fired no more. The rest of the crew followed out slowly. I watched them through my binoculars. I watched appalled. Some tanks were high up the ridge. It was the very first time I had purposefully put the Beza onto evacuating personnel. Then there was a whumpfing boom followed by a rending sound, a roar that seemed to go on for about half a minute. The tank we had hit scattered itself in fragments in the valley. I looked at my watch. In fact, we had been in action a half hour.

'Hullo NATHAN. I say all stations NATHAN. Conform

to headquarters in present formation. Over.'

'... okay, off,' I choked out in turn.

There was this thickness in my throat.

The German tanks withdrew but they would come again, I felt sure. And it was not easy. Not at all. My mouth seemed caked with salt. Briefly I reached down for the water bottle. It had to do the four of us for the day and the water tasted brackish from the chlorinating pills. Whitey wetted the flannel cover and hung it in the draught from the driver's hatch forward. That way it kept cold. Chewing gum might have helped. The Yanks said it did.

'Hel-lo, GERSHOM,' I now heard Rex saying in my ears; 'have met and repulsed small enemy force our side of figures eight two. Took a few ... ah, the rest seem to be withdrawing. Await your orders. Over.'

I wanted to hear Jumbo's voice back, telling us to engage again. I had once more been mechanically occupied, action replacing fear. I checked our position, all the instruments agreed. I scanned the fog-wisped terrain below us, where phantom shapes still moved through smoke. Now and then a flash came out of this murk as one or another of the Tigers below saw something of us, I guess.

'Driver! Close down!' I called. 'Loader, both guns!'

I could hear Jumbo acking Rex's signal and then getting onto Brigade who seemed to want us to stay out of trouble. I waited for it but it didn't come. Something was missing.

We were no longer functioning as one organism. The Panzers would appear here and there, out of the mist, easily identifiable by their peculiar turrets and six tracking wheels. These monsters had haunted our horizons for so long we felt we knew them as we knew ourselves. Even so I felt a sort of shock in the solar plexus each time one of them broke into being before us. Those bastards had the range on us and their guns could fire faster than ours. I felt a distinct draining of effort, a waste of vital energy.

We sat on the ridge for the rest of the morning, generally swanning about, getting hull down and taking a pot shot here and there to show we were still around. A sun the colour of a fresh egg yolk came up, an ominous hue, but it didn't really dispel the mist. There was a stone and stucco farm house down in the valley, just behind where we had seen the Panzers, with trees and brush surrounding it. Once I came on an overturned 15 CWT, the sturdy truck tipped on its side like a beetle and about as useful. Tich stopped to see if he could cannibalize its Leyland engine for parts but it turned out to be a total write-off. My forehead felt numb. The raw air made me weep. My goggles misted. We passed three corpses – jerry. A newspaper in Gothic script fluttered under a bloated, boyish arm, next to a spade. It was as if some invisible force had swept through this valley; I had the sense that the landscape was waiting for something. No one spoke in the turret.

Once Whitey, who had been checking the AP (armour-piercing) shells for the 37 mm, looked up at me with his face filled with alarm.

'What the hell's happened to you, sir? You're hit!'

I put a hand to my head. It came off sticky. Blood. But I'd felt nothing. Maybe just banged my head against one of the turret flaps. Then we decided I'd just had an ear-bleed. Not the first time. I'd been suffering from a certain endemic gunshot deafness we all got at times. Singing in the ears, etc.

'Let's get some bully up,' I said, and located Rex's position to pull back into a sort of protected roadway for a while. The men jumped down. While Tich brewed up, Morris, wearing that same damn scarf of his I'll swear he hadn't taken off since Kasserine, busied himself with alternately bending and bashing into true a flange of metal that had been distorted by a hit before we had taken over our new tank.

I went up to him and said, 'I'm sorry I kicked you, Morris, old man.' It sounded silly in the air.

'That's all right, sir,' he said, but he did not meet my eyes.

I could hear the stifled roaring of engines below, a tidal sound, as I stretched out on the rear camouflage netting. We could move in minutes, we all knew, even in seconds. But there was a constraint today as we ate and the char tasted sickly. If there was one thing Tich had it was sugar. Jerry had disengaged for the time being, it was plain.

Tich was stowing some spanners. I heard Whitey and Morris muttering away.

'That blighter comin' out of 'is ruddy 'atch like that . . .'

'Cap'n said to go for 'em. You heard him, mate.'

Silence.

'Pass me up some more of that caviar, would you, chum.'

I ran a hand over my face. I got down and walked along the track. I knew I shouldn't have but I did. I didn't want to hear them talking of it anymore. At the turn I was out of sight of them, still under the lee of the bank from the valley. A gulley – what we used to call a gut in Lincolnshire – led off it downwards. It was heavy in brush and I began to push into it, crouching. It was probably a farmer's former irrigation dyke for after fifty yards I could see it led right on down to the farmhouse.

After about another fifty yards of pushing the shrub aside and crouching along I came to a halt where a fallen tree spanned the banks. To my left I could see the long barren roll of hills from which we had fought and was surprised to find the other tanks of our squadrons so distant. Rex's aerial showed, its Divisional pennant whipping in the wind, but there was little else of him about. Suddenly the mist cleared and I saw them. My heart leapt. I had come far further down than I'd imagined.

It was to the left of the farmhouse that we had hit our Panzer. Its blackened remains still smoked gently, like some Indian's pipe. A burial party was trotting forward with stretchers. Neither side touched burial men at that time. Then I saw the two officers, through a hole in the mist. They were standing casually chatting by a scout car that had come up, perhaps from their Brigade. I put up my glasses. Yes, they were from headquarters. I saw the characteristic peaked cap, flat-fronted, the eagle at its peak, goggles pushed up beneath it, à la Rommel. I saw the buttoned tunics, the breeches and the boots. And yes, on one, the Iron Cross

Second Class – for gallantry where? I wondered. In the bled, perhaps? At Mersa or Agedabia? Somewhere where we had been? How splendidly languidly they stood, calm and authoritative. In that almost peaceful moment I wouldn't have wanted to kill them even if I could have. I even cursed lightly to myself. What the hell were we doing fighting people like this, for Chris' sake? Why were we bringing troopers from Southern dene and Lancashire clough and Devon cleave to kill such men? They rocked on the balls of their boots just as we did. We were *Brüdervolk*, surely. But I knew I should not think like that and as the mists closed over that immaculate, momentary vision I turned and plunged back through the scrub to my tank.

I had been to Germany for precisely one term of my school year, to learn the language at Salem Schule Schloss. To a fourteen-year-old what little there was visible of the Nazis then had been a pageant, a charade, a super-Boy Scout movement. I had not known of a fat little fairy in crumpled uniform called Ernst Röhm when he was murdered by Hitler, nor of Viktor Lutze, his successor as head of the SA. I bunked with a boy in the school of my own age called Kurt Bleyle who treated the thing as a bit of a joke. We both were more interested in playing soccer for the junior, under-XV, or Colts team of the school.

Of course, we gave the ritual *'eil'itler!* salute in this shop or that, instead of saying good morning. We hung the party bunting in our room and I myself went back to England later with several of those scarlet armbands on which the black spider of the swastika writhed.

Once we went on a hiking tour in the Harzgebirge, culminating in a climb up the Brocken in perfect spring weather. We stayed at the cheap Jugendherberge, no more than dormitories, really, with open washrooms, in which the girls joined us. As a young English boy I was amazed at the ease of mixing between the sexes and the *Freikörpergelände*, or areas for nudism. In Goslar I had my first sexual experience. Hanni (Hannelore) was the typical blonde of the time, a determined member of the BdM, or German Girls League, a physically splendid lot who sometimes sported peasant dress and pigtails. We boys had many nicknames for this Bund, like *Bald deutsche Mütter* (German Mothers Soon – thanks to their promiscuity), or *Bedarfsartikel deutscher Männer* (Necessary Articles for German Males), and the like. Hanni it was who had told me, lying back on warm pine needles by a brook, that women hung on every word of Hitler's speeches and that, for her, they were really like nothing else. Her eyes glistened as she spoke and her thick breasts heaved.

I did not know that while I was there Hitler eradicated the left wing of the Brownshirts in bloody fashion; that thirty-two of Röhm's associates were crammed into a cellar, taken out one by one by an SS man, their shirts torn open, a charcoal circle drawn round their left nipples. and shot pointblank by an eight-man SS firing squad at seven yards' distance; nor that 73-year-old Kahr (one of those who had thwarted the Beer-Hall *Putsch*) was hacked to pieces by Himmler's new SS. We saw only a few of the latter about. Kurt pointed them out to me with patent dislike even then. Himmler was appearing closer and closer to Hitler on the daises and rostrums, his sinister black crossed with shining leather.

Baldur von Schirach was leader of the Hitler Youth in those days, an ineffectual-looking man who we saw take one march-past of young boys, flanked on one side by the cruel bald head of Streicher, whose newspaper *Der Stuermer* with its pornographic cartoons directed against Jews was being put up at bus-stops. We saw the HJ posters with their clean-looking youths posturing over AUCH DU, and the brooding Wagnerian countenance of the mountebank with the moustache, above FÜHRER WIR FOLGEN DIR! ALLE SAGEN JA! It was heady stuff for those who 'did not know'.

We did not know, we did not know. We English schoolboys then were half-conscious human beings, for the most part, who looked at a lot of red on the map each morning and learnt the dates of the occupations of Quetta, the second

Maori War, the acquisition of Assam. Why, even the War House did not know – or refused to accept. When the Norfolks had surrendered after exhausting their ammunition in the heights of Calais, they were taken prisoner in the normal way (we still always hoped to be captured by the Boche rather than the Eytie); but then some men in long black trenchcoats had led them into a field and shot them, one by one, in the back of the head and buried them in a common grave. Two men escaped this carnage by feigning dead. One had got back to England, through Switzerland and Lisbon, after a year and a half. But so colossal was the blow that his story made to the code of war between civilised nations, so frightful was the outrage against decency, he was not – initially – believed. It was the first time in the West that a political apparatus had accompanied fighting men into action.

As I stumbled back up the gut, in the mist I saw some flickers of light from our furthest tanks, and heard an exchange of firing. I could see the tracers gracefully going down the long hill. By the farm the scout car started up. Whitey was waving to me with an enamel mug. We were moving off, it was plain. I had been overlong away. I leapt in after him, picked up map, glasses, headphones. To a yelping of locked tracks, and pronounced hydraulic hisses, we 'conformed'.

'Driver, advance. Loader, bags of m-g ready. Gunner, two-pounder … traverse right …'

I could say it in my sleep by now.

Of course, I knew now when I had known. Not when that extraordinary little old Jew with the wrinkled pasty face had been sent down to us at Training Battalion by some department of Intelligence; in a heavily accented English that few of our men had followed he told us about the concentration camp of Bergen-Belsen, and how he had been strung up by his arms there, on meathooks. He showed us the scars. Had we believed? Yes. Had it *entered our consciousness?* No. To me that happened in June 1941 a few days before *der Führer* released 150 divisions and 2,700 aircraft on the

Russians. It happened in a small house near Aldershot.

We in the Droghedas were frequently given high-level guard duties. I myself, as a young ensign, had never guarded Buck House, but I had the Bank (to which, for some reason, we had to travel by underground, or subway), and I had done St. James's Palace (for which the officer-in-charge got a free bottle of wine). I did not take the new duty given me with any particular interest. I was to mount a twelve-hour guard over a prominent German in captivity. I had been chosen because I could speak the language. I did not know that it was Rudolf Hess. Indeed, I did not even know that Hess had flown to Scotland on May 10th. I barely knew who Hess was. If I hadn't been to Salem, I would probably have known nothing of him at all. Such was our ignorance in those days.

It was an undistinguished pebble-dashed house up a gravel drive that our 15-men guard drew up in front of, at six that next evening. It looked like a minor vicarage. The officer I was relieving 'handed over'. He told me it was Hess. Inside the hallway of the house there were a lot of white-coated men about. Male nurses, it seemed. Our prisoner occupied a room to the left. I was to eat with him in an hour.

Promptly at seven I knocked, entered, stamped, and saluted. There was a guard left directly outside the room. Hess was sitting on an army-issue bed. He did not acknowledge my salute. It was only when the Americans came in that we stopped saluting p-o-w officers of superior rank – I think Eisenhower had put out such a directive in Africa. Frankly, from what I had seen at Salem, and newsreel films in railway stations thereafter, I had expected Hess to be wearing the brown shirt with its big bakelite buttons, dark tie pinned with a swastika emblem, party armlets, the rest. He did have his breeches on, and the customary garrison belt, but above these he wore a colourless, collarless shirt, perhaps one loaned him by our forces, I don't know. He looked like an efficient, if harmless, chauffeur off duty. It was hard to think of him as Hitler's appointed successor. But he was mad.

He was mad in a way Keitel, Jodl, Kaltenbrunner, Donitz,

Rosenberg, Frick, Frank and the others of the 'great abnormals' in our European midst were not.

We sat down either side a board table and a medical Corporal served us fish. I talked to Hess, not with him. Halfway through the meagre meal he got up, held a tiny morsel of cod on a fork and went over to his bed with it. From under the bed he pulled out a chest. He dropped the fragment of fish in this and then quietly rejoined me, explaining that they were trying to poison him, and that that was the precise piece which had been poisoned. He smiled at the knowledge.

Later, I talked to the M.O. in charge of the male nurses. He explained that Hess had had this mania since being brought to the house, that the trunk was full of rotting fish, and that, further, although the man was badly constipated, he refused all the pills he was given to relieve him. A few days beforehand he had thrown himself over the balcony of the staircase in an apparent suicide effort. Hence, all the R.A.M.C. (Royal Army Medical Corps) guards. For me that single evening he was mad in another sense. Not so much in the eyes (which others later identified as what showed – with their burning intensity), but in the movements of his hands, the way his hair grew ... *himself*. One recognised the threat to the being in oneself, that is all I could say and can say. But he was very close to being in charge of Germany.

It appeared that our 'C' Squadron had been badly strafed by mistake by some US Lightnings. The pilots were probably just out and in the mist and firing for them a tank was a tank, and a cigar a good smoke. Anyhow, we regrouped and learnt something Jumbo had perhaps wisely withheld from us before the morning's mêlée. We had suspected something wrong, somehow. The Chleuh was no fool. We had the sense that they were drawing us forward. Usually, Jerry engaged or withdrew, one of the two. Here were these occasional Panzers looming out of the murk, exchanging a few shots, and baiting us forward.

In the depths of the valley we could just see railway tracking with every overhead cable and its support for miles dynamited, also the pylons and transformer stations. What had happened was that our 10th Corps had been chucking over some pretty heavy stuff our side the river and this, coupled with the rain, had weakened the banks. Jerry had seen his chance, in his customary methodical way, and during the previous night his sappers had crept forward and blasted great slabs of the banking into the fast flowing river. The Garigliano was flooding dangerously. If they could draw our tanks forward, encircle us, the infantry wouldn't have a bleeding chance. We would all be cut off.

And we had to advance to protect them. In the desert the infantry cursed the tanks because they didn't cover them enough and we, in turn, cursed the infantry since they drew us forward onto impossible positions, to try to protect them, as at Sidi Rezegh. It was that afternoon I heard the screaming.

5

'... figures about three zero enemy tanks visible from where I am on ridge. Advancing slowly westwards and so far haven't seen us, I think. Over.'

It was 'A' Squadron reporting to our port. The afternoon was tense. The whole valley seemed to me to seethe with violence. Thirty Tigers? They were hidden from our hill by a kind of cairn. Obviously Jumbo was deciding whether to show our noses at them, or not, and thus keep our positions unknown.

'... 'kay,' I heard him say. 'Recce and B will move under ridge to intercept. ROUNDER Two, you give chase and damage as much as possible, then re-form with us up here as before. Over.'

It took us.

Rex's voice at once: '... will attack and pursue. Off and out.'

The ground to which we moved anew to hull-down positions above the farmstead was still hard as iron. Our tracks made a lot of noise on it. But it didn't send up much dust, and the mist seemed to deaden the sound. Radial engines were easily identifiable, so different in tenor from diesels. What did we have coming at us this time? I began giving orders.

'Allus gets us just before a cupper, eh, sir?' Tich's grumble came over on the intercom. He drove with his dixie handy. What would Tich do without tea? What would he ever do without tea?

'Driver,' I responded. 'Get ready to advance, slowly.'

Saturnine and dark, nose like a blade, Whitey sat draped in bands of rounds already. His second name was Miller but there were already four Millers in the regiment when he joined and since each was inevitably called Dusty, he accepted another moniker. The gunner, Morris, rubbed his palm on his thigh, his trigger finger ready. Morris liked to kill.

I looked along the line of tanks. Rex's heavy head in the flat beret was easily distinguishable to the left, Edwardson's tank beyond. Rex was looking down, absorbed. Suddenly, with a retraction of skin upon my flesh, a tightening of testicles and gut, I saw his hand come up, its horny palm outwards. We were going forward to get them.

'Driver! Advance!' I shouted, perhaps overloudly. 'Hull down behind that ridge.'

'Blimey!' I heard Morris declare, as his head went into his sights. We had had enough fighting in the last few days surely.

The vision of the low ground by the farmstead had now cleared somewhat. Then we saw them in wide line ahead. Grey baleful shapes with their sprocket wheels jouncing. Not thirty, I said to myself, dear God not thirty – as one after another emerged from the mists. These were desert tanks, I could see through my glasses, their turrets sanded. We were going to go through them and come back, I knew. Out of Rex's turret a hand was raised upright holding a beret. Then it fell forward in a bowler's swing, the old cavalry signal for 'attack and pursue'.

'Gunner!' I heard myself cry. 'Two-pounder and machine gun ready. Here we go!'

The Drogheda tanks came from the crest as one, in open order and lurching at the mortar holes. It proved steeper than it looked and, pitching madly, I clung to the turret flaps on one of which some wag had painted THIS SIDE UP. Beneath me I saw Morris balancing the breech pad into his shoulder, his face squeezed like a nut as he peered through the reek. It was surprising how long it was before we were seen. Were they deliberately drawing us forward, then? It was raining thinly still and I couldn't close down. I would have seen nothing if I had, but of course a tank commander using his specs had his head exposed and we had lost a lot that way.

I first thought the screams came from someone who had been hit near the house. But no one had fired as yet. The sounds were piercing, lonely, horrible. Both Whitey and Morris looked up at me in the murk. That was no human sound. Perhaps it was, indeed, an animal. A little fox terrier being put to death, say ... but then it came again. Was a woman in labour in that farmhouse? Bewailing her lot?

I slowed Tich till the wing tanks came abreast. That way, no one tank would limit another's field of fire. What was more, Jumbo seemed to have checked our angle of approach a little so as to get the full benefit of our fire power as we ran through them. Although I had frequently heard of it, this was the first time I had ever been involved in this particularly dangerous maneouvre. There came another frightful doglike scream and once more we three in the turret looked at each other in horror.

'Gunner! Traverse right ...'

Then we were seen as we came and the thin air crackled with shot. I saw the breech beneath me slam back and Whitey slide in the next shell quick as the smoke came up past my nostrils.

'Fire again, same target!'

I looked away as the gun vomited sullenly in its usual yellow splash, then tried to follow the line of shot. A hit, a palpable hit! But the Tiger didn't go up. There was no time left to hit it again at the speed we were going. We were down there and almost through the line. Smoke thickening the mist and a tank brewed to my left, I could not tell whose. A whole cloud of gun smoke just visible below Cerasola in the distance. Figures running.

Meanwhile, the Panzers had halted to return fire, then – some of them – spread. Shot whacked about. The ones you didn't hear were most likely the worst. Jumbo's voice came calm and cool on the net and, as we were clear through them with at least a dozen of their tanks crippled or brewing, we were to re-form on Point ESAU. We squealed around and then I saw Rex's tank halted.

As we turned, Edwardson was to the right of me, his face dark, his ears large outside his beret. His silhouette – what I could see of it, anyway – was stiff, like some cardboard cutout. His face did not change expression. Dammit, with hot lead flying around within feet of your nose you didn't just stand there looking as if you had rather a nasty smell under it, did you? Then I saw Rex's turret swivelling. The good old Ironmaster.

Running back through the burnt and brewing line of Panzers as we were, his tank was left of mine and so rather closer to the farmhouse. I saw two figures running out of that house in long black leather greatcoats, high peaked caps. A whiplash snaked across the marshland there. I saw Rex's Beza smoking. Both figures fell as if mown at the knees. They did not move thereafter.

At that moment, however, I felt myself jerked hard against some projection of equipment and then I was grabbing the Tannoy and a whining rush came from my desperate lips: 'For Chris' sake, *get some speed on, man.*'

We ran from the emptiness behind us. Strangely, the last of that line of impressive Panzers had withdrawn, rather than rushed up in support. We were not happy. Something was wrong just here. Jumbo was calling us back.

That night when we withdrew behind Hill 82 I was tired. All the talk was of whether we had been cut off. How were the banks of the Garigliano holding? Was the dratted rain never going to stop?

Yes, I was tired when we drew back. The flanks of the gritty mountains darkened above us. It wasn't a good place to play at camping out. To start off with, no one seemed quite certain to whom this terrain 'belonged', by whom it was controlled. Furthermore, one of our squadrons seemed to have got lost in the fog and had to be called in by Verys.

Finally, we were in position – night laager with all tanks facing outwards, with the Bay of Naples a long way to our left. And no sooner had we got into laager than women in black appeared out of nowhere asking if we had any washing. If we had any bully. Best of all, any of that currency of the day – fags? They haunted us. It was just like East of Suez, at Port Teufid where we had landed, with the locals scrambling for anything thrown out at them. But those had been wogs. This was different.

We set the guards and Tich brewed up and someone had a can of old sardines. We heated them up and on the flogged black bread they tasted fine. Edwardson crouched nearby with his men. The lights in the turrets glowed, for we were behind the line of hills and nothing seemed likely to strafe us now.

It was that mournful moment before wrapping up in blankets in the cold and snatching a couple of hours' sleep here and there. Just as your body sagged into total rest you got woken up for guard duty. Like that. One tank had its radio on too loud. Some comedy programme. There'd always be a BBC.

In the desert these laagers had been beautiful. We'd formed what were called boxes, back of the main 'blue'. You'd lie back under the tent of dark in the heavy relief of those incredible nights, with their endless stars staring out of the sky, an electric madness flickering away harmlessly somewhere on the japanned horizon, wisps of smoke arising from the cooking. It seemed centuries ago. Enchanted, almost.

It had stopped raining and a group, propped back against their Cruiser, were smoking and gently chanting, in strong throaty unison:

Look around the mountains, in the mud and rain –
You'll find the scattered crosses – there's some which have no name.
  Heartbreak and toil and suffering gone,
  The boys beneath them slumber on.
Those are the D-Day Dodgers who'll stay in Italee.

Odd how that tune 'Lili Marlene' had caught on, and not only with both sides ... with all three. The Eyties had a version, too – *Tutte le sere, sotto quel fanal* ... I think they put in some roses and left out the mists. The Boche themselves had made up the best parodies. Which was to be expected, after the Russian front. A figure was by my side.

'Geoff, I want you to take over command of Recce Group tonight.'

He looked smaller, more formal. Perhaps because he'd put a steel helmet on, which was unusual for him. Or perhaps it was those bandaged pince-nez. Berets had been designed for tank warfare in the desert. Montgomery had made his own famous. I looked at Rex's furrowed, tanned brow, his damp moustaches wilting. He appeared to be stuffing some grenades more comfortably into a haversack.

'What's going on?' I said.

'If Jumbo stages a sudden O Conf' – he was referring to an Order op in the Regimental headquarters ten-tonner – 'take over. Say I'm helping fix a track or something. Tell him what you like.'

'What the hell are you going to do, Rex?'

'You fought well today, Geoff,' was all he said, shrugging deeper into his webbing braces. 'With concentration.'

'Did you hear that screaming?' I said.

'A stuck pig makes less noise.' He nodded sombrely. 'Not a natural sound.'

'Maybe she was giving birth.'

'I doubt it, Geoff.'

'What's going on, Rex?'

'They were torturing a woman in that farmhouse. SS. We have positive information. One of the woman's relatives got through our lines and told Uncle.' (This was Intelligence.) 'I took two of those bastards ...'

'I saw you, Rex. Those characters in black. Are we supposed to. ... ?'

'I don't know the devil what we're supposed to do or not supposed to do, but there are said to be a couple more left down in that farmhouse and I'm going out to get them. Me and Blinders.'

I gaped. In the dark I saw a figure behind him checking a

Sten gun. It was Rex's driver, a gaunt Liverpudlian devoted to him as were so many of the men.

'Jesus Fucking Priest!' I swore. 'You can't be serious, Rex. Going out on a patrol like this alone in the middle of the night. And the mud. And what happens if Brigade tells us to scrub the laager fast?'

He thought. 'A point. But I can't stand hearing a woman screaming like that.'

'I'm coming with you,' I snorted hotly.

'You're not,' he said.

'Edwardson,' I said. 'He can take over.'

He shook his head. Smithers was over-busy checking a magazine. He was about as devoted to Rex as it was possible for any Drogheda to be to an officer who had mostly given him hell.

'I want to come with you,' I repeated.

'Two's enough.'

'Jesus, you're crazy,' I said. 'To start off with, you need some sleep. We all do. But you above all. God knows what's going to happen tomorrow morning.'

'I couldn't stand that sound,' was all he said softly.

'If you're going, I'm going with you, Rex. Squadron leaders happen to be valuable, in case you hadn't noticed. Above all, those with your savvy.'

Again he shook his head. 'Not. Two of us are enough, for what I want to do. But I'll need you to show the cut down to the farmhouse, so's we can get close.'

'You're crazy,' I repeated. 'We're at the tip of the Garigliano salient without any heavy artillery support that I know of and here you go larking around ... '

'Come on, Geoff.'

The man was beginning to really exasperate me. There had been no more crying from the farmhouse since afternoon. In any event, was he sure it was truly a woman being tortured there? Why so far forward? It was insane. As if reading my thoughts Rex stared ahead down the damp dead hillside.

'Jerry's a methodical type, as y'know. The front just rolled back too quick for the Gestapo. They'd set that house up for getting information out of partisans and so on. Tearing toenails out with hot pincers was apparently a favourite. So they just went on doing it.'

'You got two today.'

'Two down and two to go.' He slugged from a bottle in his haversack – olive oil, no doubt – put it back and called gruffly, 'Come on then.'

I led the way and watched him off into the brushy gut.

Back in laager I went over to Edwardson. He seemed to be sleeping almost upright. The guards were all out and more rain falling. Men snored harshly. At midnight there was a change of guards and an hour later we began to break bivvy. There was still no sign of Rex. I went and took a leak beneath a tree and just then there were a couple of loud explosions in the valley and the sky lit up. It could have been the farmhouse. But as I wandered back I had something else to worry about.

Some of my troopers were anxiously looking for me. Then I saw the despatch rider. At first I thought he was from Corps.

'Commanding Officer wants to see all Squadron leaders at once, sir.'

I returned his salute, trembling. That tore it. I'd have to go alone. I left instructions for Rex to be sent over the instant he got back and walked to the headquarters truck in the dark. A shadowy figure fell into step beside me. It was Felix Rodditch. We'd been at school together and he'd gone into Army class and now had a squadron. He'd done very well in North Africa. A lean, soft-skinned bloke with rather effeminate gestures and a pair of blue silk sheets in one of his bins. The type the Chleuh had totally underestimated.

'Going over to the Commander?' he asked, tucking his map-case under one arm. 'How come? What's with Rex?'

'Detained,' I said curtly.

'Well, you had a good day. Well done, you.'

'Worthy of the Light Brigade, eh. I hope to God Jumbo doesn't order another one like that.'

'That chap of yours – Edwardson. He bothers me.'

'Me too, Flix.'

'He isn't . . . showing fear.'

'I know it.'

'That's too bad.'

In silence we paced towards the slight glow coming from Jumbo's truck, parked with the other soft-skinned vehicles in the centre of the large laager. We understood each other well. If you were happy with someone for five years at an English school you knew a lot about their character. After sketchily saluting at the tailboard, we shoved aside the various blackout blankets and clambered in.

The commodious ten-tonner was dimly lit with storm lanterns and torches. There were strangely shaped bundles about. Officers were sitting on them, rubbing at their eyes and yawning. We all knew each other, but I didn't like the feeling tonight. There was something in the air. I saluted again and squatted on a camp-bed.

Jumbo Richely, tall and lean with a foulard round his throat and what appeared to be striped viyella pyjamas on his upper half, was sitting on something we knew well, an antproof tin trunk, girt with brass buckles. It had come with us most of the way from the so-called Benghazi Stakes and contained the personal effects of the very dead. One day they would be returned to next-of-kin: a trooper's watch, another's cross, a blood-soaked diary, someone's wallet with a bullet-hole clean through it. Someday such would be unearthed in attics in England and shown to the fatherless sons of these D-Day Dodgers.

There was a mutter of talk.

'Managed to brew far more than I thought . . .'

'Don't like the way they're acting, though.'

'Sergeant Ryder bought it.'

'I heard. Hard cheese.'

'Too bad.'

'And it isn't going to get any better,' said Jumbo Richely.

I looked at his endless frame entrenched behind old ammo cases, a paraffin lamp at one elbow and a tin mug at the other. There were maps in front of him, bisectors, a sun compass. The only eccentricity he permitted himself was a vast cavalry sabre, with gleaming hilt, affixed to the headboard of the back of the cab behind. It was generally the first thing you noticed when you came aboard, as a matter of fact. Despite his impression of some untidy librarian Richely had a mind like an adding machine. He had passed top out of staff college and tabulated in minutes movement orders that would have meant hours over a notebook for me. I was waiting for it and it came. There was a saying that he had seen his last G. 1098 in Libya, and it was true. He was finished with *bumf* – bum fodder from Corps. We were glad to have Jumbo around. He was not an imaginative man, but he was sound as a bell. And I knew he had something unpleasant to impart.

'Are we all here? Where's Rex?'

'Indisposed, Colonel,' I replied.

'I see.' Jumbo looked in a sombre way at his filthy nails. 'Couldn't come himself, eh?'

'No, sir. Will be along directly he can. Asked me to take you his apologies, Colonel.'

'I understand. Well, I think you know all members of the club.'

It was tacitly admitted that when Rex was 'indisposed' it meant that he was having hell with his piles, doing an agonised crap or suchlike. It was the best I'd been able to think up on the spur of the moment, at any rate. Fortunately Jumbo bought it. He craned over his map with a torch, then leant back and held up his mug. He sipped from it slowly.

'The Pope's blessing on ye,' he said, handing it to Felix on my right.

'Club have no waiters on duty tonight, sir?' quipped someone in a corner.

'Nor waitresses, neither,' chaffed another with Major's crowns on his shoulders. 'Must be a war on somewhere.'

'Best we can do,' murmured Jumbo, poring over his map. 'You look as if you could use it. All of you.'

'We'll have to indent for waitresses, sir.'

'Ask Q.'

'One issue Waitress, tank regiment in danger, for the use of. Hole in bottom. For whom it may concern.'

'In quintuplicate, John.'

When the cup of our communion came to me it was still more than half full of an amber fluid. A very, very lovely colour. I held it aloft like some monstrance or sconce, muttered a blasphemous *In nomine Patris*, sipped, swallowed, and rolled the last of the swallow around every bit of my craving tongue. The stuff cut tangibly through the dust and grime and oil and cordite with which we had been perpetually soiled so long. It was quite the best taste I'd had since last leave in the Gezira at Cairo, watching the bints by the pool, a ham sandwich shared with Rex nearby.

'Have another, Geoff.' Jumbo was looking at me curiously. 'You look as if you could do with one.'

'I think not, Colonel. Thanks all the same.'

'It's drinkable.' He still seemed to be peering, inspecting me oddly. Then he looked around. 'One more before I pitch in? Any of you?'

'Not on an empty tum, Colonel.'

'I don't believe so, thanks, sir.'

'John, Tony, Mike, Flix?'

Jumbo Richely looked down, faintly smiling, as at some inner joke.

'Well then. Here it is. The Garig is now running nearly two hundred yards wide in places, thanks to the flooding. The Queen's Light were actually pulling back to the other side. When the last Bailey went.'

'Jesus God!' someone growled.

'Yes, our line of retreat is now completely cut off. We're on our own over here. And that's what explains the enemy tactics in these last few days. Not pausing really to engage. I mean. You know the score. Touch and draw back. Not like Jerry at all. They want to attract us further northward so as to get round and destroy all tanks north of the river. Frankly, gentlemen,' he concluded sadly, 'we're in a rather delicate sit.'

There was silence. I could hear the patter of rain on the tarp.

'What a bind!' cursed one.

'Colonel, I think I'll have another tot of that scotch, after all.'

He was joking but the mug started on its rounds once more. In my hand it clattered. I set it down hastily. Then a voice from the dark outside shouted huskily:

'We're encircled, sir!'

Someone thrust back the blackout flap.

Rex stood straight in the fog. I was closest to him. The blood beat in the veins of his temples. He didn't bother to salute. He seldom did. I saw that his pockets were as usual heavy with this and that. The worry-beads slipped through his fingers rapidly, like pulses.

'It's dead on, Colonel.'

Jumbo Richely exploded.

'Just where the hell have you been, Rex?'

He was covered in mud. His face was barely human under the steel helmet.

'They're taking up positions, sir. Yes, in small groups maybe a thousand yards all around the laager. From what I heard they're eighty-eights. Yes, sir. We're in a monkey's trap, right enough.'

Jumbo: 'Listen, Rex. Did you just leave laager?'

'Yes, Colonel.'

He was breathing deeply but calmly. We all saw him. He was our elder not only by age but by virtue also of that sixth sense born of years in the desert against the same enemy. The rain pattered on the sheetings, and the steel.

'I didn't like the way they fought today, sir,' Rex added.

'Neither did I. What's that got to do with anything?'

'The Boche doesn't generally retreat in that way. Nor let a column swan along line ahead like that. If he goes, he goes. That's all there is to it. Otherwise, he sits where he is. Extrrrr-aordinary!'

Rex gritted his teeth.

'It's a mess-up, Colonel. They've got us by the shorts.'

Jumbo was listening, nodding his head, and smiling patiently, as if at some child. I noticed his eyes were bloodshot, too.

'Have they now?' he said.

'Balls and all, sir,' added Rex, fervently.

I stole a glance up.

'Their guns work too damn well with their tanks,' said Rex.

There was another silence, then we froze.

'Just *what the hell* do you think you're talking about, Rex?'

Jumbo was not given to anger and everyone in the ten-tonner sat very still.

I ventured, fearing some crisis in which things would not turn out well for Captain Davidson of Recce: 'If we had some infantry in support, sir, we could request a patrol or two, just in order to verify.'

'But we haven't any infantry, have we, Geoff?'

'No, sir.' I shut up.

The others bowed their heads.

Jumbo Richely bit his lips. He did so for several seconds. Then with a defeated air he hit his thigh, quite hard, twice, with his fist.

'How in hell's name do you think I can command this Regiment, Rex, if you act in this way? The officer in charge of my Recce Group takes it upon himself to conduct some sort of personal patrol in the dark . . . while . . . while . . .'

'We are supposed to act as scouts in a sense, Colonel,' I tried.

'Shut up, Geoff,' he said, and I did. He was about to explode again.

'They'll start coming in on us at dawn,' said Rex.

His words hung in the air, over the lamps, like an accusation. We understood them. If Rex said we were encircled, we were encircled. Jumbo awoke the first.

'All right, all of you, you can fall out. Have someone stay on the set all night, each one of you.'

Felix stumbled out first, after saluting. The other squadron leaders followed suit through the blanket hanging over the back; they saluted in the dark and went through the mizzle to pass on their orders undismayed – whatever those orders might be. To ready men for battle once more, after what we had been through, was no enviable task. I got down and stood beside Rex in the rain while Jumbo seemed to uncoil, his wet eyes enlarging in the lamplight. He gave the appearance of forgetting about our presence for a moment, rummaging around his makeshift desk for something or other. Then he did something I'd never known him do before. He came and sat on the tailboard at the back and looked down at us, legs hanging.

'Were you hit lately?' he asked Rex.

'No, sir. I was not.'

'Edwardson was.'

'Hit but not penetrated.'

'But it isn't just that. Are you . . . all right?'

'Right as rain, sir.'

'Would you like a drink? Haig and Haig.'

'I don't think so, thanks, Colonel. My piles have been playing up of late. Besides, if we're going out again, why, it would send me to sleep. I mean, with this new show coming up.'

'What new show?'

'I mean, we have to get out of here, sir.'

Jumbo stuck a dead pipe quickly into one corner of his mouth. He stared through the looped blanket into the dark over our shoulders.

'Ever had that feeling of *absence*, have you?'

'I don't think so.' Rex, cautiously.

'I mean, that sensation of . . . not being there. One had it in the blue.'

'Definitely not, sir.'

'You farmed your own land in peacetime, didn't you?'

'I did. When I could.' Rex cautious still. The storm was brewing. 'Had a bailiff. Bought freehold, don't y'know.'

'Was the going good?' mused Jumbo Richely.

'The going was very good,' asseverated Rex at my side.

'Well, you just shot up two civilians today, I saw you.'

Rex took a pace back. 'You're talking tripe, sir,' he said.

'Those blighters in black coats. I saw it. They came out of that farmhouse and you mowed them down with small-arms fire. Could have been a mistake in the heat of the moment, of course.'

'It wasn't a mistake, sir.'

'You killed two of them.'

'And I've just killed a third, Colonel.'

'They aren't Army personnel, Rex. You know AMGOT orders. Any of that kind we catch we send back to JAG.'

He was referring to Judge Advocate General's staff, a combined Central Mediterranean op.

There was a very long silence and I could hear Rex taking in his breath and then he said, 'My Beza was spraying wildly, sir. You know how it is when you can't hold the traverse. The turret was swinging round ... '.

'I hate those types as much as you do, Rex. But you didn't have to go out and get another one, did you?'

'They'd been torturing Eytie women, sir.'

'Who's sure of that?'

'Who's sure of anything?' Rex spoke in anger.

Jumbo clapped his hands. His brows rose.

'I suppose you're right. Just don't tell me you're getting premonitions, that's all. You're tired, Rex, that's the sum of it.'

Rex said nothing. He raised his worry beads placatingly.

Jumbo's eyes flashed out at him. 'I don't want to ask for a transfer, but I can't take much more of this sort of behaviour from you, Rex. All right, then. There's no infantry to get corns on their knees patrolling for us. This is what we shall do, Division permitting. And I want every man jack in the Reg to know it, too. Most of the mine fields in these parts have been effectively dive-bombed by the Yanks so we should have a clear run out. First dawn in this kind of weather won't be till after five. And with a bit of luck this rain will keep up so that Jerry won't be able to sight eighty-eights till well after six. Any fog favours us. I want it all to happen in the most natural manner imaginable.'

'What, sir?'

'The enemy simply must not know – I repeat, *must not know* – that we're on to his tactics. That we know he's going to overrun us. Each squadron will advance in turn, fall back down the hillside towards the Cerasola road, where it will look as if we are regrouping for a new position. All tanks to be no more than two hundred yards from the road itself. Not that that's much use after the strafing it's had.'

'Get out, sir, you mean? Vamoose?'

In the dark Jumbo nodded wearily. He reached back for his map-case, his dead pipe bobbing.

'No tank to start up till it's in position. We'll try to slip down the hill on our own. That will be the signal for the next to come on down. The Boche will simply think we're on individual maintenance or something. We'll move in the following order: Recce Group, A, B, C, Headquarters. Directly you in the Recce have got position, the first "A" Squadron tank will move off. There'll be just enough light to see, but not to be hit. I shall vary the intervals of approach, so as not to let on it's an organised movement. At oh-four-hundred all the regiment should be facing west. Except for your tanks, Rex. You'll be facing north. You'll have the most difficult task. Not too much of a slope there.'

'For a change,' Rex grumbled.

We smiled together. It was a novel idea. I can't say I liked it.

'Synch' watches,' said Jumbo.

Mine read just after two a.m. Another sleepless night, to add to the others.

An old desert tune came back to me:

Wanderers eastward, wanderers west,
Know you why you cannot rest?

'I'll give the signal to go,' Jumbo went on, 'as soon as you, Rex, in our lead, can see clearly your first eighty-eight.'

'Thanks, sir. Thanks a lot.'

'And remember, total silence till then. Surprise is everything. If we can make the displacement like that, without arousing attention, we've got to have at least an hour of complete quiet so the Hun won't have any suspicions we're up to something. After that, it's each man for himself. The Regiment will re-form in the village back there.'

I thought of oxen with wooden yokes, a few pathetic sheep the peasants milked for cheese, and girls in flimsy black cotton dresses with bare and shapely legs carrying sacks of fodder for their animals. On the way they would be looking out for dandelion leaves for the family dinner.

'All clear?' asked Jumbo quietly, staring hard at his watch.

'As mud,' reciprocated Rex dully.

We did not want to go out again. Not now.

'Well, see that everyone is fully alert. I don't have to tell you two that this is a matter of life and death.'

He didn't, indeed.

'Any questions?'

'No, sir.'

We saluted, turned, were about to march off, when Jumbo held us – 'Just a minute there, Rex.'

'Sir?'

'I see you tore the leg of your trousers. At the calf.'

Rex simulated curiosity, glancing down at his cord slacks.

'So I did, sir.'

'How did you manage to do that, I wonder?'

'Some projection in the tank, I imagine.'

'Of course. It couldn't possibly have been a bullet, could it? You'd have had to go back to MO for that.' He had kept all irony from his voice but suddenly he snapped into the night, almost hissing his words – 'Rex, I don't have to tell you, tank squadron leaders of your experience are damn precious in Fifth Army at the moment. And I don't have to tell you, either, that you're one of the best of all.' His voice rose. 'Get a move on, man, *get a move on*. You don't think I'm going to let the commander of the best Recce Group around swan off into the dark alone with his driver behind enemy lines, do you? You can fight twice as long as the youngest of us and you know it ...'

His voice had risen. His raw eyes gleamed.

Rex cut in, 'I tell you, sir, they were torturing women there. Didn't you hear ...?'

'I didn't hear, and I did hear,' calmly snapped Jumbo back. 'Our business is to fight.'

'But you can't let that happen, sir.'

'I tell you they were officially civvies, those two you killed.'

'So were they civvies who shot the Norfolks, sir. At Calais. It's just part of their army, that's all. I don't pretend to understand it, anyway. We didn't have them in the bled. But there was a scout car there. The bastards were getting away. I hate black leather on principle. You saw me put a couple of bursts into them. That was all. Maybe I was aiming for one of the Mark IVs.'

'Maybe,' scoffed Jumbo. 'Maybe you were knocking off a hunk of the moon, as it came sailing by.'

'And I put the beggars to rest, you see. They ... rejoined their ancestors,' gritted Rex through his teeth. He had spoken in heat, and I saw it was not rain, but sweat, that pearled his forehead.

Jumbo sat forward on his camp chair, pensive, increasingly sombre, staring into nowhere.

'That sort of thing could stir up one hell of a mess. I thought you were off your chump – right out in front of us all like that.' He tapped his chin with a chinagraph map pencil. 'Don't ever do that again. Not in my command.'

'I'd liquidate the lot if I could, sir.'

'When we get back to Martina, I'm putting you head of the list for leave, Rex. And this time you aren't declining it.'

Twice already he had given his place for furlough to younger men, more anxious than he. Over a year ago I'd taken a few days back with him in Cairo. He'd nearly been thrown out of the Gezira Club for being so unshaven – though there were Naval types with beards about. Neither of us had had a presentable tunic. At Groppi's and the Continental Rex had seemed ill at ease. Among all those base wallahs with their fly whisks and brilliant buttons he had lumbered like some prehistoric animal, useless and in the way. So I had not been entirely surprised to find that note pinned to the pillow of his bed on the third morning: *Just found a convoy going forward Sidi Omar Feel worried about that pinion-wheel Have fun.*

Cursing him I had stumbled on a three-tonner going up

the Trigh – the Trigh Capuzzo, that beaten pathway in the middle of the bled – and I had followed him back to the line, cutting short my leave by a good three days or more.

'I don't know how much longer I can tolerate you, Rex,' Jumbo was now saying in the same moody tone of voice.

'What do you mean, sir?'

'You know what I mean perfectly well.'

Rex's jaw muscles stood out in the wet and for a second I was distressed by the sight of a great pleat in his wrinkled forehead, as if pleading.

'One burst, sir. That was all. For dogs like them.'

'Do I again have to remind you that you're in the army? Not in some private shindig of your own.'

Rex seemed to have difficulty breathing.

'You mean to say, Colonel, you absolutely forbid me, should I see such types again?'

'Absolutely.'

I said: 'If Rex goes on leave, sir, might I be put on roster with him? I'm due.'

'Overdue, both of you. I'll think about it. Now you can fall out.'

We saluted punctiliously and footed it to our tanks. I think Jumbo waved a hand, in acknowledgement of the salute or out of plain friendliness: I did not know, and the last I saw of our commander there was an oriental statue, gazing into the darkness and the wet. A final gleam from the sabre followed us.

When I left Rex by my tank he was slipping the worry-beads through his fingers, the Italian rifle-bolt protruding from a chest pocket. His eyes were pressed shut and I suppose it was the rain that gathered in drops at the edge of his eyes.

'Good luck, Geoff,' he said. I felt a grip on one shoulder and then he was gone.

Now there is always something particularly unpleasant about resting immobile in silence while some yards away your enemy is sedulously preparing to annihilate you. I have never enjoyed the sensation at the best of times. I suppose it is a little like a man in the condemned cell hearing his scaffold being carpentered up, in the courtyard outside. Anyway, the sounds that came to us in the damp obscurity were similarly furtive yet menacing. The hands of my watch didn't seem to move. With everything finished, everything ready, my gunner and my loader simply waited, cramped in the tank, for the first whitening of the dawn sky. Our patience at such moments was those of animals, really, something beyond the human. And our instincts perhaps answered in an animal, tactile fashion. Morris gave me courage, stilled the stupid beating of my heart. I tried to lend some of it to Whitey, who gave what he had to Tich. Tich, Whitey, Morris, three men come from the ends of England . . . I felt a sudden indignation against fate and its presumption in calling them to this destiny. I had been lucky compared to them. Perhaps I deserved to die. They did not. What had such men done to merit a small seat in a steel cell where they would shiver until molten metal hurled through upon them, smashing tendons, muscles, bones and fibres? I looked once more at my watch. Oh – fo-uh – twenty-five.

Apparently we were effecting the manoeuvre successfully to this point. Runners came up from HQ and gave us reports now and then. The laager, you see, had been bivvied on this hill, looking out and looking down. The drivers of the individual Cruisers had aimed their tanks westwards, for the descent, before cutting motors. Then the first three tanks of our Group had let off their heavy hand-brakes and slid down the incline to the roadway. There was no sound of their engines, nor of the hydraulic pulsing of their brakes. Their tracks made a dull rumble that confused itself with the sundry anonymous explosions in the thick Italian night. Three tanks had made it down and a runner been sent up to 'A' Squadron to say that we were forming our positions. These men spoke softly in the night because it really was a matter of life and death.

It was different from the desert. That was what made us old commanders uncomfortable. That was what was worrying Rex, I knew. The bled was too vast for human habitation, that was why the wogs all crouched together in their *ksours*. So what we were going to do we had never done, and we knew that it was not something easy to accomplish. Here, we were bound closely one to another. There was no freedom of action. We were in what they called civilisation. And yet it was here, in a new war, that you em-geed personnel debouching from Panzers, it seemed, and I had done the same. They were strafing pilots who baled out of fighter planes on both sides now. In the blue we tank soldiers had not wanted to do things like that. Something had rendered it difficult for us to kill personnel. There was a sort of unformulated parenthood, a relationship, that made it really hard to turn Bezas and Brownings onto personnel. Von Ravenstein hadn't done it. Rommel hadn't done it. And yet now it was all mixed up. There was this ugliness in the beauty. I was too young to understand it all, I guess. But I sensed. There were the great tow-headed prisoners we took, who were escorted to back areas by no more than a Corp with the usual Lee-Enfield (the Boche were glad to get shot of it now the Russian front was a possibility); and there were the figures in black leather who tore out toenails, somehow sexual and disgusting. Some abortion of the norm. I looked at my watch. Four twenty-eight.

It took us next.

I began to be afraid. Heavily afraid, in a way I did not like. We all knew what those noises were. We had heard the distant shouts, the clink of limbers, the orders. The older hands among us knew, at any rate. The Chleuh was ringing us with anti-tank guns. Running down our side of the incline our Group would in fact be passing dead in front of that ring of eighty-eights. Jerry used his anti-tank guns much as a naval task force did its destroyer screen. The Shermans had seventy-five millis but not us. A Sherman had a rounder turret than those of our Cruisers, whose sloping planes were designed to deflect shot (and did so), but in every other respect was superior. I'd have given anything for their gun just then.

A host of shadows swarmed through my mind. So many

things could happen. Tich had been having difficulty with the starter motor in this new tank we'd been given. Then again, we could hit a log in the dark, jam. There was a click in my headphones. That was enough. The Regimental frequency had been established. Four twenty-nine.

I was right behind Edwardson because he had asked to go first and Rex wanted him to. Rex insisted on going last. His last tank down would be the first to start its engines, at which point we would all go hell for leather to the south. We were by no means certain of our security. It was a fluid situation, as I have said, with total confusion up in the Anzio beachhead. There could also be isolated areas of enemy infantry about, with Panzerfausts at hand. They were the same in most ways as the American bazooka and, fired at a proper angle, could go through a tank like butter. So a lot depended on Edwardson.

Four thirty at last, and the ratchets of his tank's handbrake sounded clearly through the air towards me. The hulk slipped off.

For the next eternity of a quarter of an hour I rechecked the ammo bins, the Tannoy, the gauges, the breech block. Morris and Whitey sat still like acolytes in church.

Exactly at oh – four – three – five on my reliable Rolex I realised that Edwardson had started up! The night burst to his radials. My God! The idiot! He was going to ruin the whole movement for the entire Regiment. I felt a bit of nausea, as though someone had hit me hard in the solar plexus. He was still only perhaps thirty yards ahead of me but his exhaust was blowing scarlet in my face. I had to decide, I had to decide. The night was a-roar with a Rolls Royce engine made in a heavily camouflaged factory in Edgbaston, near Birmingham. So – Birmingham steel against Essen steel. At least we didn't make thumbscrews. I picked up my Tannoy.

'Driver, start up. Follow tank ahead.'

Then the race began. Helter skelter. Would they get us before we got them? It was difficult to turn an eighty-eight – that gun for which we had developed an almost hypnotic reverence in the bled – laterally. If we had surprise, if we could get through them in time, we'd be safe. That and that only. It was all we had. So we roared through the whitening night behind the vague form of Edwardson's tank ahead. It was a sticky business. There could even be collisions in this murk, as there had been in khamseens in the desert. Were we to be condemned to a life that was, in the old saying, 'nasty, brutish, and short'?

Now this uneasiness possessed me, as though some support had been withdrawn. The darkness was a wall. Such must have been what the world was like before creation. I had to penetrate it. To make the effort. Let it close over me. I was at the helm. But I was alone, each man jack of us was alone where we stood or sat. And every form was gone, too, turret, aerial, track. There was a dreadful smoothness in that absolute night – before the first flash of fire.

Then I felt the suspension rocking under us, the sighting vanes swayed to the lay of the land and the night burst to blinding explosions. I heard the usual whistle and whiplash overhead and my face felt flayed. We hadn't been hit but there was something funny in our port track. All the squadron had started up now and were going hell for leather. Thanks to whatever it was Edwardson had done the plan for silent withdrawal on our handbrakes had been abandoned. It was a mess. Once again.

I remembered a story from the desert. We had come across a Valentine knocked out facing the enemy. It had been hit from behind near a stone sangar, and Rex had later told me it had been *funking* ... shirking fire. Would it have done us any good if I'd pumped shot into Edwardson's engine ahead? I doubted it. In the bled, or *douar*, it was different. Tich was driving well, avoiding the skyline. We'd have been sitting ducks, else. In the flash of another shot in the valley I had a sudden vision of our enemy, that enormous gun like a felled pine trunk, with little insects dashing about; it was still attached to its half-track, I saw. Edwardson's turret was skewed to the left. I got Morris to traverse right in case there was another of the bastards there. I felt very frightened.

Our fire was giving us away. We were charging in open order, and more, down a frozen hillside in Italy onto well-sited anti-tank gun emplacements. It seemed suicidal. Morris, who had worked on his traversing lever with a muffled hammer (I carried my binoculars in a sock), swore through thin lips. I knew he couldn't see. When Morris saw, he killed. Odd activity in one of normally peaceful occupation.

Suddenly, in a flash, there were men running, strongly running in the snub helmets of the Boche. We were hurtling down and Tich called back to me, 'There's summat funny with that track, sir, she's not answering when I turn,' and I'd thought it was perhaps the pin and then we were rocking to the descent and cradled in a short stretch of mud, so I let them have it.

'Gunner, traverse right! Steady ... on! Anti-tank gun, two o'clock small farmhouse. *Give it all you've got!*'

Morris got off two accurate shots, both of which hit the shield hard. Flames arose in the half-dark. I heard men screaming and to me for once that seemed a satisfactory sound.

'Small-arms ... for all you're worth!'

I shut my eyes. I squeezed them tight. But I could not close my ears.

What more to say? The Beza began spitting viciously and in the dawn Germans died. Perhaps Kurt Bleyle was amongst them.

'Hello all stations HERALD. Be prepared to move off ...'

A bail-out to my left. We left it behind.

A sudden stifling light as if from a furnace. A roar.

'Gunner! Machine-gun ...'

I did not have to say any more. Morris understood me. It was each man for himself as we thundered down the slopes to the village in the valley. I looked away as he sprayed the men in snub helmets. And then I saw something I did not like at all.

It is difficult to distinguish it now, in calm. But I was right behind Edwardson who was getting off his cannon like some crazy man and then his tank seemed to swerve to one side in the direction of an entrenchment. At first I thought it a natural gulley in the terrain, it wasn't easy to see in that light. And then they were all screaming around the demolished eighty-eight. I told Tich to keep head on.

Now it may have been my imagination, looking back on it all; after all I was controlling all the instruments in my Cruiser, but I could see Edwardson directing his directly onto personnel. That is, he was going to *overrun human beings*. I had never done that. We had never done that. Boche were running left and right. It was happening. Edwardson's tank seemed to draw up slightly, rocking on its haunches, breathing heavily. Then it ran forward fast and it crushed in deliberation two or three men in those snub helmets who tried to hurl themselves frantically out of its path. I had never seen men overrun like that before and I knew I did not want to see it again.

'Gunner! Traverse right. Anti-tank gun eleven o'clock clump of trees. *Fire!*'

As Tich held to hard ground to give our gunner more stability of shot I saw Morris get off two splendid rounds. Both struck low on the starboard shield. Whether they penetrated or not I did not know because we were swerving quickly southwards, Tich using the slight cover of a dune.

'Gunner! Give 'em all you've got!'

This time Morris understood me. The Beza started to spit and crackle, faster than a Browning, the belts feeding into it below me, and another group of Boche folded at the knees towards the farmhouse. I turned my eyes away from that sight. There was screaming near the anti-tank gun we'd hit. And then I saw Edwardson do it again. Yes, his tank slowed, dragged right on one track, then deliberately ran over a manned foxhole. I heard the yells, this time I even saw his Cruiser bump a couple of times, as it ran over bodies. I could not look at that. I tried to busy myself with my immediate command. It seemed we were through.

But not Rex. Dawn was opening the sky. I could hear the chatter on the set, the various squadron leaders calling into Jumbo. They had all seemed to have got away and were disengaging from the enemy who had certainly been taken by surprise, by our form of movement. Yet Rex had hung behind, the idiot; he had even halted at the foot of the hill, in plain range of the anti-tank guns. In the growing light I put my binoculars to my eyes as we ran, and suddenly I saw the turret of the Ironmaster turning. His gun was trained at the farmhouse. Then it pumped into the stucco of those walls, crumbling one side to powder. I saw a car come into view, it looked a little like a French Citroën Quinze of the time, and then it jumped insanely to the lead Rex hurled at it. Then his m-g swept the terrain around.

'Hallo, all stations NATHAN,' I heard in my ears. 'Hel-lo NATHAN. Have passed through cordon of anti-tank guns. Rejoin and conform as per orders. Over.'

When Rex's turn came I heard him say, 'BENJAMIN One, okay, off.'

That was all.

'BENJAMIN One, why are you not conforming? Over.'

'... some trouble with our suspension apparently ...'

'Hel-lo, all stations BENJAMIN. You are to conform and follow as per orders. Out.'

At that point I asked Whitey to pass me up the flannel-covered water bottle. Perhaps I hoped there was a last linger of that smoky scotch on my tonsils. There was none. The water tasted of good detergent.

'Hel-lo, BENJAMIN One. You have heard my orders. Off to you.'

Was Rex beating impetuously on the steel of his turret flaps? It seemed so. Tich lurched the tank ahead. I slugged thirstily at the water bottle, rinsing my mouth with the water before swallowing. I remembered the days in the desert when we had been rationed to two cups a day, brackish, heavily chlorinated. By comparison any rain we collected had such a fine taste, it was so pure it made you feel young again to drink it, although I was only just in my majority.

Dawn lit our faces. There is always something about light coming into the sky. A new beginning, really. I defy anyone not to feel sensible when rain falters and dies, and sun shows beyond the mountains. It was a good feeling, all in all.

'Hallo then, BENJAMIN. NATHAN calling. All stations BENJAMIN. Hear me now. Enemy less numerous to immediate south-east. As we do not know blind terrain beyond the Faito pass figures – seven – seffen – oh – three, follow A Squadron to heights indicated open order. Over.'

We acked. Followed Jumbo's orders. He was in control. In full control.

Was Rex?

It was a good idea. As judicious as Jumbo always was.

Given an English education, I had either been ordered about, or ordered myself. I answered to Jumbo's wisdom. The tanks of the Chleuh nearly always deployed here and there in order, first and foremost to bring out their anti-tank guns – very precious to them, at this moment. There wasn't the easy run for limbers, as there had been in the desert.

It was a good idea because we were gaining elevation.

'Good shooting,' I called down to Morris. 'You were right on today.' I patted his back and he looked up at me with a big grin and held the thumb and first finger of his shooting hand in a little circle. We were through.

But we did not know the high land beyond Faito and simply followed 'A' Squadron under Felix. I heard Rex's guttural accents on the set. He was rejoining and moving fast on my right now. I was busy following orders.

It was all quite organised now. The Boche Panzers would look after their anti-tank guns, first and foremost. They would be on our backs when they had done so, no doubt, but for the moment we had the start on them. Our Group swanned along the shoulders of the mountains, under Fuge, Furlito, Rotundo, the hill villages hatched into the sky high above. God knew how people existed there. That was probably all they did – existed. We had already gained height by hundreds of yards and the snow line was not far above us. As before, I ran behind Edwardson whose Cruiser seemed to be behaving in somewhat of an unprofessional fashion, stopping and starting irregularly.

In holding onto these sloping contours the problem was

that we could only do so fairly slowly. Twice I asked Tich how much gas we had left. It was not a good place in which to break down. I'd known better, let's say. So we continued our low-profiled ascent of the hills of the area. The sun was suddenly brilliantly shining, low and lancing at us, and the rain left the sky. Far beneath, down to our right, I could see the main road we'd used after crossing the river. It was battered to bits, with odds and ends of transport and beaten-up US half-tracks littered about it. I hope to Christ that REME could get another Bailey across the Garigliano before the Chleuh mounted a really large attack on our now precarious beachhead. Our side, there was still a depot of gas guarded by the Cheshires. When it had been bombed or shot up out of existence we wouldn't be able to move. Dead ducks, all.

Suddenly I began to feel intolerably tired. For nights now none of us had had more than two or three hours of uninterrupted slumber – thanks to guard duty, and maintenance, and the like. I reckoned we still had another hour's driving at this slow speed before we could laager at the appointed place in the plain. At that moment I saw that Rex's tank, about a hundred yards to my right, was being fired on. The first thing I noticed was, as usual, liquid spurting from a perforated Jerry-can slung in rear. More of his damn pile lotion going. And then I heard the chatter of light-arms fire from the valley. Rex's head ducked into the turret and I put my glasses up to see what the hell was happening.

'Driver, slow down! Slightly right. Ahead!'

So near and yet so far, once more. I saw a kaleidoscope of images as we bumped down and they included the scimitar shape of the magazine of a machine-gun firing. It peeked over a rise in the ground ahead of Rex's tank.

'Driver, right. Straight to small knoll one o'clock cypress tree.'

Rex's hand came up in a wave to me but I could see that he couldn't find where he was being fired on. Perhaps his periscope was shot, like mine had been. So far they hadn't turned their gun on me, perhaps due to the sighting of their foxhole, but I knew that wouldn't last long, either. For I had recognised that magazine and I knew exactly what had happened. It was a Bren gun firing on us, one of our own.

Beneath me I felt Tich locking the right track and grinding the great mass of metal round and then we jerked harshly forward. He must have thought me nuts. Morris and Whitey then probably imagined me even more consignable when I took out my handkerchief, stained with snot, oil and the odd rum ration, and began waving it hectically in the air. I only hoped they would see me in time. Another burst spattered the earth around Rex's tank, then some order was shouted out and the firing stopped. A moment later a lanky figure in battledress and British steel helmet stood up guardedly on the knoll.

'What in the hell do you think you're playing at?' I asked him as we came abreast and Tich brought the Cruiser rocking to a halt.

'I'm dreadfully sorry, old boy,' came the reply, as the Second Lieutenant swung his Webley. 'But we only took up these positions in the night. And since those Free French got surprised like that the other side, why we weren't taking any chances. Our CO said shoot first and ask questions after.'

'Okay. No harm done, luckily. But you damn near scalped my squadron leader.'

'Dreadfully sorry, old boy.'

We looked along the hillside. Rex had surfaced cautiously again and, realising now what had happened, he got his tank going. I waved and Smithers soon had his Cruiser beside mine, though at the certain distance we all observed for tanks.

Rex and I found ourselves in the middle of a green battalion of Hampshires who had taken up position among the stones and mud. I didn't envy them. We recamouflaged our tanks with their help and each of us took a mug of coffee in the cold air. Somehow they had managed to get some of that good American coffee. It cut into the dust and grime of the day. We sat back against their HQ Bren-gun carrier, chatting. The tension of movement and change was slowly rinsed from our blood. I saw a man sleeping on a groundsheet, his face extraordinarily young. What faint dreams lay behind his secret eyes? Even in our fellowship lay fear. Death haunted these hills and valleys. One thing worried me in particular.

When Edwardson's tank had come up I went over to see if all was well with him. To my surprise he squeezed out of the driver's compartment, in front.

'My driver was having some difficulty with the revs,' he said nonchalantly. 'Probably one of the petrol pumps. I relieved him. I wanted to have a fast run down there. Anyway, I seem to be able to see better than him in the dark. I've been wondering if I should send him back for testing.'

'About all I could see of you when we started was your exhaust flames.'

'I suppose so,' he said.

I did not ask him why he had started up. Let Rex do that.

'It's my hands I'm worried about,' he said as we strolled over to the others, and the boiling coffee.

'You mean, for piano-playing?'

'Yes. That's it.' Then he added with a chuckle. 'The legions return.' He stared at his endlessly long fingers and flexed their joints.

It was like that with him. He was 'off'. You didn't want to be around such people, then, nor to have them around you. I watched him guardedly. He had a grave and satisfied air. Then the pianist's fingers which had guided a Mark V Cruiser over the bodies of still living Germans grasped a steaming mug of American coffee. He poured it down in a gulp.

Rex was once again in good form, squatting by the primus on which the water for the coffee was boiling. He had a relaxed, majestic air, as if he didn't really belong here, really, his face bitten by frost, by the rain beaten, a presence. I knew I wanted no other commander.

'Sod this frigging sod of a mucking frigging...' some soldier nearby was saying, trying to prize open an ammo crate.

It seemed that the Chleuh had only recently evacuated this

hill. So there were many hurriedly dug graves, with Boche helmets stuck on crosses. Sad, abandoned, they spoke the speech of pain. In one spot, perhaps a former Spandau emplacement, there were Jerry uniform tunics, material, old cans of jam lying in disorder on the ground. A Hampshire captain told me they'd even found some women's underclothing in one haversack. There was no pattern to anything. No promise of the flower. I think I yearned for that then, like the beauty of a face. Presumably these few stunted trees would bear leaves soon, the soft voices of spring would caress these fields and hillsides. Girls as graceful as Maddelena would one day walk in these forgotten shadows, and there would be no smoke on their horizons. I wondered what the devil Rex would put into that damn log book of his this night. Above all, it was sadness which reigned over this country now.

'Edwardson bothers me,' I told him when I got him to myself as we rose to part from the Hampshires. 'He took his tank over personnel today. It didn't seem to trouble him.'

'I know.'

'Goddamit, he even drove it himself.'

Rex nodded. As we fell into step, I knew we were of the same opinion.

Before we left this solitary and vulnerable infantry outpost, they wanted us to meet their C.O. He had established himself in a ruined sheep-pen, on the far side. The place was a face-stone crater with walls at least a yard thick, for the local peasantry valued their livestock. The Commanding Officer himself was full length on some Army blankets in a corner. We saluted, and he waved a friendly hand. He was weak with dysentery, it seemed. He and Rex got on famously from the first. Apparently, they'd both been in South America – actually the Argentine – at the same time. He told us that when they'd come up the engineers had been repairing the Bailey fast and some more assistance and supplies would soon be over. He assured us we now had complete command in the air, something we had not known in the blue. Evidently his battalion had landed at Naples which he described as a 'vomitorium', being bombed nightly – often by both sides. The Anzio beachhead was requiring more and more reinforcements in order to hold and the port of Naples was a sight. Shipping lay at anchor as far as the eye could see, fighters covering it constantly in the sky, with a network of barrage balloons up also. What's more, it seemed that Vesuvius had erupted – for only the second time this century. It was no more than a slow boil-over, visible like a red worm down the eastern flank of the mountain, but the locals were superstitious and were clearing out fast around Herculaneum. It didn't help.

Before we left, the man insisted on giving Rex a Luger which he'd found in the sheep-pen on taking it over. We weren't strong on souvenirs but Rex took the tidy little automatic and thanked him. It slid into one of his pockets inconspicuously. Then we rejoined our tanks.

We soon reached Martina without incident and found the main body of the regiment laagered to the south of Monte Valle. Night was falling, we were tired and hungry. Rex's gunner was getting more and more pain from his leg. Rex took him over personally to the MO who diagnosed a fracture and splintered shin. When we had seen to our men we presented ourselves at once to Jumbo.

The ten-tonner was ringed with vehicles filling up, their crews strolling about and doing odd maintenance jobs or simply yarning about the day. It had been a full one, though not our first such. We liked the look of this area at once. We could even hear friendly planes overhead. There were some heavy battery positions visible towards the river.

Inside the truck Jumbo was propped back against the cab, with that rusty sabre winking above his head.

'I'm glad to see you,' he said straight away. 'There's some tea, if you want it, but I'm afraid all the scotch is gone. Seems that the situation has changed. A whole new Division is being pushed in to cross the Gari. 8th Indian along with our 4th. General Anders and his Polish boys are having another bash at Cassino, God bless 'em. It's that which is holding everything up. We're way behind schedule to relieve Anzio, of course. Anyway, Brigade has told us we may retire two squadrons for repairs and in order to be made up to strength. There's a REME depot now just the far side of the river and as soon as they get that Bailey up we can send them back. I hear it's almost ready now and this time it'll be far more closely guarded and held. Especially from the air. The Yanks are helping there a lot. Rex,' he concluded slowly but with emphasis, 'as of oh-nine-hundred tomorrow morning the Recce Group is withdrawn from front-line action. That's an order.'

'Sir.'

'And here's another. As of the same date and the same hour I'm sending you back for eight days leave. D'you hear? A "B" Echelon truck or other transport will take you. I'm watching you go,' he said, sitting up straight and barking it out as if Rex were deaf.

'I read you loud and clear, Colonel,' grinned Rex in return. 'My gunner has broken his leg, anyway. So we only have three tanks mobile. If you're putting us LOB' – he was referring to the term of the time, *Left Out of Battle* – 'then I'd like to ask if Geoff here could take leave with me too.'

'I take it this is a condition of your acceptance of furlough, Rex,' said Jumbo ironically.

'Edwardson can remain in command, sir,' Rex came back with a somewhat guilty smile. 'He's completely competent. He knows everything we want in the way of refitting.'

'Permission granted, Captain Davidson. Oh-nine-hundred tomorrow morning. Now dismiss, both of you, sharp.'

We saluted and went off in the dark. I felt asleep on my legs. Never had I felt so tired. It was sagging at me, bones, marrow and all. Rex's battledress jacket was caked in dried mud; all marks of identity, flashes and tabs and so on, gone from it. Looking out of the turret of a Cruiser when you were following another got you like that. Stuff was chucked up, like riding a steeplechase, in fact. With his beret plastered to the back of his head by his goggles he looked strangely anonymous, indecipherable. Yet he was still amazingly full of vigour. How the man did it I never knew.

'Wake up, Geoff,' he said, slapping my back quite hard. 'We'll just go the rounds of our men, then we can turn in and get some sleep. Amazing we got through that lot, wasn't it?'

'Half an hour later and we wouldn't have. What made Edwardson start up like that? He nearly cooked the goose for all of us.'

'Apparently couldn't get lee without. So he said. Anyhow I'll take the Group back over tomorrow morning, then we'll hitch-kitch together.'

'For Naples?'

'Why not? We could probably get a bath there.'

'I could use one.'

'I've needed one for two years.'

There was only one other incident that occurred before our leave, but it was a curious one, and perhaps typical of the crazy confusion of that time.

After Rex and I had seen that all was well with our men we walked back through the night to a huddle of houses, perhaps three or four, which showed in the starlight in the valley. It was said that 'Q' had come up – Quartermaster's – with some much needed supplies, and doubtless rum and fags. As we came up to the village, if such it could be called, we saw a pair of baggage trucks and men unloading them. The Queen's Brigade was doing the honours. A cheerful Sergeant offered us some chocolate, which we accepted gladly. There seemed to be a lot of activity further on.

Out of curiosity more than anything we entered the first house we came to and it was one of the poorest and meanest abodes I have ever been in. Two soldiers were seated on rickety cane chairs by the entrance being treated to the inevitable vino by a wizened old man in black and his crone of a wife. There was no table but I saw two more chairs hung upside down from the ceiling, each with a pair of man'sclean shoes on it. A small oil lamp flickered. The owner addressed us at once in English, with a loud American accent. He seemed genuinely glad to see us and hoped the war was over for him now. Our two soldiers had evidently given him some cans of bully and a carton of cigarettes that he could barter. His wife lowered the chairs by some sort of pulley and invited us to sit down with them.

Again, I was touched. The rudeness of these dwellings and the paucity of their possessions gave such peasant people a sort of vagabond divinity. They were the most simple people I had ever met. All the same, I remembered our last visit to one of these hovels and, while Rex sat down to drink and talk in the low light, I wandered through a door to the back premises. Here was a chair, a table, a rough chest-of-drawers, a low iron bed, two sacks of maize in one corner. A woman was standing there.

She was older than Maddelena, though like her the daughter of the house. She was nearer twenty-seven or twenty-eight. She was solidly built, buxom, with strong haunches and fine thrusting breasts. She smiled at me with beautiful wet teeth and I noticed she moved about barefoot. I talked to her a little while, feeling my desire rise towards her. She told me she had only been to a cinema twice, and only once to a dance in the neighbouring village. All summer she would get up at four and work in the fields till dusk. She was betrothed to an Italian who had been taken prisoner in Tunisia, on the retreat, and she was patiently waiting for him. Her simplicity and native eagerness made it such a pleasure to talk to her I could not bear to tear myself away. I felt certain she would remain chaste – I could read it on her brow – until her beloved returned. Such credulous and simple souls, rooted to their soil, were the most refreshing people I had ever met. I yearned to kiss her neck, it was so round and pure. But I restrained myself and rejoined Rex.

As we went out and along the road again he said, 'That man had been to America. Brook-a-lyn! But like the wog they still seem to think we're the big industrial power.'

'I think they'll soon be disillusioned,' I said. 'Look what the Yanks are bringing in.'

'I should have killed those bastards today, Geoff.'

'But it's not allowed!'

'Those SS swine are the worst of all, from what I can hear. Rommel hated them, so did Keitel and Kesselring.' He sighed and said quietly, 'It's all so mixed up. One doesn't know where one is any more. There was a family I once knew from Naples. Let's see if we can rout 'em out, heh? I say, you look half dead. I'm just going off to CCS to see they're looking after my gunner properly.'

'Want me to go with you?'

'Not necessary. Rendezvous at that house in the village, let's say, six a.m. We'll try to have a brew first and then take the Group back over the Bailey, what.'

We said goodbye. I am not entirely clear as to what did happen after that. I had a very clouded sensorium at the time. I visited my tank and posted the guards. Whitey was there, faithful to duty as ever, but Tich and Morris had sought a roof overhead in the village, or in one of the outlying houses – maybe even a cattle stall, if they could find such. I decided to do the same and took a couple of blankets from a bin, and wandered back once more. It was then there occurred one of those bizarre episodes of warfare which crop up once at least in the service of any long-time soldier, and which can all too easily put an end to your days.

The end of that shabby, half-ruined village now appeared to be swarming with sappers and fitters and the like. Dark cables snaked in the mud, something we hadn't seen in the desert much, if at all. In the blue we had lived and fought mainly from what were called boxes, fortified groups; these consisted for the most part of wheeled columns, mostly tracked vehicles of various kinds – armoured cars for reconnaissance, 25-pounders for hitting. Recce was often accompanied by a portee of this Battery, plus some infantry for night work. We tended to cast a cool eye at the apparatus and organisation of 'B' Echelon which, over here on the continent, had to accompany any large-scale move. We were wrong to do so, of course. But behind us now there always lay an entire civilisation of messes, hospitals, requisitioned rooms in good condition, forces newspapers, Red Cross, and Colour Sergeants in band-box order. They proliferated in our rear. Here in this village I saw groups of men in helmets and heavy belts laying what looked like high-tension cables. Rex and I liked liberty.

So I walked away from the few houses of this place to where stood another farm building by itself. A light came from a ground-floor window.

In the room I entered a Signals Corporal was squatting by a butane lamp surrounded by a veritable spider's web of wires. He was plugging and unplugging these into a console with mesmerising dexterity. I seemed to have stumbled on some forward switchboard. He barely looked up at me but went on working away with his set as if for dear life, murmuring messages in an inscrutable code from time to time, repeating his calls over and over, in the cold bombed building. It could have been a maniac's cell. Or a monk's.

'Sorry, Corporal,' I said, tottering on my legs.

He said nothing and I went out again.

I must have staggered blindly back to the road again and found another empty house there, because I remember climbing wooden stairs and finding myself in a fairly intact long chamber ... perhaps the top of some barn. I heard a snore from somewhere, threw down my blankets and was asleep before I hit them.

When I woke up sunlight streamed into the room. I tried to go to sleep again and would most likely have succeeded if I hadn't seen a pair of boots, equally recumbent, opposite me on the planking. I realised after an effort that these were not issue boots, and that the occupant's toes were sticking out of them in front. I had to be dreaming.

I sat up, rubbing at my eyes and squinting. There was no doubt about it, I was sharing the room with three members of the master race. At that moment the one lying on the right side opened an equally bleary eye, shouted and jumped up. Then they all jumped up. It was a ridiculous situation.

As far as I could see they weren't armed, but then neither was I, I'd left my Webley with Whitey, on guard at the tank. The three were filthily unshaven and unkempt, only two wearing forage caps, but they had the jump on me.

So when one shouted, *'Hände hoch!'* I obediently put my hands on my head. And I went down the stair slowly, the three Boches who had taken me prisoner right behind, and muttering in dialect. It became even more absurd. Out in the road there must have been at least eight Signals types hauling on a cable and swearing as they did so. They turned and gaped at what they saw.

''Ere, Sarg'!'

'Take a gander at this!'

As we emerged through the door in single file their Sergeant in charge simply stood there, hands on hips, grinning.

'Where the hell do you lot think you're going?'

Slowly, shyly, the three Germans put their hands on their heads. I lowered mine. I smiled at them and thanked the Sergeant who took them into custody. It must have been the shortest p-o-w period in military history. Who were they? Escaped prisoners themselves? Exhausted infantrymen who had somehow got left behind? I never knew. I saw them being marched off smartly and then Rex was coming along the road towards me, swinging that old rifle bolt of his in one hand. He'd dug up a new battledress from somewhere and looked very spruce and rested. I was never able to fathom his powers of recuperation.

'I've just been taken prisoner,' I told him.

'The hell you have!'

I told him the whole affair, and he laughed heartily.

'Your leg okay now, Rex?'

'Never felt better. What about yours?'

'Okay.'

'Ready to take off?'

'Ready.'

'Maybe we could get to an opera. The San Carlos.'

'Have to shave first.'

'Try that restaurant down by the docks. What's it called? Zi' Teres'?'

'Maybe we could take 'em some frogs for the pot.'

'How d'you like your lobster? Thermidor, Newburg?' We

used to make up menus for hours in the blue, against the day when we'd get back to better places. 'How about Tournedos Rossini?'

'Sure.'

'Just so long as they don't do them out of dog. Horse flesh I can stand.'

'What do you plan for the first night back?'

He didn't answer and I shouldn't have said it. That first night back in Cairo it had been the Sphinx. Four of us from the Reg. and two well-paid wog bints between us. Janine had been something from a Flaubertian dream, huddled on a hassock, nude as a slug, and giggling like hell. She made me feel so horny my teeth ached. Then all smiles had stopped together. I saw a schoolgirl's O of disbelief widen her cunt-pink lips as Rex approached her – in order of seniority, as he said later – a mottled hue flooding face and fully turgid member alike. It wasn't merely the muscular rigidity of his manhood that caused her that panicky convulsion in her belly's depths, nor the truly heroic angle from which it menaced her; the stretched silk of the ski-slope head was furiously engorged, the Cyclops eye a' dribble already, but it was the rimming of the thickest corona imaginable to man – it was almost a deformity, a ring of ruddy gristle to make even a gyppie hooker quake. Rex, however, most gently entered that gism-gristled furrow, bearded in a sole plump line, he was a veritable pedant in the saddle. He rogered as he did everything else – carefully yet with *brío*. Janine begged for more.

Now he was looking into the distance – *distrait*.

'I used to know this Contessa, Geoff.'

Gunfire growled on the mountains.

'Let's go.'

He took my arm.

A PU or Morris pick-up truck took us back, one bedding roll of personal effects between us. There were two Baileys over the river, not merely one, and we rattled across at a clip. On the far side, columns of infantry coming up and Boche prisoners going back. The latter sang strongly, as always:

Aus dem stillen Raume, aus der Erde Grund
hebt mich wie im Traume dein verliebter Mund ...

Yes, for them it was over. A cush camp under canvas, rationed by Yanks. Maybe my captors of that morning were already on their way there. Any prisoners we took who had been on the Russian front were thoroughly fed up with the war. We felt sad as we passed these reciprocal columns. Just mental fatigue, maybe.

We got to Naples by the straight road from Caserta. The Palace itself was now a combined HQ, British, American, Canuck, and New Zealand. Naples had been far more heavily bombed than we realised. It was over a year since we'd seen a big city, not counting Tunis which we'd only swanned through and that at a time when all electricity was still cut off. We felt lost in this crowded place, full of hearses drawn by black horses, their plumes black. Vesuvius glowed molten in the background. Tired, grubby, and unshaven we found temporary billet in an officers' mess near the old Parkers Hotel. That night we bunked down in a plywood-partitioned matchbox, next to which someone was playing a radio.

'*... so this BBC Programme is bringing all you fighting men out there, wherever you may be, the special request of your wives and sweethearts who are back here with us and ...*'

Music came through. If you could call it such. A songstress was subsiding slowly into marshmallow. Vera Lynn, Forces' sweetheart. Some of our men liked her. Some didn't.

'*Mrs. Morris' husband, so she tells us, is serving with our tankmen overseas, in some undeclared spot. ...*'

Rex was writing laboriously in his notebook. I looked over his shoulder:

'Arrived at Naples. See Naples and Die!'

Then – 'The world is the totality of facts.'

I could have crowned him.

Next morning the crowd in the Via Roma was bright, sharp, avid. Glossy black hair of the women, under kerchiefs, gaunt taut faces of the men in black. The desperate alleys behind, where children tried to sell their sisters for a couple of K rations. The iron sky of the Gallería Umberto where every uniform in the world, it seemed, except for that of the Chleuh, thronged. Up to the Town Major's, where we had to wait in line an hour. When we got into the first office, in order to inquire about any better lodging, a Staff Sergeant with brilliant boots made us sign the register without even looking up at us. Rex's horny hand, which had held glasses to his eyes under fire without trembling, signed and rested for an instant on the cheap deal table.

As we turned away, I heard the Sergeant mutter to a pal: 'Some of these characters who come in here could do with a nailbrush. Filthy, eh. To say nothing of a shave.'

Rex's hand tugged at my arm. His bandaged pince-nez winked.

'Let's get out of here, Geoff. See if I can find La Contessa.'

6

Naples seethed. Naples swarmed. Any morning the shine boys in the Gallería Umberto would buff the boots of the soldiers of eight different countries. From the Bank clear up to the Vomero, up what Musso had renamed the Via Roma, you had the most cosmopolitan, and corrupt, slice of Europe of the day. Everyone wanted to sell something – chiefly, their sisters or mothers, in the tiny side-streets that cut off into the refuse of this underbelly of the Axis. Churchill ought to have come out to see it, but he never did. For us it was a turning point of the war. Well, of everything, really.

From the Town Major, after endless waiting, we went to the Deputy Adjutant Provost Marshal down by the docks. We got a PU in the afternoon down the bay to a convalescent camp by the sea. The ride was really weird as the windshield was constantly pitted by what seemed like little stones, sharp and hard yet not enough to break the triplex. Evidently, so the goggled driver told us, it was from the eruption at Vesuvius. It grew heavier as we drove along.

The tented camp was filled with South Africans. Even in the back areas in the bled we had never seen such a mob and Rex decided we'd get back to Napoli and try our luck that very evening. But it was bad. They used to have those dieseline burners at street corners in Naples at that time; these sent up a thick smoke that was supposed to cloud the city in case of air attack. I don't know if it worked or not. The place was still getting its fair share of bombs. And if you were caught on the streets at the time, well no pea-souper in London could have been more opaque. Rex and I staggered through it holding on to each other. Yank MP and our own helped to steer the helpless about, here and there. And some of the Eyties weren't so helpless.

The All Clear sounded soon, luckily, and we had been standing over our bedding – hanging on to it, in fact – at a corner where we found some lodging. A huge palazzo, half-ruined with a concierge-type at the bottom who rented us a cold, duly palatial room. We dossed down, our guns beside us. The next day Rex found his Contessa.

Emilia Diobaldi was of the old Neapolitan aristocracy. Her husband Dino and she had stayed put throughout the whole Allied invasions and the subsequent bombing. They had almost no money, but a large mansion to one side the funicular which plunged through inky tunnels, down from the Vomero to the bay. They greeted Rex warmly and we were able to help them in little ways. The second night we took them out to dinner on the quays, at Santa Lucia. The *frutti di mare* was excellent, the Neapolitan wine less so. A violin mewed in the background, while coloured lights strayed (illegitimately) on the water. It was a cliché from another era.

Emilia was one of those bony Italian women who would have passed as aristocratic anywhere. Dino sat like a stick in his suit, one of shiny serge. He was immaculately dressed and, if his cuffs were frayed from too much washing, I'd bet the shirt he wore had a Sulka label. Dino was a professional 'uncle'. That is, he appeared at various receptions of what was left of the Neapolitan elite, at funerals and the like, as 'our uncle from Rome'. No questions were ever asked. Evidently it was a great mark of prestige in Naples of that time to have an uncle from Rome. They asked us back to eat with them two days later, and we accepted, hoping it would not cost them too dear. Rex promised we would bring rations, but it was clear they were offended by the idea.

The next night we scrounged tickets to the opera – it was *La Bohème*, of course, with an astonishingly healthy-looking Mimi – and then went to Manetta's after. This was the black market joint par excellence of the time. You could get almost anything there and, yes, the band had 'Lili Marlene' going practically at repeat. All around us the cunning faces of male Eyties swayed in the smoke, contrasting with those innocent countenances of young Yanks, British officers, Poles, New Zealanders, Free French, and the over-made-up faces of certain women with square-shouldered suits whose skirts were not notably in evidence.

Rex lit a cigarillo and said sleepily:

'It isn't the same here, Geoff.'

'What isn't?'

'The war, I mean.' He waved a hand. 'It's repulsive.'

We were silent for a while and I thought. At last I said, 'Do you realise I actually kicked Morris in the backside in my turret? Incredible.'

He shook his head.

'I'd never have done that in the blue.'

'Death's disgusting everywhere,' he said. 'Don't worry about it. I'm not enjoying myself here, are you?'

'No,' I said.

'Pay and get out?'

'Fine by me,' I said.

Rex signalled to the waiter.

'Thanks,' I said. 'Next time it's my turn.'

I stood up stiffly. My leg wound was playing up a bit. I seemed to have a deadness just under the kneecap, after long sitting. The waiter was spotting the bill with a flash. Rex peered through his bandaged pince-nez as he felt in a pocket, bringing up a pile of AMGOT notes of the time.

'Want women?' whispered the waiter.

'I don't think so, thanks,' I said.

'Sir?'

Rex said shortly, 'No.'

I knew that in neither case was the reply motivated by the fact that Naples of the era was infested with a notably virulent form of syphilis that was reputed to send you GPI (General Paralysis of the Insane) in six months.

At the door out we pushed through the blackout curtain together.

'Our old hero of the Sphinx?' I mocked him. 'Someone in the Reg once said you rented the whole place for a night. Don't mind me if you want a girl.'

'Not here somehow, Geoff. I learnt something that time in the Sphinx. Spent much of six months pay in a single night, too. By God, d'ye know that in that damn lupanar there was a list, a whole fucking list hung up, with the names of girls and their prices? A Canuck officer had just had a heart attack there. He was put down as *Died In Action.*'

'Better way to go than some.'

We strolled up the deserted street, our senses heavy in this solstice. Overhead the engines of bombers droned.

'But it's true,' he went on, 'yes, it's true that I'm in search of love. Love of life, love of God, death, I don't know, but I can assure you I've never really loved a woman. I would like to, but I never have. Now here I am talking too much. Let's step up. Left right left ...,' he chortled, striding.

Suddenly the sirens sounded and almost at once an impenetrable black smoke filled the street. It was generated from the burners the Eyties kept on street corners and I've never known anything more blinding; we staggered to a wall, coughing, covered in soot. *Scugnizzi* scuttled about underfoot, like sewer rats. I held hard to my gun and my pocket-book.

'The world is the totality of facts, eh,' I joshed Rex, shouting. But he was urinating into a handkerchief to tie around his nose. The stuff was as bad as tear-gas, just.

'Extrrrr-aordinary!' he muttered, before gagging himself effectively. I followed suit.

Fortunately, the All Clear sounded soon and the smoke cleared as quickly as it had started up. We stared at each other. We looked like a pair of blackface comedians. Somehow or other, I think it was from that moment that we knew we wanted no more of *la bella Napoli*.

Only on the way back to our billet did I realise I'd had another ear-bleed.

The next morning we sat sipping ersatz coffee over a Forces newspaper in the great stripped arcade of the Gallería Umberto, the meeting place of the south. At that time Naples was about as close to a cloaca as it must be possible for any city ever to be. It beat Cairo a frazzle. I mean it was the first time a boy of perhaps nine had shone my shoes and then looked up with the slick eye of a lizard, or sharp financier, and asked if I wanted to make 'facky-fack' with his sister.

'She a'better than the others, Capitano.'

I wanted to kick him, but it wasn't his fault. They had nothing to eat. The civic administration was non-existent and, to make things worse, the Yanks had started freeing all the political prisoners Musso had put away in Ponza, Procida and the other prison islands south of the bay. These men were strictly Mafia, and Musso had done the exploited heel of Italy a service in putting them behind bars. Now they were pouring out, proclaiming that they had been on our side all the time. They ruled the black market in no time at all.

'Me Tommasino,' said the boy with a wide and lovely grin.

'Scoot,' said Rex, and the boy, catching those blue eyes upon him, did.

Yank flyers, dark Ghoums, Pea-Soups (as some of us called the Canucks), Indians, New Zealand Maoris, Poles, French Caribbees all poured through this long gallery, with its cafes and souvenir shops on either side. You never knew whom you'd meet. It was quite unlike Cairo, where the situation was fairly structured still, and comprehensible. At least to me.

We sat sipping. Children edged about our legs like dogs.

Naples had officially fallen on October 1st previously. The Chleuh had retired to large-scale demolitions which were totally needless, since tactically the city was zero. This added immeasurably to the damage already inflicted on the place by our bombers. However, these (for once) had been pretty accurate, it seemed, going chiefly for the port. Hence, the Neapolitans were not ill-disposed to their new conquerors. Not entirely. Plus the fact that Jerry had laid thousands of booby traps around the place and these had claimed more victims among the Eyties than us. The Chleuh had fallen back to the Volturno, destroying the bridges at Capua behind them. Then our 167th Brigade crossed the river in assault boats and DUKWS had brought up supplies. 7th Armoured had given support (this Division included our own Cruiser Reg). The Oxs and Bucks (the Oxfordshire and Buckinghamshire Light Infantry) had crossed with high casualties, over to Brezza and Sparinese. Then the stalemate which we had been put over to relieve.

I looked around. Olive-skinned shine boys, shabby priests, drunken soldiers, souvenir-vendors and old-fashioned photographers, one or two suspicious-looking men in black and over-made-up women. Such was the mixture, in this overflow of activity throughout the Gallery. Such was their Occupation. We were matutinal incumbents of a tiny tin table and Rex had just asked the over-obsequious waiter for a couple of brandies. The man brought two of the tiniest glasses I had ever seen and poured around them from an anonymous bottle. For all the result he made he might have used an eye-dropper.

'I think I'm beginning to understand,' Rex said. 'Here you have a city in revolution. Its social structure is being transformed daily. Saw same sort of thing in South America, matter of fact.' He smiled and raised his glass. 'Here's to our tombstone, Geoff.'

'I don't want to die,' I said. 'It hurts.'

'Not always,' he said, and looked around at the sharply edged crowds thronging. 'I wonder how many deserters there are here. There was said to be a whole Division in Cairo.'

'How d'you like being conquerors?' came a voice from a neighbouring table.

It was a young American officer with close-cropped fair hair. He was lounging back with his feet up on a chair in front of him. We envied those rubber-soled Yank boots almost as much as Boche Jerry-cans.

'Cigarette?' He produced a shiny pack, and all the eyes of the vendors nearby swivelled.

'No thanks,' I said.

'I'm in the Field Service.'

'Did you do the desert?' Rex inquired quickly, for there

had been Yank AFS men – volunteers – attached to us in ambulance before Uncle Sam came in; and fine chaps they had been, if a lot of them faggots, for some reason.

The other shook his head. He took a long lean amber cigarette holder from a breast pocket above which pretty medal ribbons already sprouted. We didn't know the Yank code.

'Got to get my ass to Puglia tomorrow,' he said. 'But there ain't much to see there.'

'We saw Salerno,' Rex said.

'Fifth Army, huh?' His pale brows rose. He lit his cigarette, puffed on the holder. 'Hell of a lot of people seem to have seen Salerno. Must have been as full up as the *Mayflower*. Quite a crowd, I guess.'

'Less than here.'

'Sure. We came in to see the *Roma* sinking. Y'know, when the whole damn Italian battlefleet – all six cruisers of them – broke and ran for it out of Taranto for Malta and the Germans Stuka-ed them to bits.'

'Efficient fellow, the Hun.'

'You can say that again, Captain. Take Cassino. You ever seen that?'

'Only from a distance, thank God,' I said. 'I wouldn't want to get any closer.'

'Darn right.' He chuckled, sucking on his amber. 'What a dump! We flew over on the way from Bari, on the other coast.'

'What's Bari like?' Rex asked.

'Jesus, I tellya.' He flapped a languid hand. 'The noise. And the people.'

'What's with Cassino at the moment?' I pressed him.

He wafted smoke through the air.

'Don't ask me. Total confusion worse confounded. The krauts have got more Spandaus and Schmeissers in that monastery . . . hell, the place is a fucking fortress. I don't think they ever will take it. Your troops living in cellars and ruins of what's left of the village there. Come up only at night. And when I say your guys, I gather it helps to know some Urdu thereabouts.' He laughed and waved confidently to a friend passing. 'Living on damn short rations, too, poor bastards. Hear as how they're even smoking tea-leaves there.'

'I've always wanted to see the monastery,' Rex said.

'Well, you won't now, bud. They're aiming to flatten it.'

'Extrrr-aordinary,' Rex got out through his teeth. And then he asked, 'When are you leaving?'

I caught my breath.

'Round 'bout this time, Cap'n. You can usually find me at this table. Like, I do my business from here, you might say.'

He gave us his open honest grin again. We chatted with him a little more and I was happy that Rex didn't bring up the matter of going forward again. Cassino, ye Gods!

'We've got to go now,' Rex said.

'*Buona notte e sogni d'oro*,' said the Yank in a rippling, over-perfect Italian. He didn't move. 'Any time,' he said and boredly raised his hand as we left him. A very small fat Italian in very large dark glasses took a seat at his side.

We returned to our room above the shop where they sold lace goods and other feminine odds and ends. We had both been out to the big bath establishment to clean up. A sort of concierge sat at the receipt of custom there and you rented a bathroom by the bath – that is, you were charged for the amount of water you consumed. We consumed a lot.

I leant out the window and looked down the slope of stucco houses to the bay.

I said, 'You have the craziest ideas. Cassino, for God's sake.'

Rex said nothing. He was eating an orange on the bed.

He had been up all night reading in the flickery light of the bulb that hung from the bleeding heart of Jesus in the ceiling above us. I reflected that the man had virtually no need of sleep in him at all. He had taken watch in the desert over and over again in order to rest his men.

'We're going to see Pompeii this afternoon, Geoff.'

'We are?'

'And the Torre del Greco.'

'Better than Cassino, anyway.'

We walked out and later we ate at a fair restaurant in the Borgo Marinaro. Pollastrini and a passable Chianti. We got a PU to Ercolano but the trip was no good. The whole seaward side of that road out to Sorrento had been blasted to bits, with the debris of Jerry and Eytie trucking along it. Convoys were coming up, full of tanned men of all sorts who had been at the concamps and leave depots there. It was slow driving. Dust, potholes and above all the air – for this was full of lava shards from the eruption of Vesuvius to our left, so that we had to wear goggles and even then, in the open cab, we flinched as these minute fragments hit our faces. The windshield was fairly pitted with the stuff which grew heavier as we approached the turn-off where the road divided, one arm going up to Sorrento, the other down to Amalfi. MPs were all over the place on the south side of the road and they wouldn't allow us to Pompeii. Apparently they were evacuating an entire village further up the mountain flank the other side. History looked like repeating itself. We stared up at the lava flow which was quite distinct above us. It was like a worm of grey slag seeping down from the crater. In the daytime it did not glow, as it did at night. It looked dirty and drab. But every few hours it would pile up, in its descent, against some farmhouse or byre, and gradually shove it down. I could not imagine the speed of the eruption that had caught those trapped mummy-figures of Herculaneum, and frozen them in history forever.

So we hitched back and sat reading papers and magazines from England in an officers' club off the Via Roma. It was a solemn place with posturing statues in the main hall, the saddest spot in the world. I looked for ten minutes at the faces singled out at a Queen Charlotte's Ball in Grosvenor House – until I realised I had the page upside down. I was now taking aspirin for my headaches. Rex was increasingly ill at ease. We did not know what to do with ourselves.

So we went to the Club Nautico and the aquarium in the basement. This had survived, at least. It was a very fine aquarium and the fish looked plump and well fed. We stood in front of the thick glass looking at them for a long time.

That evening we were supposed to dine with Emilia and Dino. However, it transpired that Dino's services as 'the uncle from Rome' had been hurriedly required for a party just outside the town. So Emilia had invited her niece Rosetta, a thin pale girl with mousy hair, to be my partner at table.

It started off all right, in the large high-ceilinged dining room with the long polished refectory table running down it. Emilia did the honours, serving us wine glasses of sticky vermouth. Rex picked up. I was looking forward to the meal which would at least be a change from our everlasting suety rations; I had begun to develop quite a taste for spaghetti *al dente*, or maybe a tasty lasagna.

Rosetta was a little anxious, unliving. She wore a straight black dress with two ornaments only: a gold Venetian filigree-work brooch between her breasts and a gold chain with a cross on it. She came from a family that had property in the south, near Benevento, which had been very badly damaged. She was not an animated girl like Maddelena but rather shadowy; yet I felt she was very true, too, and I was to confirm that this was the case shortly.

Dinner began at one end of the carved formal table with *crudités* – some raw carrots, which tasted very good to me, and cold strips of ham – only it was bacon. I soon recognised this as good old Naffy bacon, of which they had presumably wangled some tins. Both women ate the cold greasy strips voraciously, against black bread. Then Emilia hinted she had something very special to follow and when she came in holding up a huge silver salver she told us was a family heirloom, our hopes rose. But when she put it on the table there steamed in the centre of the shiny expanse a small mound of what was unmistakably M. & V. By this time Rex and I had had too many tins of Meat and Veg, British-style, to have any doubt about the point. However, we did not show our disappointment, but congratulated Emilia warmly, and set to. The cob beans on the side were in fact excellent. Around nine, when we were drinking thin coffee to a truly incredible brandy, the bombing started. The lights went soon thereafter.

It was the first time I'd been in a bombing raid in a big city. I'd been stationed down in Wiltshire during the London blitz and somehow, on my few visits there before posting, had escaped any large-scale bombing. This was large-scale. It sounded as if the sky was coming down. We simply sat around the table, waiting. Hoping. Emilia was worried about Dino. Rex was playing his worry-beads. I found Rosetta's hand cool in my lap. The city shuddered.

The darkness persisted, however. Apparently the Diobaldis, better off than most, had not only blackouted their windows with heavy blanketing hung from rings on the curtain poles. They had carpentered plywood to fit into the frames. Each pane had a panel.

The house two away had bought it months ago, then a crump sounded, followed by that characteristic suck of air throughout the room, which felt as if they'd hit the house actually right beside us. In the darkness Rex said it'd be our best bet to stand against the far wall, with our backs to it. But when I got up to help Rosetta my feet crunched. Rex swore. We soon discovered that the blast had driven the windows clean through the plywood and the curtains, too. Shivers of glass lay all over the table. The window-frames were bare. We lined up side by side along the far wall and Rosetta's hand curled into mine. She was not in the slightest frightened, or didn't seem to be showing it, and then we never really heard the one that got the old palazzo itself.

When the powder and shock had settled we realised none of us was hurt but that the side of the room on the street had been sheared away completely. We stared into the coiling smoke from those bloody blackout engines ... I really doubt if they did any good. Rex got us together and we felt our way down the ornamental stairs behind him; on the way the All Clear sounded. It was very ironic.

Outside, in the street, we stood with our arms around the women looking up at the ruins of the house. We could make out the dining room up there, the table winking with glass and grub, all very formal, and there was that curious pathetic nakedness about an inhabited room suddenly made public to view, stripped of all it was made for, to house and comfort human beings.

I admired Rex more than I had ever done in those moments. He talked fast and a lot. He comforted Emilia and Rosetta, saying that now the raid was over there was nothing we could do till morning but go to Zi' Teres' and have a drink. And so we did. The place was used to this sort of thing. There was a great camaraderie about, and groups were singing. We sat together till dawn and then took the ladies back. As we did so I realised that neither of them had shown a particle of fear throughout. So much for those who said the Eyties panicked. There was the dew of tears on Emilia's bony face when Dino embraced her at the entrance, but that was all. He was a good uncle from Rome and showed no despair also. We hated that war.

I forget what we did after we had finished helping them, and using what influence we could for transport and the like. This was not our city. We felt like more than foreigners. I do remember that we went to a film in the afternoon. I could not concentrate. There were leave troops and Eyties glued to some unutterable bilge concerning piracy in the Caribbean, centuries ago. Their bloody battles did not interest us. We walked out on that epic.

So I suppose I wasn't really surprised when Rex's idea came into being. It was *in* us. I had seen it coming. San Gennaro never says no.

That night we went to a nightclub we'd heard about in an abandoned Ack Ack shelter, with all the paraphernalia still there and painted over and converted. The orchestra used the pit where the gunners had stood, blasting away into the sky above them. A nightclub in Naples at the start of 1944, that was truly something. It stank of bad gin and corruption. Officers drinking as though each moment was their last. Women like gargoyles. All I know is that by midnight I had difficulty seeing.

'I think we've done all we have to do here, Geoff,' said Rex in my ear. He drew on his cigarillo.

'Jesus, yes. What else?'

'Fascist swine,' he said suddenly.

I was perplexed. In the row from the band our voices sounded unnatural, guilty, or at least conspiratorial.

'Let's go,' he said. Then he added, as I knew he had to, 'If it wouldn't bother you too much, old boy, I'd like to take a dekko at Cassino. On our way back, I mean.'

'I knew it,' I said angrily. But there was resignation in my soul. 'Anywhere else also, Rex old scout?'

'Before there's nothing left of it,' he said. 'You know what I mean.'

'Oh sure. Just how the hell do we get there?'

'Don't worry.'

At that moment I didn't.

And the next morning I fell obediently into step beside him on the way to the Gallería Umberto. Shine-boys tugged at our elbows. Big Yank MPs patrolled in pairs, the soles of their rubber boots thudding.

The Field Service Captain was sitting at the same table. Two Eyties paying court to him, or trying to get something from him, vanished.

'Hey, fellows! Have a seat.' He waved an arm, at the end of which hung an amber cigarette holder. 'What are you drinking?'

'Frankly,' Rex said cagily, 'my pal and I, why we've had enough of Naples. We'd like to get out.'

'Sure, Skipper.'

'You said you had transport.'

'Anything you want.'

'I'm game.'

'Well, let's go.' He grinned. 'Let's paste it together.'

Rex said, 'I don't follow.'

'Why, Cap'n, everyone's had a bit too much of Naples. Of this sort of Naples, that is. The place has its points, of course, and me, I'm not oblivious to them.'

'I'd like to see Cassino before it falls.'

'Why not?' He spread his hands. 'Sure. Help yourself. So happens I'm going that way myself, shortly. I mean, I could ride you guys to Capua at least.'

'Fine.'

'It wouldn't be exactly regular.'

'It would be better than here,' said Rex.

'Sure.' His eyes searched us, blue and innocent. 'Now naturally it'd have to be worth my while, fellows. You limes have your own transport.'

I made a motion of anger but Rex held me back. He seemed to understand this type. I heard him murmur a figure.

'Sure. Very generous on your part, Capitano. How's about leaving in an hour?'

'Sooner if you want,' gritted Rex, almost snarling.

That Yank had a huge truck with six wheels and all sorts of comforts in the cab. He drove crazily. At Caserta he slowed down a bit, with all the MPs and personnel around, then turned left, northwards, up for Capua. A couple of miles along this pock-marked road, however, he turned down a side track towards the inevitable group of derelict farm buildings.

'Just want to see a few friends,' he said with a big grin. 'Won't keep you good buddies long.'

The air was fresh and pure and already we felt better. The distant gunfire was no more than a backdrop outlining this clarity. A bare-footed girl, maybe ten years old, came out of the farm.

'Eh, Bob!' she said.

The Yank jumped down, smiled at her, kissed her warmly, and went into the farm behind.

'Won't be long, fellers,' he threw over one shoulder. 'Just a few friends.'

I strolled ahead of Rex through another door, to one side of the building. It was a bedroom I entered. I looked at the bed. It was made of iron but painted to look like wood, with all the veinings and knots so well done you could almost mistake it for walnut. I opened the door of a bedside table and saw only a china chamber pot, but this too had been decorated with a pattern of red and blue flowers. There was a chest-of-drawers with a white marble top, an oval gilt-framed mirror, a bunch of artificial wax flowers under a glass bell, maybe a wedding present or the like, and two statuettes of a shepherd and shepherdess, and a blue velvet pin cushion. Everywhere I went this room followed me with the same purity. The smallest objects in the bare abode had been painted so lovingly it was like a shrine. There was a water bottle of massive engraved glass by the bed and when I lifted a box marked SORRENTO on its top it played a little tune for me.

Outside in the courtyard Rex was watching two old biddies in black working at the back of the truck. He had his hands on his hips and was staring at them intently. They went about what they were doing quite unconscious of him. The young girl reappeared and ran round to where the tailboard had been lowered onto helper springs. The old biddies loaded sacks of flour on their heads from the truck and toted them to a nearby barn.

'Jesus Christ!' I said, suddenly understanding.

I stood beside Rex at the back of the six-wheeler. It was being slowly and wordlessly emptied, by the rather grand old ladies.

There was nothing I wanted less than to go back into the line – it had to get you sometime – but I also knew I did not want to be here, where this was happening. I was just not mentally equipped, or prepared, to deal with it, I guess. The Field Service Captain sauntered out, smelling of eau-de-vie.

'What d'you know?' he said cheerfully. 'Some guy didn't check up on his load of flour.' He stared into the empty truck. 'Ah well, too bad. Uncle Sam has some more. You guys ready to roll?'

Silently we got up in the cab again. I saw that there was a pile of lire, not AMGOT, notes under a stone on the driver's seat. Our friend pocketed the pile without counting it.

'People around here are careless with their money,' he said casually.

We shot off at full speed for Capua, but the traffic started to intensify and he left us by the road near a clutter of houses and dead fields where cattle were putrefying.

Since leaving the farm Rex hadn't uttered a word.

'Cigarette?' asked the Yank, as we got down.

Rex declined, avoiding the young man's eyes.

'To hell with you then!' said the black marketeer, grinning, and he let in his clutch with a screech.

We walked off in silence, heads down. I carried our bedding roll. We felt as if, since visiting Naples, we were party to some privy secret. I was to know what it was ere long.

7

When the girl appeared on the sill of the house she seemed to hesitate. Then she sleepily smiled, uncovering her white teeth. A spicule of saliva gleamed in the sun. It seemed to me I had known Clara all my life. Her delight was infectious.

After the Yank had rumbled off with his truck and the *filoos,* some sort of strange aversion prevented Rex and me from contacting the nearest MP, or American Military Police authorities. We said to ourselves that we were still on furlough, after all. We wanted to be free. It joined us in some complicity.

'Let's go to that farm,' Rex growled uncomfortably. 'Maybe they can rent us a room.'

'Until we can get to Cassino?'

He didn't answer. And it was Clara who opened the door to us. We melted before her at once.

How utterly natural she was, so full of easy vivacity. She turned out to be the youngest of three generations living on this isolated farm, through which both armies had driven. She had two sisters, Concetta and Maria. Concetta was working near Naples. The family had been against the government since the dawn of the Fascist regime, it seemed, and they had greeted the Allies with enthusiasm. Luckily, little had come by to disabuse them since, though I wondered how long their starry-eyed version of the liberation would last.

And so it was there began the happiest period we ever knew in the soft underbelly of the Axis, a frightful pun for me then, indeed. We helped them on the farm. In the fields we rigged up braziers from holed petrol cans lying about, old German shell-crates, or simply wood we scrounged from Army cookhouses nearby. Black smoke came belching out of the oil-soaked wood and warmed our smoke-blackened hands and faces. We stood like a pair of amateur nightwatchmen, around the blazing brazier in the fields. It made it easier for us to accept the hospitality of their humble fireside of an evening.

They were such kindly people. The father had been something of a carpenter in peace, but had returned to the few fields they had when war came. His wife was good-natured, ruddy-cheeked, with great pride in her cooking and household management of their few possessions. We insisted on paying for our bunk, of course, but she made us both feel at home from the start. She had two sons. One had been killed in Eritrea, just after Wavell's great mop-up. The other had been taken prisoner in Russia, on the Orel front, back in 1941. She had never heard from him since and presumed him dead. She was a religious woman and nothing was too much for her to do for the two Inglese. She lavished her pasta asciutta on us till it was coming out of our ears.

The second day Rex and I were wandering in the fields on the slope by the brook. Stubble scrunched underfoot. The late afternoon wore down like the stub of a candle, quickly. There had been some firing in the vicinity and we walked carefully, because the Chleuh had left snipers, Nazi fanatics, in some of the deserted buildings about. Not to mention non-magnetic mines. Suddenly we saw an old woman struggling along the footpath through the fields with a sack. Then she seemed to collapse and sit down on the sack. Just then Maria came flying past, barefoot as usual and told us it was her auntie, her *zia,* who had been to fetch some flour. Rex hastened forward, saying he would carry it for her. I was about to go and help, too, when I was conscious of Clara close behind me. She had been doing some washing for us and asked me if I'd come and see if I could find some dandelions with her. These people prized them as vegetable salads, and for wine.

Of course I said yes and we wandered off down a track to a barn. She walked in front of me, her beautifully proportioned body swaying undulantly ahead. I was again amazed at the way in which these people, living in such humble and even mean circumstances, could seem so naturally dignified. It was the total contrary of the generally poor specimens of womanhood we had seen in Naples. She was easily bare-foot, too, and not in the least self-conscious about it.

We chatted as we searched and all at once I realised that of course it was quite impossible for there to be any dandelions flowering at this time of year, even though the local crocus did show early, in clumps around tree-trunks. But I said nothing about it. I told her that in England, too, the South country folk used to make dandelion and even potato wine, too.

'Ah, England,' she mused, shyly. 'Do you think I'll be able to go there one day?'

'Would you like to, Clara?'

'Oh yes.'

'I don't think it would please you.'

'Why not?'

'There are too many people, in too small a space, there's too much noise, and everyone's in a hurry. Not like here.'

'All the same I'd like to go.'

'You'd be disappointed, dear.' The epithet *cara* slipped from my lips without my meaning it to. She stood close to me in the shadow of the grange and I could see the strong curve of her hips in the cheap brown dress. Distantly a machine-gun stitched the air and my ears automatically registered Spandau by its rate of fire. 'Ah, Clara,' I hazarded (after all, as with Maddelena, I might never see her again in a day or two), 'I have seldom met anyone so pure as you are.'

'Pure?' she frowned.

'Don't give yourself to the cities. There are better things.'

She played with her necklace of shells, her best – put on for us. 'Do you mean you don't want to go back to your homeland?' She looked at me very seriously, full in the face. 'Eh?' she insisted.

I shrugged and twisted. '"The dear land of my nativity,"' I quoted from Gulliver, scoffing. 'Do you realise I was born in Ceylon, Clara?'

'Where?'

'Yes, my father was a civil servant, a District Commissioner there. It was a British possession, you see, a Crown colony.' (I found that hard to translate, and no wonder.) 'I only went back to England when I was thirteen, for my schooling. I had hardly finished that before the war came. That's as much as I know of England. Some of those out in such places even felt that England betrayed them, that they belonged more to their country of adoption. Rex said that in Malaya not a single one of the civil servants tried to escape when the Japs overran the peninsula. They preferred to take their lot with the population they had served. And that meant brutal imprisonment on Changi Island.'

'You admire Rex a great deal, don't you?'

'A great deal, Clara.'

'What is he?'

I don't know what I said. I laughed. She was too close to me. Her long lustrous blue-black hair inflamed my nostrils, it lay as if born of the wind on her creamy shoulders, heaving. Her flesh pulsed beneath the stuff. Her cheekbones showed as if she had drunk of shadows. The blood beat behind my eyes. Each one knew perfectly well what the other was thinking.

She dropped her eyes the first.

I said: 'I guess we'd better go in. You know Rex and I, why we can't live like this with you for ever. There's no chance of that, alas. These days the life of a tank commander in Cruisers is estimated at ten days in the line.'

She said nothing. Did she understand? A big gun, maybe a 240, sounded, from beyond the distant river. The first of a barrage? In the blue, Jerry had always preferred the late afternoon when the heat haze didn't distort his targets. He was a methodical bloke. The habit stuck, I guess. My mind remembered it at Bel Hamid and my mind remembered it at El Adem. Stuka time, too. But a hand had stolen into mine. The sun down. The shadows stretched. The desert full of creeks of dust. The bands of shadows grouping behind the tanks like men for attack. The floor of darkness rising.

'Come,' she said. *'Veng'*. And it was all she said.

My heart pounded as though in battle. I followed the slumbrous roll of her hips up the ladder. It was a lazy motion under belted flesh. We went into the back of the loft. It was dark. The straw was soft and she gave herself to me, her first time. We were ferocious for love and the great tenderness of giving. It was so carnal as to be spiritual. I cannot describe the happiness we felt together. Afterwards we lay and talked, the ragged tatters of distant m-g fire hacking occasionally in our ears.

'The fighting will be over soon?' she asked, nestling her head into my arm. There was such purity of living in her. Her lustrous eyes were liquid with love.

'When we've won, cara. Not before.'

'And you'll go back? To England?'

'Don't make me sad,' I said, stroking her broad forehead. Something slashed at my heart in her words.

'Your friend is Catholic?'

'No, he's Protestant. I'm Catholic. Or was.'

'What's that necklace he carries, then?'

'Oh, he picked it up in Greece. They all have them there, all the men. You see dockers slipping the beads through their fingers when they're not working. It's something to occupy your hand with.'

'And what does he believe in, Goffredo, this man in whom you believe so much?'

That made me pause.

'How do I know, Clara? I suppose he believes in the world, in liberty, in the difference between fear and terror. That sort of thing.'

'And you, what do you believe in?'

'That sort of thing.'

'In liberty?'

'Absolutely.'

We went back to the farm and though we didn't say anything I think it was written all over our faces. The mother avoided my eyes. Rex was very occupied helping Maria store demijohns or carboys of wine in the cellar.

That evening we had maize pancakes, washed down with a bottle of Valpolicella we'd brought back from Naples. Afterwards we got a little merry and they asked us to sing for them. At first we declined. Rex was stretched full-length, like a god, on the floor, his worry-beads immobile in his fingers. Clara's eyes never left mine. They seemed to burn through me.

So we tried one or two of the desert songs, like 'Waltzing Matilda' and 'The Ballad of Farida and Faruk', but they couldn't follow the words, which was just as well in the latter instance:

Queen Farida's very gay when Faruk has got his pay,
But she ain't so bleedin' glad when she's in the family way;
  Stanna shwaya! O desire!
  Stanna shwaya! Pull your wire.
Pull your pud. Does you good. Send it higher! Send it higher!

King Faruk! King Faruk! Let the swaddies have a look.
  Quais ketir, Abassia!
  Bags o' beer. Shit and fear!
Up your pipe! Take a swipe! Quais ketir! Quais ketir!

We sang that gravely and rather well, I thought. *Quais ketir* meant jolly good, and *Stanna shwaya* take it easy. It was a most irreverent ballad about the King of Egypt's sex life and they sang it from Gezira to the Turf back in Cairo. I believe the tune was actually the gyppie national anthem. We gave them the 'D-Day Dodgers' but they didn't understand that any better.

The vino started flowing – theirs this time – and we both suddenly found a supply of Scottish blood in us. I took the floor for a solo of 'Over the Sea to Skye' and then joined Rex, whose performances were improving with every glass, in 'Loch Lomond' and then 'Just a Wee Doch and Doris', into which we put our hearts and lungs and which proved very popular. We even finished with a Highland fling. Sort of.

After that we insisted that the girls sing us a song. Clara was too shy to at first but Maria gave us 'Anna Pola' and 'Torno a

Sorrento', in a lovely wistful voice. Then they joined to give us the Eytie version of 'Lili Marlene':

Tutte le sere, sotto quel fanal
Presso la caserna, ti stavo ad aspettar;
  Anche staser' aspettero
  E tutt'il mondo scorderò
    Con te, Lili Marlene,
    Con te, Lili Marlene . . .

We applauded them heartily at the end and the girls retired, blushing fiercely. But that song which was on everyone's lips in those days spoke only of death and despair and the futility of existence, and I could see Clara crying as she sang it, after the second verse. The party broke up and we turned in.

Something was changing in our lives, in our relationships with things. I was having difficulty focussing when I woke up first thing in the morning. The next day I did so fairly early, some convoy was rumbling along the road outside, but Rex was already dressed and squatting on his bed under a chromo of the Madonna; he was poring over maps and documents we had brought back with us. A tin mug of ersatz coffee steamed appetisingly on his bedside chair and I took a sip from it. I washed and shaved thinking of nothing but Clara.

She was leaning against a bread-bin when I'd dressed and gone through to the main room. We couldn't do anything, but our eyes met in an intensity I'd never known. Somehow or other she'd got some eggs and Rex and I had a super hot breakfast of eggs and corn bread and coffee, served by the girls who looked after our every need. Rex's eyes were anxious this morning, however. He had something on his mind. I decided to say it for him. I no longer cared, I was so in love.

'We're two days A.W.O.L, Rex,' I said.

'Absent without leave, eh?' He mused, the beads sliding through his fingers like amber water. 'Jumbo will take care of it, I expect.'

I laughed. 'And Brigade? And Division? You think you can get away with anything, Rex, don't you? As you've hardly ever been on leave I suppose you've never been absent without leave. In the C.M.F. I'd remind you it's a court martial offence for an officer to A.W.O.L.'

'I got in to Capua this morning,' he told me calmly.

'You're crazy,' I said. 'Why the Reg' has put up with you for so long beats me. We're *absent without leave,* man.'

'There was some MT going there. I hitched a lift. Convoy of 9th Lancers, new chaps all.'

'Well?'

Somehow I knew what he was going to say. Clara was listening savagely, trying to discern what we were saying. For a moment silence raged within that calcined chamber. Maria was wheeling barrow-loads of logs up to the house outside.

'You don't have to come with me, Geoff.'

'Oh sure.'

'No, I mean you can go back on your own. You could even stay here a few days more and say I detained you. They can't do much to me at my age, you know. Well, I met a Polish Colonel there.'

'Where?'

'In Capua.'

'Don't tell me you can also speak Polish, Rex,' I blurted angrily.

'Chappie by the name of Pieniazek. They're a little less regimental than us in the Droghedas, y'see. Said he'd pick us up on the road tomorrow.'

'Us!' I exclaimed.

He shrugged.

'We're A.W.O.L., Rex,' I half shouted. 'Don't you realise what that means? Am I not getting through to you loud and clear?'

'You don't have to come,' he said.

'Jesus Christ,' I said.

I stood up. The atmosphere in the room was strained. Clara was watching me like a cat. She didn't understand our words, but she *felt*. She went out to the well and drudged noisily with a bucket. I joined her there.

'You're going tomorrow. Goffredo, aren't you?' she said. It was her resignation that undid me. My eyes burnt at their edges.

'I could stay,' I said.

'No. You're going. With him.'

'What else can I do? We've exceeded our leave, Clara. Our permission.'

She said nothing.

'He's my senior officer.'

'You wouldn't go if you loved me, 'Tenente.'

'I love you with all my heart. I'll come back.'

'You'll never come back, Goffredo,' she said and she was not crying.

I didn't mind who saw, I took her in my arms and hugged her. I gave her a great big hug to console her, to try to thank her for everything they had all done for us in these past few days, and her especially. But I knew that Clara had instinctively understood our different destinies. The war was a bitch.

That afternoon something odd happened. I'd been helping Maria at the well, I was scared of coming too close to Clara again. After I had finished hauling up the buckets I packed our bed-roll and then wandered over to the main road. Desultory firing was coming from the distance and a column of infantry were swinging northwards up it. You could tell they were just out by their faces. This was clearly the first close firing they'd heard. The officers looked particularly green as if they'd just exchanged a swagger stick for an umbrella, a tin hat for a bowler, their Colonel being their new bank manager.

When they'd passed I crossed the road to a field where stood a few of our three-tonners, spaced out, with their canopies down. Camouflage nets all over. In this way they made a couple of makeshift offices either side the truck. There was a rough *G* scrawled on the side of the tenting nearest me and an unlit red lamp hung inside. I had been wondering whether we could scrounge some scotch from Q, actually, when I caught sight of the MP Corp standing near a stack of petrol cans, on guard. It was the first time I'd hesitated at sight of military police, but I did so then. However, the man saluted smartly and I sauntered on, playing calm.

Two captains were crammed in one corner under the canopy peering at a map-board. Across from them sat a Colonel. I saluted when he looked up, but he did not interrupt himself. His face was leathery, with hard blue eyes. From what he was saying I realised this was some sort of G.S.I. Information Headquarters. The Colonel was briefing the two Captains.

'One great thing: never sneer at the enemy in the summary. 8th HQ does it sometimes but it's not a good idea. Front-line troops get the pricker if you sneer. If you've lost cobbers in a scrap and are likely to get walloped yourself, you don't want to hear what a stooge the enemy is. That's for the man who's done the fighting to say and no one else. And while I think of it, watch out for expressions like heavy shelling. The front line man's idea of heavy shelling is shelling that's heavy ...'

I wandered off. That G.S.I. Colonel was all right.

When I got back Rex was having a bath in front of a wood fire. It was an old-fashioned enamel sitz-bath and the water had been heated in an even older-fashioned way, by having hot bricks dropped sizzling into it. In the bled there'd be no chance of a bath, of course, though we'd managed to find an old bath establishment going through Tunis. So the chance of a real scrub-down now was a great luxury. Rex sat like a pasha in the steaming tub and I soon joined him. We scrubbed each other's backs like saucepans. The girls tactfully absented themselves but their mother bustled in from time to time, to see we had everything we wanted. Something odd was going on in the doorway.

I was wrapped in a heavy towel and I saw Rex, nearly dressed with his top half in issue flannel undershirt, watching closely. One of the girls' uncles whom we had met was sitting on a chair talking to a thin young man with his brown hair cut in a peculiar way, as if someone had driven the clippers straight through it from back to front. He wore a cloth coat and a pair of rough canvas trousers, of the sort of material such people made tablecloths. He was talking in an animated way, gesturing a lot, and Rex and I drew closer to hear. The old *zío* looked at him guardedly, without saying anything very much. From a string bag the man produced a pair of heavy boots. Suddenly I recognised them as issue boots. Then I identified in his bag the short spade Italian troops carried on their knapsacks. I glanced at Rex.

'What's going on?' I asked

'He tried to sell some pipe tobacco to old Tonio,' came the cautious, growled response. 'Now it's boots.'

'Who is he?'

The question became academic as the type drew out of his bag a battledress jacket.

'Lire,' he hissed. *'Lire!'*

'It's a deserter,' I said to Rex.

'Perhaps,' he said. 'Yes, perhaps.'

Rex watched him closely.

'We ought to turn him in. There are MPs on the other side of the road. There's a whole G Section there. It could be one of ours.'

'It is one of ours,' said Rex, looking at the man's bent back, watching him struggle with his pidgin-Eytie. 'It is one of ours.' His voice sounded tired in the room.

I wondered why he made no move, why he carried that slight smile on his face.

'Is it a Drogheda?' I whispered.

'No.'

Just then Tonio turned in his chair and winked back at us. The stranger took a step back, suspicious, alert. Rex looked at him calmly, without saying anything. The game was up now and the man knew it. He recognised a British officer when he saw one. He looked like a regular, a long-term man, perhaps thirty-six, and his chin was covered in stubble. Suddenly Rex said softly in Italian, 'Eh, Tonio. Give him a little pasta. And some coffee, see.'

The man looked at us, on the defensive, fearful, indecisive.

He must have been asking himself what the hell we two were doing there, anyway. Flogging a bath in a peasant's farm? Why weren't we with our unit? A craftiness entered his eyes.

'Oh-kee,' said Tonio, and got up to fetch some pasta. In this household it was nearly always simmering at some time of day.

'Come on in,' said Rex. 'You must be cold out there. We've just been having a tub.'

The man shuffled in, his limp bag hanging.

'Thanks, sir,' he said.

'Rough time, eh,' said Rex.

'We were bombed and strafed for forty-eight hours without cease, sir,' came back the other abruptly. 'I wasn't able ...'

Rex's wave cut him short.

'What did you do in Civvie Street?'

'Construction, sir.' He said it eagerly, gratefully. 'Mason in Perth. Then back from Cerasola I went to a farmhouse at the corner of a field and asked an old woman if she'd do the washing for our crew. That was ... when it started.'

'What were you?'

'Loader-operator, sir. Since Sollum.'

Rex sharpened, visibly.

'Since Rezegh, sir.'

Immediately there was this complicity among us. I can't describe it exactly. We belonged. And we spoke in low voices together, like conspirators. Clara came in with some steaming pasta and a bowl of coffee. The trooper sat down to it as if he'd never eaten in his life before. When we'd finished, and we'd yarned with him about the blue, he looked up at us with gratitude, not knowing quite what to say, what to do.

Then he stood up straight and clicked his heels.

'I'd like to tell you my Regiment, sir. You can turn me in.'

'No,' said Rex softly. 'Not necessary, really.'

The man stared at the flagging floor.

'I couldn't help it, sir, really. It got to me.'

There was a sob in the voice and I didn't want him to cry. Rex was pulling out of his pocket a roll of lire, not AMGOT, notes. God knows where he had got them but there must have been hundreds of pounds' worth there. I fairly stared.

'Here. Take it.'

The trooper hesitated, then took the bundle with a kind of craven fear.

'You know. The Capua road goes pretty straight back, all the way to Caserta. You'll find something there, old chap. *Go!*'

The man stood there, stupefied, for a second. He shot me a last desperate look, as if perhaps I could help in some way. Then he ran for it.

'Extrrrr-aordinary!' said Rex, staring at the flooring.

I hitched my towel higher about me as Clara came through to remove the dishes. She knew I was leaving on the morrow and I knew she knew. There was nothing I could say to her. It had all fled, like the deserter in our arms. The best I can say here is that all this was an astonishing manner of behaving in an officer like Rex of the time, a man so sure of his duty. It was unhinging. Yet today it seems to me to have been right – just, even. No other solution. The deserter had chosen his destiny before we had entered on his scene. He was a proud swimmer striking out on his own, now. God forgive him.

That night Rex wrote with great labour in his diary:

The world is determined by the facts and by the fact that they are all that there is.

Great, I thought. A big help. I wondered how far we'd come, what a different leave it'd been from Cairo. I remembered reporting to Town Major, Cairo. The largest Moslem agglomeration in the world at the time, with over a million inhabitants, Cairo had been surrounded by huts, dumps, camps. Pyramids of cans had festered on the fringes of military installations, while in the city itself bodies fouled alleys and night convoys dazzled the darkness. General Sir Claude John Eyre Auchinleck, Grand Commander of the Indian Empire, Companion of the Bath, Commander of the Star of India, Distinguished Service Order, Order of the British Empire, 1914–15 Medal, General Service Medal, Victory Medal with Palm, Jubilee Medal, Coronation Medal and Croix de Guerre, was said to have got through more work, and exercise, than most Cairenes knew in a week, by six every morning. Rex had admired the Auk.

I went to sleep with the tune humming in my ears, trying to forget Clara walls away and probably weeping:

There's the Auk, there's the Auk
And although some bastards talk,
  Och, he didn't do so bad
  For the Eighth Ar-mee!

Once more we set off in the dawn – against it, as it were. Clara was standing outside the house under the dead orange tree; she made sure I had everything I wanted.

'Don't worry about me,' she said, with her hands on my shoulders.

'I'll come back,' I said.

'No you won't,' she said.

And I didn't want to lie any more.

'Think of me at springtime, Geoff,' she said and I felt her lips dry on mine and the scent of her like newly baked bread, the purity of her being in the flimsy cotton dress as she stood barefoot and shapely in the fields. I could not look back as we left. We had already thanked the others. I simply walked behind Rex who took great steps ahead; I followed, in my newly washed socks. We walked to the road in the direction of the still snow-covered mountains where the great guns already played. Down here the last snow had melted and I walked with difficulty and Rex didn't say anything to me about it. And I knew I would never forget that moment with Clara, when she had taken my hand and said the one word 'Come!'

'They were good to us,' I said to Rex, stumbling.

'They were all good to us, all. This way. We'll pick up my Polish chappie near what was the station. I think his brother flew most of the Polish air force out in 'thirty-nine. I don't know. We're in good time.'

For what? I wondered. For what?

8

That Benedictine monastery was our jinx. It was the still centre of all our violent campaign. It was the hinge of the road to Rome. And in the distance it looked like a giant's tooth sticking stiffly up, lonely on its mountain. It was the charnel house of the time. When we alighted at the town itself, on the lower hills, its fate was already sealed, really. Under General Freyburg, the 2nd New Zealand and 4th Indian Divisions, both of which we had known in the bled, relieved the 2nd American Corps who had suffered very heavily in the approaches to the higher village.

Then our 78th Div. joined in the fun. On the night of February 15th a Maori battalion crossed the Rapido and hacked their way through mined wire into the upper town, capturing the railway station, but the Chleuh counter-attacked from the hilltop and threw the Maoris back. Jerry then began a perfectly fanatic burrowing around the base of the monastery, surrounding it with a network of nebelwerfer, mortar, and m-g nests so that it seemed to our lads, huddled half-frozen in their shallow rabbit scratchings, that literally every inch of the approaches was fortified. In particular did the infantry of that time dread the five-barrelled nebelwerfer rocket mortar, or 'moaning minnie'. Subsequently the Chleuh reinforced the monastery garrison with their First Parachute Division, the pick of the German Army, dedicated to fight for Hitler to the death. This had been formed by 'Butcher' Heydrich, slim and ruthless.

From a distance the place was like nothing else in the world. The walls had been holed and breached over and over, but all these apertures were now put to use for gun emplacements. It was for us of the blue a new kind of war and

I shall try to explain this in a way. For it provoked within us some profound alteration. You could say that it was really our end, rather than the beginning of it all. In the desert the tank armies of both sides had some, if only slight, descendancy from the cavalry of old, and we fought by former cavalry rules. We were to pay heavily for this mentality, to be sure. But the heritage was there, in the back of the mind each time you saw a line of enemy tanks ahead, even after we had learnt our lesson and we had seen the first of those excellent, but non-cavalry, tanks of the Americans, the Stuarts and, above all, the ten-ton Honeys. A last legacy of chivalry, if you will. Whatever they may say now (wherever Kurt Bleyle may be, God bless him) it existed, it existed. At least for a time. At Cassino it ceased to exist. That was what Cassino meant for us.

The mud was heavy in the lower approaches as we arrived in the town in the Humber scout car. There were just us two, and the Polish Colonel with splendid moustaches, and his Orderly. It was raining, the Rapido was flooding once more and we saw all sorts of MT and medium batteries marooned in the mud in the fields about. But no firing came from the sinister shape of the distant monastery. Rather, all was menacingly silent. The Colonel took us to his bivvy, in the usual ruined cattle byre, and gave us some extraordinary German wine he said he had captured. He lived in some comfort, comparatively speaking. And as we sipped the heady Bernkasteler Kurfürstlay Auslese he briefed us on our ascent to the ruins beneath the abbey – which were, indeed, our most forward positions. For Rex would be satisfied with nothing less. He wanted to go to the end of the journey. So it transpired that we would go up with a night convoy of mules, carrying rations from 'B'. Absolute silence was of the essence.

That afternoon we saw our first Cromwells. These new tanks were clearing mines in the river bank. Each had a drum of wire stowed forward in front of the round driving visor (Tich's was a slit by comparison); when a mine was found a man got out, quickly unwound a length of this wire and attached it to the protruding head of the mine. Then he ran back in through the mud, the commander closed the turret and all visors, reversed the tank and pulled the mine clear. It exploded noisily, but harmlessly, on his sides. They were the best tanks we had at that time; two camouflage nets were rolled up to the right of the hull gunner's Beza and above these were housed two smoke generators. These could be ignited, on command, by the driver inside in order to provide a screen to cover movement of the crew. Rex and I saw them working and talked to some of the men aboard them and we wished we'd had them in the blue. I wished we'd had one of those smoke generators that day by the ricks in front of Three Balls.

The Pole Colonel left us for the rest of his battalion who were holed up in a sort of quarry back of the village, and I know when he went we both thought him a grand chap. Our rendezvous was in full dark at a place called Monkey's Bottom where the mud wasn't so bad. The mule convoy was in command of a REME type, it appeared, and I again wondered what the hell we were doing. I'd already heard Rex murmuring something about a fellow he knew in G.S.I. (Intelligence) who might let him go on one of the bombing raids over Yugoslavia. As an observer, Jesus Christ.

We began our ascent of Castle Hill shortly before midnight. It was pitch dark and raining steadily. The mules were lined up with the rations strapped on them, in the charge of some Eytie civilians. Most of our men accompanying them wore denim overalls with leather jerkins. Blankets, water, ammo, rations and other stores were going forward. Stretchers, too. We went along slowly but surely, the mules padding silently as cats in the mud. Once we had left the town behind we realised their importance – just so long as one of them wouldn't bray! – since all wheeled transport was stalled at the start of Castle Hill. Above this towered the monastery and beyond that Monte Cairo, another 'soft underbelly' of the Axis. Quite what we thought we were doing playing tourists here I did not know.

As we climbed we began to pass posts of our own troops who for months had lived in a misery of snow and ice, of blinding rain and biting wind, to say nothing of constant bombardment. We passed silently upward to the hill that was two hundred feet higher than Gibraltar and just as steep. The fellows saw us go and did not envy us.

We now moved slowly upwards, occasionally hearing soft chuckling in the darkness around. Maybe Poles, maybe Gurkhas, maybe Indians. There were at least a dozen nationalities encamped around Cassino then, waiting for it to fall. And the Boche held them all at bay, including the Yanks. The old irrigation dykes had swollen and engorged and there were huge bomb craters full of smelly, stagnant water. Our trouble soon came to be keeping up with the mules, whose sure-footed progress forward never stopped. There was no firing around at the time and they knew no war, poor beasts. The last part was the worst.

The objective of our convoy was the courtyard, then the keep, of the old castle ruins, just north of the village. It was a good hour's climb behind the bluff of the hill in the dark, with the aid of ropes in several places. I was soon sweating hard, though in pretty good shape. We had to go in single file as there was only one track. Luckily the Chleuh held his fire all that night. The only thing that bothered us was the smoke from what were probably our own smoke shells sent up supposedly to help us, by friends. One landed, softly hissing, almost at my feet and I had great difficulty breathing for a while thereafter. One or two rifle grenades, and maybe stick grenades too, but that was all – and it was all we wanted for that night. The smell of unburied bodies – of God knew which side – was very bad as we emerged into the area of the keep itself. Here a couple of infantry companies were leading a troglodyte existence, in cellars and sangars, never venturing out by day. Jerry fixed-line firing had every exit to such places fully covered. There were white tapes guiding us, to indicate cleared mine lines. Otherwise it was the normal nightmare.

Out of the darkness emerged a bedraggled figure. He stood

before us outlined against the black mass of Monastery Hill and the broken scaffolding of the old rope railway up to it, looking no more in the dark than a series of scaffolds. We had reached a rubble path, and fallen masonry. The man was a Corporal guide. The mules were to go on round to the left of the keep where a ration party was waiting to unload them and hoist the stuff up. We two could follow the soldier back. He was attached to Brigade Staff.

Although it was a short distance it took a half hour to get to the Company Headquarters to the north. We crept through a blanket-covered mousehole in what had been the gaol, turned up a rubble incline, went through another blanket curtain, then crawled over fallen masonry until we reached the ruins proper. I remember that once my hand rested on some ruined statuary, perhaps the head of a Saint. There was another bank of rubble, then we slipped down a chute into a double blanket screen, and so through into a long underground room.

We were challenged here, as we had been at all the platoon positions we had come through for we were now in (or under) the courtyard of the main castle ruins and there were German positions literally yards away, just beyond the wire that actually closed off this broken yard. Rex had wanted to come this far, and he bloody well had.

So we slid down the ramp into the room. There were two hurricane lamps and the bodies of snoring soldiers all about. This subterranean den, which reminded me of Poe or Hogarth, was a Battalion Headquarters, housing the Commanding Officer and his staff, signallers and intelligence personnel. It was merely a cellar of a former house with two holes created for exits and entrances. Above it was a kind of sangar of rubble, now made into a sniper's nest.

Rex and I hardly knew where we were at first. To a sudden menacing rattle of light arms fire we hit the floor as one, but the soldier nearest us grinned and tugged at my shoulder. Apparently we were safe in here, though the orange line of tracers outside was visible through one of the holes. The burst, as always, started some reciprocal firing and for a moment we simply sat on our fannies trying to orient ourselves, listening to the kraark-kraak of big bullfrogs, the pop-pop of those smoke shells, the odd bursts of m-g fire and the whistle and crump of moaning minnies coming over. It was a weird way to win a war and we didn't like it one bit. The mist-hung night outside was strange, malodorous, hostile. We weren't used to hugging the earth at all. And while Rex was still swearing in the silence that followed a particularly venomous crump, the voice that came to us was so ultra-Brit as to make me want to laugh.

'Delighted to see you again, old top. What brings you two here?'

'Advance one and be recognised,' he chaffed, as we peered into the dark in his direction.

'Take off your boots, sir, would you,' said another voice.

It was straight Goya or Bosch, all right. All air outlets had been blocked up with masonry and covered with blankets, to keep fragments from coming in or light getting out. Cigarette smoke coiled to the invisble ceiling. The hurricane lamps guttered. There was a smell of stagnant water, wet uniforms. We struggled off our boots. Apparently sound carried through these ghostly domains that now comprised Cassino town and the enemy could identify movement in this manner. I saw a smiling face in front of mine, a finger to lips. It was the Hampshire CO we'd met in the ruined sheep-pen, the one who'd given Rex that Luger he carried with him now. I sketched a salute and felt myself drawn forward to a niche where his bed was. A second later there was a mug of good coffee spiked with rum in my hand and we were sitting talking to the man again. He'd apparently got over his dysentery and seemed thoroughly at home in this Gothic decor.

'Sorry about your boots,' he said. 'But we have to. During the day very little can be done except for improving lines of fire, from info brought in by patrols, and the general revetment of strong-points. This is the time when we get stuff done. I have four patrols out now, trying to discover Jerry's movements.'

'So you're all living in these cellars, sir, is that it?' Rex looked at him closely, the light dancing on his ruddy cheeks.

'That's right. Radio communication almost uniquely. We know where all our platoons are, but I haven't seen some of them for days. A runner comes in every now and then, but it's certain death to move around towards the monastery.' He added, 'You two'll have to be out of here by three. Dawn at four thirty.'

'So it's like this you live,' said Rex dully.

'Absolutely, old boy. Nearly all our Brens are on fixed lines. Might as well be a bloody pack of robots, eh? We're waiting for the day when some poor bastards can get round the hill and up the Boche's arse. Until then we're stymied here.'

'You mortar them?'

'We strafe the bejesus out of them. From the start it was my policy to harass Jerry up there as much as we could, allow him no peace at all. For every shell landed in our area I promised I would put five back, with our three-inch mortars. It's not difficult to wireless back the map number where we've heard their troops and our gunners can guarantee to have bombs on the spot within three minutes. The trouble is their position. Have you seen air photos of the hill?'

'No, sir.'

'It's perfectly sited for defence. Anything we send up there either hits one of the forward walls, or goes right on over down the other side. That applies to air strafing too, very largely. We feed at night and cook on smokeless fuel lamps. Most of the men in HQ are still noshing.'

'And Jerry is forty yards away?'

'Sometimes less,' said the Colonel, frankly grinning. 'We've got to know each other pretty well, by and large.'

'And that's what it's like, the war,' said Rex.

'That's what it's like. Around here.'

'Somehow I didn't think Cassino would be like that.'

'That's because your war was in the desert.'

'You're right. I recognise that.'

'Our trouble is recharging wireless batteries.'

'I can see that. For a Tac HQ.'

Rex panted; he was sweating as I was. It had been an arduous ascent and I wasn't looking forward to the return. A sudden malevolent burst of Spandau fire beat upon the walls of the sangar overhead, but it did not disturb the sleepers. A few turned, in their blankets, that was all. It was clear they were fairly impregnable in here.

Rex leant forward.

'There's something I want to tell you, Colonel.'

'Shoot.'

'That day when we met you, I mean. The first time.'

'What of it?'

'Well, something happened.'

'What?'

'Something that drove me crazy. I couldn't seem to understand it at all. I mean, it was beyond reason. Why, they were torturing women in a farmhouse down there. So I killed two SS with the Beza. Now my CO says they were civilians.'

'And you're for the high jump?'

'I don't know. I don't think so. But it's confusing.'

'Rules change,' said the other with a shrug. 'I've never seen any SS. But I can tell you we're using partisans here.'

'Eyties who've come through the lines and collaborated with us? The ones who were leading our mules?'

'Right. M.M.I.A. – that's the Military Mission to the Italian Army – they've said we're to co-operate with those Italians who were provenly working against Jerry, all along. I expect we'll get a directive about it all soon.'

'A directive.' Rex laughed shortly. 'More bumf. I'm sorry, Colonel, but I'm beginning to think I simply don't understand this war.'

'It's a rough billet, I agree, but at least it's better than Anzio. I hear that's hell.'

'Don't wish it on us,' I said.

'I don't know quite how the hell you two managed to get permission to come up here but now you've seen Cassino, and you can die.'

'No permission, sir,' said Rex. 'I just wanted to see ... for myself ... the facts.'

'Well, you're going before dawn. Both of you. That's an order.'

So we ate some M. & V. with a couple of subalterns and the mortaring grew a little sharper. I began to curse Rex with all my heart. What was going to happen when we rejoined the Reg A.W.O.L.? Finally, the time came to leave. We would be going down with some stretcher bearers and wounded. At least they would show us the way.

There was no moon to assist us as we left the cellar to a final tot, passing outside it a pocked portrait of Hitler complete with Iron Cross and swastika. It had been put out there to draw fire, and reveal positions, obviously. We slid down the rubble and waded through the irrigation dykes to the croaking of frogs and whistle of mortars behind us. The darkness was almost tangible, thick and fumy. We had no idea where we were. A runner came past and told us there was an ambulance waiting lower down near the quarry. And that was how we left Cassino. In an ambulance smelling of gas gangrene and a soldier groaning. We didn't like that sort of war at all.

9

We got back to our billet, picked up our bedding roll, and hitched transport back to Capua. It looked remarkably intact, after what we had seen. The place was a hive of activity. Tank carriers, troop-carrying vehicles, gun limbers and all sorts of MT were moving steadily, if slowly, forward. Overhead the 12th Tactical Air Command was up in waves of bombers. It looked as if some offensive were on the way. I had no desire to be part of it.

But by now it was clear that if a link-up with Anzio could be effected, Kesselring would be forced to withdraw from Rome. Defending that city would have taken most of the German Army in Italy. The Chleuh would simply fall back to another line.

Some Pioneer platoons were out sweeping mines to one flank of the road with their electronic 'vacuum cleaners' and I saw Rex talking to the commander of a 25-pounder going up, self-propelled. Just then he waved to me. There was a despatch rider right behind it, booted, guantleted and goggled, and it was with him Rex was actually talking. I crossed over, an exclamation on my lips. I saw the clenched-fist patch of our Armoured Division on his right shoulder. It was in fact a man from our own Regiment, a young chap called Dorset who'd been a steam-fitter before the war.

He told us he was bringing up an urgent message from R.E.M.E. We were being refitted, it appeared, and parts were badly needed, ranging from sighting vanes to spare tracking. It seemed that our Group, plus one other Squadron, was being seconded to 'marry' with some Lothian and Border Horse going up to Anzio.

An hour later Rex and I were saluting at the footboard of

Jumbo Richely's ten-tonner. He acknowledged our salute without a word and we jumped up. Expecting the worst.

Jumbo spoke through his teeth:

'I won't ask where you two've been, but I suppose you know that it's an extremely serious offence for an officer in our Regiment to go A.W.O.L.'

Rex said: 'I was a little indisposed, Colonel. Else, we'd have got back sooner. Geoff was helping me out.'

Our Commanding Officer bit his lips. For a second I thought he was going to fly at Rex, then he shook his head, in a kind of numbed calm.

'Jesus Priest, I don't know why I've put up with you and y'r rotten piles as long as I have, Rex. And you needn't think you're getting away with a thing this time. You're both on my Memorandum when you come back. At the moment you're needed urgently. Anzio. You're to bring the Lothian and Borders up to strength.'

We expressed polite surprise, well-feigned in both cases, I think.

'You will be in full readiness as of first light tomorrow morning. Your crews have all been warned to stand by. Ammo stocked and all maintenance done. You'll leave when the tank-landing craft are in place in Naples harbour. It's a matter of co-ordinating with the Navy. Is that clear?'

We nodded.

'Synchronize watches.'

We did so.

'Apparently it's a final bid to crack the Gustav Line. Get through to Rome. The infantry on the beachhead have suffered heavy casualties and badly need tank support. You'll land at the southern end of the salient and endeavour to stabilize the sit there. You know the drill for mounting infantry, I think.'

We did, but we didn't like it. We had done it only once, as a matter of fact, at Elaroussa and it had been a hell of a shambles. The code word for mounting infantry at that time was 'Magnum'. Troop-carrying MT brought them forward and a complete infantry section was carried on each tank; a platoon of three sections would work and fight with a troop of three tanks. But it was damn hard to see anything with all those bods clinging on your turret and I hated having men dying, unprotected, so close to me. It went against the grain, somehow. But we were more than used to these sudden departure orders – Tich's agonised face as he tried to bolt the last of some boiling char and men all over leaping onto moving vehicles, brandishing cookers, dixies, Jerrycans, the like. Having taken our maps and received our frequency orders, Rex and I slipped guiltily off; I'm sure Jumbo was heartily glad to get rid of us.

I went to rejoin my tank.

The first thing I noticed, as I greeted the boys, was all the waterproofing that had been done. We were going to be taken to the beachhead in LSTs – Landing Ships, Tanks – the larger version of tank-landing boats. We would run off a ramp into shallow water and it was necessary to fix a kind of big chute coming up from the exhausts at the back, also to build up a cupola for myself, through which air for the engine was drawn, swathe the gun mantle in tarp or other waterproof sheeting, stow the rope around the turret, and so on. Of course, we had never so much as practised the manoeuvre and I know none of us were looking forward to it.

'Spick 'n' span, eh, sir?' said Whitey. 'Even gave her a lick of paint.'

'So I see.'

I was standing staring at the front of the tank where, beneath the driver's visor, a series of signs had been touched up. Each of these had its significance. The first, on the left, was a white 45 on a blue and green background meaning that we belonged to an armoured reconnaissance group. The yellow 26 on a black background that came next in line was a bridge sign. All bridges were classified and numbered by the engineers to show what load they could safely carry. Our vehicle could not use any bridge marked lower than 26. Then there was the white square of the Regimental sign, then the Squadron, and a further sign denoting that I was 2-i-c, or second-in-command, of that Squadron. Last came the Divisional sign, the clenched mailed fist already mentioned. I must say these had got a bit knocked about of late and the old heap looked the better, though I say it myself, for the dressing-up.

'We'll be going up on LSTs,' I said.

Morris moaned. 'I'm always sick as hell on the sea, sir. 'Tain't my element, you could say.'

'When are we leaving?' I asked.

You might think they would ask me that, but I had been away and out of touch, and, truth be told, the men had a habit of knowing movement details long before we officers got them. They had a positive grapevine of such information. This time, however, none of them knew and this was for me a sort of omen, or presentiment. I didn't like it, told myself I was being a superstitious fool, and thrust it from my mind, trying to think of Clara. It wasn't good to have ideas like that in tanks. But then something happened to deepen that inward warning. I had got up into the turret, to try out the raised cupola, when I felt someone looking over my shoulder down into the hull. It was Rex. A new Rex – sombre, even gloomy.

'Everything tiggerty-boo, Geoff?'

'Everything ay in order. They seem to have done these turrets to a T. We should get through.'

'Just so long as it's not too far a run through the water. Tell your driver to let her run easy. Steady as she goes without any change of speed, even if you're fired on. That way we won't splash saltwater onto the ignition. We'll be carrying infantry with us. I don't like it, Geoff.'

'What's wrong?'

'Everything. You know we've never fought like this, hemmed in and with infantry all over the shop. My God, I don't like it.'

And I didn't like it that his voice shook.

'I've got a new gunner, too,' he said. 'Completely green. Had the other laddie since El Adem.'

'You still have Blinders,' I consoled him.

'And that Edwardson's worrying me, too. He's a weak link, I know it, can feel it in my bones. I want him between us as we debark, with you on my right. The thing is, it's going to be difficult seeing, let alone commanding, with all those men aboard.'

I knew Rex well enough to know that he wanted to tell me something. Otherwise he'd not have been on my turret in the first place. He could have contacted me by radio. His right hand came up, heavy, and I heard him sigh deeply.

'If anything should happen to me, Geoff ...'

My heart fell. It was just what I didn't want him to say. I wanted him to shut up. This was the worst of luck.

'I require you instantly, do you hear?'

'Don't say it, Rex.'

He rubbed raspingly his moustaches, into which seemed to have crept a tinge of snow. I hadn't noticed that before. He looked like a broken eagle and I watched him unhappily.

'What is it, Rex?'

'Well, you know that I ...' he began, half-apologetically.

I was thinking that never in all the time we had fought together had he spoken of this. We had sat under stars from Benghazi to Bizerta yarning our heads off about this or that – but never the ultimate. It just wasn't done. It had not needed saying between us. Other officers, yes. Rex, never. He had always seemed so full of vigour, so sure of living. I couldn't imagine him dead and yet I had seen quite a few dead men. I felt profoundly uneasy. He was too close to me for one thing and he seemed desperately old all of a sudden, with his scraggy neck from which some wire-like hairs stood up. Christ Almighty, he was old enough to be my father!

'Listen, Rex,' I tried.

'If I shove off ...'

'You know perfectly well you're going to bury us all, I've always said so.'

'It's your duty, I remind you,' he said with sudden severity. 'That's an order. I have a feeling. This one has my name on. You see, if I'm hit, if I do buy it,' (how hard, I realised, this was for him to say) 'well then, there's my daughter, you see. My agent has her address.' Here he grinned to hide his emotion. 'Young girls, they're terrible, aren't they? I mean, they're always a worry, they tend to make you anxious.'

'Nothing's going to happen to you, Rex, because nothing can happen to you.'

'My dear chap, I'm mortal!'

He struck the turret a savage blow with that old Eytie rifle bolt of his.

'I didn't know that you had family,' I said to him. Nor did I. During all this time together I just hadn't put personal questions to him, nor he to me, it would have been vulgar somehow. That was one of the aspects of the blue we both liked, I suppose. Domesticities belonged to another world.

'She's very pretty!' he tossed off suddenly – just like that.

'I'll bet.'

'She'll marry one of these days. I would like to think someone was taking care of her.'

'I'll see to it,' I muttered gruffly, under my breath.

I was really worried, still. In one way we'd never been so close. But I was shocked, horrified even, by Rex's having also had the same warning. If I hadn't felt it myself, perhaps I wouldn't have given the matter much thought. In any event, one had to be realistic. It was said that the average life of a tank commander on the Anzio beachhead at that time was all of four days. But his confirmation shook me, in my heart.

'Any rum around?' I asked.

'I think they gave out the last tots before we got in.'

'Too bad. Think Jumbo will cane us for those days over leave?'

'Who knows?' he shrugged. Then he added wearily, 'My reactions just aren't what they used to be.'

I looked closely at him then. We all depended on Rex. And how! Before he hopped off our hull onto the hard ground he looked all at once his age. A vigorous but very old man. And I think that was when I learnt that I would not want to be around without Rex, and his friendship. What was he going to write in that notebook of his this night? I watched him go with a great sense of loss. A strange pillar of shrewd sayings and eccentric courage. A man made for myth. Then I picked up my map-board and tried to clue the men in – on 'Fanny Adams', for that was all we knew. We were at the southern end of a two-divisional front, on terrain we had never seen and knew damn all about.

We rumbled off in the dark before dawn. Searchlights from either side of the Caserta road swept the sky in pocket pencils high above, and lighted us a little. But no moths played in those reaching beams. The docks at Naples seemed complete chaos, with cordons of Yanks and our own MP keeping the bambini out, and the bambini trying to climb on our tanks and beg for filoos. I wondered what they thought of this transformation of their town and the lawless world we had now made their law. Just whose side were they on?

Guides embarked us in the flat-bottomed LSTs. They were American boats with very shallow draught, holding thirty tanks in three rows of ten on the lower deck, with an hydraulic lift able to take lighter wheeled MT to the top. Our men were in good spirits, all except Morris who immediately started to be seasick. I told him we were still tied up at dock, and even went aloft to verify this for him, but it was no good. He couldn't stop vomiting. Finally, I played cards with him and it seemed to help take his mind off his allergy a bit. All the same he landed weak, even though the voyage was calm.

I knew the time we were set to debark and we were all in our hulls, with the infantry mounted on us, when on the dot I heard the anchor dropped astern. This would be used to haul the LST off the beach at the next high tide. The ship simply ran on the anchor until she grounded. With an immense clanking the two doors in front of us opened and a ramp was lowered to the sand. It was nearly full daylight.

Our group was in the second wave and we saw the first Cruisers dip out, laden with infantry, plunging quite steeply down the ramps. The shore looked about a quarter of a mile away and was covered in an ugly low smoke. But the sea, we soon saw, didn't even come up to the sprockets of the tanks and we had an easy run onto the bench. There we immediately came under enemy fire – and lost our infantry in short order.

If the ground around Cassino had been shell-holed, that at Anzio resembled a Swiss cheese. I've never seen so many craters, most of them filled with water, odd bits of equipment, and many dead bodies. The Lothians got off the beach all right, without loss, but frankly I was so fully occupied hanging on and receiving orders from Rex that I could hardly see where we were going for a while. The artillery from both sides had had a go at this beachhead and the cratering was ridiculous. It was slow going. I caught kaleidoscope glimpses – a bloated leg, a spade, a Jerry helmet – bodies in the definitive postures of death. There was no way to bury them here, I supposed.

'Hallo BADGER Two, BADGER calling. When you have reached field three-three-oh move rapidly to my right. Cannot stand here. Have sighted two enemy tanks probably refilling north of ruined windmill . . . cannot quite identify . . . do not engage, I repeat *not*. Figure two. Over.'

'BADGER Two, okay . . . ' I shouted.

I heard Edwardson ack and then we were plunging roughly southwards either side of what had once been a road. Infantry were in the ditches around it. The usual tactical sweep was what had been ordered, and was now developing. The only way you got through a screen of Boche anti-tank guns was by going around them. This we were doing – racing to the southernmost tip of the beachhead and trying to get behind the considerable armour the Lothians were engaging.

For engaging them they were already. Their guns were spewing forward at something or other. They were trying to deepen a hole already made, in the confusion. We had been given the task of turning the southern flank. Just too bad we hadn't been able to rehearse the manoeuvre, nor even seen photos of the terrain first (as we had at Salerno).

I saw Rex's gloved hand go up in ironic salute as we careened off to the right. He was clearly in his element. The Ironmaster was *at it again*.

Then a crackle in my headphones.

'Hallo BADGER, this is BADGER Three.' Edwardson's voice sounded definitely edgy. 'Those are Tiger tanks we see. I identify figures eight. Oh-eight. Stationary. Possibly ex-hulls dug in. Over.'

I heard no more. There was a lurch of the tank and a sudden screech of tortured metal. I popped my head out of the raised cupola. The waterproofing exhaust port had been ripped off the back of our engines while in motion by shot whose source I could not identify. Apart from the scare the sound had given us, it did no harm.

I was waiting for Rex to come back. In the desert, damaged Jerry tank hulls had dug themselves in, like so many pill-boxes, for the gun to be used against armour, then abandoned when necessary. I could not see the Chleuh doing so in a killing ground like this, where mobility was of the essence, and I got my glasses onto those hulks. It was a cardinal rule of desert warfare that a tank refilling was a sitting duck. It was highly unlikely a forward Panzer would do so here. Rex was simply wrong.

Then a mine went up, a big one to our left, and all I heard was muddled voices.

'... have knocked out one gun and crew ... '

'... Three has knocked out anti-tank gun on ridge to flank front. And crew. Please appreciate ... '

'Over to you, Over!'

'... and advance on present bearings ... '

It was the worst set scramble I had heard in my life. We were all working so damn close. And the whole frequency went dead. I heard some static, then an old man's voice chortle happily *'Si, senor!'* and then nothing at all. My phones went dead. And those were Tigers, all right. The Tiger was the biggest tank sent against us at that time. It was fifty-six tons with an eighty-eight milli leering out of its characteristically squat turret. I saw the black cross on the side of this, the thick-weaved tracking, and the cobra-like cowl of the barrel perforated for reduction of recoil. And the bastards had the sun.

It was as I thought. The Tigers weren't refilling. Some details of ground infantry seemed to be attaching tarp or rabbit netting or something or other, behind. These tanks had been in Africa. It was a trick to raise dust. And I could now see why. High overhead out to sea, I saw four slim darts descending. At first I thought they were Focke-Wulfs and that we were for it. The light made it hard to identify them with certainty and then I saw the peculiar swept-back wings and knew them for fighter-bombers of ours. They were coming over to strafe the Chleuh. Then my breath was taken, sucked from my lungs, by the blazing vacuum of passing shot. A hot blast seemed to thrust at my face.

'... have identified in front, figures two-zero-zero ...'

'Suggest all tanks BADGER organize to ...'

Then the planes dropped their bombs and you could see nothing of the enemy at all. We had drawn down to the right of the beachhead while the Lothians had been badly pinned down, some of them even re-forming closer to the beach itself. I could see a pillar of flung-up sand hurling itself at the frontplates of two of their Cruisers, and then subsiding slowly. Rex had got us out, southwards, and I reeled in my mike, like a fisherman his line, as I saw him waving from his turret and giving us the old cavalry signal. Advance and pursue. So it was to be then. It was to be something we had done in the desert. I was familiar with the tactic.

The main area behind the beach where we had landed was all brewing and bombing, seething swirls of oily smoke and dust obscuring any shapes at all. We would drive a wedge up behind them, and force those Tigers to turn (since they did not have 180 traverse), and expose their engines at the rear. Rex gave us the sign. In the old A6's we had fought in first in the desert, our guns had been useless against those of the Chleuh. Both Boche Mark II and III easily outgunned us. So a drill was devised whereby each tank was autonomous. The line advanced, the gunner selecting his own target on the crosswire of his sights and then when the commander gave the order to halt, the gunner fired when steady. As far as the gunner was concerned, that is, the Tannoy order to the driver to halt was also the order to fire. Then, directly he had fired, almost before the breech bounced back in the turret, the driver would accelerate. In this way we tried never to stay in one spot long. It had worked then. Whether it would now, in such different terrain, I did not know. Rex still had Blinders as his driver and the two of them worked virtually within one head. Blinders knew what Rex wanted to do before he did himself. Halt, fire, advance. I saw what seemed to be a Tiger in the murk, and its snub turret already leaked a healthily growing oily smoke. Then, to my left, Rex's exhaust port blew off to a great wake of shot.

Feeling our own Cruiser lurch to a strike, I reached blindly for my other phones, only to hear Edwardson's excited chatter in my ears.

'Hullo BADGER. Uh-hullo. This is BADGER Three. My loader has been hit. Having trouble operating the set and commanding myself. Over.'

Rex's voice: '... just do your best, Three. Keep on attacking. They should swing soon. Have taken one. Out.'

I hated this thing from the start, though at the time I suppose I did not know it. In the dark smoke of ununderstood explosions I think we all wanted to get the living hell out. Several eighty-eights could be heard, with their characteristic accurate cracking, and putting my glasses up I could see two of the Tigers, perfectly untamed, making for higher ground on the flank. And for some reason, seeing those great menacing shapes, their driver's hatch low and, on the other side from ours, the spare tracking forward, I thought of those men in black, whom Rex had mown down, kicking. My mind left the immediate ordering of the details of the engagement – which I don't believe it had ever done before – and I remembered a line from Dantë read on a punt on the Isis at Oxford. *E cortesía fu in lui esser villano.* A sultry, fly-hung stretch of the Cher near Magdalen, punting to pick up a girl who'd known my father in Ceylon and was now studying at Lady Margaret Hall, a Malayan Chinese who easily translated the line for me, explaining that it meant that lies and treachery were too good for some people, like the Nips.

In our case, like the Nazis. Then a crackle in my ear, all protocol abandoned.

'Geoff, can you see those muckers? Do you have them in range?'

Not a potato, I was about to return, but suddenly on a high-pitched note Edwardson's voice came on the set:

'Hallo BADGER, this is BADGER Three. My loader's badly hit about the shoulders. High velocity shot entered. Rex! Sir? Can you hear me, man? This is BADGER Three. Send out an artillery SOS. Where the hell are any OPs? For God's sake let's get some counter battery fire onto those ... Dammit, my loader's dying I tell you ...'

It was horrible.

Rex's voice came back correctly cold.

'Hello BADGER Three, BADGER calling. Do not understand signal. Heavy Relations unable to get on ridge in time. Over.'

Then a thunderous explosion somewhere.

It was a haughty reprimand, public on the net and terrible, one to which I acceded. It mastered Edwardson for a minute. His voice had sounded dreadful, almost as if he'd gone round the bend.

Fighting like this, moving to get hull down northwards, in order to engage those higher Tigers, and thus release the infantry whom we could see crouched in dykes and ditches all over, we sweated in our hulls. It was no war. It was what the learned doctor had called 'confusion worse confounded'. My God, what a mess! Crates and trucks and half-tracks and what have you, dispersed in all directions, most of them with men lying behind them seeking cover. I would seriously guess that ninety per cent of them lying in the mud, our chaps or Yanks or Pommies or New Zealanders, had not the slightest idea of what the general plan of battle was – other than to thrust, somehow, inland. Mortar stuff was coming down all the time and I'd seldom seen such a concentration of confused infantry, mastered with so little co-ordination, anywhere. For a moment, though, no one was firing on us directly. I mean, not particularly directly.

I write this now because at that moment something happened. I mean, our tank stopped. Before Tich braked. Where the damn thing came from we never knew.

Our tank was moving forward for another hull-down firing position, behind a grassy knoll, when it stopped as if it had struck a wall. The whiplash crack that then went through my marrow came infinitesimally later. I remember hunching panting, staring down hard into Morris' greasy, thinning hair. To his right, perspiration lay thick on Whitey's astonished face. A cordite cloud spumed up in the turret and we were all coughing and choking like hell. Then Whitey's jaw hung slack.

Tich bawled back, 'What's the mucking frigging fuck 'appened, sir?'

It was extraordinary.

But it happened.

The tank was tottering fitfully forward again and as it did so, a lump of shell – doubtless still hot – toppled through the rent it had made in our turret and plopped apologetically to Morris' feet. We all stared at it aghast. It was not explosive. A fluke had happened. One always did, in the life of any tank commander over a considerable time. We had been penetrated but not hurt. Trancelike, the eyes of the three of us in the turret stared down at it while the engine picked up speed. I was ready to inform Rex, the Regiment, if necessary, when it all became a matter of giving – and hearing – orders again. Chill wind whipped through the rent the eighty-eight had created in our starboard side.

For a moment, at any rate, we were not being fired upon.

Now there was incredible confusion to our left, in the direction of the beachhead. The Lothians were drawing back. Light-skinned traffic was swanning every way, God knew whose some of it was. Shelling was constant in that vicinity.

'Hallo all stations BADGER, this is BADGER One. Heavy Relations appear not to be able to get on ridge in time. Continue direction with me. Off.'

I then heard Rex asking the Lothian commander for

permission to hold where we were, and to try to enfilade the Jerry flank, such as it was.

'Hello BADGER, DIVER answering. Situation very confused over here. Am sending DIVER One and DIVER Two to figures oh-four-fife-seffen to protect landings there. Hold your position. I repeat hold your position till I contact FEVER.' That was Brigade. The message faded with firing all over. Then some infantry ran to the back of us and the lead Sergeant shouted up to us that there was one hell of a mess and that some American Honeys had been firing on the Lothians. No losses, luckily. The Chleuh were drawing back to try to secure higher ground, as per. The Tigers were skulking away.

''Allo all stations BADGER, BADGER calling.' Rex's voice was assured now. 'Position stable where we are. Keep hull down at ease unless they counterattack. Have one man on the set continually. Over.'

'Okay, off,' I said.

There were deafening explosions northwards and Whitey was clicking switches like crazy, keeping our frequency established, clearly. I could see Rex's head atop that new tall cupola of his – the Ironmaster transformed! – and just the shoulders of that IZ sweater and damned if the old gypsy hadn't put a tennis visor on, against the sunbeams. There was a man riding on his tank with him and I reckoned it was probably an Artillery O.P. – Rex liked to tell them they could ride on the outside of his Cruiser, that'd teach them to be accurate. The figure seemed to be operating a 38 set, or trying to, at any rate. Then a couple of sections of someone or other doubled past us carrying needle-nosed P.I.A.T.S., Projector Infantry Anti-Tank as the acronym went.

We left Whitey operating and Tich and Morris and I got out to do the necessary. En route we examined the hole where we'd been penetrated and I remember that none of us said anything. Now Tich could brew char in the back of beyond and he soon had a cupper steaming. The dixie burnt my fingers. So our breakfast was a bar of chocolate and biscuits and I handed some up to Whitey, who was duly grateful. I was stretching out my map case on a port bin when they came.

Now, either by good luck or good management by Jumbo, our lot had never been Stuka-bombed and here they came in two formations, the sky around them momentarily empty. The first one peeled off and we got the impression, characteristic as it happened, that the bastard was coming right at you, had seen you in his sights personally, I had time to yell up to Whitey to close down and then as the first of them came down looking even more like a grasshopper than our Lysander and whining like crazy, I heard the clang of the two turret flaps and then we all hit the ground. Almost immediately it bounded beneath us.

'Fuckin' Priest!' cried Tich in an audibly agonised voice. 'There goes the char again!'

We survived the thumping of the first formation and I could see the second circling to swoop in when a bit of the dust and smoke flung up had cleared. I longed to see a Spitfire really go for those buggers. But I knew we had to save the tank. Without that we were useless.

'Mount!' I yelled in the lull.

We acted as one. I got in last. There was a deep indentation in a division between the fields to our right and, though it was cutting our retreat off from the shore tanks, we had to use it. There was even a ruined building there. We had perhaps two minutes, I calculated, before the second wave of Stukas would also pay us a visit.

'Bye bye, breakfast,' grinned Morris beneath me. He now could not see what was happening.

'Driver,' I shouted into the Tannoy. 'White house two o'clock brewed tank ahead. Depression behind it. Quick as you can now.'

Rex, I saw, had anticipated me. The Ironmaster was on the way, jerking over the shell-holes ahead, as he also made for the protective ditching. We might just make it.

'Get this beast into top!' I called to Tich, sweating.

For a second I saw the Stukas resting suspended on the sky, like slots in that morning's heavens. I saw young hands clasped on the joysticks, I imagined the men in them twisting in the roaring cloud, and coiling to come down at us. I saw the holes for eyes in their helmets, I saw their heads bent, fair and thick, over their controls. All the instruments agreed that they were a precise race. And I saw the huge deaf head with bristling brow of Beethoven there, coming down straight at us.

Luckily, we just made it. The Stukas came down like angels of death, ploughing the landscape directly ahead of us. There was harsh longing in their engines, the apt desire to kill. We responded to it, like troops to drums. And then my skull and dream split, the lights blotted out, black earth fountained in front of me.

When it had subsided I turned my periscope anxiously around to see what had been hit. We had somehow survived. Rex looked all right. Edwardson? Had his tank made it? Then I saw him stalled and despite the clamour in the air I heard the familiar starter whizzing and whirring. In a minute the cripple would attract its customary ration of concentrated fire.

'... elders now in declivity north of ...' It sounded meaningless in my phones.

By transmitting on Brigade frequency some local set had effectively jammed all other signals and then all I could concentrate on was a whooshing rush, the flight of another giant bat out of hell, snapped short by the usual dry needling crack, the ever-ready whiplash that took your soul away, as if all the air in the universe had been fissured, physically. It was a close call but, though we seemed to bounce, nothing hit hard. Just a few odd clangs low down on the tracks.

'... have knocked out one ...'

'... be prepared to move quickly, Two ...'

'... confirm hit,' said another voice I did not recognise. 'Advancing on present bearings. Over.'

What the hell was going on I did not know. All I knew – all the poor blighters in my tank knew – was that we were under fire but had not been fucking hit. It was all we begged the old man of the mountains for. A bit more luck like that we'd had with the freak penetration. I saw German gun crews in the rear distance dashing about a truck with a gun mounted on its back, and I was going to ask Rex for permission to fire – I did not know if he wanted us to reveal the new position – when his voice sounded quite clearly and deliberately in my ears.

'Hel-lo BADGER Three, BADGER calling. Are you hearing me? Are you hearing me clearly? Is something wrong? Over to you.'

It was all very calm and methodological (as always with Rex in emergencies) and then my blood froze as I heard the response. The Stukas had come in screaming but this was worse, much worse. Edwardson's voice was clear also and it had reached some end of terror. I listened to it horrorstruck, ashamed.

'BADGER ... my engine's ... hello, Gunner, traverse ... what's wrong with ...?'

It was all blurred, confused, mired with the hebetude of fathomless fear.

'I say Three, pull yourself together and ...'

There was another deafening explosion and then I stared down at the floor at the dud shell between Morris' boots during all that ensued. The hole in our turret swept warm cordite past my face.

'Urgently needed ... twenty-five pounders ... plenty of figures two five two five two five ... hallo any station BADGER ... I mean figures two two is what I said ...'

Edwardson was babbling. The man had come apart. What had happened was that he had picked up his wireless mike but was using it like the Tannoy, blathering away to what was left of his crew. Suddenly I thought I heard him give a great guffaw and my blood froze anew.

'My loader's dead! D'you hear me, Rex ... *he's dead*!'

Thank God the others beside me couldn't hear this. Rex and I had made the wadi. Edwardson hadn't. That much was plain as a pikestaff. Evidently he'd taken all the Stukas could give. With the turret flaps closed over my head I could only see through the periscope – small cut-outs of the incredible confusion around. Rex had his turret open; that I could see. His head was inclined, his arms folded, balancing himself and listening to a man at the end of terror, the extreme of emotional degradation. I flung open my turret flaps too.

But as I did so a crushing surf of flung-up earth hurled itself at our plates, like a gritty sea smiting a rock. I ducked down as this cataract of stone and sand belaboured our sides for several seconds, hanging on to the gun baffers, and now the deflector guard, and now to Morris' neck.

'They're *coming again*!' Edwardson's voice was the anguished whine of a chastened child. It was very terrible to witness it. 'Driver, what's gone wrong? There's water in the turret, I tell you. Why don't you answer, Driver? My God! Quick! Rex, he's gone, too ...'

I do not want to transcribe the rest. Edwardson, the stoic, the monk of our Group, who showed no fear when you cut flies off his nose with Beza fire, had simply broken apart. I had never heard it before and I never want to again. I would have torn my phones off if I could, but I had to keep them on for any orders coming from Rex. Amid the horrible stammerings in my ear I could now hear the Stukas coming in again. I banged down the flaps once more and hoped to God that Rex was doing the same. I crouched for death between Whitey and Morris. I could not see, in that steel cell, but I could hear.

'Where's my left hand? My God, *where's my left hand?* Gunner, what have you done with my left hand! There's no more fingers ...'

Then the Stukas were upon us, I was almost glad to say, and I could hear Edwardson's sobbing on the set no more. Sitting waiting for the explosions in those split seconds, I prayed that death would be quick for him if it had to come.

All we heard for a minute then was the screaming of the Stukas and the avid bursting of their bombs. Our tank rebounded to these, but this time I heard no clanging on our sides. Even so, it was close. They only had to crack a track and we were dead ducks. Then when they had gone I opened up once more and stood high in my cupola to try to get a sight of Edwardson, to see if I ought to dismount and help. And all I could hear was his sobbing in my ears.

'I'll never play the piano again!'

I had never heard a man break down in public before. The bombing had hit some petrol tins, I suppose, because there were flames ahead and the usual dark smoke going up all over. I couldn't even see Rex through it now.

'Hello BADGER, I say they're all dead ...'

The smoke was rushing through the rent in our turret wall and I got out to let Morris and Whitey come up for air. A strangled kitten mewed in my ear.

'My God, I can't stand it, I tell you ...'

His voice was unrecognisable and I wanted to see Rex, to get a hand signal to see if I should get back and help. We could take the man aboard, at least, if he was indeed the final survivor. At last I got a sight of Rex's Ironmaster, maybe no more than fifty yards ahead. He was still in the gulley between the fields but I thought I saw blood on his face and on the powerful binoculars he had taken off a Jerry Colonel near Sfax. He did seem to be looking in my direction. I waved. He did not respond. I knew that we were both listening to the end of a man.

'BADGER, where are you ... Three calling ...'

Rex's voice trying to break in on the babbling: 'Now Three, BADGER calling. If you have been hit and hurt, advise that you abandon tank and ...'

'Rex? Can you hear me, man? Send out an artillery SOS. Where the hell are the OPs? For Christ's sake let's get some counter battery fire onto those ...' It frittered into sobbing again. 'I've lost my hand. To hell with the lot of you!'

Now I saw him. By standing up high on the waterproofing cupola I saw his tank. It was brewing. Badly holed about the engine vents it was leaking dark smoke like a hungry tongue. The Stukas hadn't missed, after all. They'd got him. And I could see their sinister grasshopper shapes making out to sea, northwards up the coast, with what looked like a squadron of Spitfires criss-crossing behind for all they were worth.

'Never again!' Then the word, 'Mozart.' Then a sob. Then silence. Indistinct noises. Then a detonation that ripped through my eardrums. Then only the ritual hum of a set sending. Rex and I stared at each other, over that stretch of foreign soil, and I knew we were both interpreting the sound that followed as that of a body falling to the pit of the turret, dragging the mike at its lips. Edwardson had killed himself. Then there was a gigantic explosion and we both ducked down in our turrets. Our crew huddled bent for those moments while the spasms of a blown-apart Cruiser Mark V flew overhead. That poor devil Edwardson had remained free of the final indignity, at least. His had been a sobering end. I think of it often as I write now. It haunts me. You will understand why in good time, I believe.

Then I heard Rex's voice in my ears. It was calm, considered, even lethargic in tone.

'Hallo DIVER, BADGER calling. Have been bombed by Stukas. Lost one tank. Over.'

'... keep in contact ...' The message back was weak. 'We hope to make a hole through this lot and laager in ...'

The voice faded.

Rex gave the Lothian CO our map co-ordinates in code.

Things calmed. All that afternoon we recce'ed, just the two tanks now, Rex's and mine. It was a lonely vigil among battered fields and broken houses and demolished vehicles, many still burning. There were great piles of 'B' Echelon material lying in chaos all over the place. We held closer contact with Diver, the Lothians, who had also been badly mauled on the beach and apparently divided into two. Jerry armour had retreated as usual, after having hit and hit hard. We awaited the morrow.

At one point in our swan, I remember, we passed back not far from Edwardson's tank, what was left of it. It was the engine compartment that had gone up chiefly. The turret looked somewhat intact and Rex halted his Cruiser and got out and took a look into it. When he got down he put his hand to his head and seemed to stagger a pace. That was all.

Night came on and we bivvied near some Royal Engineers who had been brought in to help ford rivers. The Chleuh had left this forward area less than two days previously, we learnt.

We parked near a house that had been split gaping open and took the opportunity of its humble hospitality. Even Morris and Whitey and Tich and Smithers felt the sadness of these places, I know. There is something humiliating, indecorous, about looking into a stripped house like this – I had felt the same of the Countess's palazzo in Naples, after that bomb there. The wall against which I leant now in the half-light had family portraits of happier days hung crookedly upon it. The room was strewn with rubble, burnt furniture sticking through it. An old Victorian iron bedstead with oval cameos set in its front hung down from a half-demolished bedroom above us. Crude dadoes and frescoes of the Madonna and the Saints were painted on the walls. From the cracked and bullet-splattered remnants of one ceiling the Son of Man looked down on us as we ate our M. & V. There were what appeared to be a lot of insurance documents and certificates in one place, and some letters too. These I pocketed. Perhaps I could hand them to GS later, and help them on their way.

Rex and I took first guard. Night was a veil of sadness. The stars stared down. All the time we heard Boche engines starting and restarting in the distance. We knew their note. Jerry didn't miss his maintenance. We were both dead tired after the day, and anxious. In the blue, night encampments had been sacrosanct, never attacked. The worst fighting came with dawn, a low light in the eyes. But here it was all different; it was all muddled and saddened and diffused. Different. We couldn't recognise the problems which the terrain posed. We – the old veterans – were at sea. We sipped our char. Under the stars, under the night, with half a building behind us.

'It wasn't any good,' Rex said at last.

'What?'

'Well. Burying any of them, I mean.'

'Edwardson?'

'The lot. I looked in. Any burial party'll have to hose out that turret to get the remains. A biscuit tin or two would do for the lot of 'em.'

We had buried more than one in a commodious can of the

kind, courtesy Huntley & Palmer, in the bled. There had been a padre – I had never met him – who had apparently gone round the bend, gone bonkers, off his chump, since his duty from dawn to dusk was burying particles of men in this way, and praying over them. I could see his point.

'D'you think it was a sort of jinx, Rex, maybe?'

'Our *guignon,* as the French say?' He did not discount it. No one in our Regiment would have. As in World War One the ordinary soldier did not disregard the place of wisdom's other children. He had learnt the speech of pain. He had studied hands that had given death. The dying soldier, like a straying lover, made no mock of premonitions. Some had come all too true.

Rex said nothing.

I put my head back on the wall.

'Do you think it was Jumbo?' I asked.

'What?' Rex's voice was a growl.

'Well, I mean. He sent us here. He could have chosen another Squadron.'

'You mean – as a punishment for our independence?'

'Sort of?'

'I don't know. I've never thought Jumbo vindictive. What's bothering me is I can't get clear to Diver.'

'Want me to have another shot?'

'No. There's wireless silence till dawn. Then all hell's to pay. You can hardly scramble out who's talking what.'

We quieted. It was better than nothing. We were men astray, and we knew it. This was not our world.

Round about one a.m., when Tich and Smithers came to relieve us, so that we could curl up in a corner and try to get some sleep, our own infantry started coming through – quite inexplicably. They splashed and cursed in the dark. They must have just landed because the Number One of a Bren gun team I spoke to had a wreath of flowers round his steel helmet and another flower stuck in the muzzle of his gun. We were liberators – and had been so sent off from Napoli in such guise, in a number of cases. We also exchanged words with a Major, asking him to leave a standing patrol in the vicinity, in order to clue us in better as to what was going on, but he seemed to have only the vaguest idea of where they were going himself. Man after man poured through patiently behind him.

When they had gone I was tired. With the first whitening of the sky before dawn I knew I was deathly afraid. Something was going to happen. It was in the lightening sky. I knew it but didn't know what it was. I felt like a schoolboy before a caning.

So I sat on the side of my tank and, with the aid of a torch in the first light, I looked at some of the letters I'd picked up. It was something to do, to quiet what I was feeling. They were rain-sodden but legible. They were mostly written by two people, one the soldier's wife, the other his father. The wife wrote from near Leipzig in a beautiful hand, some of the finest writing I have ever seen. She wrote that she was working long hours, seven days a week in a factory, and was feeling very worn out and exhausted; apparently her soldier-husband was close on fifty and she was glad to have had his letter telling her he would shortly be posted from front-line infantry to a rear unit, because of his shoulder problem. All she wanted was to have him back with her and embrace him. After I had read those letters I could not look at the ones from the father. The first I opened seemed simply to contain lists of the soldier's friends who had been killed in Russia.

There was a sort of diary among these effects, presumably the soldier's. It too was smudged and torn but I was able to read some of the entries. Very succinct and bare. Laconic.

21st February – All is chaos. The march goes on southward. Here we shall soon meet Tommy.

25th February – In the night a direct hit. I was lucky.

2nd March – We push forward as an advance post without communication right or left. Heil Hitler! Terrific noise everywhere. Terrorists in the rear. English A/T Gun 100 metres to our left.

5th March – We attack towards Anzio now with increased force. Shoot an English DR [Despatch Rider]. Put a mortar in position but do not have opportunity to fire it. HQ destroyed. A lot of crawling on our stomachs ...

I put the letters back into the little bundle I had made of them and crammed them under the cellophane of my map-case. I was struck by the mention of terrorists. These were presumably Eytie partisans we had begun hearing about lately. Directly our advances got fluid and looked like liberating Rome, the Italians got their courage up and some of them blew up Boche emplacements and stores behind the lines. As yet we tank corps men knew very little of this activity, how authentic and useful it was, and so on. We were soon to learn much more.

Dawn came up as it always did, and with it hope. I very badly wanted to do something. I called Rex, illegally breaking set silence while doing so.

'... desire recce north of Hill figures five-seffen. May I have your permission to move off on ...'

'Hello BADGER Two. Okay. Maintain contact. Off.'

I was pleased. I did not know that this decision of mine to investigate what lay beyond an empty squared-off hill – possibly a former olive plantation – to north-east of our present position was to be a turning-point. I think at the time I wanted to get out of my head the thought of that woman waiting in the fields near Leipzig for her vanished husband – *'wie einst Lili Marlene, wie einst Lili Marlene'*. A throw of the dice and, instead of being permanently immured in the mud of Anzio, he might have been in a hospital, sitting on clean sheets at the side of his bed playing cards with a Sapper from Melton Mowbray. Both of them Blighty's. Out of it. No more 'shoulder trouble'.

Whitey had been on watch, but all my crew were awake. As I told them to mount, Morris said to me, 'Don't like the look of this lot today, sir. Not at all. It's too calm for its own good.'

It was. He was right. Something was up. Some desperate counter-attack. We stretched and piled in. A distant mortar crack sounded. Then a rattle of small-arms fire. Maybe a tommy-gun, own troops.

'Driver, start up. Good. Loader, check your ammo. Gunner, traverse left – on.'

As ever, these men acted automatically, asking nothing more of life than to be left alive – for twice, as the poet said, no man dies. Morris sat easily in his seat, padded with old balaclavas and the like, cradled the loosened breech to his armpit, thrust his eye to the scope. Good old Morris, I so hoped he would live. His view on life was now an O traversed by sighting lines. Might it not always be so. The very fact that these considerations were flowing over me was an anxiety in itself.

'Driver, close down!' I shouted.

This was not necessary. A self-reassurance. I heard the flap clang down as if on a coffin.

We did not know this country over which we were moving, over which I had decided to move alone. For Tich it was now no O but a rectangular slit right in front of his bony nose.

'Driver, advance slowly ... hull down by shot-up tree ...'

In the slow Italian dawn we moved alone. There were Pioneer Corps men working away to our right, but that was about all. To our left and north were mottled patches of armour, vehicles, stores, with men already seething about them. We could not see the shore.

I was thinking of Edwardson. His death had been a shock. More of a shock than I dared to acknowledge. That kind of a death changed something. I was beginning to discover it now, giving orders for the first time since it'd happened. I cannot exactly explain it but there was something different in our relationships. It was as if something amongst us had been soiled – yet I know we all felt pity for the man. There had only been one time similar in the blue and that was when we had gone through a Regiment of Lancers who had withdrawn, wisely, from a slugfest with eighty-eights. Their brewed tanks lay out in front, where we took up our positions. But one of them, a hundred yards behind the others, had been penetrated *from behind* ... from the direction, only, of 'friends'. It told its own story.

In front of us now, as we ascended the crest of the ruined hill, firing increased. It seemed to herald an unpleasant day. Then I slowed Tich down and we crept to the crest, where I could see and still be hidden behind our camouflage nets. Morris, too.

What I saw was a long plain. Two roads ran through it at an angle to each other. There were hedgerows and shattered houses but the general impression was of calm, as if an army of death had just rushed through. Many of the lighter-skinned vehicles, of both sides, were toppled over and smoking gently, as if snoring in their sleep. In the distance, on another rise, there was definite Boche activity. I saw Jerry helmets in tree branches. Other signs of OP posts. There had been a bad tank battle here. Yet I was comforted to see, perhaps two hundred yards ahead, two or three of our own Valentines in place, with infantry lying behind them. The sky was growing lighter. Then Morris tugged at my trousers.

'Sir!' He pointed hectically ahead.

I saw them too, now. They were Tigers, all right. Five of them, low, with the squat turret and moving fast northwards beneath a sort of scarp. Not breaking the skyline. Despite its weight the Tiger could move at over forty miles an hour on solid soil. It was terrifically reliable, giving very little mechanical trouble. It also carried well over a hundred gallons of petrol. The Cromwell was the best match we had to it to date, and there weren't many of those in Italy at our time. As it was, the gunner in my bus was crouched between my legs. The loader to our right operated the wireless, in touch with me on one communication system and with the so-called outside world on two others. Whitey presided over seventy-five cylindrical bins of heavy-shot ammo, all of it heavy, while across his knees lay draped the coils of the Beza belts. In some ways the loader-operator's lot was hardest of all. Certainly he had to be fit and strong. Whitey was. And it was cold. Air whirled through the turret and a small gale whipped in through Tich's slender slit visor.

'Driver, right. Steady, halt. Okay.'

I wanted to inspect what was going on personally, at the same time not hit the horizon so that those Tigers could calibrate on us. I got out of the built-up cupola with my head-set on and brought the glasses to my eyes. A sense of dizziness overcame me for a moment. Then chaos took form, in a certain sense. You got to know it. I could see what was left of the battle that had been fought in the valley and it wasn't very pleasant at all. Bodies, rations, stacks of ammo, overturned or smashed trucks – all caught in that loving type of Eytie mud which starts at your boots and somehow or other, before the day is through, works up to your armpits. And then there were those damn tanks, three unmoving Valentines.

I wish I'd never gone near them.

The tanks were half-on to me and I wondered why, now that it was full light, some Jerry anti-tank guns hadn't taken them. There was no question of our firing at anything, it would only have given our own, highly perilous position away. So I did something I had never done before. Handing over command of the Cruiser to Morris I jumped down and went forward with my pistol drawn. It was a little walk.

Who were all these men lying in shallow foxholes behind those tanks? I could not see them clearly. Why were not the tanks, in open view of the enemy, traversing? I directed my steps to the little Valentine silent on the right. An officer stood in its turret, I could now see, staring directly ahead. He was hatless, bald, and seemed to be sporting a monocle. As I came closer I saw he was also smoking a pipe.

I think it was really that touch which did it. Here was the epitome of the base wallah, the man whose tank corps beret had just replaced his City bowler. The docility of suburbia hung about him. I gave him an angry shout. The man's stance did not alter as I approached. And now I could see his face. Gazing ahead, it wore the expression of someone listening to an interminable anecdote.

'I don't know who the hell you think you are,' I shouted. 'But for Christ's sake you can't sit there bloody smoking and making a dead target for Jerry like ...'

The face did not turn. The gaze did not waver.

'Look, do you think you could get your men together and we could all reform behind that ditch?'

For a second it appeared to me that the unknown officer was about to answer, but he did not do so. His jaw muscles tightened on his pipe, that was all.

'You'll be brewed for sure if you don't . . .'

Still the eyes looked ahead, into some non-existent distance.

It was the monocle that did it. Yes, the farcical monocled faces of two vaudeville brothers I had seen before the war came back to me in those moments. They had had a song:

You can always tell a gentleman wherever he may be,
And if he's dressed in any sort of garb –
There are just three institutions I am sure you will agree
That always tend to make the pukka sahib;
There's the private school, the public school and the varsity . . .
Produce the type of chap of which there's a scarcity . . .

I thumped lustily on the nearest sand shield. There was something so indecently complacent in that winking round of glass. It was like some dead convention of the vanished western world, a piece of self-conscious 'Britishness' as out-of-place as an off-colour story in a cookbook – and as vulgar as those songs by the Western Brothers at the Palladium. I found myself putting a boot on a sprocket wheel, preparatory to hauling myself up. Such sublime indifference had to be broken.

'There happens to be a war on, old boy,' I cried.

Again I thought he was going to speak. He was much younger than I'd thought. Then the clutch of his cheek again, a spasm of skin to grip tighter the eye-glass, I reckoned.

'Chris' sake! This takes the bloody biscuit. *Listen!* There just happens to be . . .'

Starting to raise myself off the ground under the man – the Valentines were high of port – I found my temper suddenly deflating. The eyes of the monocled officer met mine. They had fallen a fraction, with the august gravity of a Ritz concierge assessing a new client – or some king of old contemplating an unruly courtier. And it was I who averted my gaze first. I had seen the full suffering in the face. The man was in some sort of agony and trying to suppress it. To a sudden shrill yapping of Spandau fire in the air and a sound of angrily tearing bushes I stifled an exclamation and ran to the rear of the tank. Its engines were dead, wrecked. The side of the Valentine I should have seen was a colossal gash, a cutout of avant-garde theatre, an imbecilic rent in metal. The shudderless and total immobility of this thing created for a battle's rage testified to some atrocious suffering. I knew I hated war.

'Oh!' was perhaps what I feebly said. Then, 'I see.'

I did. With all my being. For a long second I stood riveted, hearing firing thicken somewhere, automatically registering the rate of that fire. How crude my life seemed to have been. Would it ever be possible again to hear without fury the selfishness of cities, the scruples of 'place' and position, the poor conditions of this or that labour, rich women complaining of the shortage of nylons, bankers demanding collateral of returning vets, ministers mouthing religion, poets bleating about the states of their souls (plus the lack of public support) – in short, the ugly appurtenances of what's-in-it-for-me? I stood crushed by that presence. It had happened. I think I tried to take some control by frowning and breathing deeply. For what I was looking at was the Bismarckian end, the spirit of autocracy, of violence and fatality. It was almost puzzling it was so absolute.

For what I stood looking at – what was *there* – was a Valentine with one side staved in. The tank had probably been backed out of battle, to keep more healthy armour towards the enemy, till it had been struck again. By some fluke two figures, driver and gunner, were visible through the rent metal in postures of patent death. Yet – more than death. As usual, the driver had been ripped backwards, the gunner was inextricably and forever intermingled with his breech. They lay at the feet of their commander.

For he stood above them all, alive. Alive enough to die. The monocled officer had his left leg anchored to the bloody base of the turret and, half unbelieving, I saw that he was wearing a kilt. It was one of the Lothians, all right – such eccentricities were common in that Regiment. It was the damnably complete outfit, sporran, tasselled stockings, the lot. The only exception to the ensemble was that most of his right foot and shin had been shot away. Bloody bone was visible. It was only then that I saw that his fingers gripping the useless flanges of his turret were doing so convulsively. Those fingers were what I should have looked at first. I gave a last horrified glance up at the bronzed cheekbones, the fierce full moon of the monocle, and it seemed to me the head bowed a little, but calmly. He too was waiting for the end.

And looking wildly to right and left I saw that the other tanks had also been knocked out, their crews within them doubtless dead. The recumbent figures behind lay like those overtaken by the lava at Pompeii. They were distorted, scorched, I now saw; one in a posture of running still, an S of humanity on the ground. Then a screech of air made me turn. The rigid outline of a great Mark IV showed on the distant hill. I turned, holstered my .45 and began running. I did not stop until I reached my tank. I did not vomit, I don't think I threw up, but my face must have been ashy by the expression on Morris' when he saw me. I leapt into the turret.

'Driver, start up!'

We roared alive and swerved back down the plain to where Rex had wandered to recce. I desired nothing more in the world at that moment than to see him in his turret, Olympian, with his great burnt forehead, the beret belonging to that human head, the phones wound around it and the mike pressed to his lips like a lover. I did not make wireless contact. I did not trust my voice at the time. I thought back to the officer smoking his pipe and staring into the middle distance. Shock had clearly anaesthetised much of his pain but when the nerves awoke it would become intolerable. I knew somehow that he too wanted to die. I signalled a CCS, gave them the tank's position, and told them to try to get a stretcher forward as soon as possible. I was sweating, I was cold, I was scared. I did not want to go into action again.

Under the scowl of that sky the two Mark IVs ran very confidently up the rise on our right.

'Gunner, traverse right,' I began; once more decision was taken from me. Those tanks could outgun ours by several hundred yards. Whitey had loaded, all was ready. We would fire moving forward as we were, if necessary. But to my infinite relief, as I saw Rex's gun turning to engage also, the Mark IVs seemed to disdain our presence and swanned off back over the rise from which they had run down. A minute or more later I was walking up to Rex who was leaning on an evidently abandoned scout-car by which his own tank had drawn up.

'Damn glad to see you in one piece,' I said. 'What a mess over there.'

'Yep. Hasn't been too pleasant, has it? What I'd like to know is where the nearest petrol depot is. I'm getting short.'

I was contemplating telling him about the officer with the monocle but he seemed to have such relaxation in his pose, leaning with both elbows back on the flanges of the scout-car. Maps were strewn about on the radiators. I'd heard of a Cruiser commander who'd shot a mortally wounded driver in the head in order to get him out of the hatch – but nothing like what I had seen.

'Take over, would you, Geoff. I want to take a crap.'

He sauntered off with a spade. It was a crazy war.

It was a new war.

And it was a nasty war.

When Rex returned he said, quite casually, 'Well, I suppose we'd better recce, eh? We're a Recce Group, after all. Your men okay?'

'Okay,' I said.

'One of the Lothian troops appears to be missing,' he said.

'Yes,' I said.

'Some young officer in charge of them, I guess.'

'Yes.'

'In theory they should be somewhere about here, now.'

'In theory, yes. Possibly they're going to stick wings on our backs to try to fly us to Rome.'

'So, that's all you know about it?'

'That's all I know about it, Rex.'

'I agree with you. Since we landed in this god-forsaken dump, I haven't frankly received a single order that makes sense.'

'Well then. Let me give you one that does make sense, Captain.'

An officer – one of ours – was approaching in dishevelled garb, equally tatterdemalion as Rex's and equally with a spade in his hand. A big soldier-servant followed behind.

I was perplexed. I said nothing.

The newcomer, a shortish man with a black eye-patch over one eye, approached the battered scout car in a loose duffel-coat. He seemed sedulously to study the stripes on Rex's washed-out cricketing sweater. The man's face was divided between a palish forehead and lean cheeks beaten crimson by sand and grit.

'What the hell's happening here?' said Rex. I think both of us sensed a desert comrade.

'Wish I knew.'

Over folded arms, bush-shirt out at elbows, the man grinned ruefully. He wore no beret, nor other head covering.

'Who are you?' he said.

'Recce Group, Third Droghedas. What can we do you for?'

'Where are the rest of your tanks?'

Rex bristled. Then laughed.

'Ah, recently we've had some rather disobliging encounters. I mean, for quite a time. Since we've been landed.'

The man's eyes narrowed.

'So this is all you've got. Two tanks? I see. You laagered here? Well.'

'Frankly, we've been so buggered about since landing at Salerno that the only instruction to make the slightest sense . . .'

'As I said, I'll give you one that does, Captain. You will cross that line of hills – you see where I'm pointing – and report to the infantry CO you'll find digging in on the other side. He's just over the end of that feature. And he needs help.'

'Sorry.' Rex shook his heavy head. 'We're under orders from Brigade.'

'Then you've just got yourself another order, Captain. I happen to be your Brigadier.'

The man's big driver grinned. Rex blinked. I straightened. The scout car's identifying flashes had long since worn off. All at once I realised – the eye-shade, the duffel-coat, the peremptory manner. I hardly needed Rex's elbow in my solar plexus.

'Great Scott, Sir. I'm terribly sorry. I didn't recognise you at first.'

'That's all right. I didn't recognise you. I would suspect you're the infamous Captain Rex Davidson, of Third Droghedas. Very well, then. There's a battalion of Bedfords and Indians over there. They need all the support you can give. Stay with 'em. Now I'd like to talk to your Commanding Officer. Lothians, eh?'

He jumped up and slipped himself into the operator's seat. A gaping Trooper Denster came out onto the engines. I sketched a salute. General Stainton-Sims, of Greek reputation, could be heard crackling away into the mike. I did not like to tell him I had just recently seen the man he was attempting to contact – with his right boot shot off.

'Still no contact, General?' I asked him, watching him manipulate the set from above.

'Not a sound.'

'Maybe they withdrew, sir.'

'Not Knocky. I'm going to see for myself. Yes, in this dingo.' He waved to the scout-car.

'Jerry has some Tigers that way, sir. You'd better be careful.'

'I know the area, thanks. I just want to see that you are attached.'

Rex and I exchanged glances. We saluted as one, impassively, as our Brigadier with the beaten and scoriated skin, and the black eye-patch, finally drove himself off, his driver beside him. He seemed to make fast for the landing-ground, infantry – on the beachhead leewards. Dark smoke arose from this and from time to time it was traversed by cutting edges of light-arms fire.

'Still no communication with DIVER?' I asked Rex when he'd gone.

'Not a noodle. I suggest we go try to find 'em.'

'And if there are Tigers in that direction?'

'There's everything in that direction.'

'We don't know the terrain.'

'We don't know anything, Geoff.'

'What a mess,' I said.

'I know. I hear that two more squadrons near the disembarkment beach got it at dawn. Dicky, Andrew . . .'

The usual litany continued. I had heard it before, in the blue, but these were the names of men I did not know. Something was coming to an end. I knew it in my blood. We were two lone Cruiser Mark V tanks cut off from practically everything, on a relatively small beachhead in southern Italy, encircled by an efficient enemy. The prospect was not pleasing.

'There was an officer over there,' I mumbled, stumbling. 'Very seriously hit. I left him but tried to get . . .'

'If I only knew what the bloody hell to do,' Rex's brows were thunderous, his light eyes lowered.

We were close to his tank. I noted the usual surrealist arrangement of sighting vanes thereon. He had ripped most of his water-proofing equipment off for better visibility. I decided to do the same. My exhaust had been shot to hell, anyway. Rex's eyes looked tired, older than I had seen them.

'Do you think I ought to go back and get him?' I began. 'Then I could rejoin . . .'

'Follow me.' Then he looked up, grinning. 'Want me to draft out an op order?'

I was grateful to him. I needed that firmness. I ran back

and jumped up on my tank and into the turret with renewed courage. The crew had been brewing. As usual, something hot always made them feel better. We mounted again. Distantly, the sounds of battle at Anzio resumed: mortar, m-g fire, Spandaus, Schmeissers, a Breda somewhere. It was impossible for the ear to sort them all out accurately. The air over the inland hills was thick with fighting now. One explosion among many. That was all that was needed. Our morale was low. These men had seen our tank brew, been given another, been shot at, pursued. They counted on me. I felt the responsibility.

So we set off for Point figures three-four-seven across what had once been fields, where once men had grown vines, and in the evening drunk their yield under doorways. The buildings were all beaten to bits. There was a broken mesh of tracer fire ahead. Good soldiers, the Chleuh. They advanced side by side, but with fields of fire carefully worked out so that never did one tank obscure another. Own troops lying in sangars and trenches about, some of them changing clothing and equipment. Along the roadside camouflaged trucks, some of them still burning. The ground troops were getting set for counter-attack. They were New Zealanders, here.

'Good on you!' they shouted up.

'Good luck, Kiwi!' we called back.

'Any wire ahead?'

'Don't know.'

'Personnel mines?'

'Don't know!'

I waved hopelessly.

Then as we drove forward I was happy that Whitey, at least, could not see what I saw. We coursed down the reverse slope of the valley and the configuration of the broken ground was already unfavourable to us. Stretcher-bearers were picking up bodies. A battalion to our left was moving gradually up the ridge like a shoal of fish moves, responding to no visible signal but yet moving as one. Here and there someone going over a dead Jerry for loot, or identification. A smashed mortar – theirs. Curls of signal wire dumb now –

likewise theirs. Man in a khaki jersey handing out grenades – ours. We swanned ever more purposelessly forward. I left it to Rex. Presumably he knew what we were doing.

A kind of despair was starting to come over me. We had come so far, got through so much in the blue – to come to this ... this nonentity of chaos where no one seemed in command, but death. In warfare, we had always felt, there was a certain limit to what you could ask men to do. We were tired, dirty, beaten. If you removed all chance of success from a military enterprise, a man died. The future is bound into our language itself. Deny it and an aspect of existence goes. This whole situation had seemed to me to be fated since the start.

Indeed, as we rode forward inland (ever forward!), we passed foxholes in which the men did not look up at us, and from which no hand was raised. Tired phantoms beside their spent Lee-Enfields. I assumed Rex knew what he was doing. Presumably he was looking for the other half of the divided Lothians.

He drew me forward to an observation knoll where a battered PU stood flying a yellow pennant. We dismounted together and went over to salute a small, tired, bearded officer who was seated on a shooting-stick, looking vaguely into the distance. Two other officers sat on the hard earth around him. The man wore a belted battledress top, without any visible insignia. His right foot was heavily bandaged.

Rex said: 'General Stainton-Sims told us to report over here.'

The other did not answer. He merely looked up with his eyes bloodshot from lack of sleep and incomprehension.

'Recce Group, Third Droghedas,' Rex added quietly. 'Or, rather, what's left of them. Two tanks, to be exact. If we can be of any assistance ... '

'Assistance?' He sounded perplexed.

'To be affected to you, sir.'

The little officer looked up at us with a dreamy and disconsolate air. The other two – one of them trying to set up a canvas basin on a tripod – paused to stare at us also. One of them had on a green sweater.

'Who are you?'

Rex repeated slowly, 'Third Droghedas, Second Independent Tank Brigade.'

There ensued a long silence. Spandaus stitched the distance.

'I can't give you anything to drink, you know,' the little officer said.

We hesitated. I looked closely at the man.

'Of course,' Rex said. 'Our water-bottles are full, thanks.' A distant whistle shrilled. No one moved. We seemed frozen into immobility of an artificial kind. 'I saw you had some AT guns placed on your right flank, sir,' Rex continued. 'If you want us to take up position in support to the east of ... '

His voice died. We were not communicating with this man. God knew where he had come from, where he was going to – he remained motionless, strangely abstracted from our world, as if half-comprehending our words.

'East?' he said. 'Where's east?'

The whistle shrilled again. It might have been the cry of the second whip, hulloing above the wood.

'We were pasted rather badly yesterday,' said one of the officers, washing.

'We were put in the bag actually,' the other added, apologetically.

The air shivered. Over on my tank I could see Morris taking the muzzle cover off the Beza.

'The whole of Brigade HQ were put in the bag, as a matter of fact,' went on the other. 'All of two hours, actually. He got through our lines, you see, we retreated encircled and were put in the bag. Then, thanks to air action, Jerry vamoosed. Spitfires, Tomahawks, and Hurricanes, actually. Frankly, there's not one of us here knows his arse from his elbow. Actually.' He made a shrugging gesture at his CO.

'Actually,' said Rex.

'But from which front do you expect to be attacked, sir?' I asked this odd Commanding Officer.

We had to get some sense out of these men.

After a long moment, and with a profound sigh, as if

impatient at some child's persistent nagging, the crippled officer answered, 'We are being attacked. At this moment.'

It was, as the French say, exact.

Some hundred yards forward of us earth bounded, in the customary theatrical effect.

Something was being prepared.

'Let's go,' Rex said, taking my arm, and I knew I wanted to get shot of that lot as urgently as he did. They had death about them, too.

We ran to our tanks. I threw a last look back at that bitter, deserted trio. They had *given up* – no doubt about it. All I knew was that I never wanted to see men like that again. I cannot describe it now. There was some infection in their presence. We set off to take up some sort of co-ordinated position eastwards – I could hear Rex desperately striving to reach DIVER or other elements of our Brigade.

'Hallo, Geoff.' I was happy he abandoned the habitual formalities, now that he and I were alone together, in a sense. 'Do you hear me, do you hear me?'

'Yes, Rex.'

'Let's make for that plateau. Nine o'clock cypress by ruined building.'

'Okay, on. That will force them to fire from skylines. How many do you think there are? Do you see them clearly?'

'BADGER okay. Watch my position. I shall try to give covering fire if they engage you first. Must hold that low ground. Otherwise, as you've seen, friends southwards could be completely overrun.'

He didn't say they had been.

I was instinctively aware of the usual evil stabbing of the air to our left horizon. Ruptures in the earth along which we were advancing. Then the silhouettes we knew so well, the squat hulls (their sighting vanes whipping) crawling crablike through the rise of trees. More and more of them came into my ken. They moved so sure of themselves that I felt a faintness behind my knees – that feeling of being 'sent for' by the headmaster at school.

'... I would say figures one-five,' I began to Rex.

He cut me off: 'About twenty-two-oh moving across our central front, direction of small circle of trees ... '

'Read you, Rex.'

They were new, good tanks. But this time the sun was with us. All that awaited us was the most powerful army ever prepared for war by a single nation. In its forms and forces. Whitey was pulling a new shell ready out of its bracket, below me. Morris' right eye was glued to his scope. Again the ground trembled beneath us.

'Figures two-oh,' said Rex, in my ears.

Morris turned back his head.

'Thirty, sir.'

He put up three fingers. Eloquently.

I flung up my glasses. The hill quivered. Thirteen, fourteen, a whole line of livid steel, their dual-purpose guns bumping like the antennae of ranging animals. Low sunlight lit them and gave an eerie orange cast to their tracking.

To my left Rex had not closed down. I was glad of that. I still kept some physical vision of him with me. And yes, my God, there must have been thirty of them making slowly down for us, like confidently hunting animals. I searched in vain for our own bazookas, our own AT emplacements. Perhaps they were there, I could not see them. I was thinking: What the hell! We might have been in a couple of sardine cans, so far as that line of Panzers went.

Then I saw the infantry troops, blunt-helmeted, moving behind them. I looked at Rex and saw that he had seen them also. I wondered if he was as afraid as I was. As Edwardson. There was nothing for it. We were scuppered. Two against thirty. Coming at us slowly.

'Driver,' I said, for something to say. 'A few degrees right. Move slowly down incline altering direction as you ... '

I hardly needed to say it. Tich knew. I knew it. We had to do something. The first shot from those Tigers was falling over us, splitting and cracking the cold air around. There were no desert tactics we could use here. We were, rather, part of the infantry we had infiltrated, whose AT guns, to our left, now began to dart out orange flames. I did not think they were in range but for them also it was a thing to do. They were shifting their positions cleverly.

'Geoff!' In my head-set Rex's voice was unusually anxious. 'If unfriendly types get amongst us, shall try to contact PANTHER' – he was referring to Brigade – 'for orders to withdraw.'

'Okay, out.'

PANTHER was Brigadier Stainton-Sims. No one in his right mind could possibly ask us two Cruisers to take on thirty Tigers, but if we were seen running – in Rex's view, I suppose – it would be all up with us. All up either way, was what I thought. And how the hell did Rex think he was going to locate on net the man with the black eyeshade in his scout car? I felt a strong stream of air, a whistle. The explosion was spectacular. I ducked so hard I knocked Morris into the breech which shut automatically in a slam beside us. It was nearly comic.

'Jesus!' I said as we rocked. 'Sorry, Morris old man. But that one wasn't too far off.'

'Not too far, sir,' he echoed, dully.

As for myself, I felt I'd been damn near gelded by that breech; I stood up and to my left saw a six-pounder anti-tank gun shattered wildly, its crew dead about it. The frontal shields of that gun were not far anyway. I averted my eyes.

''allo PANTHER, BADGER calling. This is BADGER. Hal-lo? Do I hear you, PANTHER? BADGER calling ...'

Rex vainly trying to contact Brigade – and get that all-important order to withdraw. Skedaddle. At least I thought it all-important.

There was a smell in my nostrils, an odour of fumes on my forehead. No respite, no respite.

'... PANTHER, you are hearing me? PANTHER?'

I was about to tell Tich to keep on going when a small but lovely butterfly posed itself on my periscope. At least, I thought it was a butterfly, though I suppose that at that time of the year it could not have been. There it was, in any case, on the turret. I saw its broad soft wings palpating on the steel. Perhaps it was a moth. One of the heavy, slothful South

Italian moths we had seen. Where had it come from, where was it going?

Again the earth spewed in front of us. I began to swear. I do not know what I said but I began to swear. It was intolerable. It was – how you made war here. War took away your little country billet, it took away your mother, your father, in short it beat the hell out of you, and then presented you with contrasts like this. Two against twenty, thirty. Clara and destiny. Chaos.

'Hel-lo PANTHER, BADGER calling ... '

Suddenly I heard the wrenching clash of shot on metal and knew by the wincing of the men in the turret that we had been hit again – yet not penetrated. The strike had been close to me. I searched all skylines around to see what was responsible. There was a certain amount of smoke in the turret but nothing serious and I did not think much of it when Whitey tapped my knee. I immediately donned the interset earphones.

'Hallo PANTHER, BADGER calling ...' His voice was perfectly calm. 'My loader has been killed. Will act as loader-operator personally myself. Over to you.'

There was no answer.

The Tigers were drawing closer. To our left another anti-tank gun emplacement had gone in a flash of infuriated metal. I did not myself see any further possibilities available for defending ourselves.

'Let's get out of here,' I cried to Rex. My voice stuttered in the mike. I did not know if it came over clearly. 'We haven't a chance in the world ... and you know it.'

'Okay BADGER Two, over to you.'

The response was virtually languid.

The Panzers were slipping down the hillside now, drawing closer to us. I saw one of their turrets dissolve in a blast of black smoke. One hit, at least. From somewhere. But more and more of them appeared to be coming over the hill.

There were then three explosions. Our tank stopped. We rocked on our tracks. What was going on here? I looked down. Morris had his right eye sealed into the rubber ring of the scope and I saw that in the concentration of the moment his teeth held a half-eaten biscuit.

'Fire!' I yelled at him.

I did not even know the target. He would, out of experience. It was like that with us, at the best. The Cruiser bounced back, vehemently, and when I next looked up the butterfly or moth or whatever it had been had gone for good. I was happy in a way, I would not have liked to see it die.

'Fire!' I yelled again.

Rex's guns began to speak. Both of them. Then the Ironmaster started to turn.

'Hallo, Rex,' I started, 'do you hear me clearly? Tiger Tanks figures three-oh in position ... as you see ... do you hear me clearly? All we can do ... well, we can brew some and go. What do you say, Rex?'

There was no answer.

'Rex? Rex? Figures three-oh ...'

His gun answered me. I saw a Tiger struck. Rex's gunner began firing in a remarkable manner, a copybook exercise: after the shot the driver moved, the Cruiser squirmed on its tracks, the turret traversing. I imagined Rex cramped in his turret, his brow pleated as if over some complicated long-division sum (which is what it was, really), waiting for death to enter his hull also.

'Let's go!' I shouted to Morris. 'Pick your targets and fire as you wish.'

I trusted him entirely.

'Can't see nothin' but shovin' dust, sir.'

'Fire when you can!'

I put on the other phones, tried to get Rex to answer again. All he gave me was a guttural growl, a sound from a ditch.

'Fire!' I shouted at Morris.

We hit again. And again.

But what amazed me was the way Rex was behaving. Imagine if you can that he had to be crouched in the hull himself, seeing damn all, and feeding the rounds into both guns from bin and belt alike.

'For God's sake!' I shouted to him over the set one last

time. 'Don't you see? We can never hold this lot. Let's take what we can and get out.'

Again his gun answered me, belching bleakly. Another Tiger stopped, stalled. I waited to see if it would brew but it didn't. The great log of its eighty-eight could be seen juddering as if trying to traverse and not being able to.

'Go ahead then,' I shouted down to Morris, in final furious exasperation (I had known this thing had had our number on it from the start), 'choose your targets. Stalled tank right of brew. Fire!'

We were on a good slope and I saw Morris' shot clearly plunging, in that characteristic curve or lope of heavy lead. At the same time it was as if a genie had tapped the turret of the Tiger Rex had stopped and drawn up skywards inky black smoke. The crew baled out. But Morris was pulling on my pants leg.

'Look, sir.'

Through my binoculars I saw that the line of Tigers had stopped on the crest. To this day I do not know why. Oddly enough, it was almost as alarming as their advance. Had they changed their mind about mixing it? Were they simply amazed at the gall of two light Cruisers standing toe to toe with them point-blank? Yes, you could have said there was a sort of stupefaction in those giants of the plain, as they hung over us like thunder.

They didn't stay still long. No Boche tank does. These could outshoot us by a thousand yards.

'Driver! Left a bit more, steady.'

I looked down and saw Whitey pulling a new shell out of its bracket, holding two now ready in his lap. The German pause had been sufficent for Rex to brew one more. Then Morris scored a hit but it merely glanced off. But I should have known better. Panzers like to fight back. They weren't going to take this kind of a pasting from inferior armour. So far we had had outrageous luck. It ended.

I felt the hit before I heard a thing. It was as if some giant maddened stallion had kicked its hoof at the front of our tank. Then I was fighting to see in the cordite dust blowing through the turret. At the same time I was aware of the tank starting to roll slowly forward. It was at that point – I am quite clear of this – that Whitey screamed.

'It's Tich, sir! *They've got him*!'

'What ... who?'

'Tich, sir. Look, he's 'ad it!'

The loader continued to tug in a panic at my right battledress trouser. We seemed to be gathering speed.

'Look, sir!'

My God, he was right. With our downward movement the wind whipped through the driver's visor – what was left of it – and cleared the turret of smoke. I was kneeling down on the serrated base of the turret and just by the look of Tich's back I knew he was dead. Very dead. His head formed an impossible angle with his body. It was as if some enormous weight had pressed the former jockey backwards into the turret. To his forward front a jagged hole had been forced by the high-explosive shot. Somehow or other the tank had stayed in gear and was now advancing, out of control, straight on the enemy. God knew what they thought we were doing. They must have imagined we'd gone insane.

I squirmed back up into the cupola. We were leaving Rex's tank behind us, to the left. I saw his head out of the turret examining a dent where he'd apparently been hit again, and I bellowed through funnelled fingers:

'They got my driver ... tank out of control ... don't follow!'

But I saw him ordering a turn on his tracks to do so. Even as I swore at him I looked ahead at the line of Tigers and seemed to stare right down the throat of the biggest gun I'd ever seen mounted anywhere. It was a plinth, just. In seconds it would be firing at us, and *buenas noches*. There was only one thing for it.

I unholstered my pistol and ducked back down into the turret. Whitey gave me an aghast grey look. What did he think I was going to do? We couldn't traverse, not without mangling Tich's body in two. Even then, it wouldn't work. As I squatted down sweating I was wondering why the hell it wasn't coming, the shot that was to put an end to it all. It was like waiting for the next stroke of a caning at school. I had time to wonder who was in that Jerry tank, with his sights on us. Was he a lean, tanned, close-shaven man, his sand goggles pushed up his cap with the eagle stretching its wings on the peak, the Iron Cross at his throat – like our hero of the desert? Born half a century before on a quiet Sunday in Heidenheim he had been the master of tank tactics, able to get within twenty miles of Alexandria with a handful of tanks, only to run out of gas. Why had we all secretly admired Rommel so much? He had piloted his Fieseler Storch himself through heavy sandstorms, he had breakfasted in the foxholes of forward troops in a dirty squash cap, he had flown low over his ships set on fire in the Mersa el Brega bight. Bavarian Medal for Bravery, the Max Josef Order ... but Ritter von Thoma, his good friend, wounded a score of times in two World Wars, had had those distinctions also. Why not then von Thoma, Kesselring, Gause, Westphal, his GSO 1, or even Pastor Dreyer, his bald priest from Hitzacker – no, it had to be Rommel, the schoolmaster's son with the eagle screaming on his cap; I prayed it would be Rommel himself who would kill us. And I took careful aim, holding my .45 with both hands.

The shot echoed through the speeding hull. I had not missed. I had aimed over Tich's ruined shoulder. I had aimed for the clutch plate, and got it. The gears jammed. The tank shuddered and went still. I'd stopped the beast. When I put my head back out of the cupola I was amazed. We were right on the huge Panzer, maybe under a hundred yards. To my left Rex's tank had halted, also close, and with a dreadful smoky leak coming from its engines. It was the end. At the curt sparing signal from the P.Z.K.W. commander ahead I got out with my hands up. Whitey and Morris followed suit. I know we were all damn relieved to be put in the bag – certainly by Jerry. At another signal we put our hands on the tops of our heads and trotted round to the rear of the tank line where all sorts of Boche infantry were about. They appeared to be digging in mortars among dead cows and horses. The Chleuh were very good at slowing enemy armoured advances by simple demolitions, destructions, and non-magnetic mines – plus accurate sniping. Such seemed to be what was being prepared for us here. I surrendered my weapons, binoculars, maps, and was motioned back behind a Jerry half-track on the hill. I was trying to see what had become of Rex.

To my horror, his tank seemed to give every evidence of brewing. Smoke was thickening from his port engines. What the hell was he doing? Why wasn't he abandoning tank while there still was time? He wasn't really playing Don Quixote, was he, and trying to get off a few last rounds from a dying Cruiser? Answer: he was. We ducked as the shot laced the sky above us. Close.

Confusion intensified. The Tigers were clearly preparing for an attack towards the beachhead again. Infantry was riding on them and forming up behind. No one took much notice of us beyond motioning us angrily to the rear.

'Quick, sir.' Morris tugged at my sleeve. 'This way.' I had no desire, either, to be shot up by our own troops – as seemed highly likely. It had happened in the blue. We jumped into an old mortar hole and clung to the earth, breathless. At that moment I heard a colossal explosion and, poking my nose over the edge of our hole, I saw Rex's tank go up. The turret was wrenched off, then it subsided awkwardly, its tracks ripped to ribbons. The Ironmaster was dead. Morris had to hold me by the arm then, hard. There was no sight of Rex or any of the men anywhere. Boche infantry was coming past us more rapidly now. We changed position, so as to shelter behind one of the tanks Rex had earlier brewed and I found it impossible, staring down the incline at that blackened hull, to think that Rex had gone. Impossible! Impossible! I found myself beating at the earth. Then the firing thickened as those vulture-like Panzers went in for the kill, backed by bazooka-bearing infantry. Already, away over to the left, two of our own AT positions had prematurely given their positions away, and been cleared up. I saw some forward sections of what were probably Bedfords running behind the Tigers with their hands on their heads. The firing intensified to a point at which it was hard to know where it was coming from. Then two silhouettes could be seen making along a hedgerow to the right of our rise.

'Rex!' I yelled out. 'Rex!'

For it was him. There was no mistaking that gait. It was the old eagle himself, with his bushy hair and commanding allure. The other was Smithers. They had hit the ground when I called out. Then they ran towards us - literally through Jerry infantry.

'Rex!' I cried. 'Are you all right?'

'The two others bought it,' he said. 'Smithers and I just made it out in time.'

'Bloody muckin' lucky to do so, too,' said the driver, whose face was as blackened as a clown's.

'Tich didn't have your luck,' I told him.

But then a Jerry Corp started waving us furiously back and I could see prisoners being herded onto a truck, to be taken off quickly. P-o-ws could get in the way badly at moments like this. I shouted back to the man in German, which seemed to surprise him a bit, then we were climbing up the tailboard of the truck. It was full of prisoners, mostly infantry types, but some from tanks, I could see. We'd finally been put in the bag.

10

If the areas behind our lines at Anzio were confused in those days, the German rear was more so. Every house seemed to have been pulverised to rubble by either artillery or naval guns. Trees dynamited and then axed to form tank barriers. Anti-tank trenches of vast proportions dug. There was a lot of wire about and our truck, I'm glad to say, drove strictly through taped lanes. It was impossible to imagine that in peace Anzio had been something of a fashionable place.

I was jammed next to Rex on one side of the truck. We were moving at speed through shelling, past blazing vehicles and fat puffs of smoke, perhaps some thirty of us in all, guarded by this kraut Corp. The tank men were mostly US, I think, off Honeys and Grants. I saw a harnessed horse dashing about, neighing in terror. There was a heavy British Major seated in front of me slowly tearing the identifying flashes off his battledress jacket. A real mess. Then I saw the campaign medal on the German Corporal's tunic. He'd been in Africa.

So I started talking to him and, though suspicious at first, he relaxed at my German. He was the typical Hermann Goering trooper of the time, fair-haired, long-limbed, looking as if nothing would ever tire him out. We swapped yarns. He had been hit at Gabes and hit again at Maknassy. I told him what we had been through here, without revealing any specific information, and he agreed that it had been better in the blue.

'Where's the cage?' I asked him.

'You'll see soon enough.'

'Big one?'

'You'll see.'

Then he offered me a cigarette, which I refused, saying I didn't smoke. For the time being I was so tired any bunk would have done. Then we stopped at a farm where there were a whole lot of Jerry back troops. They told us to get down – all except officers. So we said farewell to Smithers and Whitey and Morris and to this day I have not seen them again. I often wonder how they are, and if they came through it all safely. I hope they did.

The men went off in a truck guarded by Eyties and, while I was glad we had the Boche instead in charge of us, I knew he would be harder to escape from; and it *was* our duty to escape where possible. So we drove off once more and I slept with my head on Rex's shoulder; after a while in the blue, you could sleep anywhere. I woke up when he gently shook my arm. I scarcely knew where I was at first, in that bumpy truck. Then opposite me I saw the fat Major's finger pointing upwards. I realised it was dark outside. The sound in the sky was all too familiar to us all. An ominous drone, the regular throb – vroom-vroom – of Junkers. I glanced at the Jerry Corporal sitting on the tailboard. He too was looking up, searching that starry sky. The bombers were high enough, by their sound.

'We've passed Rome,' Rex whispered.

'You mean, we've been through it?'

'No. Bypassed. Ran along the Tiber a while. Terni, Todi, Spoleto, that way.'

'What time is it?'

'After ten.'

'Christ, I was dead out.'

'I let you sleep. They distributed some bread. I saved your share for you.'

'I'm thirsty,' I said.

Rex passed me his water-bottle. Only when I'd taken a deep slug did I realise it was lightly laced with rum and lemon. It tasted like the nectar of the gods.

'The Corporal searched us all for arms while you were out. He even went over your body. You never woke up all the time.'

'Jesus!'

Rex sounded depressed or, rather, as if he were concealing

something. Once more I was convinced that he was gifted with a sort of second sight, in matters of war, at least.

Outside the drone of the bombers increased. They were getting lower, surely. It seemed wet and misty out. Some of the men around me were shivering, covered in mud, beplastered out of all semblance to human beings. The truck driver was moving in sweeps, rather than at a steady speed, rowing along the road – sudden dashes, then slowing, then revving forward again. The tactic told its tale.

'Jesus God!' said a voice. 'Their own shit.'

The Germans knew it then. There was a swish, that vacuum in the air which invariably took the marrow from your bones, pith and all, then the crump of butterfly bombs straddling the road. And then you were fighting to get the deafness out of your ears. Everything happened. The truck screeched to a sickening halt, throwing us all over the shop, there were more explosions and that mad swishing of wintry branches by falling flak. The Boche guards jumped down, showed us the noses of their tommy-guns, told us to jump out. There was a mad stampede in the dark as the truck doused its lights. We were towards the back and got out last and ran for cover. Another bomb fell as we did so. Rex grabbed my arm, hissing. I hit the earth the moment he did.

The Junkers were spraying the road and it was all foggy and the Jerry guards started swearing at their own muckers up in the sky, too, and brandishing their tommy-guns and telling anyone who had not got down to stay in the truck; then they too made for cover as another burst cracked the air as if some giant were trying to splinter that element forever. Something whistled close overhead. My fingers dug into good Italian earth.

'Quick, hey!'

Before I knew it I was crawling along this sort of irrigation dyke in the milky haze with Rex's backside full in my face. He moved remarkably quickly. There was a cluster of houses, blacked-out, ahead. It wasn't easy but we could maybe get there. After the bombs had passed by we heard the krauts shouting and yelling, telling everyone to get back into the trucks, and I was working fast on my elbows along that muddy ditch.

Suddenly we had a spot of luck. In the dark behind us we could hear them counting the officers mounting the backboard of our truck when another in front of it went up in a rush of smoke and flame. God knows what it was, but it blew up in a spectacular fashion and I heard what sounded like a stuck pig screaming. That was understandably enough for Jerry and as soon as they'd loaded the prisoners the whole convoy roared off. Suddenly there was nothing but silence and the stricken truck smoking on the road behind us and this swirling fog and the dying screaming. There was a narrow slope of sleety field ahead, then the houses.

'Wait,' said Rex, a finger to his lips.

On his knees he looked around. Our ditch was only a few feet deep, heavy with mud hardened by hoar-frost.

'They're going to come back to see if they can salvage that truck. Quick, Geoff!'

I realised what he wanted to do and from the first I didn't think it a good idea. He started doubling back to the road, the screaming, and the smoking truck. Bodies lay all around it. I even tripped on one. In the cab we found two Jerry, both badly dead. No one in rear. The truck was carrying rolls and rolls of barbed wire and ammo. We stripped off a couple of decent-looking German greatcoats and forage caps. Then Rex found a loaded Luger on the driver and I picked up two of those excellent stick grenades the Boche invented. We put on the greatcoats and made back for the buildings. Three children came out of the nearest as we approached and then went back in again. The screaming stopped.

Rex shouldered into a cold dark room ahead of me in which a woman with a round face was apparently doing some sewing in the lowest of low oil lamps. A pile of plates was stacked at her side. I remember thinking she must have been there all that time in the dim light while scalding lead had ripped around that road and lashed the trees and buildings. Perhaps it had helped her to hang on to sanity in some way. Then a man in the shadows behind her made a quick motion and said something in patois. The two of them looked at us immobile, with hatred.

Rex took a pace forward, said something else, and opened his greatcoat to show we weren't Germans. He talked to them in dialect and they realised at last we had been taken prisoner at Anzio. Even so, they were suspicious. Rex explained to me it was because they were afraid we might be deserters – Italian deserters, that is. Rome radio had just sent out a decree of some sort ordaining that deserters from the now thoroughly demoralised Italian Army were to be shot on sight. They looked for black shirts on anyone who came, and asked questions after.

So they sat us down and gave us dried figs and wine and I was suddenly ravenous with practically nothing in my belly since the landing and I wanted to thrust even their cold maize flour into my mouth, just as it was. They gave us a hunk of their precious parmesan cheese and a few old rotten walnuts, but they were afraid. They were not naturally hospitable, as Clara's brave family had been. They wanted one thing only – for us to get the hell out, and our greatcoats with us. They'd let us sleep the night, they'd even show us where we were, but in the morning we'd have to leave. The man insisted on it quietly, in a tense voice that concealed a lot. We had to get out. Somewhere. No matter where. But not here.

'Actually,' Rex said, as we sacked out on some straw in a cellar later, 'I still think they're scared we might be deserters. My Italian maybe. How do I know dialect, as an English officer, eh? They'll probably turn us in, anyway. I don't think they thought we were Germans from the first. We were simply something they didn't want. We've got to get out of here.'

'Where the hell are we?' I asked, stretching uncomfortably on the itchy straw.

'According to Giuseppe – that's the husband of the fat lady doing the sewing – we're somewhere up near Terni. Well north of Rome.'

'I only wish I didn't feel so darn bushed, Rex. Don't you

ever know what it is to feel tired?' As he answered with no more than a chuckle I went on, 'So you mean we ought to try to hit through south somehow?'

'I'm not so sure.'

'What do you mean?'

'Well, I'll tell you, Giuseppe's brother sells the olive oil these peasants press here, and a bit of their better vino. He could be persuaded to take us. He's driving north tomorrow.'

I sat up. 'North!' I exclaimed. 'Are you nuts?'

Rex sighed.

He wasn't nuts, but he was incorrigible, as I was to learn in a second.

'Florence,' he breathed. 'You ever see the Uffizi, Geoff?'

'You can't mean it,' I said. 'You know perfectly well it's our duty to rejoin our lines as soon as ...'

'Our lines,' he mused, in the dark. 'Ever seen Bologna? Whole damn place is arcaded, see. When it's raining you can walk all over under these arcades without getting wet. The people are among the kindliest, the friendliest I've ever ...'

'Ah shut up, Rex,' I said, rolling in irritation to one side. 'We're both damn lucky to be alive after what happened today, and you know it. And now you want to go waltzing about behind Jerry lines ...'

We drove north the next morning, fortified by a surprisingly excellent peasant breakfast and watched by three children with practically purple thighs. We lay in the back of a rickety Fiat and were covered in sacks of corn. The womenfolk were taciturn. Giuseppe's brother drove and drove. It began to rain a lot and my head was bruised with the bumping since he went by side-roads most of the time, to avoid the Chleuh. Towards noon we stopped at a low stone house by itself and had good cheese and bread and some wine with the peasants there. There was no one about. After we had eaten, one of them showed us a large sheet of printed paper, a Boche order to evacuate. On such occasions these people were not allowed to take any possessions with them, only a tiny amount of food. Deportation to slave factories in Germany or simple shooting awaited any who wouldn't obey. They were longing for the Allies to break through and send the Hun packing. Everything would be just fine then. So they thought. We couldn't share their optimism exactly, but of course this all worked in our favour, such people would take risks to shelter us.

'Do they say the Germans seem to be starting to leave Rome?' I asked Rex at one point.

'Perhaps.' Strands of straw still stuck in his shaggy head. 'Who knows? Actually this war begins to disgust me.'

'I can't say it ever enchanted me exactly.'

'No, but it wasn't so bad in the blue, admit it, Geoff.'

'Where the hell are we now?'

'Out of the blue, somewhere in the Chianti hills south of Florence.'

'You don't seriously intend to go swanning around Florence?' I was stupefied; if Rex had this extent of self-destruction in him, I'd better get shot of him for good. The thing was: he seemed to be reasonably indestructible. 'Florence is going to be crawling with Jerry.'

'I know.' He nodded his leonine head. 'Giuseppe said he knows some relatives. Small farm in the mountains. Place called Marradi.'

We were then signalled back to the truck as some Germans had been sighted. In a matter of moments we were huddled under the sacks again, nothing but the tips of our noses showing behind the cab. We set off shakily but safely enough. There was only one bad moment before we reached our destination.

Marradi was a tiny hill village apart, at the crossing of two country roads, skewered to the earth by the usual bell tower. There was a pewter-hued stream flowing over rocks beneath it. At the Borgo San Lorenzo crossroads leading up to the village we heard a loud and menacing "*Alt!*'

The old Fiat ground to a stop.

Actually, though I held my breath, it was not a road-block searching vehicles. Some Boche had simply stopped us to cover a mechanised column moving southwards. They didn't search the back where we were, at all. Just a lot of orders and boots and tank-carriers coming by. Giuseppe's brother would undoubtedly have lost his life on the spot for smuggling prisoners like this. Instead he got a cigarette.

But then the Fiat wouldn't start. I began to sweat at each racing of the starter. Some Jerries sauntered round to the back. I felt Rex grip my arm. Someone laughed. Another asked if we had enough gas. A hand came over the back and stirred the sacks. I nearly passed clean out. But the footsteps went away. Finally (so we learnt later) a kraut M.T. Sergeant lifted the hood and got the old crate going again. We put-putted up the hillside.

So began our stay in the hidden farmstead of Marradi. But it was not at all as it had been with Clara's family. To start with, we had to live clandestinely and thus couldn't help, as we would have liked, with the work. We lay up by day. Moreover, the family was mercenary and cruel, even though anti-Fascist. In fact, I came to feel their anti-Fascism was a form of social resentment bred of the moment, and itself perhaps basically opportunist.

The family was called Borselli and consisted of the farmer, Luigi, his brother Filippo, and three women: wife, sister, sister-in-law. There were the usual numerous children who got frightful beatings when within range – usually with an old soup-ladle. These children rarely washed or were washed, and whimpered and fought each other all the time, in the most disgusting manner. Most of the time they had running sores on their faces. The men washed their feet in a bucket when they came in from the fields, so that we ourselves were able to get pretty clean for the first time since Napoli. They fed us with constant hints concerning repayment when the 'beloved Allies' broke through.

But the beloved Allies, so far as we could learn from their rumours, were still well and truly stalled under Cassino. We were at the end of March but it was bitter cold and we were glad of our greatcoats, which also, of course, served as protection should a Jerry see us from a distance.

Then they put us out in a hut apart, low and filthy, literally a pigsty, the remains of the original occupants smoking in the main room in strings of sausages and black puddings hung high up, and watched over by the anaemic sister-in-law called Concetta, who spent much of her time weaving. She worked that loom endlessly, with a sort of idiot monotony that kept the kids mesmerised. They'd stand there hour after hour in the cold, watching her.

As for us, we kept apart, mistrustful of them, and washed now in a tub in the mud. Old onions and loosely baked bread were our fare and after we'd been there a few weeks we knew that Concetta was keeping a tally. They expected to be paid back when the 'beloved Allies' came by. I didn't intend to disabuse them of the idea, personally. But still I didn't trust them.

The country here was wooded and sweet, and the first buds were greening the shrubs. A line of oak-scrub led from our hovel to the bed of the river where the pebbles shone white in the sun. April had come, the stream was swollen from winter snow, and we sat there and talked in the spring afternoons. Sometimes we talked to two peasant girls, Maria and Natolina, and helped them carry their sacks of fodder for the oxen, which were much prized in those parts. They would be carrying a sack of clover or armfuls of the tall reeds which grew down by the brook. In their flimsy cotton dresses they were eager and they were lovely, with bare and shapely legs. But for me they did not rival Clara. They would ask us the time. Rex showed them his watch. Neither of them understood so-called Roman figures. Natalia did all the needlework for the family and she mended our shirts and underclothes for us. Mine were getting threadbare. I badly needed a new issue.

And chatting there we would see the dust rising from the columns on the distant roads of the plains. We could not distinguish what was moving – thanks to losing our binoculars – but the convoys continued to roll south while we sat there, and they glinted like leaves in the sun. There would be men aboard those tanks and trucks, gunners and loaders and drivers, all making for the front. While we sat there alone on the banks of the brook.

Out of it.

I could not keep from commenting on it to Rex.

'You'd hardly know there was a war going on,' I said.

'Hardly,' he agreed, dreaming. He reclined on one elbow, sucking a straw, his huge head dappled by shadow from the stream-bank.

'Hell, it's full April,' I said. 'Here we are, living with these paisanos, doing damn well, seeing nobody when we ought to be trying to escape. Do you think we're not going to have to field some tricky questions when we rejoin?' I added, in a surly tone, 'If we do.'

'They pass us off as evacuees, Geoff. To any local who asks, that is.'

'The place is stiff with spies,' I spluttered. 'We ought at least to make one try – to get through south.'

They were words, that was all. I knew it too well. I'd go where Rex said – that was all there was about it. To myself I rationalised it by the fact that he was my senior officer, that I was merely taking orders. I was relieved to see his great leonine smile.

'I'm interested in the north.' Then he said, 'You aren't scared, are you, old boy? I mean ... *losing interest*?'

'Nope. Don't think so. Only, I hardly think, I scarcely feel this is really war.'

'Did you think Anzio was, then?'

I said nothing.

'It wasn't my conception of war at all. Extrrr-aordinary!'

Ahead on the plain below was the growing sunshine and the white road and I was glad he had replied as he had. The shade of the evergreen oaks was heavy already, it was April and living. Yes, we were alive, dammit, and the stone he tossed into the water beneath our boots was round and clear.

'I don't know if I agree with this kind of war at all,' he said, stretching. 'Over there' – it was a term he was using more and more for the desert these days – 'out there it was comprehensible, somehow. Didn't you think? It was black and it was white. We knew our adversaries. We knew where we were going. Then this kind of slow progression right up the Italian peninsula, with all these rotten types involved, well I can't somehow conceive of the spirit who organised it all. I mean, the Boche and us, that's one thing. You know where you are. Frankly, I don't know what it's all serving any more. We're killing some of the best of men. My hair's growing grey. I feel old. All this blood. I know I'm not what I was, Geoff, no one is, but I still feel I can sense something good, and just, in these woods.'

I looked at him sharply. 'These woods?'

'Something I have need of. You don't get the same sensation, heh? Have you seen the first convolvulus? What a blue! Almost an acid colour. It makes you weep. May God be praised for His flowers. They fill me with such pity. Why, why? If only I could *learn* something here.'

'Well, we can't stay here forever, Rex,' I said discontentedly.

'I know. Besides, I promised my girl I'd live. That I'd see out this war, if only for her. Tell me, Geoff, is that some kind of bird of prey up there?'

I squinted. An oxydised flash came through the branches. Yet I had not heard anyone moving. I looked up into the sky, seemed to see a sliver of greater light.

'Looks like an old Hampden limping back. Probably been pasting the Po.'

'I sense something in these woods. Wild pinks, already. Even this little straw. I tell you, Geoff, this meagre thing distresses me. Did you see footprints on the way down?'

'I don't think so.' But I was momentarily distracted, distraught. I thought I had heard a soft whistle in the bushes behind us. I sat up, saying, 'Well, I'll tell you something, Rex. I do believe Emilia has fallen for you, how's that for a lark?' Emilia was Luigi's sister. She was worked like a slave by the other Borsellis and I had several times caught her throwing soft eyes at my friend.

Rex gave a distant nod, hitched himself up, slung an arm over my shoulders. Then suddenly his arm tensed.

A black cat, half-blinded by the farm children, padded timidly out of the undergrowth towards us. It had taken to following us from the house since we spared it more to eat than the Borsellis ever had; besides, we encouraged it to sleep in our hut, to keep down the large rats there.

'It was only Lucky,' I said. It was our name for the cat.

'No,' he growled thickly, 'someone's coming.' And he cocked his captured Luger.

I did not even have time to move. We were both covered from behind. By an impressive-looking shotgun. Three men had emerged from the bushes. The first, who was carrying the gun, was a tall pale youth in canvas overalls, wearing gilt-rimmed half-spectacles. The second of them had red hair and was in his thirties. He too wore dungarees. The third was a misshapen, dwarf-like creature with a mass of dark hair, his trousers loosely belted under a prodigious torso. We stood up slowly. Rex pocketed his Luger.

'Aha, the evacuees!' laughed the red-haired one.

'Welcome to our humble province.' The dwarf grinned, bowing low.

We said nothing. We did not know what we were getting into here. These men were too much at ease, somehow.

'Come, you needn't worry,' the redhead went on, as if reading our thoughts. It was he who appeared to be the leader. 'Let's all sit down and have a little wine. *Un puo' di vino!*' he laughed, tossing down a haversack which seemed to have a bottle in it. We sat in a cautious circle, our own backs to the brook; the bottle went its rounds in the sun. 'We heard you two gentlemen were here from Filippo. You don't have to worry. Rather than give you away, if anything we would help you.'

The dwarf was nodding and beaming. The wine ran down his powerful neck and chest.

'Glad to hear that,' said Rex. I realised this was town-Italian we were speaking, not the peasant brogue of the Borsellis which was still giving me a lot of difficulty. Where were these types from?

'As a matter of fact, Capitano, we'd just been over to the farm to warn them that there are a few unpleasant fellows in the area, searching for deserters.'

'Fried Tomato here,' grinned the dwarf, indicating his carrot-cropped companion, 'he can smell out a Blackshirt at a mile.'

The red-headed one spat. 'Deserters! Pah! Scoundrels, what?' But he said it looking straight at us and laughing in the shadowed sun. 'Deserters deserve to get their desserts, eh, Tenente?' He turned to me. 'Deserters deserve to be shot.'

'Maybe Blackshirts too,' said Rex.

'Why, there we agree,' replied the other, still steadily staring at him. 'Why, there we are absolutely of your opinion. Not that it's a too healthy one to hold in these parts.'

There was something about these people. We hadn't yet fathomed it out and I know that we both mistrusted them. I saw that Rex had a casual hand in his right trouser pocket.

'Let us talk, Captain,' said the pale-faced youth, and he said it coldly, almost with dislike.

'I thought that was what we were doing,' said Rex.

'Closer to the stream. More in shadow. We can be seen from here.' He looked uncomfortably about, through his thin spectacles, as we all shifted position to the bank. The pure water gurgled below.

'Here, sir.' The dwarf offered us hard pears, very sour. We gave them the last of our cigarettes, which we had hidden from the Borselli family.

'Who are you?'

'Just men.' A grin, a shrug.

'Where are you from?'

'We are simple refugees,' Fried Tomato answered, still grinning. 'At the moment we live out there.'

He pointed to an outgrowth of rock – or so it seemed – not far off in the valley.

'Sort of cave, you might say. Quite thick. Boom, boom!' he proclaimed delightedly. 'We are safe. We are living there and, like you gentlemen, waiting for the Allies to arrive.'

'You may have to wait quite a while, then.'

'We are not so sure. Two days ago your 4th Division, sir, crossed the Gari' to join up with your 8th Indian. The Poles . . .'

'What do you know about our Divisions?'

'Do not be angry, Capitano!' He held up his hand. I confess I dropped my eyes. I was uneasy with these people. They seemed to know as well as we did that we should not be staying here so long. The way they pronounced the word *deserters*, for one thing.

But Rex was probing again.

'So when do you think the Allies will arrive?'

The other shrugged. 'We have a little radio down there. Quite good one. We get the London news now and then. The Poles will take Cassino soon.'

'You think so, eh?'

'They have to, Captain.'

'You ever seen Cassino, chum? As it is now, I mean?'

The answer was evasive. 'General Anders a very clever General, Signore. What's more, the American 2nd Corps are getting ready to cut the Rome highway.'

How did he know all these details? I was willing to wager a hell of a lot that the men in tanks being prepared for that operation hadn't a clue about where they were going.

'What's the news from Rome?' said Rex.

'This is what is interesting us very much, Capitano. Very much, indeed. Yes, you could say that we are most highly interested in the manner in which our capital is taken. All the documents, all the archives, records of the past ... yes, it is most important to us that these be preserved. For the future of our country, you might say.' He broke off to munch a pear. The dwarf was playing with the cat. 'The entire situation is mixed up, of course. But there are certain – shall we say? – formations interested. General Orlando, our Minister of War at the moment ...'

The pale youth sat up straight, cursed, and spat.

'At the moment,' he repeated, looking carefully at his snot-green gob.

'Fascist pig!' said the third, in an equally expressionless tone.

'Come, Mario,' laughed the first speaker. 'Orlando has his difficulties, too.'

'And you boys wouldn't mind increasing them, eh?'

At Rex's frank sally they all three smiled. The ice had been broken between us. I began to understand who they were.

'Well then, good luck to you.'

'If we hear of any way of getting you south,' said Fried Tomato after a moment; he was leaning forward as he sat, earnestly uttering the words. 'Carmelo here' – he pointed to the dwarfman – 'he has contacts. The only thing is, he's a trifle conspicuous himself, you see.'

They smiled at that. There was silence between us.

I know I was relieved when I heard Rex reply, 'Thanks all the same, but I'd rather stay hidden here a little longer. Until the weather improves.'

'But the weather is beautiful, Capitano.'

'I know. But I think I chipped a bone in my skull before being put in the bag. Get dizzy spells.'

And he showed them the scab of the latest place where he'd knocked his head on the turret in the last days of fighting; then, in case they knew (as I did) that nearly every tank commander carried such scars, he also pointed out the bump at the back of his head where he'd caught that mortar splinter in the blue. They seemed satisfied, nodded sympathetically, and after a little more talk went away. The cat stayed with us.

'Partisans,' I said when they had gone.

'What I'd like to know, Geoff, is if they're good partisans.'

'I suspect such types don't carry three-star credentials about with them. I don't believe they'll betray us, Rex.'

'I wouldn't be too sure.'

We moved back to the hut through the grove. There were a few lemon trees, on which the hardy leaves were out in force, the green pods visible amongst them.

'They'll be ready in June, just you see,' said Rex, touching one gently. 'Maybe July.'

Will we be? I wondered.

So we got back to our byre in safety, Rex carrying Lucky all the way, simply by stuffing him comfortably into his shirt. The cat made no visible protest. As we walked in the sun I think we both knew that that meeting with the three men by the brook had again altered our relationship – that something was coming of that nothing. There was a sense of mission in those men, something inevitable, I knew we would see them again. They carried a purpose we no longer had. But as usual I left all the deciding to Rex, always rationalising such inaction to myself by claiming that he was my senior officer, in charge of my destiny, whatever that might be.

When we went into the house for supper, it seemed to me that Emilia looked long and glowingly out of liquid eyes at Rex's regal head. He himself went to the kettle on the charcoal hole. We had taken to toasting the stale bread of the place, which was always full of holes. The Borsellis had never seen toast before but after a while they grew to like it, too, Luigi dunking his elaborately into both his coffee and his soup and noisily lapping the mixture. We had collected a few first apricots from the trees and, though these were far from ripe, they softened when heavily stewed, and made at least a contrast with our usual watery diet.

That night I stayed awake a long time. I thought of all that had happened to us since landing on Italian soil, that heroic land of the past. I thought of Rex – of that gun-limber he hadn't brewed because of a small fox-terrier. The deserter – one of ours – he hadn't turned in. The Eytie spy whose radio he'd destroyed. Again I saw Cassino in all its devastation. I wondered what had happened to my old gunner Morris, one of the best. Was he in a prisoner camp in Germany somewhere, tired, fed-up, and hungry? Would I see him again after this lot was over? Had anyone been able to bury Tich?

Look around the mountains, in the mud and rain –
You'll find the scattered crosses – there's some which have
no name.
Heartbreak and toil and suffering gone,
The boys beneath them slumber on …

I hummed it to myself, seeking sleep. How absurdly important to us it seemed at that time to bury bodies. Why?

The burial parties in every battalion were numerous, they could have been used in other ways. Why was the last token so essential? Did a man have a soul, or was he just so much chemical matter? I closed my eyes but sleep wouldn't come. Outside, the tramontana breathed strongly, the wind from the south stirring branches against the slate roof overhead. I could hear those blasted rats scratching. Where the hell was Lucky? Rex worried me. I knew I had to get out of here soon.

11

That April we helped in the fields. Chiefly we helped dig the irrigation ditches deeper, to water the few fruit trees owned by the Borsellis, for that work gave us some natural cover. The ditches all connected up with a stone reservoir higher on the hill and this was shared between several farmers. We saw the three partisans more than once and one day Rex gave them an old leather poncho he had worn through the winter. They still lived in the cave lower down, but they were men who worked by night, and left few footprints.

Occasionally we saw our own planes coming over to strafe the road, once recognising Spitfires and Mustangs of the old Desert Air Force, now so much stronger here than they had been in the blue. Once a medium bomber squadron of Marauders pounded the hills to the north and we saw chutes of men who'd baled out coming down, with their comrades circling in protection. Once an Auster recce plane swanned low down the valley and not a shot of Jerry ack-ack bothered it.

The farmer's sister Emilia was by far the kindest of the family. In the warm April days she would wash herself in full view of our hut, for she was always scrupulously clean. The water would slide over her long sloping shoulders and heavy breasts, with their horn-shaped curves. Then she towelled herself vigorously, after. She had a great vigour and strength of flesh and I knew she was proud of her body. She had taken to coming in to us for English lessons after the evening meal; she would sit opposite Rex, her oval face fixed in an attention long lost by more urban or civilised peoples. Her memory was phenomenal. Her soft intense face would watch Rex reading, the bandaged pince-nez astride the raw bridge of his nose. She was secretly in love with him, I knew, but he was impervious to this tempting morsel of woman-flesh.

'Hell, m'hair's growing grey, I'll be white soon,' he would say. 'Besides, I want to know what the hell's going on here. I don't trust that Luigi. If you interfered with any of these women he'd see it as a breach of hospitality, all that. Vendetta. I wouldn't blame him. What are we to them? We'll be gone tomorrow, and he knows it. What's more, the woman doesn't really move me.'

'Not like those bints in Cairo?'

He shook off the memory in a motion.

'I feel there's something else I want . . . that I want to learn here.'

'We've been here long enough,' I said.

'Scared?' he asked, mocking.

'Sometimes more than I was in battle,' I avowed. 'Anyway, stop trying to test your courage, Rex. Let's see what a spot of cowardice does for a change.'

'Hum. Yes. I suppose I ought to take into account your feelings more, Geoff.'

'My feelings, hah!' I kicked a stone. 'What about our duty? We should be making back towards our lines. And you know it.'

Rex said slowly: 'I'm not everything that I was over there.'

I felt indignant at this unnecessary expression. Our combats in the desert had been . . . quite *other*. Rex regarded himself as a chronometer which needed winding up again. He seemed to think some event was needed to set him going again. Otherwise, he would continue running down. Something in me wished this to happen, too, but yet when the event came to pass I wished it had not. I could have gone on quite happily lying stretched out on those sunny hillsides, under the shadow of olives whose exposed roots resembled the muscles of some drunken wrestler.

'Few more days, old boy. I'm going to make a real effort. Our friend Fried Tomato will probably come up with an idea.'

I wandered off by myself. I was annoyed, did not know

quite why. An unresolved irritation. The plain beat below, a brazen bowl. Fried Tomato had told me – Carmelo had told us both – that the SS had executed seventeen young 'Italian patriots' in a blocked-up former bridge, far below, and that the bodies were there still. We ought to see them, they told us.

Well, I wandered down, I do not know why. I had stood with Rex near El Ada looking down once into a wadi into which the guns of both sides had played all day. I had stood with Rex, streaming with sweat, hushed to death at the edge of that mutilated and forbidden statuary. It had hurt me to touch the back of my neck. At least the stench had not started, thank God. Here it had. The sickliness led me down the tawny hill, up the next crest, and over. For a second, before entering the gallery formed by the ruined bridge, I stared at woodlice marching up a tree trunk. I guess the Chleuh thought this would do as a burial pit – and just left it at that. I know I heard my breath rasping like a horse's.

The opening to the ruined bridge – the other side having been blocked in by bombardment – was already somewhat overgrown with lichen when I reached it. But there was no doubt that it was here it had happened. That it had been what Rex would have called *the case*.

I pressed into the bricky shadows. I told myself it was important to bear witness. Suddenly, without quite knowing or absorbing it, I realised I had been staring for minutes on end at a fattish head with heavy curls. It lay at my feet. It had not been severed, entirely, but in a blob of blood the left eyeball had leaked, had tumbled from the socket down the cheek. Still, I saw no sign of suffering on the relaxed lips, nor in the other widened eye. Then, remembering Fried Tomato, I compelled myself to stagger forward to look, and look again, register this abyss of hell or danse macabre of the machine. The SS had rounded them up and assassinated them all here, one in front of another, and left their bodies to rot, chucking in as they departed a few stick grenades for good measure. Rags of the dead, poor peasant rags, white bones, tight breeches, holed boots. The poverty of what had been their costumes undid me. It was some acme of catastrophe, mosquitoes buzzing on those trunks and limbs. I remembered that I opened my mouth, as if gasping for air – before I felt my way out.

But I had to tread on inflated skin to do so. It yielded, rubbery. Oxen they might have been, those splayed rachitic corpses, Bismarckian offerings to Mars, pinkish fragments, leaky organisms, peripatetic spillings, loins and shreds and ruptured shoes, all illumined by the receding sun, creeping off to die also, it seemed to me, and mingled with the things that did it, precision of machinery, exactitude of Schmeisser and grenade.

I stood at the gate of those dead, hardly able to think, to move. This was much, much worse than anything I had ever seen. Besides, they were civilians. I couldn't comprehend it. My foot fell on some split plum, or sutured wound, some hair-edged hole sprung apart in an expanse of nudity never meant to be shown, white as a loaf in the light. A greedy, lush appearance. Newspapers in Gothic print. Beneath, a veinous bulge from some dun shirt. I stood at the sunny verge of that tunnel and literally panted, like a dog. Those shapes, those intolerable postures of death (if not the features of those earthly doomed) personified atrocity for me.

Staggering from the sight I felt there should have been some belling yell since surely this was hell itself, natural chaos, the centre of an idiot's dream. But words, sobs and cries are but air. I said nothing. On my way back to the farmhouse I plucked a flower. A white convolvulus. They grew on mountains. The gesture was somehow artificial and I was annoyed with myself at it.

April turned to May before we saw the partisans again. There were flashes of firing in the valley but whether these were field guns in practice or earnest we did not know. Emilia received a letter from a cousin, a young man fighting apparently in Poland. And once, resting under a tree, we were told to hide at the sight of a couple of elderly Italians approaching the manse with guns. But they did not see or hear us. We hid in a loft. The couple were not Blackshirts but they were good friends of the local Mayor, thus powerful and worthy of suspicion. Their guns were for shooting game, a special permit in these parts. They gave the family a pair of rabbits before they left – wretched, stringy things we ate smothered in a thin tomato sauce. But it was good to eat meat again and we thanked the Borsellis heartily. They ate with relish.

The sun flamed in the sky that May. The horizon of the plain reverberated with light. The oak woods bloomed and shuddered. Emilia's body showed through her cheap cotton clothing. We lay in the shade with Lucky, our cat, and talked about all things. Chiefly about life – life that we loved and revered. What it meant. Rex had grown a small light beard in order to save razor blades and, well tanned, looked more like a god than ever. Or was it some pagan priest?

'Everything's simple again,' he said on his stomach in the reeds by the brook. 'Like it used to be when I was in the Argentine.'

Ants crawled before me. Lucky stretched a leg, licked. From the valley came the sound of a bell. Heat-haze shimmered on the rock outcrop below.

'What's simple?' I said. I couldn't get the sight of that tunnel of dead out of my head these days. 'What's so bloody simple, man?'

'Take this fly. Or maybe this blade of grass. It can do what it likes. Our world is fated to be overturned.'

'Theirs isn't?'

'When it comes down to it, we don't have much power. And look … where we are now, there's no one else, and everything's calm.'

I said nothing. It was the way he would talk. 'Don't you understand?' he said.

'No. Yes. Maybe. Let's see what you wrote in your notebook last night.' He reached into an inside pocket and handed me that battered old black book. I looked at the latest entry for a long time. It ran: *The facts in logical space are the world.*

All I knew was that I heard the whisper of blood in my ears, the summer day gave a grace to being alive. I could even hear myself breathing. And then a fir cone fell with a thud. Rex whirled with Luger in hand. This time their approach had been soundless – but it was only two of them, Carmelo and Fried Tomato.

'Buon' giorno, Signori!' came the cheerful call of the first. *'Buon' giorno, Naso di Cane!'*

Such was their new nickname for Rex. They squatted down and passed around a gourd of wine that tasted good in the sun.

'Where's Mario?' I asked.

They dropped their eyes.

'Mario, he ... how you a'say, he met with a little accident, did Mario.'

We said nothing. I thought of the pale, fair-haired youth with the dedicated eyes behind the half-spectacles and I hoped that the end had been easy for him.

Not like under that bridge. Not the men in black greatcoats.

'In fact, Tenente, *in fatto*, we have just lately lost rather a lot of what I may call our . . . friends.' he looked steadily at Rex as he spoke. 'Yesterday, Capitano, we heard that Sant' Angelo has fallen.'

We sat up straight. God knows how these *partigianios* knew as much as they did concerning the campaign, especially about the monastery and castle, and the major positions like the Massa Albaneta and Sant' Angelo. But the latter was the key, not only to Cassino itself but to the whole Liri valley. The Jerry flank at Anzio would be wholly exposed after this.

'Those Indian types ...'

'The Gurkhas?' I volunteered.

'Yes, yes, they took it, Tenente. I'm glad I was not a German there.' Carmelo hitched at his leather belt. His chest seemed to stretch to his hips. 'On the 13th. According to our information,' he added, punctiliously.

So Cassino had fallen, or was falling. No one in their right mind could hold it if Sant' Angelo were taken.

'Fierce fighting. No quarter either asked for or given.'

'Yes,' I said.
'The Poles were eager to pay off old debts.'
'Yes,' I said. 'I can imagine.'
'It was very bloody. Hand-to-hand fighting. They felt they had at last met the adversary on equal terms. Cisterna has fallen also.'
'How's Anzio, then?' asked Rex. 'They must have enlarged the bridgehead. We were not so far from Cisterna before the break-out.'
'If the Fourth can link up with the Anzio pocket,' I exclaimed, 'then we're through to Rome.'
'Exactly, Tenente.'
'And beyond,' put in Rex thoughtfully. 'If you ask me, Kesselring's got far too much at stake. He'll haul out and he won't stop this side the Prato hills.'
'Yes, precisely,' clipped out Fried Tomato. 'The rats have already started leaving the sinking ship.'
The other giggled. Then there was silence for a while. Somehow, talking about it like this, the war seemed a million miles away. Down the slope of the hill beyond the stream I could see a figure carrying what seemed to be a mattress. He was moving through a ragged field in which were both poppies and cornflowers. A cricket chirped. All at once I heard a vicious click. The dwarf had shot out a small spring-like knife. He looked at the blade affectionately, and stropped it on his palm.
As if at a signal Fried Tomato sat straight up.
'Thanks for the duffel coat, Naso di Cane.'
'An open shirt's all I need these days,' said Rex. 'You're very welcome.'
'For the clothes we will see to that.'
Carmelo said, 'It is not if you do not want it, Naso di Cane.'
At this I sat up brusquely, too. I did not quite understand them. What was it they were saying now? I thought I had followed the entire exchange. Yet something seemed to have been agreed upon between them.
'It may be in a hurry, Capitano, you know that. A last-minute affair. You would have to be prepared for that. We

only get short notice ourselves. And with what is happening …'

'You know where to find me, gentlemen,' Rex said shortly, 'and my comrade.' He reached for the gourd and slugged several gulps. 'We shall be ready.'

'Your friend the Tenente, too?'

'What is this, Rex?' I said.

'The time has come for us to leave, old top. You were right all along.'

'How?'

'It is not if you do not want, Naso di Cane,' Carmelo repeated softly.

I stared from one to the other of them. What was going on, for Chris' sake? Then I glanced down at the fields below. The man with the mattress seemed to have gone. The earth lay plushy in the hot sun and the water rippled with all the clarity of innocence below. But now the war seemed no longer so far away. It had come up close before my eyes. again. It had been thrust in front of me once more. I felt something akin to what I had when sighting a long line of advancing Panzers in the desert, their outlines blurred by dust. It was like being struck in the solar plexus. I realised how easily a human being can dig in. We had become part of this place. Too much a part of it, Rex had decided. Loneliness as a condition of existence was once more threatened. This war would not leave us alone.

I said drily, 'You want us to give you a hand in some way?'

Carmelo exchanged glances with his companion.

'Nothing may be so necessary, Tenente. But our numbers are being extremely depleted. Our arms also. That is the chief thing these days. There may be … a little de-ratting necessary.'

Rex said: 'We'll be in this grove – one of us – every day at this time. When you need us we'll be here.'

'Carmelo knows Bologna like the back of his hand. You don't have to worry.'

'I won't worry,' Rex said.

'And you speak like a native, anyhow.'

'Just like a native from the Abruzzi,' grinned the dwarf, jumping up with alacrity.

The two slapped us on the backs and shook our hands and drank more wine to our health. I hoped it would stay good. Then they crossed the brook to the plain. Once more I let my second self decide for me. I remember that we sat in silence for some while and then I asked him: 'Ought we to do this, do you think?'

'Fried Tomato strikes me as an honest fellow.' Then he turned to me with his most roguish smile – *'The woods will avenge themselves!'*

And just what the hell did that mean? I wondered as we traipsed back to the house where there was a bowl of polenta on the table and Emilia had washed her dress.

'You've heard the good news?' she said brightly.

We nodded cautiously. We did not want the Borsellis to know of our assignations with the partisans.

'The liberation,' she said eagerly. 'They will be here in a few days – the Allies.'

'Perhaps,' was all we said.

Yet we noticed the mood of the family alter perceptibly towards us from that moment on. And when on the 18th it was reported that a Polish flag had flown from the ruins of Cassino monastery, their enthusiasm knew no bounds.

They feted us – and themselves – with the largest meal we had had there: pasta, with butter and grated parmesan (two strong swipes of Emilia's sturdy arm against the grater producing clouds of it), chicken fried with local herbs in the olive oil we had helped to press ourselves. After that, maize cakes, bread and a brutally harsh goat cheese, lots of wine to wash the taste of this last away, and even coffee at the conclusion – best American coffee, at that. It was a gala occasion, but this time we did not sing for them after. The war was over, the Borsellis thought. We were not so sure.

Finally, even the children did well, and got happily sleepy on watered vino. Only the cat went hungry. It was their policy to starve that poor blind cat so that (their theory was) it would be a better ratter and mouser. But we looked after

Lucky later. We had no milk to give it but it loved the soft cheese we had both squashed surreptitiously into our pockets. It licked its paws, then Rex's beard, and made us laugh softly at its antics in the hut. I would like to think it lived up to its name, and brought us luck, but today I am not so sure.

According to Rex's latest prognostication we were to 'undie'.

Quite what this meant I did not know.

The days dozed by in pleasant torpor. There were flowers by the brook and the heath by the oak grove was in full blue bloom. Rosemary, cystus, the whole marquis. *E macchia*, they remarked with a shrug, uncaring. But we loved those wild things. The strong sun of late May made them quiver, as in some mortal intoxication. The nights began to grow hot in the pigsty pen and Emilia's softly called *'Buona notte'* hung languorously on the velvety night air.

She said to me once:

'Your friend has this wild animal look. Why is he so cold? When he looks at me it makes me mad. It is as though he touched me.'

'He does not want to belong,' I said. I don't know why I said it, but once out I approved of what I'd said.

'How you mean – not belong?'

'To remain apart.'

'Then he is indifferent, you mean?'

'Not exactly.'

'Away from us?'

'In a kind of way – yes.'

How smoothly those days passed. We were indeed the undead. One day I was coming down the hills to the grove and I saw an old hunchbacked crone with a kitchen knife uprooting dandelions. The locals went out to get dandelion leaves – *caccialepri* – which they boiled as we boil thin cabbage; then they ate them with polenta, the meal pudding made with maize flour. Or else they would eat them in a sort of sandwich form between the flat insipid pancakes they scorched on an old iron plate. And I thought of Clara then, and wondered what she was doing. I saw again her rosy skin, dark hair, and clear, wide-open eyes – eyes always soft and questioning.

There was much more air activity now and the road in the plain was filling with convoys heading north. Even so, I don't think either of us was prepared for the moment when it came. Carmelo came with Fried Tomato behind him through the trees by the brook that afternoon and by the way they walked I understood them to be different. They looked resolute, skilful, and organised.

At first, however, they chatted with us on the bank of the brook in the shade, giving us the latest news. The Canadians had broken through with part of our own Division at Pontecorvo. Heavy losses. Aquino had fallen to the 78th. They knew all the numbers. Our 2nd Corps had also taken a pasting but had succeeded in cutting the Rome highway near Valmontone. There was now a definite, if fragile, link-up with the Anzio force.

'A regular briefing,' I said when it was over.

Then Rex, leaning back against the bole of a fir tree, said shortly: 'Come to the point, fellows. You want something. Tell us, Fried Tomato.'

'Yes, it's hard to hide anything from you, Naso di Cane.'

'Don't try then,' said Rex.

They exchanged guilty glances, then the first shook his carroty crop and began, 'Well yes, it's urgent, all right. The day after tomorrow, in fact.'

'We're ready,' Rex said.

There was a pause.

'Ready, Capitano?'

'Yes.'

'Ready to kill?'

'Well, yes.'

'It won't have been the first time,' I said.

'Very good. Then most kindly listen. Cenedella is escaping. We've had information, solid information, he's burning the archives, all papers in the Ministry. General Cadorna is going to be appointed Chief of Staff of the Italian

Army, thus we shall see justice done.'

'You mean, he's one of yours?'

'Yes.'

'And Cenedella isn't?'

'No, Capitano.'

'Files and files going up the chimney,' said the other, miserably.

'Who's Cenedella?' Rex said sharply.

'Why, him of the War MInistry, of course. He is directly responsible to Orlando. He and Colonel Baudino, that is. He is what you might call the second-in-command,' the man finished in an excited, irritated tone.

Rex said: 'Let's get this straight. Your Ministry of War in Rome is cracking up. Right?'

'Right, Capitano.'

'This character is making a bolt for it. Is my understanding correct?'

'Yes.'

'And you want to stop him?'

There was silence.

The dwarf broke it: 'To kill him, Naso di Cane. To kill him.'

I said quickly, 'We're not killing civilians.'

There was another silence. The two partisans looked nervously at each other. The brook flowed beneath us.

'A Fascist swine,' broke in Fried Tomato in an imploring tone. 'A pig.'

'A torturer,' added the dwarf. 'There are photographs. We have seen them. Torture of women.' He made an expressive gesture. 'In the genitals.'

Rex seemed to sweep fog off his face.

'That may be possible, but we don't want to have anything to do with it. We'll go along with you fellows in any op you care to name – blow up a bridge, ambush krauts. Myself and my officer under me here, we are at your disposal for that kind of mission, gentlemen, and for that kind only.'

I was heartily glad he had said it.

Rex concluded: 'But there are certain articles of war. We

will not go beyond those. You cannot take us beyond those.'

'Naso di Cane,' said the dwarf, spreading his hands in an open pleading gesture, 'see reason. Make the Tenente here see reason also. It is the *General* Cenedella whom we wish to kill. Whom we are going to kill.'

'With your kind assistance,' added his colleague.

'General Cenedella,' Rex echoed thoughtfully, after a moment. He pulled at his moustaches. 'Yes, that of course is different.'

'What are you talking about, Rex?' I said.

'Thirty of our senior Generals have run for it,' said the dwarf, watching him closely.

'And you partisans want Cenedella rubbed out?'

'All Italy does, Capitano. Necessary action.'

'Absolutely essential, Naso di Cane.'

'The day after tomorrow?'

The next silence I broke.

'What the hell is this, Rex?'

'Put it like this, Geoff,' he said. 'Most people have a very mistaken idea about the fighting capacity of the Italians. They judge 'em by their conduct in this war and the last. You should remember that those soldiers fought under practically every condition non-conducive to morale. Absolute damn opposite of the Jerry. The Eytie organisation was bad, staff work poor, mails from home a rarity, food scanty and intermittent. Equipment antiquated. No wonder Wavell did what he liked with them. I put it to you that here are forty million people with a traditional friendship for Britain and America, living not too far from what's going to be communism. After all, old boy, we have killed or been killed by pretty well every nation in Europe, when you come to think of it. Just a question of *amour propre*. We don't harbour animosity against the Frogs because of Napoleon nor love the Boche because of Blücher!'

'What's this got to do with Cenedella?'

'We have to help these people get on their feet. They're forming new Combat Divisions ...'

But the red-headed maquisard was leaning forward in the

sun – 'Signore. Tenente. This is of the greatest urgency. We have it on unimpeachable authority that Cenedella will be passing through Bologna the day after tomorrow.'

'You know his chauffeur?' questioned Rex.

The man dropped his eyes. I realised there were limits to what you could say to a dwarf.

'The General Cenedella is making north, probably with important papers and no doubt for Germany eventually. His aide-de-camp has reserved a table for luncheon in a restaurant we know.'

'Where ... you are known?'

'Where we are known.' He nodded again, biting his lip. I could see how wound-up he was. 'Yes, yes, Naso di Cane. The proprietor is not to be implicated. In no way. But we will take you and the Tenente to Bologna tomorrow and you will work as dish-washers in this restaurant at once.'

'I see.'

'A new job,' I said. 'Maybe it's got a future. For Civvie Street after the war. We could rent ourselves out as mercenaries.'

'Shut up,' said Rex.

'Shut up, yourself,' I said. 'Sir.'

'These types are serious.'

The partisans let us handle it and then went on:

'The kitchen is right behind the dining-room. Okee? So we will enter from the front. We ourselves are too well known. Carmelo here, there is a price on his head ... every single German military policeman ...'

'How many did the aide reserve luncheon for?' asked Rex.

'Necessary action,' said the dwarf, chewing his lips.

The redhead took a deep breath; he held up a placating hand.

'Now not to get worried, Naso di Cane. It will all work out all right. We have it planned. In fact, it is really too simple.'

'That's just what's worrying me,' I butted in.

'How many?' said Rex.

'Twenty.'

'Jesus Fucking Priest!' I said. 'You can't be serious.'

'Figures two-oh,' said Rex. 'Gentlemen, I share my colleague's point. So far as we can see, you're proposing a tricky job in a tight spot. One stroke of the axe in a forest. Four against a whole roomful, most of whom will undoubtedly be well armed; not to mention the difficulty of getting away in the streets around.'

'This is crazy,' I said.

'But surprise, Tenente!' The partisan again looked at me in a manner I thought pleading. I ought to have taken heed of it. 'Surprise. You see, Cenedella will be sitting at the head of the table, that is – with his back to the kitchen. We will cover them from the door. Enough time for you two to come through from the kitchen ...'

'Oh no!' I said.

Rex said, 'Wait.'

I said, 'I'm not fucking shooting any man in the fucking back of his head, civvie or military.'

There was a long pause after that.

Then a despairingly whimpered *'Mamma mia!'* met my ears.

In the silence that continued I looked up at the house. Gemma, the wife of Luigi, was struggling with a sack of fodder for the oxen. I remembered the time we had seen oxen yoked to pull out a 15-CWT on the flooded banks of the Garig'. Different weather now. Different times. I thought I had heard a twig break nearby, but it must have been a bird. Then I remembered there were very few birds in that part of Italy. They had nearly all been trapped and eaten in the war.

Rex was saying in an undertone, 'I tend to agree with my colleague. All the chances are against us.'

'Except surprise. We shall have the advantage of surprise.' The partisan was looking at me in an imploring way, his hands pressed together as if in prayer. 'Surprise, Tenente. Cenedella at the head of the table with his back to the kitchen, as I said. We will show you photos of him first ...'

'And listen, Naso di Cane,' said the red-haired one. 'If we ourselves can get in easy enough, then it'll be us who'll do the shooting. From the doorway.'

'Sure,' I said bitterly. 'Take care of us too, that way. How do you think we'll be, with you spraying bullets around point-blank from in front?'

They ignored me, appealing to Rex, my senior. I think they sensed that I would do anything he said.

'Just so long as nobody escapes.'

'Above all, not Cenedella,' said the dwarf. 'Cenedella must not escape. He cannot. He may not.'

It seemed to me I heard another rustle in the bushes, but it must have been my imagination. When I swung I saw nothing; besides, Lucky was with us and gave no alert.

And then Rex again: 'All right, what weapons do we have? I'm pretty happy with this little Luger I picked up. Eight rounds intact.'

I sighed. So it was decided. We were going to kill a man. We were going to fight side by side again – perhaps for the last time. Yet, while the partisans pored over a tattered map of the Bologna streets which Fried Tomato produced from somewhere on his person, I found it hard to believe that this enterprise had our end in it. We had come through so many incredible experiences together ...

'The best we can do is a motor-bike,' I heard redhead explaining to Rex.

'Motor-cycle combo?'

'No. Just a put-put. Now here, look closely here. Down the Via delle Moline,' he was tracing it with a filthy finger. 'You'll have time to study it all tomorrow. No check points so far as we know after the one by the public gardens ...'

Rex nodded quickly, his huge head moving over his collarless khaki undershirt. Half royalty, half workman, I thought, as I studied his profile then. I had given myself up to him. Put everything in his hands, all to the excuse that he was my senior officer. It was a new kind of operation, something we had never done, and which I myself did not want to do. We were going to help them to kill, a little like (I consoled myself) those commandoes who had managed to get into Rommel's headquarters in the desert only to find he had just left with Westphal. Only to find themselves all killed. Now it was being explained how after it was over, after the killing had been done, we'd drive hell-for-leather on the bike to a man who had a garage near Ravenna. It all sounded unreal. Like a movie. Doomed! I listened in the sun, relaxed, disbelieving. What if the bloody bike wouldn't start up – like that Fiat truck which had brought us north? Did they expect us to get a Jerry to get this one going, too? It was ridiculous. I let Rex attend to the affair.

'One thing,' Rex said. 'Don't thank us.'

The rendezvous for the morrow was made. They shook our hands and left.

We stretched in the shade, chatted over the matter a bit more, then went back to our cabin. It was useless my arguing with Rex any more about it. All we had to do was to tell the Borsellis that we'd be leaving the next day. And just whose side were they on in this affair?

'By the way,' I asked, 'where's Filippo?'

'Haven't seen him for two days,' said Rex.

'They told me he'd left for Florence, to sell some produce for the farm. We'll have to pay these people something for our stay.'

To my surprise, however, the Borsellis learnt of our intention without curiosity or even much interest. Had they been somehow or other prepared for it? In any case, the liberation was a matter of days away, in their estimation. The war would be over soon. They were beginning to worry over relatives, a brother fighting abroad, another who had been taken in Africa. Stories and rumours, all. They made me recall those interminable columns of the Ariete Division we had seen going back to captivity in the blue, great hordes of human cattle, thousands and thousands of them guarded only by a couple of Corporals with Sten guns. Here the first peach trees were in bloom and the almond blossom was the most delicate pink I had ever seen. Leaves of the trees were green velvet against the sombre blue of the sky.

Rex told the family that we wanted to give them something for their hospitality so long. He tugged out of his multiple pockets a vast sum in AMGOT notes. I had no idea he walked around with this much on him, but apparently he did. I suppose he'd probably saved up over the years to blow it all in a single bash during our leave, but in Naples we had not felt in the mood. The Borsellis accepted the small fortune that he gave them with gratitude, but at the same time I know they would assuredly have preferred provisions. We did give them some soap after we had had a final wash and put on the peasant pants and leather jerkins given to us by the partisans for disguise, and said goodbye to Lucky. Only one incident disturbed our departure.

Fried Tomato had told us that the Hermann Goering boys defending Valmontone had been pushed back by the Yanks (actually the US 2nd Corps) and so, that last evening, the Borsellis gave us another festive dinner in celebration of the 'victory'. I think only we knew how much hard fighting was probably going to lie ahead. We knew the Chleuh.

We started with spaghetti, very thick, in a heavy red sauce. As usual, Rex drank some olive oil for his piles and as usual the three women served us first before sitting down to eat themselves. Filippo still wasn't back and we two grew a little worried. Where was he? Outside, in the dark, we heard Dorniers moving through the sky. Neither of us drank any wine, we had to be alert on the morrow, and the evening was far less gay than its similar predecessor. Rex and I were nervy, taut. And what happened the next morning didn't make us any less so. The business started badly.

Ordinarily, the fields around the little farmstead were bare and deserted. By this time we knew by sight the few peasants of the district, whom we watched climbing the mule tracks behind their animals laden with maize sacks. You can thus imagine the start it gave me when I awoke to see, just outside our pigsty, a young German soldier sitting in the fields fifty yards away, near a grazing cow. We had overslept and it was already sunny.

'What the hell's going on?' I hissed to Rex, tugging him awake. 'Take a look at this.'

He came to the window.

'They've betrayed us' – was my first thought.

But Rex shook his head. We watched the soldier. He was such a young and friendly-looking kid. Maybe even a deserter himself. Certainly a countryman, by the manner in which he now got up and felt the cow's thin udders. He smiled so gently in the sun that I did not want to get rid of him, yet I knew full well we had to do so.

Had the Borsellis seen him?

Rex cocked his Luger. But to fire, we knew, would be to wake up the whole area, and what with the possibility of Boche about, now there was this retreat ...

I then heard a noise coming from the main house and saw the dwarf Carmelo. So the partisans were already here. The dwarf stood in the shadow of the door. We could see him but the young, fair-headed German couldn't. Carmelo looked suddenly sinister, lost, quite different, and I regretted having undertaken this mission with him. There was something not so much menacing as disturbing in his pose. I cannot quite explain it. But if only I had taken note of that new presentiment of mine ... Then he disappeared as if he had never been.

For Emilia was striding from the house, walking with that classic majesty of her people of old, the kind of gait civilisation has destroyed in women. I saw her full, sure body as she carried a demijohn of wine on her head, on a little twist of dishcloth there, the hair falling down her back. She balanced her hips thus in a studied way (was it to please Rex for the last time?) as she passed by our place, her thin cotton skirt taut on the hieratic hip-roll of her body, her calves strong. She radiated, a goddess in the sun. I don't think I shall ever forget her as she was then, and as she will always be in my eyes, unaffected, barefooted, with that purity of living in her that I had known in Clara. She was transformed in those grave and desperate moments for us. She served us, with herself.

Emilia came forward, her eyes on the soldier now again lying on the ground in the sun. He had not seen her yet. My heart was beating faster, the advance she made on him was like some primitive ballet. Then the German turned brusquely and on his young face was a frank and innocent smile. He scratched his head and watched Emilia advancing to him – on him. The sun showed through her skirt. Her whole desirable body was over his. Her white teeth shone in the sun as she smiled at him – would the young soldier like to come to the farm to drink a glass of wine? The young soldier would, but first he pointed in an embarrassed way at the cow. Emilia tied it to a stake and he followed her.

I found the whole scene profoundly troubling somehow. The soldier was so young, so fair. He exactly resembled Kurt Bleyle, my chum at Salem. So I covered my ears with my hands when he entered the house after Emilia, but I did not shut out the forsaken cry, one of betrayal as much as of pain.

Later Rex told me it had been done on the instant, the fellow hadn't felt a thing.

'Another Agamemnon dead!' – was how he put it to me.

Later still, sitting on the pillion of the bike which Rex was gunning for all he was worth, I had a sensation of nausea, a splitting headache, at sight of Carmelo ahead, equally striding his saddle; once he turned and grinned back at us, holding up the knife that he kept in his belt. I felt sure I saw blood on it.

At the curves I clung to Rex in front of me. He had shaved. It was as if he knew the way already. He made vague gestures, but seemed fully confident. A man who refused to know any pettiness. Despite his bravura, I don't think he had appreciated that assassination in cold blood any more than I had. And it would be the same in Bologna. I had never killed a man in a city, let alone in a crowded restaurant, it was not my *métier*, you might say. In short, I had never killed like that and I had no desire to do so. We sped along the empty plain. Voyagers once more. But to where ... to where?

12

The inhabitants of the charming city of Bologna are lucky. Not only is the town the site of one of the oldest universities in the western world, the people who live there do not have to get wet. Thanks to the arcades which rim the Piazza Maggiore and then run off in all directions, there are natural shelters from the rain. Nor had the town at that time been badly hit by bombing. We were taken down into a sort of hutch behind a shoemaker's stall in a back street. Our bike was hidden in a back yard, the wheels chained to a tree. There was one low plank bed which we shared after a final check of the maps with Fried Tomato. Rex slept, but my night was sleepless.

Promptly at eleven o'clock the next morning we went to the restaurant, which was off the Via G. Petroni, not far from the fine arts building. It was far posher than I'd expected, a long narrow main room, connected by one swing door with an equally long and narrow kitchen. This door had a peephole cut in it, so that waiters wouldn't bump into each other coming and going. Through this hole you could obviously see all the guests in a glance. In the middle of the restaurant was a large hors d'oeuvres table, empty so far but for some bowls of suspicious-looking fish salads (*ïnsalata dell' 'mare'*), but stuff soon began pouring in from outside. You could have fed an army on what we saw.

The proprietor was not there – wisely, I reflected – but we met the cook, a jaundiced individual with a limp. Evidently the restaurant was originally a 'Dopolavoro', or Fascist civic club, for a while. We prepared the tables and Rex put on a white apron and helped served the lunch and I washed the dishes with him afterwards.

'There's not enough room to *work* in there,' he said as we

hurried back to our hideout through the thronging evening arcades. I had my collar up and felt a shiver of fear every time we saw one of the Boche military about. I had never before been in a town behind enemy lines like this and had never truly known what occupation was; but Bologna was calm and prosperous compared with *bella* Napoli.

'If I hadn't seen that order they had,' Rex went on, 'I don't know that I'd have gone along with this.'

'It's tomorrow,' I said.

'I know it. This character's supposed to have been Orlando's right-hand man.'

'I've never seen Orlando,' I said.

'I know. But you told me you saw those poor devils killed under that bridge, too. You owe it.'

'And you shot those SS in front of that farmhouse, Rex,' I reminded him.

He groaned.

'I don't like this thing, Geoff. Let's sleep in turns tonight. One of us awake all the time.'

'Okay.'

We mingled silently with the active crowds in the narrow bustling Ugo Bassi street.

Rex was right. It was not a good killing. And he was right for perhaps the last time in his life. I myself was nervous and irritable, the headaches hitting me more and more. Then there was this feeling of being unmoored. There was no reality to which we could respond, in which we could believe. We got back to our hutch through the narrow streets without trouble and did not go out again that night. We slept in stretches as Rex had advised. Around ten Fried Tomato came.

The plan was this. Evidently the restaurant proprietor was away and again I didn't blame him. We understood that this was all to the good. Everything was proceeding as prearranged. No difficulties, no difficulties at all. Cenedella's party would arrive around one. They would be duly seated and start to eat. At shortly before two a group of partisans would sabotage military police transport near the San Felice gate (where there was a barrier), and then Carmelo and Fried Tomato would enter the restaurant from the street side.

Now this was what we wanted to get quite clear. Our job was to block any of the party from escaping through the kitchen. Strictly speaking, it was not to do the shooting – though obviously that might be necessary. Fried Tomato's automatic – it was a Heckler & Koch, out of the Mauser stable – was destined to put paid to the evidently unspeakable Cenedella. What worried me was that there were only two of them – and of those two one so small he could not properly dominate a crowded room with a gun, short of climbing on some table. Fried Tomato told us, moreover, that the dwarf was suffering from the raging pain of an abscessed tooth. Naturally this cheered us up a lot. As it transpired, my fears were well founded. And it is for that reason I sit here today, trying to understand this story, while the sun plays jovially through the bars on the windows. Along with Rex, I have come to thoroughly detest the feeling of being locked in.

Next morning he was stirring ere I awoke. Then I leapt out of bed, imagining it later than it was. The sun shone outside, it was a perfect day. There was the scent of coffee in the air and a girl with a satchel walked softly by on sandals. I wished we were back in the mountains. I did not want to bring death to this place. But Rex had on those pince-nez of his and was studying his Luger on the bed. It lay all over the blanket in tiny pieces, slickly oiled. Good old Georg Luger's 'Pistole '08' with its 9-mm Parabellum ammo.

'I want to be sure this thing works,' he told me.

There came a tap on the door. I jumped back. But it was only the cobbler with whom we'd been quartered. He had produced a fine breakfast. A condemned man eats well, so they say. Yes, I had the feeling that the guns of Bologna were in other hands today. I was bringing death not to Cenedella, but to myself.

Naturally it will seem, in retrospect, that this whole operation was hopelessly hastily conceived and totally unprepared. True, it was. Yet it was the best that could be done at the time. And Rex had apparently seen an order from the Colonel commanding local partisan activity authorising the attack. So he told me. By this time the peninsula was subdivided into territorial regions by the partisans. The Colonel had signed himself *Principe del Giudice*. It had satisfied Rex. That satisfied me.

Moreover, when we arrived at the restaurant the cook was in a kind of idiotic ecstasy and this too boded no good to our enterprise. He told us that Rome had been entered the day before, that is on June 5th, by the Americans, after a last stand by Jerry forces at Tivoli.

'French and Americans ... the Tiber ... boom, boom!' he crowed expressively, throwing up his hands like a Pagliacci tenor. 'What is more, gentlemen, there has been a landing at Normandy this very morning . . . six thousand planes, four thousand ships . . . boom, boom, *boom*!'

He went on repeating the figures with absurd monotony, capering all over the place, trying to cook up the gala meal while Rex and I stared at each other. Operation Overlord (as we later heard it called) had finally been let loose. Our first thoughts were naturally for our brothers-in-arms in Italy, the D-Day Dodgers who would hear this news with the relief of a man on his knees who can finally stand up. We thought of Smithers in the bag somewhere, and Whitey and Morris and all the fine men we had known along the way.

Rex went to the Judas eye giving into the restaurant.

Something was coming to an end for me right there, I felt.

My job on that fateful day was to be the getaway man. Directly I had helped Rex (the hit man) to serve the dinner from the back quarters I was to leave the rear, or service, entrance and get the motorcycle going. I must have tried the kick starter at least a dozen times before noon, to see it was answering properly, and indeed the little put-put came alive valiantly each time. But I could see there was a lot of Boche transport about. I really didn't like the look of things at all.

Cenedella came in with his party promptly at one. He was quite the most sinister individual I have ever seen. Small, bald, with little glittery eyes and a great deal of gold about him altogether. He had on a pale shantung suit and everywhere you looked there seemed to be something flashing – on his wrists, fingers, lapels, a tie-pin here, eye-shades there. A metallic man. There was even gold in his grin. I felt an instinctive animal antipathy to his very existence the moment he appeared.

The party consisted of a number of civilians and several high-ranking Italian military. They sat around their table in easy posture, relaxed and gesticulating, and ordered aperitifs. It was '*Subito, Signore*' all the way then. Cenedella, I recall, sent for a Campari bitter. Perhaps it would have been better to have poisoned him. The luncheon prepared was to be, if anything, less lavish than usual since officialdom was supposed to show an example in public, and so the kitchen had prepared a *brodo,* a chicken broth soup, then *lasagna alla bolognese* of course, a fillet of *manzo* with salads and cheeses to follow. Not bad, all in all. A rough Sorbarese Lambrusco had been picked for the wine. Cenedella made a waiter taste it first. Aha.

The central buffet table, however, was for some reason groaning. There were towering aspics and terrines, many made in fancy shapes – to simulate animal or human heads as well as swastikas. The Italian and German flags were represented side by side on a terraced cake nearby. There was only one flaw – Cenedella had a woman with him.

Now there had been a girl in the cashier's stall in front. She had sat with her full legs close together, her short skirt of the time revealing knees upon which enviable and seductive black-market nylons made white patches by their tautness. On her upper thighs the indentations of stocking tabs showed alluringly under her skirt. She had left, too. They had got her away. But Cenedella had a woman with him.

At first I did not see her, she came in after the others, then I heard Rex get out through his teeth – 'There's a bint.'

I went to the window slot to see.

She was the classic kind – I mean, for Cenedella's type. For she seemed to be so ostentatiously his companion, buxom, with white teeth, solid breasts, tanned cheeks, altogether vulgar and theatrical in appearance.

'That's all we need,' I said.

As I spoke behind the door she kicked off her shoes and, with a crisp clap of hands, padded across the room to inspect the buffet table. There the chief waiter, in his greasy Sunday best, paid homage to her. A marinated herring slid down her over-powdered, throbbing throat and I turned away.

'For Chris' sake!'

I was edgy as hell.

'Damn the bitch!' said Rex, by my side. 'I've never been mixed up in a mess like this before.'

'Me neither.'

'Fried Tomato's going to do the killing, I'm sure of it. We'll only have to cover them.'

'Well, I hope to hell this cook'll calm down a bit first,' I said.

'Don't worry.'

We looked at the man. His eyes were dilated, even frenzied. He looked ready to take off any second. But time was moving on. At twenty past two, with the meal in full progress (Cenedella sitting, as predicted, with shaven skull back to our kitchen lookout), I heard a distant explosion. Rex and I exchanged glances. The partisans? If so, they were ahead of time. What if the whole party here took this for an air-raid and decided to clear out before Fried Tomato even got here? Would not everything then devolve upon us?

At a nod from Rex I went out and again started the bike. It broke smoothly into life as ever and I stood astride its softly purring cylinders while detonations grew from the direction of the San Felice Gate. My heart was pounding into my throat and I was already eyeing the street into which we would turn. A shopkeeper was lowering the *rideau de fer* in front of his window display, but that was all. Bologna had begun its siesta. That was the idea. The time had been so chosen. Then I heard a strange rattling sound, then shouts, then something overturned within the restaurant. What happened next was only related to me later, of course.

'What I first heard,' Rex said, in his eventual account of those confused moments, 'what first got through to me was that dummy of a cook, tugging at my sleeve and saying, 'Patron! Patron!' or something of the sort. He was positively hissing with fear and I realised our boys had got in. The man started running in circles back there, so I gave him a hard kick in the arse, which stopped him in his tracks a bit, and then I pulled off that apron I was wearing and went through with the cocked Luger in my hand. Fried Tomato was there, all right, just inside the door looking scared as hell over the barrel of that Mauser thing of his. What chiefly worried me, of course, was that if he'd fired like that I'd have had it. Darn funny, what? Someone back in England telling my daughter, 'Daddy died in action coming out of a kitchen in Bologna.' That dwarf Carmelo looked a lot more in charge of things, I'm glad to say, holding a pistol properly and not aimed at me for a change, but his face looked terrifically swollen. That toothache of his was giving him hell. Well, apart from the War Ministry crowd there were only two others in the restaurant, both men, and, jeepers, the whole set froze. I've never seen a bunch so petrified in all my born days. Just so much statuary, too, that's all they were. Why, I'll swear the back of that bastard's head in front of me went white. He'd just been cramming in some pasta and he sat up straight staring at the guns covering him, with little bits of it coming out of his mouth. The whole bloody bunch were paralysed. Cenedella knew he had to die, each one of those s.o.b.'s – even that silly whimpering woman – had guilt in their eyes large as life. They were like so many schoolkids caught in the act. But those two jackasses of partisans, I tell you, Geoff, they had some perfect genius for ineptitude. Extrrrr-aordinary, sport! To start off with, Carmelo jumped on a table – the man had clearly seen too many movies – and it toppled directly.'

This had been the first sound I'd heard outside.

'He recovered but looked pretty foolish and Cenedella called out, "Just a minute there!" in what was meant to be a commanding voice and it made everyone hesitate, Fried Tomato included. I wanted them to get on with it and I was aiming to stay out of the forthcoming load of lead, 'cos I hadn't an ounce of confidence in that lad's ability to handle a spitting Heckler-Koch with a kick like a mule and keep it down on target. Let alone the ricochets. As it transpired, I needn't have worried.'

'Why?'

'Because the gun didn't go off. Those 9-mm submachine guns can be tricky as hell. Jam at the drop of a hat. Well, it was typical. All of a pattern with the futility and incompetence of the whole affair. I've never been mixed up in anything so inadequate in all my life. What happened was this. Cenedella raised a finger at the ceiling and called out in a high-pitched voice, "Wait! I know who you are!" Carmelo fired and a bit of plaster spat in my face and something buzzed like a bee and then one of the bastards went for the dwarf – sort of low tackle round the knees. Football nonsense. Nuts! At first it didn't work. Carmelo was a cat. The man went down in a crash with Carmelo on top of him, the revolver went off again, and all sorts of limbs and things writhed. The dwarf stabbed with his knife from the groin and there was this redness and wetness and the other guy's hand started scrabbling at the floor. At the same time I saw Fried Tomato covering the table and – by God! he was backing towards the door. The dwarf got up but in the mêlée he had lost his revolver and now he was holding hard to the swollen side of his face, so perhaps he'd had a blow there and his toothache had flared up. And I wanted them to get it over with, when suddenly I knew what had happened. That Mauser had well and truly jammed.'

A subdued chuckle was Rex's accompaniment to this communication.

'Y'know, the geezer was wearing those old canvas slacks and sneaks of his and clamping the butt of the gun to his thigh for dear life. But he'd gone dead pale in the face. 'Naso di Cane!' he was shouting to me. "Naso di Cane ..." And I knew he couldn't go any further for fear of giving the game away to that entire table, many of whom were armed. But I'd seen his finger on the trigger. Squeezing like mad and nothing happening. Holy Moses, it was white to the knuckle with effort. He couldn't get that damn gun to fire and in a second someone at the table would see what I'd seen and twig. "You ... *you*!" he yelled at me from the door. And then suddenly I knew I had to do it or the whole horrible business would break up about us and go bad. In which case we'd both be back in the bag with a vengeance.'

He paused at this point. Then – 'Dammit, you saw the set-up, Geoff. There are certain moments when you have to act.'

'When you *know* you have to act, Rex.'

'Right. Now as I told these guys, I wasn't shooting anyone – not even the second-in-command of the Fascist Ministry of War – through the back of his head. So I got a good hold of him by his lapels and swung him round and let him get a good look at me and then I pitched him backwards for the kill. The fellow was just disgustingly terrified. It was horrible to see, a god-awful face. That filthy woman of his was moaning about like a cat and then with his gold teeth chattering the idiot lurched into the buffet. I believe he sat in some foie gras or something. Anyway, I shot him there and saw the blood flow over those teeth of his and then I gave him another – two, three, four – till he made a heave, a sort of lunge back of his body into the trifles and patisseries and whatnot there and I knew he'd had it. He was still jerking a little when I left and he had that sort of mortal cry or gasp on his face. You know it, old boy, well enough. I even think there was a large blob of that pastry cream, or custard, on his pate – just about where my third shot got him. That Luger really worked.'

Such was the story of those intervening moments. Rex, when I saw him, looked calm and collected. He had stuffed the gun in his belt and straddled the pillion behind me in a flash. We were off.

We tore through that town in a single scream of scalded rubber. A few faces turned to look at us, but no hue and cry went up. The back way out was the best and I was glad not to be with Fried Tomato any more. By that time I had cased these streets and studied the map by heart and I made fast for the Carducci square out. It was clear. We were through. What's more, we had calculated that if Jerry was nicely engaged in one of his rapid retreats, to take up new positions on another line of hills, then established road blocks would be unlikely. At least before Ravenna. He'd want everything open. We might get snarled in some of his convoys, but that was all. Ravenna was ninety kilometres off. The San Felice gate thing might have aroused suspicions, though.

Suddenly I heard Rex bellow in my ear – 'Look out!'

We had swung down the little Via Guinizelli far too fast and I'd misjudged the bend, owing to the extra weight on behind. We'd tied a blanket roll to the bike as well. Ahead of us a huge high kraut truck was double-parked by a tiny Fiat and the road the other way jammed by an Eytie half-track. Vaguely I was aware of the entrance to some garage or repairs shop, Boche soldiers lounging about in their squash caps, and damaged equipment, and I knew we were in trouble. We were in trouble if we stopped – and the road was so clogged we couldn't get through in any case. I had split-seconds to decide what to do. My decision was made for me. As I slowed the bike a bit, a burly German came forward in his galluses, angrily pointing to some sign at the entrance to the street. German writing on it, I'd seen. And just at that moment I had my inspiration.

The Jerry truck ahead was high and wide with a heap of clearance underneath and what's more, there was oil slick on the cobbles. Now, in common with many Italian side-streets in those days, these cobbles were of wood. At least a sort of wood. With anything on them they could be slippery as hell. Now once, too, as a student, this same situation had befallen me on the way out of Reading. I'd pulled up a bike so sharp it'd skidded at speed and before I'd known what was up I'd actually slid under the wheels of the vehicle ahead. That, too, had been a high truck.

This time I was all instinct. I gunned the throttle on the grip and gave her the juice, then I floored the brake with my right foot on the lever, staring open-mouthed at the arm-flailing kraut – a Sergeant I saw – as if I'd just seen him. I guess Rex caught on. Anyhow the long and the short of it was that we shot forward, I wrenched the bike hard to the right, and sure enough it started sliding and yawing from under us. I put out the clutch on the grip and slid with it, slinging my right leg over – as did, I was glad to feel, Rex behind me. He had cottoned on quickly, as always. We were hauled along the slippery cobbles for yards and when the bike came to a halt we were actually under the cab of the truck!

'Quick!' I called to Rex.

He helped me shove out the bike from the front of the truck and, when we emerged, oily and dirty, we shook our heads ruefully at the two Boche mechanics standing there.

Rex even called to them in Italian, *'Dío mío!'* Then he wiped his brow and said, 'Lucky scrape,' also in Eytie. They came forward, gaping at us, but I waved a hand in friendly fashion, kicked at the starter, and we roared on. There was a shot or two, but that was all. The bike was in good shape, or as good as it ever had been, and would be.

'Nice going,' Rex called behind me, one arm slung about my waist for balance. 'I wouldn't have liked them to have searched me and found a warm Luger. Go like hell.'

'I'm giving it all it's got.'

'Sure we're on right bearings?'

'I'm damn certain we're not,' I gave him back on the wind. We had come out of the town the wrong way and were on a road leading into the hills.

'Keep going,' came the growl back. 'I didn't care for that set-up one bit. Let's stick on our own. We can make it together.'

'If you say so,' I told him. But it wasn't prudent to be shouting out English where we were.

So I pushed the bike through the sunny afternoon and crossed the Arno east of Florence. This whole area was seething with military, some of the Jerry soldiers looking incredibly young, and we knew we ought to pack it in and take to the hills. But at the same time we wanted to get as far down these side-roads as we could without discovery. To the ordinary kraut soldier, of course, we looked like a couple of local labourers returning from work. I'm sure that Rex's moustaches helped allay suspicion. Too bad they didn't now.

He looked facially exactly like the typical Carabinieri type, under the famous three-cornered hat designed by Napoleon for the senior Regiment of the Italian Army. Fortunately for us most of those we saw around were still armed with the old 1870 musket.

In the evening the fields we passed were full of green maize and sturdy corn and there were even orchards linked with brilliant vines. It was a good country. There was no sign of any fighting at all – except for a comfortable-looking squadron of bombers overhead, ours. So we pulled off the road to the north of a still lake, a Turgenev lake, circled by cypress trees. It was the sort of deserted stretch of water over which a girl's song should have floated.

But all that was over now.

The sun was already lancing low at the sentinel cypresses and the hills of Italy were turning mauve, as we hid the bike near an abandoned villa and sauntered up to a peasant house on a rise. Rex reckoned we were a little more than a hundred and fifty kilometres north of Rome. As the crow flies.

So near and yet so far – was what I thought. We did not mean to make one last foolish mistake and I went alone to the door, covered from a tree by Rex's last two rounds. We need not have worried. A woman fetched a jug of wine at once and began scraping some corn from the cob of a *granoturco*. Her husband would be back in a minute. Everything was in turmoil. The Germans were pulling back in numbers, perhaps out of Italy altogether, she surmised. We could have what shelter we wished for the night. We began to feel that things were going to go more easily for us than expected. Another mistake.

The husband came back, a man with a purplish fattish face and a sly expression. A mean-looking guy. He welcomed us, however. He told us that according to the latest radio news the ground won by the Allies in Normandy was being extended. D-Day had been successful – thanks to the Americans. All Russian soil was freed. Above all, he seemed to want good news for Russia – before anything else. He sounded like a dedicated commie but whether he was or not we did not know, nor did we care. The types we were afraid of were the retreating and escaping Fascists.

That night we slept well on an old four-poster facing a religious chromo of many figures clustered round a central figure. I think this Saint had arrows in the side and the others were shooting point-blank.

Already on the next day we felt improved. The guns of Bologna began to recede into the past – one increasingly misty for me, with my headaches and all. Yet seawards there were flashes and we stayed with this paisano two days and a half. At the end of it Rex dished him out more money. He eyed our boots but we couldn't give him those. At the same time I think we both realised how easily we could have been betrayed by this item from our Quartermaster's stores, so different in appearance from the footgear of other armies.

This farmer passed us on to another far south of the lake, still closer to Rome. We moved by night on our bike with its light in blackout hooding and met no difficulty at all.

The summer air was soft and these people were glad to be seeing the backs of the Boche for good. It was only a little later that we knew we had crossed, however. A British bomber had crashed in the vicinity, an old Hampden (memories of our seventeenth-century Civil War!), and a peasant hurrying out of a vineyard beckoned us to come and look at it.

We did so cautiously, from the distance of another hill, and a great clump of dark orange trees. Then suddenly we realised that the Corp standing guard over the colossal wreck was one of ours, some poor bastard dug out of Durham or Lincolnshire fens, maybe. At just that moment we heard a strong chorus of male voices:

On the way to Florence we had a lovely time.
We ran a bus to Rimini right through the Gothic Line.
Soon to Bologna we will go
And after that we'll cross the Po –
And still be D-Day dodging, way out in Italee.

We hope the Second Army will soon get home on leave;

For after six months' service it's time for their reprieve.
But we can carry on out here
Another two or three more year –
Contented D-Day Dodgers, to stay in Italee ...

It was a platoon coming along a track, in good order, possibly to relieve the single sentry on guard over the Hampden. We ran down the hill towards them shouting, 'We're English! We're English!'

13

A week later we walked past the heavy Gesù church together. We had just been to an extraordinary ceremony.

Rome was a sad city in those days, almost without hope, you might say. It soon got back on its feet, but I am thinking of just after its liberation, when we were returned there. It was far more orderly than Naples, but much more sombre... less living. Its atmosphere seemed charged with an uneasy oppressiveness. A place of scarcity and yet luxury and high prices. Napoli was a free-for-all by comparison. At the time we got back there, Rome lay under a melancholy despair, its people seemed listless and indifferent, resigned to a hard future. Moreover, its male population was sullen and humiliated, rather than ingratiating, as in Naples. In Rome they seemed ashamed of seeing their city occupied, and many were openly resentful of our presence. This soon died down. But it was a feature of our first days there. And I got to know Rome well. I walked almost every inch of it – except the *trastevere* – on foot.

But directly we got to the Eternal City together, Rex and I footed it for St Peter's. Almost every other soldier on day's leave in Italy had the same idea. They too made a beeline for Vatican City, that state within a state. We did a little better. First, I was Catholic. Second, Rex seemed to know everyone. There was a Consistory taking place, the first for years, and the Pope was giving the Red Hat to no less than twenty Cardinals in St Peter's. It was the largest ordination since the inception of hostilities, indeed for centuries. Somehow or other Rex wangled an audience in. It was an impressive occasion after what we had been through.

To start off with, all the aristocracy of Italy, plus

womenfolk, was present. The Diplomatic Forces came resplendent with their stars and decorations and sashes. All the ladies were in black with their best jewels and wearing the traditional black mantilla on their heads, customary for such ceremonies. Rex and I had two good seats by the Diplomatic enclosure, quite close to His Holiness. He pointed out to me Schuschinigg on one side and General Anders, the Polish C-in-C who had taken Cassino, on the other. I also remember Major-General Theron upholding the honour of South Africa, his lovely daughter Jacqueline, or Jacky, beside him. She was to become the 'pin-up girl' of the Assembly of Nations at the post-war Paris Conference.

Rex also showed me the Turkish Ambassador and the Afghan Minister (at some time in his checkered career he had been in Kabul and could speak *poshti*, that northern dialect of Urdu), and I remember thinking it strange that in the Hall of Audience there were only two paintings, both concerned with killings by women! One was of Jael, wife of Heber the Kenite, driving a nail into her sleeping visitor's head. The other was the picture of the head of John the Baptist in the charger.

There was a wave of cheering as the Pope was borne in on his sedan chair, on the shoulders of his guards. He bowed right and left and blessed everyone as he passed. The garb of the Swiss Guards was very colourful after what we had known in the blue and Rex told me the costumes had originally been designed by Michelangelo. Princes of the Pope's Guard, like Count Aluffi-Pentini whom Rex knew, stood on either side of the Pontiff with drawn swords. The dais had been erected over the actual tomb of St Peter and the new Cardinals (including a Chinese one) went up one by one to receive their Red Hat. They made obeisance and kissed the Pope's right toe, then bowed and descended the steps from the throne with acolytes carrying their long red trains. I so well remembered performing that office at school. Bach's B Minor Mass, and carrying the candles. All Cardinals are equal. For this very reason most old palazzi in Rome have several doors into the main reception hall so that if more than one Cardinal is invited they can all enter at the same time. You can also escape at speed in case of vendetta. Even at meals each course is served at exactly the same moment, and with the same flourish, to each Cardinal.

'Today I heard,' said Rex, turning slightly towards me, 'that our forward tanks have got as far as Perugia. Imagine. Think of where Jumbo is just now.'

'Where?' I said.

'Somewhere round there. Another university city.'

'That's a big help.'

'The IRTD Major says we'll be posted back to them in short order.'

'Good.'

'You think so?'

'Yes.'

'Why? Those poor buggers at Sidi Rezegh, the ones who've come all the way? Don't you know, Geoff, they're already forgotten? In five years' time no one in the world, let alone England, will even know that place existed. A dot in nothingness, that's all.'

'The facts ... in space,' I mumbled, watching him closely as he strode past the souvenir-vendors of the Colosseum.

Yes, Rome was sad in those first days. Esedra, Barberini, Piazza del Popolo, I had a feeling this was to be converted in time into a vast parking lot. Civilisation had written this upon ROMA AMOR. The palindrome might persist a century more. But the city would be in service of another mentality. We both sensed it intimately, I think.

I felt it upon each step of each staircase, passing each rubber-booted Yank, snapping snapshots. We were now in the happiest quarter of Rome at that time. The town was coming back slowly, its inhabitants seemed to have thought all would be well, all would be solved, directly the Allies arrived. After all, one could fine Yankee cigarettes outside the Forum and good thick eggs in the baskets of vendors in the Via Appia. But at what a price! It must have been like Germany after World War One. Besides, a number of these Yanks were Eytie in origin, and they were said to be the cruellest of all to the locals.

And no one knew exactly what was going on. Ourselves, least of all. C.M.F. bureaucracy was worse than anything we had ever seen. After medical examination, and outfitting at a Q's, we had been sent to an I.R.T.D. consisting of five thousand officers and men, on the fringes of Rome. Strictly speaking, the acronym stood for Infantry Reinforcement Training Depot and we were not infantry; however, it was a catch-all for types like us waiting to get posting forward to our various units. It was a vast tented plain run principally by an extremely anxious Major of the line who didn't know what the hell he was supposed to do with a couple of Droghedas who'd been put in the bag and had got back through enemy lines. I think we made him feel uncomfortable, particularly since he hadn't himself seen a shot fired in anger as yet. He was not interested in our exploits, only in passing bumf across a table and getting the okay from someone for us to go forward. In those days all such orders were copied longhand into a sort of ledger. There was plenty of time.

So in those first days back we lay in the sun, read old newspapers from back home, and wangled transport out to Ostia to swim. We enjoyed Rome. The Arch of Constantine. Tasso's oak, all that. We even went to the Criminal Museum in the Via Giulia which had been the Fascist police HQ under Musso.

'That's the man,' said Rex suddenly, and stopped me in a side-gallery. The photo was in a small passe-partout frame, a group documenting the fall of Rome already. Cenedella's face stared at us oleaginously. He had on his shantung suit.

Then San Clemente, Santa Cecilia in *trastevere*. The Baths of Caracalla next. The celebrated 'Typewriter', or monument to Victor Emmanuel II, with all its aching steps. A place of pomp, and sadness.

'That one they really finished, eh,' said Rex of the monstrosity.

Endless galleries, some bad basilicas, lots of gilt framing and paintings signed Ignoto. So it went.

Of course, we tried to find someone who knew where our

regiment was. Rex knew a Countess who lived in a sinister Gothic addition to the Palazzo Pennini, a boneless woman in British tweeds who advanced towards us over a watery floor about the size of an average parade ground back home, holding up phthisic fingers. She introduced us to a mournful Colonel in the darker barathea of the Rifle Brigade who told us he thought the Third Droghedas had been practically all massacred at Anzio. The Town Major might know. The 2nd Tank Corps were said to be swanning around a place called Toschi, what was left of them. When we returned to our I.R.T.D. camp that evening, Rex and I calculated that probably two-thirds of those of us who had survived North Africa had been killed or wounded by now – what with Salerno and Anzio. We felt in no vast hurry to rejoin the Reg, but we did what we could. Unlike myself, Rex had always hung onto his bakelite identity tag, strung in greasy string around his neck. I looked at it as we undressed. The numbers still stood out on it, but the letters of his religion were effaced. I joked with him that no one would know whom to bury him with. A joke that turned out to have a sting in its tail.

We looked odd, I guess, in our brand-new, unmarked, and medalless battledress that we'd drawn up from Q. Rex, in particular, looked gauche, I thought, vulnerable. He spent much of his time hunting up old opera records in the little shops around the Pantheon. He even found some Caruso. Maybe he was going to send them to his daughter, I had no idea. We had made few friends at the Depot where we were simply told to report daily. It was like an extended leave. We kept to ourselves.

At the top of the Spanish Steps at that time there was a bust of the Duce which had been overturned and disfigured. A lot of Yank GI's were photographing it. They told us that after the Normandy landings, Cherbourg, Caen, and the Orne estuary had been taken, the advance had temporarily stalled there. Looking down at the Duce's swollen head I felt suddenly happy that we'd killed Cenedella. It was the same sort of face.

'Let's get out of here,' said Rex, and we took a horse-drawn carriage to the Borghese Gardens.

Here the almond blossom had gone, now that it was full June. But it was better. There was something stagnant in Rome those days; the corruption and perverse activity of Naples seemed preferable to this sad torpor.

'When are we going to tell our story?' I asked him as we lay back on the faded cushions.

'I'm not saying a thing till I'm sure of whom I'm talking to,' was his response. 'Preferably a senior officer in our Regiment. Preferably Jumbo, if he's still alive. And I want you to be there when I get it all off my chest, Geoff.'

'I will be. But I wonder what happened to Orlando and all those other Eytie Generals in the Ministry they were talking about. Did they try to get away, too?'

'God knows.'

'I suppose we could try to find out.'

'How?'

'Well, there was this other type they mentioned called Linardi. Another Fascist swine, it seems. They wanted to get him too, if you recall.'

'For the time being, old boy, silence of the tomb.'

He put fingers to his lips. And indeed it made sense. We had to wait until things cleared a bit. No use hurrying it.

The Major at the Depot was so fatuous he'd probably have taken off like a hen in hysterics if we'd made a full report of it all to him. Jesus Christ, what a wet-bag. Now of course there were some interrogation centres, they'd been set up for escaped prisoners-of-war, which is what we were, in a sense, but if there were any in Rome, well we hadn't heard of them. It was then something odd occurred. The hand of fate, you could say. It happened the next day.

Food at the mess at the I.R.T.D. was getting worse and worse in measure as its numbers grew, so Rex and I had taken more and more to eating out in Rome. We had decided to binge the tidy sum of back pay due to us and received after filling in more forms than I knew existed, in that Major's Orderly

Room. We had taken to going to a spot called Lucrezio. It lay at the top of the winding Via Quattro Novembre and was quite the most sophisticated joint we'd set eyes on since the roof bar of the old Continental in Cairo. Our usual waiter greeted us at once and seated us at our favourite corner table. We ordered Tio Pepe sherry. The place soon began to fill up.

The Lucrezio had a splendid cellar. Rex was a connoisseur. He ordered a '29 Liebfraumilch and, with the tournedos, a Carruades de Lafite which he classed as a death-bed wine. I only hoped his phrase was not to be taken too literally, it was in fact the last bottle of quality we drank together and I, too, found it a good mouthful.

'A robust claret, but elegant,' he remarked, and I felt that the description applied equally to himself; he was passing judgement not so much on his wine as on his person.

'I give you life!' he said, raising his glass.

'To lots more of it,' I agreed, lifting mine.

'Odd how you come to appreciate it after you've seen a spot of death, eh, face to face.'

'You can say that again.' All I wanted was to get through the rest of this campaign in one piece. But sitting next to Rex you couldn't be too sure. 'I thought you were never coming out of that damn restaurant, you know, and all the time I was scared stiff the bike wouldn't take off.'

'Ugh!' he said with a grimace. 'Horrible. But look here. Take a dekko at these types coming in.'

A good deal of brass and braid had just been let in, then installed with much circumstance at a reserved table not far from ours. We looked at them with the same mild amusement we had at fly-whisk-wielding Majors in desert boots at Shepheard's in Cairo. They ordered French champagne and were served with comic-opera obsequiousness. We admired the sheen of their Sam Brownes, the newness of their medals, and returned to our wine.

When time came for us to leave, this party of base-wallahs, for such they appeared, were in fine form, one pretty drunk. At the table next to ours there were two RN officers, one of them a submarine Captain, I could see. We had exchanged a few words with them. Rex now paid the exorbitant bill, then tipped back his chair in their direction.

'Don't know who these brass-hats are, do you?' he inquired. 'Commander-in-Chief, Central Med Forces, or what?'

'Christ no,' said the younger of the two. 'That's Allied Commission, Italy. Actually we're attached to strength. Debarking procedures, all that. The one in the middle is our C.O.'

We turned and saw a tall, thin British General, bronzed and distinguished-looking, with a thin moustache. There was something in him caught me. It was not only that he was obviously aristocratic, but he had that assurance, that clarity of vision, a fulfilled look in the eyes which only comes from having seen bullets fired at you in anger. I liked him at once. Just near him was a squat and swarthy Eytie with medals practically down to his ankles.

'And who's he?' I asked. 'The ice-cream merchant?'

'Oh him,' said the other, grinning. 'That's General Orlando.'

Rex and I froze.

'The Folgore Combat Group, you know,' we heard. 'He and Casati come under Rear Admiral Stone.'

'And who's the Johnny on his right?' Rex asked coldly. 'The one with the monocle?'

'Think he's called Linardi. You have to watch it, with them. They're touchy as all getout. Frankly, I salute every Italian I see in uniform above a bottle-washer.'

'They like it,' said his friend. 'They really are sensitive these days. After the surrender, I mean.'

'Did you say Orlando?' Rex asked.

'Minister of War and Commander-in-Chief of the Italian Army – what's left of it, that is. Sure, that's his name.'

Rex thought. He said cautiously, 'But Orlando had that post under the Germans.'

'So I gather.' The submarine Captain shook his head. 'Don't ask me. He must have come over. You know how it is these days. Bury the hatchet, forget the past. That's the policy we get handed down to us. Higher command probably knows what it's doing.'

'It didn't at Anzio,' said Rex.

'And it didn't at Salerno,' I said. 'Goddam shambles.'

The naval types looked at us quickly. They didn't want to get involved with what probably seemed to them a couple of embittered desert rats. They left, smiling.

We were not smiling.

Outside, there was a new moon. Rex walked up and down the empty street, his hands behind his back, and his worry-beads moving through those hands at the rate of knots.

'I can't believe it,' I said. 'Orlando was a Fascist pig, a torturer. We knew it. Had all the proofs ...'

'Is there a fucking Italian Cabinet or something?' said Rex with sudden fury. 'If so, we'll go to them.' In the night his lion's head seemed fringed with snow. He had been right. He was going white quickly. Then, with a sob, he said, 'What have we done, Geoff, what the hell have we done?'

'We've done what we had to do, Rex. That's all.'

'But Orlando sitting there, pleased as punch, proud as a turkey cock ... I ask you, I bloody ask you. No, it couldn't have been him.'

'We'll find out tomorrow.'

'Tomorrow I'm going to Allied Control Commission. Whatever happens, I'm going to tell our story and tell it straight. Before someone else does.'

'I'll come with you.'

'You'll back me up?'

'Of course. All the way.'

He put his hand on my shoulder. We started to walk down the street together. Once he stopped and turned to me.

'The higher the jump, the better the horse you need, Geoff. Never forget it.'

'I've never forgotten Alamein,' I said.

And it was all that needed saying between us.

14

The next day Rex wasn't feeling too well – his usual complaint – and I stayed with him in the camp. For two days he seemed totally grounded and I was beginning to think we ought to get our story in soon, otherwise they'd ask us why we'd held it back. So with Rex's consent I went there alone.

In those days the Allied Control Commission building was in the Via Veneto. It was an old palazzo in the usual disorder. Several military agencies were moving in. No one seemed to know which branch was occupying which floor. Workmen were busy dividing up baroque rooms, with fantastic fireplaces, into plasterboard cells for offices. Already the typewriters were ticking in some of these.

So I wandered around the marble staircase and on the fifth floor I found a Brigade of Guards officer with the old eggs-and-bacon Africa Star on his tunic and a long amber cigarette-holder in his mouth. He seemed a pleasant enough fellow and I asked him if he knew where I could find someone responsible in B.L.U.

Now B.L.U. stood for British Liaison Units, the idea being to have our reps at the headquarters of every new Italian formation. Rex and I had decided that because of their obvious contacts with Eytie forces behind the lines the B.L.U.'s was where we should formally deposit our report. In the Italian Combat Groups, the B.L.U. numbered at that time only about fifteen officers with each group headed by a G.S.O.I. Lieutenant-Colonel. He sat at the right hand of the Divisional Commander, so we felt that like this we'd have a fairly economical and direct route to the powers above. We wouldn't be dizzied around. The B.L.U.'s could corroborate our report for us better than anyone. They had a picture of all Italy.

The Guardee looked at me, quizzically grinning. He extracted his cigarette-holder.

'Jim Dakesworth's the man you want to see.' He pointed to some ladders in front of a white-and-gold door on the landing below. 'Holes out down there.'

A Colour-Sergeant met me at the door indicated. The place was being set up for a series of offices. I thought: God, how the bumf grows behind the lines.

'Major Dakesworth is presently in attendance on King Umberto, I believe, sir,' said the Sergeant doubtfully. 'But if you have anything of official importance you could perhaps communicate it to him through me.'

'It doesn't matter,' I said. 'I'll come back another time. I want to see someone who knows something about the underground movement. I have a rather serious report to make.'

'Or else you could submit the whole thing in triplicate.'

'It doesn't matter,' I said.

'Unless you wished to see the British Ambassador himself, sir.'

I did not think he had spoken ironically. He had sheaves of papers in his hands, a pencil stuck behind one ear. I started down the vast stair.

Now, on the way, I saw some red tabbing on a tunic, the baton and sabre crossed beneath a star on the lapel nearest me, and automatically saluted. Suddenly I realised that by a bit of luck it was the lean British General who had been at Lucrezio's with Orlando. He acknowledged my salute absently enough and turned to the officer beside him, evidently an aide.

'Might I have a moment with you, sir?' I asked.

He stopped.

'What is it?'

I gave him my name and number and other particulars. It had been a long time since I'd spoken to brass. I thought his eyes picked up a bit at mention of the Third Droghedas.

'I'm presently attached to an I.R.T.D. waiting to go forward, sir. I have a deposition I'd like to make concerning important Italian underground activity. I got back from Bologna through the lines not long ago.'

'Did you now? Put in the bag, eh?'

'At Anzio, sir. I want to make an official report, together with the squaddie who got taken with me.'

'Well, you do that through the usual channels, surely. Your own. I'm not one to step on the Droghedas' toes.'

'It's just that . . . well, sir, we wanted to be sure to make this official. We happened to see you dining with some important Italian officials the other evening, sir.'

'Lucrezio's? Fantastic smoked salmon, eh?'

I left that at that.

'And as far as we can find out there's no one of our Regiment in Rome at all. They're all in the line.'

I didn't like to add – What's left of them.

'The devil!' He gave me a kindly look, pressing his swagger stick into his chin. 'I tell you, I have the greatest respect for the Droghedas, but I've only just got out here myself. As you can see, there's quite a bit of organising to do to get this place ship-shape first. But I'm sure my aide-de-camp will take care of you. Alec!' he called. The officer with him, who had turned to talk to a heavy-headed Italian workman in white overalls, came up.

'Sir?'

'Would you route this young officer on to whom it may concern?'

'Certainly, sir.'

'Good luck, old chap,' said the General, jovially continuing up the stairs. 'You're in good hands.'

The aide led me into a side-room with a worried expression on his face. The room was almost entirely bare of furniture but with the usual achingly high scrolled ceiling, completely intact, as was most of the 'open' city – *città aperta,* as Rome had been declared by both sides. The man collected two small seats worthy of Versailles and we sat facing each other in the middle of the gleaming expanse of parquet.

'What can I do for you exactly? What's the trouble?'

I said: 'You don't have an Orderly or something . . . to make a transcript, I mean?'

'Not an earthly, I'm afraid.' But his interest had sharpened. 'What's up?'

'All right. Do you know General Orlando?'

'Of course I do. He happens to be the Italian Minister of War.'

'Does the name Linardi mean anything to you?'

'Certainly does. Present Italian Chief of Staff.'

I took a deep breath, wishing Rex were there and not floored with those bloody piles of his.

'As members of the ex-Italian Army they are of course your prisoners.'

The aide hesitated. I looked at him, wondering. He was a Captain in the Sussex with an almost oriental face, under silky black hair, now that he had taken off his cap. I could sense that his indifference was alien to me, bureaucratic.

'I don't think you quite understand,' he said, looking down at his boots. 'Linardi comes from the province of Palermo.'

'What's that got to do with it?'

'Now take it easy, Lieutenant. I know you forward fellows have had a hard time of it. Get jumpy easily, so on. We were warned about it.'

'About what?'

'Shell-shock. Battle fatigue. No, all those high-ranking Italian officers surrendered to us unconditionally when we entered Rome. The whole Italian War House came over, as it happens. Why, did you know that nearly a quarter of a million men surrendered to us in Sardinia alone?'

'Meaning what?'

'That they were expecting an invasion there, of course.' He turned up his palms in an expansive gesture. How soft and sure they looked. 'But, more than that, the way in which such vast numbers laid down their arms – or just cleared off on their own into the hills, why that's encouraged higher command . . . Sir Noel Charles . . .'

'Who's he?' I snapped.

'Our Ambassador,' he replied coldly, after a minute. Then he went on, 'We have been encouraged to send a mission out to resuscitate the Italian Army. That's what we're doing here. Personally I think it's a fine idea.'

'And the Fascist regime?'

'Oh, most of them were against it, in any case.'

'You sure of that?'

He shrugged. 'You know the Italians.'

'Their change of heart seems a trifle sudden, surely.'

'Listen,' said the aide with more an edge of irritation in his voice, 'all I can tell you is that two days ago there was this big State lunch. Ever had Italian boar? Oh yes, there are still some about, you know. In the Abruzzi. Well, for our purposes it's going to be best to let bygones be bygones. Save us a lot of time and red tape in the long run. The political prisons on the islands – Procida, so on – they're all being investigated at this moment for possible amnesty of prisoners. Musso simply confined his political enemies there.'

'Also most of the Mafia, too, I hear. Dammit,' and here I struck my knee so that the flimsy chair perilously wobbled, 'some of us were taught to fight them. Some of us died fighting them.'

The aide dropped his eyes. After a second he said, 'It's the future that counts, old boy.' I saw that he was looking at my fingers and that my fingers had one hell of a shake on. 'Battle fatigue is said to be a damn unpleasant business. We've heard about anxiety neurosis in returned p-o-w's. Listen, if I were you, Lieutenant, I'd take it easy for as long as you can at that depot of yours. Why don't you talk to one of your own people? Y'know, I have a pretty good hunch you fellows are going to have all the fighting you want before this lot's done. It isn't over yet, you know. Not by a long chalk. We want all the allies we can get.'

'All the fighting we *want*!' I shouted and my words hung histrionic in that still chamber. 'Jesus Christ, man, do you know what you're talking about? Do you know how many tanks I've seen brewed while you were sitting on your arse counting cheques in the City?'

It was ignoble and I knew it and I regretted it instantly. He was looking at me attentively, as a scientist looks at a specimen.

'Poor chap,' he said. 'You've had it rough, you fellows, and no mistake. It's precisely for that reason I urge you to take it easy here while still you can. Maybe you should see a doc. Frankly, I don't see how we can help out at all.'

That stung me.

'Ever heard of a General Cenedella?' I asked him.

'Hm.' He paused. After a second he said, 'Name seems familiar. I believe I remember someone like that in briefing.' He undid a shining button, Brasso'ed to blazing point, and reached into a breast pocket. From this he extracted a neat notebook or diary. 'Name seems familiar,' he said. Then, 'Nope. Sorry. There's no such person in the Ministry at the moment.'

'There isn't,' I blurted angrily, 'because not so long ago we killed him, that's why.'

The aide-de-camp closed his notebook very deliberately and painfully, and then restored it to his pocket. There was no doubt but that he thought me round the bend, or joking. Anyway, it was out now.

'The name seems familiar,' he said gently as if to himself.

'Shot him stone dead at Bologna,' I pursued, though a trifle less hotly. 'That's what I've been trying to tell you, goddammit. Cenedella was second in command to Orlando, according to the information given us behind the lines. And that's where we want to lay this,' I concluded. 'On the line.'

The aide's lips pursed.

'You serious?' he said.

'Deadly.'

He gave a leisurely whistle.

'Not pulling my leg, I mean?'

'No.'

He tugged at his nether lip.

'I can't see why you've come to me with this,' he said. 'There are the proper channels.'

'I didn't come to you. I was handed over to you. By your C.O.'

‘Well, I must say it merits thought,’ he said, rocking forward and studying the pattern of the parquet. ‘It certainly merits thought. Frankly, it’s all a bit beyond me. As the General told you, our mission’s only just arrived. We’re supposed to dish out co-operation, sympathy, bags of compassion.’ He looked at me sharply. ‘You feeling all right?’

‘Perfectly.’

‘It is a little hot in here.’

‘I hadn’t noticed it.’

‘The Eytie makes a damn good soldier, you know.’

‘What’s that got to do with it all?’

‘All right, all right.’ He stood up, slapping a thigh with his stick. ‘I think we’d better get a G3 in on this. Maybe some US.’

‘I shall be happy to accompany you to G3 Intelligence,’ I said, ‘but I would like to do so with my senior officer in the affair, who is presently . . . indisposed.’

‘Very good. Let’s make an appointment here. Day after tomorrow. No, can’t manage that. Friday?’

‘Very good.’

But when I got back to the depot Rex was not there.

15

A week later we were following the young aide-de-camp along a wing of the edifice. Rex had given me a scare. Actually, all he had done had been to change tents, telling a rather stupid soldier servant to bring my things over. I found him on a camp-bed twiddling those worry-beads through his well-worn fingers. I told him all that happened.

'I'm sorry I spilt the beans, Rex,' I concluded. 'But that blighter got under my skin.'

He waved a hand, recumbent.

'It doesn't matter. It had to come out some time. Let's go and do it together now.'

'Rex, I've always thought how like a rosary those beads are.'

'So have I, Geoff. They pacify my mind. After all, if you go through the Mysteries, I mean ain't it exactly what you and I faced up to ... in the blue?' He started to tick them off on his fingers: 'The Annunciation – humility; the Nativity – poverty; the Presentation – obedience ...'

'The Agony in the Garden,' I put in, 'and how!'

We paced, steel-heeled, behind the aide together, warm in our comradeship.

To my right a blinding view of Rome became suddenly visible from a sash window. I thought: what an incredible city, after what we had been through! How calm, how confident its tufa looked, as the great birds swooped and dived.

Up short stairs, up wide steps, past workmen carrying crates, soldiers clumsy in boots. Electricians up ladders in sandals, replacing light bulbs. Eventually our cicerone, more formal than when I had first met him, rapped on a particularly ornate door and we were ushered into another palatial chamber. The Sussex Captain seemed glad to have got rid of us. Good Droghedas, we stamped our salutes resoundingly, though Rex – I would have wagered – had seen ten times the battle than had the white-haired figure in tunic and Sam Browne, smoking a PX cigar, and talking stage Italian to a grey-suited individual wearing a knitted black tie. Everything was muddled here.

'Yes, yes, Cavaliere, you needn't worry. No, we don't have the figures yet. We'll fix it. Have no fear.'

The British officer – a Major, I saw, who looked as if he'd just been outfitted for the first time – bent to the other's ear. I saw the Italian make a snap of his fingers when the word Cenedella came up.

'Very well, Cavaliere, we'll see what we can do. Yes, of course, the man's entire police record. If possible, bank statements, so on. I know.'

This was double-dutch to us.

'But of course, as I said, Major.' The Italian reached for his grey suede gloves, fondled them a moment, and stood up. 'Naturally, the whole dossier. Anything of use.' He hesitated, and with a bow left the room. I saluted again. Whether Rex did so I did not know. He stood slightly behind me. We had agreed beforehand that I would do most of the initial talking, having seen this base-wallah area before, and he would look on, act witness.

'Do sit down, gentlemen. I'm Major Dakesworth.'

I remembered the name, introduced Rex and myself. We sat down stiffly.

'I was informed that a Major Dakesworth was in attendance on Prince Umberto,' I said. I didn't call him the King.

'Actually, yeah,' he said, slightly impersonating the then 'in' American accent. 'Actually, yeeeh!' He shook his head apologetically. I thought he was drunk, or somewhat so. In any event he seemed to find the whole thing a vast joke. Which we certainly did not.

Dakesworth inhaled, grinned, gave me an avuncular look

and slapped, a little limply, a book on his desk. I saw the spine – *'Lafcadio's Adventures'* by André Gide. I had read it as a schoolboy. Also, something of the same sort about cholera and a cute kid in Venice. Thomas Mann. Both in the original. Easy stuff, and without great interest for English schoolboys of my age – more addicted to swastika pennants than erudite prose, you could say. Actually, one of our young officers, a fervent admirer of Gide, had got leave back to Alger and seen the great man in the flesh, then installed at Blida. Our friend had, with several others of his ilk, awaited for pearls of wisdom at the feet of the sage, but Gide had spoken of nothing but royalties, of what his agent (Mori) was getting for him in Japan, what England was sending over, so on. I didn't get it. How could an author be that commercial, that vain? What the man was really concerned about was how his books would go in Germany after the war. I couldn't believe it, never having been an author myself. I supposed they had their problems, too. Rex now seemed to me to be looking at it all with an air of indifference. Sands no longer moved beneath our feet. Perhaps we should never have come here in the first place.

'Smoke?' said Dakesworth, inhaling luxuriously.

'I don't, thanks,' I said.

Rex said nothing, staring ahead.

I felt it time to begin.

'Does the name Cenedella mean anything to you, Major? General Cenedella?'

'In a way, yes.' His response was cautious.

'Ever meet him by any chance?'

'No.' The G.S. or General Staff Intelligence Major puffed on his cigar in a satisfied manner. 'Listen. That character was sent on a mission by his superiors a little while ago. At least, so I understand.'

I went on, 'His superior in the Italian Ministry of War would be General Orlando, am I right?'

'Yes, that would be correct. But frankly I don't deal much with the ex-Italian Army. Thank God. We have other problems here, chiefly political but also military. There's a complete new mission just established to liaise with those guys. I would advise you to go and see them.'

'But we seem to have been sent from them to you?'

'Very well then, Lieutenant, perhaps you would get to the point. Just what is it you imagine I can do for you?' He buffed a well-manicured nail on his lapel and studied the result. 'Please be brief.'

'You mean, the General's aide-de-camp didn't tell you anything?'

'Only that you had some sort of science-fiction story to tell me.' This time he smiled at the nail.

Rex and I exchanged glances. We were in perfect accord. We realised that in Africa we had been continually involved in manual labour; this was not the same. We had also arranged that, as senior, he should finally say it and he did.

'We killed Cenedella,' he grated out.

It did sound oddly melodramatic and impossible in the empty room and I noticed that Dakesworth made no move at this information, still continuing to study the polish of his fingernails. He knew, then? Was he playing with us?

'We shot him in a restaurant in Bologna on the sixth of June,' Rex added.

'D-Day, eh. Remarkable coincidence. Now look here, Captain Davidson, just what kind of delusions do you think you're wasting our time with?'

'So the aide did tell you, then?'

'Now don't get excited. I know what strains you people have been under in tanks here. In fact, if I were you I'd take these tales to an Army psycho-doc. Quite a few around these days, I gather. You know, trick-cyclist. Physi-Christ, that sort of thing. Frankly,' and he grinned, 'I've always felt that the best kind of therapy of that kind was Axel Munthe's speciality – strong kick in the seat. No, after prisoner escapes like yours you ought to have been checked by one of those blokes, anyway.'

'You mean, you don't believe us?'

'Just breathe deeply, Captain Davidson, and keep your dander down.'

'I'm going to make you regret this,' Rex said softly, after a long pause.

'Be my guest.'

We stood up as one.

'Then I am sorry to have bothered you, Major Dakesworth. Possibly I chose the wrong time and the wrong place. In my eventual report I shall have to say that I applied to you, but was not listened to. That I was dismissed cursorily, without due attention to the facts. The General's aide-de-camp will corroborate that, as will my second-in-command here.'

The Intelligence Major waved his hand again – this time not quite so limply.

'All right, don't get your balls in an uproar, Captain. As I say, we fully understand what you boys have been through up front. There's no need to get snotty, though, just because I tried to rattle you over your story. I had to do it. Afraid I was purposefully abrupt. Now sit down, both of you. That's better altogether.' He dropped ash in an alabaster bowl. Then he took a gold pencil and a pad of yellow legal paper.

'Third Droghedas, you say?'

'Second Tank Corps.'

'Embarked for Anzio as a Recce Group to help make up the Lothians? I hear they've been having a tough time.'

'On the fourteenth,' said Rex.

'Taken a day or so later?'

'Right.'

Rex gave our story in detail and from time to time Dakesworth checked it by cross-questioning me. He did a good job of what he had been trained to do. But it wasn't our job and we didn't like him, or it.

'This gets interesting,' said the Major at last, stubbing out his cigar and looking over what he'd written. It was in an immense scrawl, covering pages. 'I'm glad you came to me. Of course, it is rather serious.'

'So serious,' said Rex, 'that we propose to confront General Orlando with what we know – here in your presence, sir.'

'Now wait. Not to be so hasty.' He gave an uncomfortable

wiggle and shot up all sorts of coy smiles. His white hair had flopped over one eye, giving him a fake 'boyish' look that I found curiously repellent. 'This is a pretty delicate matter. We're walking on eggs, you might say. There isn't all that hurry.'

'I want everything to be above board and in its proper order,' said Rex solemnly. 'I intend to be quite certain that you have all the facts in their place before I go forward into the line again. I would not be able to.... able to ... function, if I may put it so, without having clarified everything first. To the proper authorities.'

'Where does Orlando hang out?' I asked hotly.

'No call to be precipitate, Lieutenant.'

'Why not?'

In the room the atmosphere was getting sticky. Picture it for yourself: cigar smoke curling to the scrolled ceiling from the confident white head of an Intelligence wallah while two tank corps officers stood there, hostile and contemptuous but gradually beginning to realise the can of worms that lay underneath their story, and now in those elaborate notes. In restaurants in England men in their right mind do not mow down others with pistols – at least, such was what the expression on Dakesworth's face said to me then.

He piloted us to the door.

'You know, one of our main headaches is this matter of the partisans. It's a very controversial question, you know. On the one hand, any effort by the Italian underground hurt the Boche and of course helped the war effort. But, on the other hand, the partisans were the cause of the most frightful reprisals by the Germans who without hesitation shot whole families if they thought they'd had anything to do with the underground movement. Moreover, all this present cheering of the partisans on, telling them what a marvellous job they're doing, so forth, this has made them feel they were the real saviours of Italy. This feeling threatens to grow to such a ridiculous extent that when Italy is finally liberated in toto, then these partisans are going to demand all kinds of recognitions and rewards, forgetting that it was the Allies who did the real job. According to our information, there are probably less than 50,000 partisans at work behind the lines. We are rebuilding an Italian Army our side of the line ten times that size and they fear that, if the partisans get all the publicity, they'll demand the disbanding of what we've created and try to become enrolled as the official Italian Army themselves. Now I suspect this Italian General you want to see is pretty busy. Rather like English Generals, what! How's this for size? I'll make an appointment for you to see him. Directly I've got one I'll send you a signal at that Depot of yours and we can all rendezvous there together, eh. At the moment I'm just snowed. Horribly busy. The liberation of political prisoners in those perfectly ghastly island prisons ... you've no idea.'

'A man has been killed,' said Rex, stopping him at the door.

The other gave a nervous shrug which again flopped his thin hair forward over his noble brow.

'*Major* Dakesworth,' added Rex. As I have previously remarked, promotion was slow in the Droghedas. Rex could have been this man's senior officer any time he wanted to; he could also have been sent back to base offices like this, too, considering his age and experience alone.

'I hope you two realise there's been a change of government in Italy,' said the Major carefully. 'We're still kind of sorting out who's who, you know.'

'I hope you do your sorting well,' said Rex.

'Well, so far as I can understand Orlando is a highly respected individual.'

'According to our partisans,' I came back coldly, 'he was a Fascist swine. And so was Cenedella.'

'I shot him down like a dog,' said Rex whose erect bearing contrasted with the somewhat furtively bowed shoulders of the Major, now trying to usher us out of the door.

'Yes, yes, of course, Captain Davidson. All this will have to be authenticated. You'll have to submit an account of this to the new Italian G Staff as well. Officially, of course. Before rejoining your Regiment.'

'I answer to my own government and to my own country,'

Rex returned. 'Just as you do.' Then to my surprise he added, 'I acted under orders. And for my daughter.'

Major Dakesworth crinkled his forehead. A lot of hammering had started outside.

'What on earth's your daughter got to do with this?'

'That man was *de trop* on this earth. No space for him here.'

It was clear that Dakesworth was growing more and more puzzled by Rex's arcane utterances, and more suspicious as he grew more puzzled.

Through the hammering I shouted out, 'I am happy we did what we did.' And I looked the Major full in the eyes.

We were being seen out to phrases – 'Devilish tricky moment in international relations, I agree, Lieutenant ... will of fate ... no one wants to have backed the wrong horse ... anyway, the secret police is totally dissolved, we can be thankful for that.'

'We did our duty,' said Rex. 'Let that be clear, Major.'

'Of course, of course.' He held open the door. 'I'll let you know if I can arrange something. Naturally, this is all in confidence between us and I consider the matter of the highest importance.'

The door closed in our faces. A little civilian in horn-rimmed spectacles was apparently waiting to go in. We wound our way back through the building, threading through the workmen and painters; we went down the great stair in a sort of mirage – I've never known a better one even in the blue.

'Christ on fucking Crutches, Geoff!' Rex said at the foot of them. 'We were right to do what we did, weren't we? Weren't we?'

'Yes, Rex.'

'Then we're innocent.'

'Of course, we are. Who said we were guilty?'

'He said that the government has changed. The one we fought for doesn't exist any more. Geoff, we're in a pickle.'

We made our way over some planking to the double door out.

'That's nuts,' I said. 'You can't predict events in time, for

God's sake. The facts', I said, musing, 'in space.'

'Unfortunately, old boy, the facts in space tell me that those in time have changed. The result being that the old values no longer hold and that the man we killed may have been part of what is now the dominant power structure.'

There was a tree in the street and he put his hand out and touched its bark, then held it hard as if to steady himself.

'We're in trouble, Geoff. Make no mistake about it. As I read it, we have assassinated the right-hand man of the new Italian orthodoxy. It's going to fall back on our heads and I don't see why it should on yours.'

'Nonsense. I'm in this with you to the end.'

16

In the days that followed I began to find the affair less and less funny. Perhaps, I thought, we ought to abscond, make it somehow back to the Regiment – now said to be fighting around Cortona – and take it from there. But we couldn't be certain that Jumbo and our other allies would still be with them. Besides, was Jumbo such an ally by this time? Rex wanted the whole matter cleared up here in Rome. He had got the bit between the teeth – as he put it – and wasn't going to let go till the course was done.

So while waiting for Dakesworth to contact us for the important appointment, we spent our time strolling through Rome. All the monuments and museums and churches. It was in doing so that we realised we were being followed. I think the conviction first came to us in the Piazza Navona, after a rather poor lunch on the square. But that we were being followed with ill intent only came to us a few days later.

I remember so well the mangy cat rubbing against Rex's ankles. He had on the usual humble canvas battle-dress gaiters and the cat was scratching its back against one of them and purring. We were just coming out from some ruins – made by another Caesar – and the yellow tufa was warmly lit by the late afternoon sun – what the men had called in the blue, 'the good old currant bun'. Already someone had stuck a *Provi AJAX, Signora!* ad on one of these walls. It was just behind Rex's head. VICARIUS FILII DEI was inscribed in the brick, and the swallows of Rome swooped in the dying light. A pneumatic drill was going full blast in the road we were just about to join and effectively drowned out all sound. It was that which made it hard to identify the direction of the shot.

I had been trying to listen to the sound of some lovely cracked church bells above the din of the drill in the street when part of the wall cracked, smoked, right there behind Rex's head. We looked at each other and in that interval another invisible bird pecked a white hole in the mossy tufa and we hit the ground.

'For God's sake, what was that?' I asked, panting.

Neither of us knew. There was no one in the ruins. We had been the last visitors for the day, it seemed. The caretaker with the false nose and limp had disappeared. We had been fired on in broad daylight in a fairly crowded capital city. That much was certain. No one who has known lead passing his face in the turret of a Mark V Cruiser in the bled can doubt the sensation. So we clung to the rubble, feeling idiotic and not a little scared. Sniping was not our particular forte.

'Don't get up, Geoff. If we crawl towards that arch the angle will be different for that blighter. If he's using a window he won't have too much field of fire, anyway.'

'Christ!' I exclaimed, looking up at the hole in the plaster. 'He wasn't using a popgun.'

'Could have been a Walther. Probably some maniac. Elbows and knees now.'

I followed him, scrabbling along, and after the arch we were able to get up and climb over to what turned out to be a fairly busy street down which pedestrians and vehicles were passing unconcernedly.

To be shot at in the streets of Rome! What a crazy idea. So crazy that that night we decided to say nothing about it to a soul. Already our Intelligence friend, the reader of André Gide, seemed to have some doubts of our sanity. As I joked to Rex before we fell asleep – if we weren't careful the man would stick us in a loony bin somewhere.

'Perfect end to my war,' he said. 'Most fitting.'

He was snoring in a minute.

And God knows he may have been right, at that. In the days that followed our world at times seemed to come apart in our fingers. What was the point? I kept on telling myself that someone had fired on us, in the open streets of Rome. That seemed 'exact'. Then as the days passed, the memory paled. Perhaps we had been mistaken? And were we truly sure? I once suggested to Rex that it might have been some erratic ricochet from a shooting range nearby. Something of the sort, no doubt. Rex looked gloomy, in response. And we were to learn that it had been nothing of the sort, we were destined for death by someone not a million miles away.

For at the end of another week or more, since nothing had happened, we returned to the headquarters house in the Via Veneto. It had completely changed since our first visit. On the great rectilinear staircase someone had placed a ridiculously narrow red carpet. Workmen were complaining about it as we passed and complaining about the absence of spare parts too, I remember. What the spare parts were supposed to be for I do not recall. But the phrases stuck in my mind. All those spare parts. The whole of Rome, and no spare parts. Only all those 'works'.

And then we had the sensation – I know I did – of many more doors and odd rooms here and there, all half finished of course, nothing very certain and old-fashioned soft sofas herded into passageways, impeding the passing soldiery in an absurd fashion. A whole apparatus undesigned for these parts had been unleashed here. All these modern machines, the roneo machines, the typewriters, the filing cabinets, the files, the telephones. Dakesworth's office seemed simply to have disappeared. We could not understand it. It was not . . . where it had been.

So we began to give up hope, nobody seemed to know anything very much, but then on a third floor of potted plants as we began to retrace our steps, a flimsy door opened. We got a glimpse of a voluptuous woman, highly lipsticked and in a cartwheel hat, leaning back on a desk with her skirt round her thighs and laughing fit to die. At that moment our old friend the Intelligence Officer came out, holding a bunch of papers. He drew up short when he saw us, shot Rex a sharp look, then relaxed and smiled.

'Ah! Our good friends the tank corps officers. What a pleasant surprise, gentlemen. How glad I am to see you. All those partisans. Yes, yes, I haven't forgotten your affair.'

'Nor have we,' I said.

'We didn't hear from you at the Depot,' Rex said.

'The wheels of justice advance slowly, Captain.'

'Just so long as they advance justly.'

The man looked at us with expectant, shining eyes. He was at ease. We were not. I had less and less confidence in this consummate dummy. He closed the door behind him.

'It's still a little untidy in there,' he said, shutting out the vision of hot-house nylons, rustlingly crossed. 'We're not quite fully installed in there as yet.'

'Is there a chance of seeing General Orlando, Major?' Rex asked impatiently. 'That's what we'd like to know.'

'Really?' He paused. 'Really?'

His eyes creased, they seemed to watch us with a kind of malevolent, all-knowing triumph – like a parent watching some refractory children. 'Very well. Then perhaps I may be able to render you this small service. Would you do me the courtesy of waiting for me down below? Yes, by the entrance desk, if you please.' Lines crept around the edges of his eyes. 'I'll take you to see General Orlando, right away. Not to worry.'

He vanished back into the room with a laugh.

I hope I have been able to convey something of the unreality of the situation. In any case, the feeling was increasingly haunting us at the time – as it haunts me now. Frankly, it sustains, it makes possible, what I am to do now, what I have to do, directly I have completed these notes.

Major Dakesworth descended the staircase some five minutes later, cap on head and humming to himself. With a gesture he led us out and across a court to a garage. Here was his spanking new jeep, a much envied morsel of transportation at the time; I had actually been 'offered' one by a green GI in Tunis in exchange for a Mauser I had taken off a Jerry but it was not a good trade and I rightly declined it – the fellow would simply have reported it as a theft to his unit, and there'd have been all hell to pay. Now the Major's chauffeur got the jeep out and Rex and I climbed in the back.

'Yes, yes, don't worry. I'll introduce you to this famous Orlando of yours,' Dakesworth was clucking away to himself, swagger stick under his chin, as we drove slowly across a sunny Rome.

We said nothing. Rex sat with head in hand like some oriental god, or Rodin thinker. From time to time I caught a glimpse of the chauffeur's face in the rear-view mirror; Italian drivers use rear-view mirrors for rear views – of passing girls. Ours didn't. I remember being a little surprised by the thin wrinkles on the man's temples, the crow's-feet around the eyes. Usually such Orderly drivers were young, and he had looked young, at first, with a well-tended face, rather flat and shiny, quite untanned. Yes, like a face watching itself in a mirror, I thought of a sudden. Like a false face. Then I saw that of the Intelligence Officer. It rang a bell.

Now we were in some street apparently empty of anything but military vehicles and a lot of police about, too. I saw the Divisional signs on the tailboards of such transport and wondered at how many of them had been culled from the animal kingdom – the cat, the kangaroo, the rampant boar, the antelope, the rhino. It was quieter here, only the vague muezzin of some hopeless vendor's cries. The sun was a sword overhead and cropped urchins darted almost under the wheel of the jeep. Nothing was safe from those *scugnizz'*.

At last we parked in front of a building heavy with ornate iron bars. Dakesworth beckoned us through cool hallways, past green-uniformed officials of a type I had not seen before – the new Eytie Army, or museum guards? In a wide upstairs corridor some US MP stood guard, legginged, scarved, soft-footed. Big men. Heavy-bellied. Dakesworth showed a pass. Then through a set of double doors he led us into an ante-room full of photographic equipment. At that moment, indeed, an Eytie civvie with a very antique camera was blocking the way in front of us to the main room. We pushed in past him.

Inside, all the curtains were drawn. Artificial lighting poured from chandeliers and wall fixtures. The room was reminiscent of an early von Sternberg set. To me it was filled with corruption. The walls were hung with dusty damask, lurid with nudes. There were black frames and long tables. This ugliness was anonymous. It reminded me in a way of the Musso post office in Naples.

We entered preparing to salute the Minister of War but, standing just behind Rex, I realised that we saw no Orlando. Because he wasn't there. Instead, what the three of us stood staring at – under the baleful eyes of an MP guard – was a number of wrinkled splashes in mirrors and windows – somewhat similar to the lines about the eyes of the young-old driver who had brought us here and who was, in fact, lingering in a rather proprietary way by the door. An ornate chair was smashed, riddled by obviously close-up gunfire. One lordly pillar had been flayed by a burst from some automatic. Glass lay all over.

'Who did this?' Rex spoke in a sullen voice.

'Happened yesterday morning, it seems,' came back Dakesworth in an assured tone. 'We are still attempting to assemble all the evidence, obviously enough. Yes, yes, Commendatore,' he said to an Italian civilian who glanced in for permission to enter. 'Only don't touch anything, if you please.' To us he added, 'They still haven't taken off all the prints, though I doubt if there'll be much to help in that way.'

'Why not?' I asked.

'There just aren't the records available – with half the country still divided.'

'Holy Cat!' said Rex. 'What did the fuckers use in here? Must have had a couple of Skorps, at least.'

'Yes, you see, I was going to send for you two officers just as soon as a few further developments had been checked out.'

We had moved back somewhat instinctively towards the door. It was a very sinister palace and I, for one, would be glad to be out of it.

Rex's head came up, his mouth slightly ajar.

'Then General Orlando ... we can say he is no more?'

'How do we know? Who can tell anything these days? All we are sure of is that we are not calculating,' and Major Dakesworth limply grinned, 'very much on his being alive.'

'He wasn't killed here, you mean?' Rex inquired. We had seen no marks of blood in the room.

'We don't believe so, no. But he hasn't shown up. There are absolutely no personal traces. His apartment was apparently cleaned out lock, stock, and barrel.' He ran a finger under his collarband. 'In short, General Orlando is no more.'

Out by the jeep in the street again I sensed some complicity between the G3 and his driver – as if they shared a joke we two weren't in on.

'Who did this?' Rex repeated.

'Who knows? The whole of Italy's in shambles at the moment, as you well know, Captain. Situation snafu.' His pale eyes scurried over us searchingly for a second. 'Of course, you are aware of that if you really have come back from Bologna, ha! ha! The country's divided into a number of Allied Military Districts and each and every one of them seems to be growing its own private internecine feuds and vendettas. On top of all this, my office has been given the task now of relocating Italian prisoners repatriated from England. It's one hell of a headache. Our hands are completely full.'

'Then it looks as if ...'

'General Orlando was a Fascist?' The Major completed it for us. 'I suppose so. Linardi's lit out too, you see. Yes, yes, I don't know anything about this Cenedella you say you ... had some difficulty with. But I'm filing your report, it will pass through appropriate channels.'

'So we may take it the matter's closed?'

'Suspect so, yes. We're uncovering some pretty nasty things about friend Orlando during the German occupation. A lot of the archives we wanted to peruse are missing.' Buffing a fingernail, he stood there staring into the sky through whose royal blue a three-engined Savoia was gently nudging. 'The man we're really trying to contact is a certain General Benchivenga, who commanded the underground in Rome. Pretty busy linking up with the partisans at the moment, I gather. No, so far as I can see, this all lets you two gentlemen firmly off the hook – if that's what you're worried about.'

'All right, let's go,' said Rex abruptly.

The Major put us off just the other side of the Cavour bridge and we walked a bit in silence. We walked through Tomacelli to hit the Corso high up. The pavements were crowded at this hour of day and they hadn't got most of the chains up to keep the pedestrians off the roadways, so that there was this constant spill-off into the streets. A lot of horns sounding, too. There was always this pleasant loose informality at the end of a day in Rome, I found, with the trams honking their way through the vigorous, active Eytie crowds. So we sat down at a tin table of a caff' that was also a great-bellied cheese shop, just next to the P.B.S. Officers Club, and I knew the vision of that room – that murder-chamber – would be with me always. I have never liked shooting inside houses. We ordered wine-dark expressos and were happy to be able to dunk big bolts of sugar in them.

'Well, it's over, thank God,' I said.

'I wonder,' said Rex.

'What do you mean?'

'I didn't see his body, did you?'

'But it all hangs together, Rex. Orlando must have sent Cenedella on ahead and stayed behind to destroy the documents, leave no evidence of what they'd done behind. But then he was taken. He didn't get away quick enough. I've heard it's happening all the time. So what did he do? He deceived our G Intelligence into taking him for a firm Italian patriot. At which point word got through to the partisans. They tried to get him. Either they took him, or he escaped.'

'I wouldn't mind seeing that General of ours who was with him at Lucrezio's, just to make sure of all that, but I don't know if I have the courage to face all those typewriters again, Geoff.'

While he spoke I asked myself – and I do so again today – what was the magnetism this man held for me. For those passing by, I would imagine, what they saw was a rather run-down tank corps officer, no longer young, his face tired, sensual and intelligent all at once, the black-and-white mailed-fist patch of our Division on his right shoulder.

'Okay,' he said at last, tossing back the tiny cup. 'The world divides into facts.'

'Going to put that in your notebook tonight?'

'No, I don't think so. Though I could.' For a moment he shovelled sugar into his bitter, irregular mouth. Spicules caught on his moustaches and I thought he looked *real* – in the old sense of royal and he said something I shall never forget – 'It's become too sombre, Geoff.'

For a few more days we strolled the streets of The Eternal City. Neither Rex nor I knew quite what to do. In a General Hospital – No. 92 – I found a trooper who'd been blinded with our Regiment near Cerasola and we took turns in sitting by his bed and reading to him in the afternoons, but I knew we both felt lost, unmoored. St Peter's was still off limits in those days but Rex knew this Count attached to the Vatican and he let us in. We stood for a long time admiring the great bronze Baldachino and then the Sistine Chapel. But looking up at all those figures on the ceiling made me giddy. Rex had to help me out through the narrow stone passages.

No posting order came through for us. We were not wanted, it seemed. But our presence must have existed somewhere, on some sheet of paper, surely. We heard that south of Arezzo the Boche had deployed more than a whole new Division and, according to the rumours (mostly from men in 'dock', or hospital) it was a hard land for tanks. There was not enough space. It was even said that flame-throwers had been used by forward tanks, to clear a hill village where snipers were holding up an advance. The story filled us with horror. We had not even been trained in their use. I think it must have been a good week after seeing that shot-up room, where Orlando wasn't, that there was a second attempt on our lives. And this time there was no mistake about it.

One morning we finished some horribly sugary ice-cream in a caff' and walked through narrow streets we didn't know. More than once the black spider of the swastika writhed in charcoal on a wall. I was reminded of the Jerry armband I'd taken off a prisoner in Cap Bon and managed somehow to keep with me all this time. I'd used it for wrapping up my binoculars at night. It was not much more than a rag by now and I sometimes used it to buff up my boots. These days I had taken to looking at it with a sort of affection, so brazenly scarlet and black it was.

Well, we were in this little pagan street with the blistered shutters and small shops full of animated life, if not selling very much. There was a group of young men with dark curly hair and open-neck shirts at the foot of the street and I remember wondering why they weren't in uniform, as you got to with any young face at that time. They seemed to be watching us from under a broken lamppost.

Then Rex said, 'Hey, I wonder if good old Pentini could get us a pass to visit the catacombs. I've always wanted to. And the Sant'Urbano church.'

'What I'd like is to get the hell out of Rome,' I said. 'But whatever you want. We might as well.'

So Rex got the permit. How he did it I don't know. I think he could have wangled his way anywhere. Don Juan in Hell. In fact, only one of the five catacombs was fully open at the time, but Rex wished to visit the deepest, that of San Callisto. I knew nothing about those old tombs and corridors underneath Rome and did not feel much desire to repair the omission. Nevertheless, while Rex betook himself to his friend's flat near the Villa Borghese in search of yet another permit, I bought a much-thumbed second-hand guide at a stall and mugged up what I could from those famous authorities on subterranean Rome, Bazzi and Celda, while waiting for him at the cafe.

He took more than an hour and we set off, duly furnished with a pass, shortly after noon. You turned off the road down a rather shabby gravel path, passed a shed selling cheap mineral drinks and came to a gated entry. Also two tin WC's, as I recall. A moth-eaten and almost toothless old gardener appeared to be the only sentinel when we banged on the grille. He opened to the pass and, after a princely tip, locked behind us, and said he'd see us out. We only had to call for him, he'd be there. But he was too infirm to go down with us the whole way, so he sold us some candles – matches we had – and warned us against getting lost.

'Should have brought a flash,' Rex said, as we left the aged gardener at the first level.

Rex led the way with breaking matches, and a hand cupped to a candle. We moved slowly down the corridors honeycombed with hollows for the bodies – a few hollowed pathetically small, to house babies.

'What's this smell, Rex?' I asked him.

'The oubliette of the centuries,' he said, shading his candle.

I wasn't so sure. I knew the smell of death. There had been death here recently. The stench increased. The ceiling was now invisible.

'They didn't waste any space here, eh,' he was saying ahead of me. 'Economic, huh.'

I stumbled and swore. It was like being at the bottom of a big dustbin. Rex was too far ahead. I could barely see him.

'You can get lost in a dump like this,' I called. 'Hey, hold on a minute. That guide book said there were literally hundreds of kilometres of these passages under Rome.'

'Over here,' he called back urgently. 'Quick, Geoff.'

I plunged forward. But there was little light to see by. Rex had the candle, not me. And why was he laughing now? I passed the case of a Saint in what seemed to be very small pieces. And suddenly I remembered that tank at Bir Tella.

Yes, it was still a blinding memory. A year, two, a century ago? It was as present to me then, at any rate, as it would be to me all my life.

As usual, Recce Group had been alone, out in front, testing Jerry positions. We had stopped to take on water, I think it was, and while the REME boys were topping us up all over, I wandered off for the usual, with a spade.

After I had relieved myself – as the saying goes – I strolled over to what looked like, and was, the remains of an old A6, one of ours that must have really caught it. Not the first such relic we had passed in that advance but a singularly arresting one. I felt an urge to examine it before the sand covered it for good. Sometimes that happened quite soon. This time my heart beat quickened as I approached the wreck, it was such a raddled ruin. So grossly incongruous there. I gave a whistle as I jumped on what was left of the starboard sand shields; baking in that sun – the great machine was nothing but silence, a silence beyond death, the silence of these catacombs. Useless to wonder what had happened to the driver. I peered down into the shadowy turret.

At first, after the blaze of the blue, I could see nothing. It was all dark as a well. The driver's seat had been torn to bits. Then suddenly I saw the head. That was all there was. They had left the head. Or someone had. The Bedouins? I'd never forget it. *Nor* the old bone, some thin thing, yellowish, which Rex, when I caught up with him, persisted in holding to his face and light.

'For Chris' sake, put it back, old man,' I told him. 'At the very least you can get excommunicated for fiddling with these relics. They're holy, you see.'

He giggled.

'I stole it when the Duchess wasn't looking.'

I stared at him. What the hell was he talking about? Candlesmoke wreathed. I trod on a stone.

'They used to hold services here,' I whispered.

'Sacrifices, you mean?'

'It was the only place they had for them, Rex.'

'The communion's a sacrifice, isn't it? Read your Freud.'

'Who's he?'

'All right, they weren't allowed to hold them above ground. They still were sacrifices, chum.'

Suddenly under the candle I saw that what Rex was now holding, had somewhere unearthed, was an antique hunting horn of some sort. How lovingly it had been carved. Diminutive mermaids wound around the handle. Such care produced a toylike simplicity. A virginal slimness in the figure, adolescent articulations with the connivance of art, the charm of girlish forms, and boyish buttocks, and all dreams and longings and eternal atavistic springs ... no, it wasn't a bone at all.

'All this smoke. It's fusty in here,' he said.

He chuckled again and put the horn to his lips.

'Imagine being under the sentence of death,' he said.

As if we hadn't been. For so long.

I remember standing on that A6 and a few minutes later Rex had joined me ('Anything *wrong*, old boy?'). It was a *vanished* head, I do not know how else to describe it. There wasn't a single feature visible in that porridge of strawberry jam. I might have glimpsed something else that resembled, equally vaguely, a hand, but I didn't look too closely. That was all there was. I'm not an imaginative person, I suppose, but, in the life we had lived, imagination was hardly necessary. There were the facts in space. Most tank men would have been able to tell you what had happened. At the last minute, the ultimate moment, when the explosion had taken place within the tank, the Tannoy lines to driver and gunner had been ripped brutally backwards and thus had decapitated the commander. What was for us the fantastic element was the superstition with which the burial party must just have left that head, now royally covered in flies. They had not wanted to touch it, though they had doubtless delivered the body to the sands.

I was beginning to stifle in these catacombs. In the candlelight, in the smoke, Rex actually put the horn to his lips. Prepared to blow. What was it going to be? Yoicks? Tally-ho ... *loo on*? I remember thinking that in the writhing smokelight he resembled no more than a pagan priest.

'I hope to hell you know the way out,' I said thickly. Frankly, I was feeling dizzy again. It was a matter of getting to the main exit out before throwing up. I'm sure it was that smell. Of course, it might have been the severed head. That

that sort of butchery should become the manner of procedure of civilised governments – the German, the British – required a state of mind, an act of imagination inaccessible in the milieu of my boyhood, in the way I had been brought up. I suppose that's simply a House of Lords' way of saying that the end of a tradition was at hand, even without any humble assistance from me.

It was the high wall that saved us. Rex was beginning to pass by me to return to the opening. He staggered, gasping, seemed to stand still for a second and then the explosion resounded, echoing, through those nations of the dead and out up to invisible scraps of the untainted sky.

'Again! Get down!'

We couldn't hit the dust, all we could do was throw ourselves into the nearest graves, hug the walls there like lizards, while the echoes of ricochets went on for simply seconds.

I called to him, 'You hit?'

'No. I don't think so. But let's get to hell out of here.'

'All they need is one grenade.'

'I'll swear there's someone around who doesn't love us, Geoff,' he chuckled mordantly, then he must have put that damn horn to his lips again. A last nostalgic note, a challenging sound (eradicate me if you can!), went trembling towards Rome's tufa. We made it back in individual rushes and emerged to a stone-coloured sky, pebbled rose at its edges. I saw that Rex had his Luger in one hand. He shouted for the guardian of the place who came limping along, in old carpet slippers.

'Where is he?' Rex grabbed the man's throat.

'Who, Signore, who?'

'The one you let in after us, grandpa.'

'But I didn't let anyone in, sir. I swear to it, Signore. Impossible. Forbidden by order.'

His teeth chattered. Rex let him go.

'The only permit I had today was for you, Signore. From Count Aluffi-Pentini. One from Prince Umberto yesterday. That is all, Signore, I swear to you.'

'And of course you heard no explosion a moment ago?'

'No explosion, Signore. Well, maybe some sound. Underground is not clear. I hope you are not discommodated. The Germans left mines down there, you know, sir. Yes, against the partisans who utilised the catacombs. I meant to tell you to take very great attention.'

'Mines!' snarled Rex. 'Let's go, Geoff.'

On the way out I used one of the twin WC's. I thought the gated end of it was a possibility; a slim man, a boy, might just be able to squiggle under, and get inside.

When we got back to the Depot we again decided to say nothing about this second evident attempt on our lives. It would remain a secret between us, a mine that had been set off close and nearly killed us, during the war of the catacombs. We also decided formally to request our posting forward to the front the very next morning. There was a kind of obstinate *cafard,* a boredom, within this camp. We made an appointment to see the Major at midday.

But we were forestalled.

The next morning we were instructed by a Colour Sergeant to see the Major/Adjutant at figures oh-ten-three-oh.

I am sure that was the time. From this point on I want to be especially clear about things. A young subaltern on strength, with a cement face, came over to give us the instruction. Rex duly nodded, shaving. We would report in the Orderly Room – a Nissen hut – at the hour given. Which, by Drogheda time, meant five minutes before five minutes before.

The prefabricated and insularly English construction stuck up insolently in one corner of the camp. There were the usual groups of soldiers standing around, the non-comms barking orders, and then a military jeep – I saw from its flash that it belonged to our MPs.

We went inside the hut and saluted.

The Adj got up with a concerned expression on his face. He came round the corner of his table, with its IN trays, its OUT trays, very slowly – almost in slow motion. At the same time a man I hadn't seen before rose from a wicker chair behind us.

He did so with assurance. A Captain, I noticed, a man with a cruel, clean-shaven face and the red band of the Military Police around his cap. I remember thinking I'd almost never seen MP officers in our Army (the Yanks were stiff with them) ... Sergeants, Corporals, all the NCO's, yes – but never an officer. Here was one. He didn't salute.

'Captain Davidson, R.?' he asked.

'Guilty,' grinned Rex.

The man then named my name and I acknowledged it. I wondered what role officer MPs took in that infamous 'Glass House', or military prison, in Aldershot, a relic from another century, it seemed, where only the very hardened cases were sent; not only were the inmates brutally caned there, but evidently all chores had to be done at the double, so that a visitor might see a brass rail being polished by a soldier running beside it – running to drop the Brasso on, running to polish it off. In any case, the summons was for me too, no doubt about it. His fish-eyes never left our faces.

'It is my duty,' he said slowly, and with a certain satisfaction, I felt, 'to put both of you under close arrest.'

There was dead silence in the room.

According to King's Regs there was arrest and there was close arrest. The latter was far more serious and only employed in exceptional circumstances.

The Major goggled uncomfortably. I looked at him with loathing.

'Say that again,' said Rex softly. His head had gone back and he was watching the other sleepily. 'Say it slowly, old boy. I'm a little hard of hearing.'

Now we had all heard of those very rare occasions when one of His Majesty's officers on active service had been put under close arrest, but frankly I'd thought most of these cases fictitious. Certainly no officer in the Droghedas had ever been so treated. For this reason I began to sense the unreality streaming through me throughout this scene. It just wasn't happening.

But it was.

'You are both under close arrest. Committal papers have

been given to your Adjutant. I am acting under orders of M.M.I.A.'

'Who the hell are they?' said Rex.

'Military Mission to the Italian Army.'

'I'm not in the Italian Army, chum.'

'In co-operation with J.A.G.'

'Who are they?'

'You'll find out,' said the MP officer curtly. 'In the meantime, get your things and come with me.'

17

Peasants rode mules in those hard hills. Through the bars of my window I could see a birdless land, beaten by sun. One deserted road, going nowhere, a few dun downs, very silent and still. The usual hill terracing and some occasional embittered Eytie peasantry about.

The base itself, however, was all order. A number of gravel roads ran at right angles. There were frame huts, well guarded, and a prosperous car park, shimmering with military pedigree of the day. Cactus shadow-boxed along the face-stone wall in front of my window.

We were, so I understood, a little more than thirty miles north-east of Rome. It was hard to be more precise since this camp where we had been guarded all these months was sort of in the midst of nothing very much at all. It was not very large and we were the prize tenants, it appeared; they certainly looked after us very well. The place had been taken over by J.A.G, in fact.

'What's J.A.G?' Rex had again asked the MP officer in the jeep who took us there.

'Judge Advocate General,' came the curt reply.

'What's that?'

'Chief legal division of C.M.F.'

'Can you tell us what the charges are?'

'You'll be charged,' was all he said.

'Yes but for what?' I chimed in from behind.

'There's a new Commandant,' was the only answer I got to that one. 'He may take a little time. He's not used to our ways here.'

'And you? Can't you tell us?'

'How could I do that? It's quite impossible. I can neither help nor hinder you.'

When we arrived we settled down to a long captivity. We both knew the tergiversations of Army bureaucracy.

But no more than two days later we were summoned to the camp's central Orderly Room and arraigned in front of a J.A.G. Colonel, plus two US staff officers, for some reason. The charge was that we had on our own confession murdered, or been accomplice to the murder of, a partisan officer in General Benchivenga's underground resistance movement. Actually, like all such arraignments in the Army (at least in ours), I think they got about a couple of dozen counts each out of the matter – deserting, intention to incite to desertion, the like – it got boring after a while. The whole thing was such an Alice-in-Wonderland world that for the life of me I couldn't see light for a week. That was when the man from Texas came.

You see, when you take an officer into close arrest in the British Army you are involved in little more than a formality. An officer has to make the arrest and be present with you throughout, that's all. A mere Second Lieutenant or Ensign can be detailed to take – should it ever happen – a full Colonel into close arrest, but out of courtesy such would not be done. There are no cuffs, no searching, or even heavily locked doors. None of the apparatus of prison as is the fate for Other Ranks. It is assumed that the officer will stay put – in his own interest. King's Regs simply prescribe for a fellow-officer, of some kind, to be continually in company with the accused. The reason for the bars on my window was that this wing of the building had once been used for certain mental patients, chaps who'd gone round the bend in service. The bars were not to keep me in. In fact, I could walk out of my room at any time, down the hall, and into the similar room that Rex occupied further down the corridor. However, there was always a young officer sitting reading at a table in that hall. He read thrillers, chiefly. And of course I could not walk out of the camp itself without him. Besides, there was nowhere to go. It was all explained to us by the Texan.

Major Woodward was a mild-mannered man of close on fifty, silver-haired and with those rimless pince-nez I always somehow envisage as American. In peace he had evidently taught international law at Stanford. That sort of man. I could see him in tweeds smoking a pipe. He impressed us at once. He was to be our advocate, our defence attorney throughout.

Actually I remember that he lit a cigarette and sat on the edge of the bed in Rex's sunny room and came to the point at once.

'Look. I've been assigned to your case, but you don't have to have me. J.A.G. is a joint Anglo–US thing. They're getting ready for the prosecution of war criminals and the like. That's how they got mixed up in this Benchivenga business. J.A.G. is committed to prosecuting your case. But, if you wish, you can call on a non-combatant officer of your Regiment for your defence.'

'I don't know any non-combatant officer in our Regiment,' said Rex. 'Besides, I don't want them mixed up in this muck. My Regiment has nothing to reproach me for.'

'The President of your Court Martial has to nominate someone to defend you. I got my law degree from Columbia and I was working on a book in precisely this area when the war broke out ...'

'Which area?' Rex growled.

'Political assassination,' said Major Woodward calmly, glancing through a sheaf of notes.

We let that lie in the air. I think we both liked this man from the start. We felt we could trust him.

'I'm interested in your case,' he said.

'So are we,' I said.

'Our case is this,' Rex said. 'I shot a Fascist swine and I didn't shoot him through the back of the head, either. I'm not ashamed of what I've done. I saw an order for his execution from this same underground movement you talk about.'

'Unfortunately, we don't have that order, Captain Davidson.'

'I saw it. It was signed. By Principe del Giudice.'

The Texan drew on his cigarette. He looked out of the window. Orderlies were walking briskly about in the sun, file folders in their hands. A fattish British officer was parking his bike in a rack.

'There is no such person, Captain,' came the reply. 'He does not exist.' There was a silence, then he went on, 'As you know, Giudice means judge in Italian. There are hundreds of Giudices in this country, a couple of pages of them in the Rome telephone book alone. But there is no Prince of that name.'

'The Italians are given to titles,' I suggested.

'Not to Princes. There is Prince Umberto and that's that. No, I'm pretty sure it was a sort of partisan pun and you two didn't catch it.'

'Cenedella was a beast. I know a swine when I see one,' Rex persisted. 'I caused him to disappear. I rubbed him out. A human louse.'

The Major shook his head ruefully.

'I'm afraid that doesn't accord with the facts.'

'What are the facts?'

'Do you want me to take your case?'

Rex looked at me. I nodded.

'We'd be grateful,' said Rex.

'Very well, then,' the other continued in his homely way. 'I'll do the very best I can for you. There's only one prerequisite. I require from you two gentlemen that you tell me at all times the entire truth.'

'I never lie,' said Rex contemptuously.

'That goes for me, too,' I said. 'We have nothing to hide.'

'Good. In any event, there is this deposition you made to that G3 in Intelligence in Rome, Major Dakesworth. You can hardly go back on that.'

'We don't intend to,' I said. 'It was the truth.'

'Let's get Dakesworth here, damn him,' snapped Rex.

'Unfortunately, that's impossible. He's gone.'

'Gone?'

'No longer ... with us. In short, gentlemen, he has joined the majority.'

I must say neither Rex nor I was used to American death

euphemisms and it took a moment for it to sink in that Dakesworth was no more.

'What the hell happened to him?' said Rex.

'Heart attack. Very sudden. Died before they got him to hospital, I hear.'

'That's ridiculous,' I said. 'He wasn't an old man.'

'Whether he was old or not I don't know. And in any case it doesn't matter,' went on our new-found advocate. 'Your deposition was already in the files. Dakesworth couldn't have altered the price of fish for you two. Besides, any claim that you fired in self-defence has to be out of the question, not only by virtue of what you said but owing to the fact that Captain Davidson fired so many shots.'

He paused to look out the window again and I think we both felt he was completely in our corner.

'All right,' said Rex, the worry-beads slipping through his fingers, 'what is the situation? Shoot.'

The man from Texas smiled.

'Just this. General Cenedella was a double agent. It is thought that he may have gone up north for any one of a number of reasons – perhaps to go underground and help organise further resistance among the partisans there, directly Rome fell. He would have known that the Germans had plans to pull back fairly far north at once. And it is now believed that he took with him important War Ministry archives. Apparently he gave out that he had some pressing negotiations in the north, such as would take him out of Rome for a week or so.'

'But that means that Orlando would have got to know of this in a matter of time, in any case.'

Major Woodward smiled from his perch on Rex's cot.

'Orlando was having his suspicions already. But he was pretty busy himself. Rome was almost encircled, the Allies near Tivoli, oh he had his hands full, all right. And by the time he'd found out, Cenedella would have been underground.'

'But this is fantastic,' I said. 'We saw him surrounded by Fascist brass.'

'And why not, Lieutenant? He hadn't shown his hand by then.'

'So our friends the partisans,' Rex said solemnly, 'chopped down one of their own chief men. I've seen that happen in action, but the way it works out here, it seems highly unlikely to me.'

But the Texan Major was still smiling. His pince-nez twinkled.

'Cenedella was not one of their chief men at all, Captain. You don't seem to follow me.'

'Me neither,' I said.

'Cenedella was working closely with *our* Intelligence – in particular, with some agents in Sardinia. That cell of partisans near Bologna which contacted you was completely independent. They knew nothing about him at all except that he was a respected member of the Fascist Ministry. It was naturally in Cenedella's interest to maintain the integrity of that role. No, tragic but true. You stand accused of the murder of Cenedella on your own word, and you' – he pointed to me – 'of being accomplice to that murder. It seems that the new establishment, responsible to Benchivenga and the monarch, consider Cenedella to have been one of their heroes. They are formally insisting on the full prosecution of his death. It is part of their – shall I say? – mystique.'

'What's that?' said Rex, but he got no answer.

A tide of black bile was rising up my gorge. I stared out the barred window into the sun. Surely there was some clarity there. This was all so absurd and impossible, but somehow it was one with the ineluctable logic that had changed our lives since landing in Italy, and lately tightened its hold about our very steps. The trap was closing. I thought of Tich and Whitey and of the sombre silhouette of Edwardson, erect in the turret of his tank and getting off that final shot with the one hand left to him.

'This is going to be a slow business, I'm afraid, gentlemen.' The Texan rose to his feet. I found his accent picturesque, redolent of old movies seen as a schoolboy. 'In your case all papers will have to be referred to London for approval. It may take months.'

'That would give you some chance to pick up a witness,' I said.

He shot me a look.

'Precisely, Lieutenant. That's the whole trouble with your case. Witnesses. Indeed I am actually going to argue that it isn't a legal situation at all, since you are your own accusers, and we have no chance of finding witnesses.'

'There was that dwarf,' said Rex. 'Not everyone in Italy is a dwarf. Plus that the poor bastard had his face practically puffed double by that dicky tooth.'

Major Woodward seized on this. He began scribbling hard.

'Toothache, you say. Now that's interesting. Someone in that situation would have had to consult a dentist. Tell me what you know.'

'An impacted wisdom, in my opinion,' Rex said, and we told him what we knew, but I had the feeling it wouldn't help.

'The longer I can spin this out the better for you,' said our attorney finally, as he folded up his notes. He smiled in a kindly way, his glasses winking. 'For the time being the Germans have formed another line and are holding us there. The Normandy landings have taken higher command's interest off Italy a bit - certainly that of Churchill. The Germans have most of the Arno valley well registered by their guns now, but there'll be another breakthrough one day, and if we can only find someone ... anyone. The trouble is, Benchivenga is really burned up about this.'

'Burned up?'

Major Woodward gave a watery smile.

'I suppose it's an American expression. Sorry. But I mean that Benchivenga's furious. Yes, directly the underground people got a report rumouring that Cenedella had been killed, in corroboration of your story, they started putting every possible pressure on us to prosecute the matter. As fast as possible. It's a matter of urgent policy for them right now. The Italian Army is being resuscitated, several units of them have already been sent northwards. Oh, mostly on digging missions and the like. But news of this will encourage more

Italian desertions behind the Germans' backs. And creation of Cenedella as a hero is essential to their new image. If they could secure a conviction of you two, it would add enormously to their "face". They'd feel ... well, that they were in charge of things again."

'I see,' I said.

Rex said nothing. There was the rattle of distant m-g fire. This time almost certainly from some range.

'I don't have to tell you, Captain Davidson, that there are plenty of monarchists about, and they'd be more than happy to be able to turn this to the advantage of the King.'

'Long live the King,' said Rex in a sarcastic tone. He seemed to be smiling to himself as he crossed to the barred window and looked out. How old he seemed, how tired. Something had drained his spirit. How useless for such a man to try to justify his life in these new terms, I thought. We had been well and truly trapped – yes, by our honour.

'Well, everything has to come to an end, Major,' he said. 'It seems we just backed the wrong horse.'

'We couldn't have backed any other,' I said heatedly.

'No, but a soldier, a fighting man,' he went on, 'someone in combat ought to be able to anticipate events. It's a sort of curiosity, really. We are deeply grateful to you, Major, for taking on our case but I'm sure you know what I mean. The mind has to stay elastic. It's a matter of reaction time. I had it in the desert. Everything was simple there. A child's colouring book, really. Here, I no longer know. Something's been missing since the start of things.'

'We were ordered to kill, and we killed,' I said.

But the attorney was watching Rex. Watching him with that kindly smile, and a sort of strange complicity, maybe.

'It wasn't just that, Geoff. We lost touch, old boy. I mean, of the standards – from which events originate. We ... *let go.*'

And I knew what Rex was trying to say. We had been haunted by the mood since Salerno. Poor Clara had been my only sanity since then. It was like two men going up an increasingly steeper flight of stairs, always hoping to find a landing, a resting stage, then finding it – only to discover it was no more than a turn in the endless stair and that one had to move ever more wearily on. On and on.

'Don't worry,' Rex was saying to the Major now. 'We won't give you any trouble. But just supposing things don't go so right. Let's say, if we can't find any witnesses, I mean. And that crowd you mention manage to push this thing through – for the glory of the new Italy, so on. Well then, what's the worst that could happen? Look to the end of the tunnel for us a moment, huh?'

The slender, scholarly Texan drew back his shoulders by the door. His face went solemn and a steely light flashed like fire from his specs.

'In that case, the Court – as presently constituted, that is, and I intend to make certain objections about that, too ...'

'Come to the point, Major.'

The other paused.

'Well then, the Court would have the right, as presently constituted, to demand of you, Captain Davidson, and of your accomplice ... the highest penalty.'

Rex's lion head went back. It was as if he were suddenly searching for some purer form of air. But at the same time that wickedly suggestive smile of his, with its sybaritic dimple, appeared like a scar on his face.

'Death, you mean?'

'By firing squad,' was the answer.

18

At times we walked through the fields to the road. There was a scruffy track on the ground heated by that sun of July. It wound beside the terraced fields down to two villages. We never went so far as the villages. An officer always came with us and when we came in hailing distance of those houses he said it was time to go back. And so we did.

Rex liked to stroll outside the camp these days, and go by the vineyards where the peasants were pruning and the dark grapes grew heavy on leaves. There he would look at the distant lake, steel grey at twilight. Our food was copious if boring, we were not allowed even beer, but a Red Cross van came up now and then with books. Different officers relieved each other on the twenty-four-hour guard. One of them had on the cherry-coloured trousers of the Hussars and we remembered the valiant Second in the desert. But this spindly fellow had been at Sandhurst at the time, training. There was no one with whom we could chat about the blue, it was as if those days had never been.

Major Woodward came to see us from time to time. He gave us the latest news on our case, which was really dragging along these days, and he left the latest Eighth Army newspapers with us. Actually, they said nothing about the fighting, but the Texan told us progress was slow. Shortly after mid-July, however, good news came through. Ancona and Livorno had both been taken. The Jerry front had been cracked once more and Florence was menaced.

We should have been excited, but the days passed so slowly for us, in that sunny encampment with its shiny barbed wire. We got out some maps. The Germans would certainly make use of the Chianti hills. The good old 'soft underbelly' of the

Axis would still prove tougher than they'd expected. Someone told us our Regiment was straddling Route 69. The Gothic Line looked like staying solid to us for several months, and that would be frankly all we'd need. It would be all up with us soon.

'They're really putting some pressure on J.A.G. to get this Court Martial going,' said the Texan one day, with his sad professional smile. 'Land Forces Sub-Commission, Allied Commission. Under our own Rear Admiral Ellery Stone, you know.'

'They're after our hide, you mean?' said Rex.

'Not exactly. Stone's not the vindictive sort. But there's little sympathy for you on the Via Veneto. They're reforming the Carabinieri and a finding against you would be a boost for their morale. What with all these political liberations in Sicily, the Communists coming in like that at Palermo ...'

He continued to talk away. By this time I had become quite resigned, it was almost as if I no longer cared. In any event, I was having more of these dizzy spells and often had difficulty in following him. It was all so complicated and, in a sense, irrevocable. We had done what we had done, in good faith, and that was all there was to it.

'Yes, they're making the partisans out to be the real saviours of Italy,' he went on. 'And the new army doesn't want them usurping their role.'

'Do you remember that old General Maletti?' Rex asked me. 'There was a valiant Italian for you.'

'Who was he?' said Major Woodward vaguely.

'Died firing his automatic out of his own tent at Acroma. Badly wounded beforehand.'

The man from Texas closed his notes. He had not seen the flash of shot japanning the horizon, the snub short-barrelled seventy-five pointing from a wadi to get you.

And it became like this. We had ... *lost interest.* And when, a week later, we were told that there was a Drogheda officer to see us, Rex refused to see him. I went in his stead.

It turned out to be a senior officer from Headquarters in London. I did not know him. He appeared extremely anxious and talked in a low tone, as if to a dead man already. His eyes were heavily wrinkled as indeed was his whole face, which looked as if it had just been pushed up hard against chickenwire. His expression was hesitant, to say the least. Well, I suppose priests look in much the same way at condemned men whom they have to visit.

I think the part of the charge that upset him most was that for 'behaviour unbecoming to an officer and a gentleman'. This was the commonest one against an officer in King's Regulations. I would have thought it somewhat redundant in the phrasing but there must have been some dusty forensic logic to it. There were wags these days who referred to themselves as 'officers and temporary gentlemen', and a lot of them were right.

Anyway Rex hadn't wanted to see him because our affair had apparently become a sort of shame to the Reg – however it should turn out. This HQ wallah was doing his best to mitigate that feeling on our part. He had come out on a kind of paternalistic mission. If there was any way the Regiment could help us ... one of their most respected sons ... etc., etc.

I could just see him in those carpeted rooms at Wilton Crescent where they barely knew my name and for whom Rex had long ago become no more than a cypher on a pay sheet. Rotten luck that this had happened to the Droghedas, of course. Hard cheese, old man, hard cheese. My visitor sighed. He would have liked so much to have had a word with this Captain Davidson. He was 'indisposed', I told him. I didn't mention piles. Well, the poor fellow shook his head. In living memory there had never been anything quite like this. I gave him a comforting pat on the back as he left.

That evening, while the officer on guard in the passage read Graham Greene, Rex's voice lowered in his room – tired, dream-ridden, lost, like a sound dying among vast spaces. He began talking of his daughter.

'She took after her mother ... colour of the eyes, and all.'

'You realise, Rex,' I said awkwardly, 'for a long time I never even knew you were married.'

'Mrs. Davidson was ... how shall I put it? ... a passionate

person. She had her struggles too, you know. Dead now, of course.'

'A long time ago?'

'She deceived me, Geoff.'

He closed his eyes, blind Samson, and I began to understand something in him I had never really known.

'How could I have left the child?' he went on thickly. 'There were times when that was all I held onto. Half my pay is sent to her each month, to pay up the insurance.'

'And yet you can't have seen her ... in so long.'

Something happened then that I would like to forget. Rex's tanned face turned red, under his now white hair. At the corners of his half-shut eyes I saw tears forming. I quickly looked away.

'It's not a sin to love one's child, is it?' he said, adding, 'She always took her mother's side.'

I heard a strangled sob and wished I hadn't. Coming from a man like Rex, whose life had been the facts in space, it was the equivalent of a roaring cry. I knew what he was going to ask of me, then. I don't know why I knew, but I did.

'You've been a good friend to me, Geoff, and I don't want you sharing my guilt in this business.'

'If I am a friend, I am just as guilty as you can be, Rex.'

'You won't fail me, I know. You never have. You'll do what I ask you to. It's been a good innings but my time is up. I've felt it here more and more. That child took after me in more ways than by the colour of the eyes. I haven't the courage myself ...'

'You have courage enough for a regiment,' I told him, but I did so despairingly.

He was giving me the secret of his heart.

Outside, in the corridor, the officer yawned over his thriller. I didn't blame him. The facts in space were so very much more frightening.

Rex put a hand on my shoulder. 'When this damn thing is over and done with,' he said, 'there'll be the girl, you see. *I adore her, old boy.* I can't think of never seeing her again. She's the only one who remembers ... who loved my wife, too.'

Silence then. Silence of the tomb, indeed. And despite all we had gone through together, a feeling of loneliness overcame me. Rex was taking himself away. I had felt it lately, and I could not bear it.

'She's over there?' I asked, trying to sound nonchalant.

'Well, in the Argentine, yes. I haven't seen her since the separation, you see. Her mother took her with her. But everything I've done – if I have done anything – it's been for her. And I'm not talking about money, though God knows that hasn't been easy, on our pay. The insurance, always that insurance. The agent has been looking after it. He keeps in touch with her and will hand over everything to her in good order when the time comes. I have confidence in him. Name of Bringas, Buenos Aires. Everything's arranged. When I shove off ...'

'We'll find a way out,' I cut in, revolted.

'No. They've got me, Geoff. This has been coming a long time, somehow. But she'll have plenty to live on. I've seen to that.' He was quiet a moment, then, biting his lips, he sobbed out, 'Too late, too late.' And then he said something terrible – 'After all, I couldn't ask anyone else to do it, could I?'

Then it was I saw the Luger. He had managed to keep it. They had not searched us, though they might have. From the first they had reposed a certain confidence in our being officers. It was like that in those days, and one did not betray the trust.

So in the dying day I took the little Luger which he extended to me and I slipped it in a trouser pocket. The officer in the corridor barely lifted his eyes as I walked out past him towards my own room. My eyes were full and I seemed to have to feel my way. This man who had been so much to me ... no, no, it was impossible, he couldn't ask this of me.

To start off with, I told myself it wouldn't be necessary. Something would come up. I could give him some hope of that. I did my best to do so.

When July turned into August there was fighting reported in the outskirts of Florence. Bloody battles were taking place along the Arno and they said it would be another month before the Gothic Linę would be broken. We could well believe it.

Meanwhile, our situation worsened. A new President was assigned to our case, a Brit lawyer who had been a vigorous prosecutor for the Crown in peacetime, a Colonel in J.A.G. The Texan told us he didn't like the man who was clearly out to gain promotion at our expense, that is by getting our scalps.

'If only we could find that woman who was with Cenedella in the restaurant,' Major Woodward said to us one day.

Rex lounged on his bed.

'That bitch,' he said bitterly.

'Pretty, dark, well built.' The man from Texas diligently consulted his notes.

'In all the right places.'

'Full profile.'

'All the way down.'

Rex's cynicism didn't deceive me.

'We've checked the names of everyone in his entourage,' went on our advocate. 'The damn thing is, the only contacts we have with Bologna these days is via the partisans. That means we have to contact Benchivenga and his boys.'

'Who are out for our blood,' I put in.

'They certainly wouldn't lift a finger to help you,' said the Major.

'That's true,' said Rex, his head against the wall. 'Yes, yes.'

I was not feeling my best, it was as if I were riding some ocean swell, and then I heard the man from Texas say something that meant our case was really grave, and that little time was left us.

'I have an appointment with Sir Noel Charles on Friday,' he said quietly.

Sir Noel was the British Ambassador.

By mid-September our troops were drawing close to Rimini. But winter came soon in those mountains, growing ever higher to the Alps, and the Chleuh would try to play for time, what with what was going on in France. Jerry would hope to try to hold us down until our advance was enmired in the first rains, the first snows. He had abandoned Florence long since but his new front, hinged on the mountains of Verro and Battaglia, was still quite a way south of Bologna and it looked like remaining there. We knew his guns. The new V1s and V2s were falling on the south of England and I for one was not surprised when, one chilly evening in October, Major Woodward drove into the camp to announce to us the worst.

'We have a date,' he said, taking off his cap as he entered Rex's room. 'It's finally set. No more postponements, I fear.'

'When?' Rex was immobile as a statue.

'The nineteenth,' came the calm answer. 'In a little less than two weeks. That is, if my last objections to the constitution of the Court are not sustained.'

'They won't be,' said Rex. 'This has our number on it – as you Yanks say.'

He was not wrong.

So no quietus in a bare bodkin for us. The wheel of fate was turning too inexorably for that. According to all educated bets, our chances were very slim. The Court would sit in Rome, actually in the Via Veneto. The days during which Rex and I had lived in an absolute present were over, denatured, turned into worse than lies – into farce.

'No luck, eh.'

That was all Rex would concede.

Later, when the Texas Major had left us, I whispered:

'I can't do it, Rex.'

'You have to,' he said.

Imagine! He was talking about killing a fellow officer in cold blood. One I'd soldiered with through thick and thin.

And that is why I can't write any more about the matter and why I have somehow to finish this whole story of a strange man, a singular character, one who was important for me. I have tried to recount the events as they happened, I have tried to make a just recital. Now I must break off because tomorrow at oh-eight-hundred Major Woodward, from

Texas, is coming to take us to the Court Martial in Rome. Where we shall face our accusers.

But that won't happen, will it? Since at this very moment I am looking hard at a cocked Luger on my bed. Its safety catch is on, but can easily be released. I shall walk down the corridor, pass in front of the officer reading at the table, enter my old friend's room, and kill him at his request. That will leave one more round.

Nemesis had walked too quickly behind us since landing in this country, reducing all our actions to the absurd, making a mock of our lives. I would not kill myself, would I? I would simply kill my brother officer and then I myself would stay alive in order to give witness to the truth, especially about Rex, and the facts in space.

Under this vesperal Scottish evening, in this strange hospital at Duncanford, I see again the short squares of grass at the entrance to our compound. A jeep has just crossed the gravel to the park. They have put broken Eytie urns of the wall by this park; already these look sombre. The jeep is a particularly modern vehicle, its motor an almost intolerable mechanism. But for me that brutal sound is like the music of the spheres, expanding through the oceans of the heavens. And in their depths there reigns a crown of pearls.

I want to be merciful.

Towards myself as well as Rex.

19

They are hangin' Danny Deever, you must mark 'im to 'is
place,
For 'e shot a comrade sleepin' – you must look 'im in the face;
Nine 'undred of 'is county an' the regiment's disgrace,
While they're hangin' Danny Deever in the mornin'.

So ran Kipling's famous lines. And yes, it was the most unimaginable crime to have killed a fellow soldier. How often had it happened in the British Army?

My recital of the facts in space approaches its end. The director told me to try to write it all down, word by word. Besides, I am running out of loose-leaf books here. Even in Scotland there seem to be shortages these days. It is Cripps' England, all over.

And my account has not been composed, really, just a lot of words assembled together. They asked me when I came up in front of them for the first time here to imagine it all, and I'm not a very imaginative type. An Englishman of my background and education, entering military service as little more than a delayed adolescent not long out of one of those monastic British schools, does not often stumble into the events that I had encountered.

'Now, then, chaps, all together. On the knees, *down*!'

Bones creaked in the misty Lowland air. The squad in its navy shorts, brown canvas shoes, jerked like a set of sticks in the exercises. Beyond them green swards stretched obediently towards the river below. Heavy rhododendrons massed the flanks of the gravel drive, from which these decent lawns curved down. In the main buildings were lodged the administrative offices of the clinic, the director's suite facing the hills directly.

'One, two, one, two!'

In front of the squad stood a powerful man, the clinic director. Two sagging dewlaps on the hefty chest, a bull-neck, suggested a fit fifty. Major Peat believed in physical fitness as a prelude to mental, plenty of good fresh air.

'Give it hell now.'

On the caged porch an RAF officer detached himself from the group one end and came over to me.

'My name's Wilson. Got in last night. I see the Africa Star. What's yours?'

'I don't know,' I said.

'Psychosomatic or dry martini, eh. Well, I suppose one soon finds out.'

'On the feeet, *up*!' Dismissed, the squad trotted off. 'Inside for cold showers now. Last one in's a rotten egg. At the double there.'

'Here comes Major Peat,' I said to the newcomer. 'He's in charge here.' I could feel the officers on the porch stiffening. The big man came along the gravel path, his arms swinging. He was humming to himself.

'Morning, chaps. Feeling fit? Brigadier, Ankroyd, Teddy, Geoff?'

'Morning, sir ... fine, thanks, sir ... much better today, sir.'

'Good night's sleep, all of you? Done your beds? Set out your kits? Good, good.' His eye fell on the newly arrived RAF tunic. 'Let's see, you got in last night, didn't you? Name of Wilson, eh?'

'Yes, Major.'

I was aware of bulbous eyes, snub nose, blue veins cross-hatching porous cheeks.

'Well, we'll be seeing more of each other, Squadron-Leader. Don't let 'em get you down.'

A well-dressed Naval Commander came running round the building.

'Fisher?'

'I'm very sorry, sir.'

'You cut PT. We can't have that, Commander, can we?'

'No, sir. I overslept, sir.'

Major Peat frowned.

'No idle excuses here, mind.'

'The Orderly gave me an overdose of formaldehyde last night. I'd like to be taken off that formaldehyde, sir. It's not doing me any good.'

'I said, no excuses.'

'The treatment's wrong.'

The voice was almost pleading, desperate. Major Peat hit him on the back of the head. It could have been taken for a piece of friendly horseplay, but then it couldn't – the expert chop caused the Commander to stagger. No one on the porch moved.

Major Peat cleared his throat, gave one deep laugh, tapped the Commander on the back.

'Don't say that again, Frank.'

'No, sir. You're perfectly right, sir.'

'Be on parade tomorrow and we'll say no more about it, eh?'

'Thank you very much, sir.'

Major Peat threw an amused glance up at the group of us on the porch and we froze. 'Just goes to show, what, one daren't let you fellows out of here too soon.' He ticked, wagged a reproving finger. 'Possibility of relapse, slip back no end. I want everyone out for Physical Training except my celebrated band of shockers.'

Those of us on the porch were under insulin treatment. One started quaking with laughter.

Peat gave another booming laugh and strode away, his feet turned in. He made for the noble sweep of stone leading up to the clinic's main building. Pedimented, ornate, it might have been some Whig retreat, some *nid* of the eighteenth century. Balustraded wings ruled the beds, on which Major Peat, M.D., lavished so much care.

As the little group of insulin 'shockers' wandered back inside for their special breakfast, myself included, I felt my arm gripped.

'He hit him,' said the RAF man.

Someone among us said, 'Frank should have known better than that. He's been here some time. Went down in the *Penelope* do, in fact. He knows our Peat.'

'Wait a minute. He struck that man.'

'Playful clout. Peat runs this place. Peat and Levoutier, that is. Responsible for our papers, therapy, the admin business. They claim Duncanford's the best-run service nuthouse in England. Though as a matter of fact it's in Scotland. I suppose you knew?'

He passed in to a giggle. 'Remember Patton,' said another. Breakfast was ample. No knives were provided. After breakfast I tried to write again, to bring these notes to a conclusion.

I have said that in the British Army only one officer in hundreds of thousands ever gets put under close arrest. And of that number how many are charged with murder? So I try to imagine that young officer who was myself again, sitting on the side of his bed in that J.A.G. camp, holding a Luger as if it were infected. Everything had been 'agreed upon', the time (full daylight, please), the method, the aftermath.

So what happened?

On the appointed hour he had gone down the corridor, walked past the table where the officer doing guard duty was reading, and entered Rex's room. Naturally he couldn't fire. There was something so indestructible in the image of Rex waiting there, on a wooden chair, the worry-beads slipping through his fingers. Thus, after a moment's hesitation, the young officer who had received the best of British educations reached into his pocket and tossed the Luger on the bed. Without saying anything he returned to his own room.

Almost at once had come a knock at the door. Major Woodward had come in, close followed by a short, dapper Italian Army officer in high spirits. The man from Texas seemed to be in haste and I assumed it was some last-minute detail concerning the evidence I was shortly to have to give.

'Sit down,' said the expert on international law, drawing up a seat for himself and motioning the Italian to the bed, on which he sat beside me. 'I want you to pay particular attention to what I have to say, Lieutenant. This is of the greatest importance. I had to come at once.'

I think I said, 'Oh hell, what can you do now? Let's pack this in.' I glanced at the little epauletted Eytie beside me. 'Does your friend . . .?'

Major Woodward nodded impatiently. 'No, of course you can speak quite freely in front of us. In fact, that's the whole point.'

'Well, you know there's no way out now. You've said as much. We killed Cenedella and that's that.'

'No, you did not,' said the Italian.

'What the hell are you talking about?' I said crossly. 'What do you know about it?'

'Quite a bit, as a matter of fact, Tenente.'

'Such as?'

'I know quite well you didn't kill Cenedella,' he said with a smile, 'for the simple reason that I am that man.'

'You!' I started up.

Still smiling, the Italian also bounced up off the bed, saluted in a rather histrionic manner and came forward, taking off his gloves.

'General Cenedella, at your service, Tenente. I got back from Padua a few days ago. It wasn't too difficult, on the whole.'

There was a long silence, then I think I put my hand to my head.

'What is this?' I said to Woodward. I was feeling giddy again.

The man from Texas was grinning broadly.

'The truth,' he said.

'What truth?' I no longer knew what anything meant any more.

'Yes, that's right,' went on the Italian, resuming his seat on my bed and speaking with the same winning accent, 'you people seem to have got badly mixed up with our beloved Mafia. Orlando was too, of course. I knew that. But he was becoming suspicious of me at that moment also. It sounds very complicated, and I see you are confused, but it really was quite simple. He ... what is your American expression, Major?' He looked to the Texan for assistance, then got it. 'Ah yes, he *fingered* me. I went north on a so-called mission for the Ministry and he planted an assassination attempt on my person. Not too difficult these days. Leaked information through a stool-pigeon. You see, Orlando believed that if I was working for Allied Intelligence behind his back, that fact would not be known to our own partisans.' The Italian tapped out a slim cigarette. 'Very largely, it was not. No, Orlando was preparing to go over to the Allied cause directly Rome fell and he wanted to do so intact, topdog, with all the records destroyed.'

'Fortunately,' put in the man from Texas, 'General Cenedella saved quite a number of archives. They corroborate him a hundred times over. It was when Orlando found that those had disappeared that he must have become uneasy.'

The Italian grinned. 'Most uncomfortable, to be sure. However, not as uncomfortable as I myself was nearly made by his kind attentions. What happened was this: by a bit of good luck the leak got through to one of the few cell leaders who knew I was secretly working for them. That I wasn't a Fascist swine, about to flee the country for Switzerland, so forth. Well, this partisan leader was an ex-Sard, a Communist, he works with a fellow called Togliatti you may hear quite a bit about one day. Most intelligent chap. In my own interests he didn't want to give me away. So he sort of substituted a *fake* Cenedella. That is to say, he let the plan go through and then that couple of Bolognese toughs organised the rubbing-out of a singularly unnecessary and vicious Mafia crook, a *capo* who most of Sicily has been trying to get rid of for more than one generation.'

'And who'd probably have been given amnesty by Washington at the rate we're presently proceeding,' laughed Major Woodward.

The Italian nodded. 'Yes, it's remarkable how all you have to say in certain quarters these days is that you were against

Mussolini – and before you know it, you're in office.'

I stood trembling all over.

'What's wrong?' said Woodward. 'Anything wrong?'

'We were fired on in Rome.'

'You never told me that.'

'We never thought it was necessary or relevant to do so. It all seemed so weird anyway, you'd have probably thought we were going round the bend. And then a mine went off when we visited the catacombs.'

'The catacombs, a mine!' The Italian General seemed to rock himself into laughter. 'Yes, yes, the ways of our most honoured society are certainly devious. *Omertà*, all that. Absolute mutism. Amazing how complete deafness, blindness, amnesia overtake so many witnesses to murders in the Catania courts. It is extremely difficult to bring those *mafiosi* to trial. No, according to my information, they would be doing their best, Tenente, to give you a hard time.'

'I was just thinking,' I said. 'In the restaurant that gun of theirs jammed.'

'I find that very hard to believe. Fried Tomato knew too well how to look after himself for that to happen.'

'You speak of him in the past.'

The Italian lowered his eyes. 'The poor chap is dead now. No, I'm sure his gun was working. It was just that he wanted your friend Captain Davidson to be the assassin.'

'So … what? You mean, the whole thing …' I stumbled out the words.

Major Woodward was smiling broadly.

'Don't look so anxious, Lieutenant. The case is dropped. You're quite free now, you know.'

I hurled myself to the door. Too late. The detonation resounded – alarmingly loud – throughout the whole building, it seemed to me, as I ploughed down that passage. The officer on guard was already at the door, pale and frightened in appearance.

'I didn't know,' he was mumbling. 'How could I have known he had an arm?'

'Get out!' I shouted.

I entered first, but the other two were close behind me. The body had toppled back on the blankets, hurled down by the heavy explosion and the shot through the left temple while he was doubtless seated on the end of the bed. His right hand still held the Luger, as if with love or despair of love, the veins on the back of the hand nearly black with effort. Under the snow-white hair those imperial features I had known and loved so long were not disfigured in the least. They were, if anything, more striking than ever before, the chapped lips parted as if in some final sarcastic grin or ecstasy of peace, which he had finally found, by honour. The only concession to mortality was that wet red velvet pressing almost surgically through one temple. Although I had no cap on, I saluted. The Italian General followed suit and crossed himself. I picked up the worry-beads from the floor. Nothing to worry about now. Edwardson's end.

For a little while after that I did not know very much. Then they shipped me back here, to this decent civilised place run by Major Peat in Scotland. Male nurses wore white coats over battledress and we called ourselves 'The Nut Brigade' or 'The First Fruitcake Lancers' and suchlike.

Major Peat saw me the day after my arrival. There was a colonnaded entrance hall to the main building, under a sort of fluted dome, and behind a breasted desk a VAD typing amicably. His office was full of flowers and he came forward and shook my hand like a piston.

'Delighted to see you, old top. Now you won't find any trick-cyclist stuff here, I believe. No, no, trooper, what I'm going to give you is the proper authorised version, believe me.'

I was scheduled first for 'bathe-therapy' for two weeks. In the afternoons they wanted me to write, to put together as comprehensibly as I could this account ... of the facts in space. I did my best, though pushing the pen isn't exactly my forte, as you can see. It was an effort. Peat read parts of it as it went along. He sent for us all for 'interviews' from time to time. I came to dread them as much as once I had the sight of an eighty-eight.

Tapping his teeth with some spatula or probe, or maybe ice

tongs, he would tilt back his swivel chair and send me roguish winks across the desk.

'Now then, how's the great author coming? I like your last instalment a lot. Delusions, tricks, masks and imaginings I'm up to all of 'em, scout. Get it all out of yourself. Only, let's not make it too complicated, shall we, son.' His pencil provocatively protesting. 'I mean, this little dream of glory of yours, of operating with these Italian partisans behind the lines ... some of it beats the biscuit.'

We patients were given an option of 'therapy' tasks and I chose gardening. It was something that was real, at least. One morning the director had sent for flowers for his office and I was in fact clipping some daffs right under his window when I heard them talking. Them was Levoutier (he was the insulin expert) and Peat.

'Fantasies, hero-illusions,' I heard the latter chuckling in the summery room, 'at this point they're routine. But I think we're getting some focus. That dirty old swastika armband of his, for instance. Homo-erotic psychoneurosis, probably. All this stuff about having "executed" a said-to-be Fascist behind the lines in Italy, who was really working for the Allies *sub rosa* ... I tell you, it's a real rib-tickler. On D-Day, too. Can you imagine anything more phony?'

Levoutier said something incomprehensible and I went on cutting the daffs.

There is only one more incident to report.

We were allowed to have visitors on Sundays and I was surprised when they told me a young lady had come to see me. I straightened my tie, tugged down my battle-dress blouse, and went into the waiting-room. She stood up with the light behind her. She was in black, very thin and frail, and somehow I think I knew who she was from the moment I set eyes on her.

She held out her hand. 'I didn't telephone ahead, I wasn't sure whether you would wish to see me.' Her voice had a slight foreign accent to it. 'I'm Maria Davidson.'

'His ... daughter ...?'

'Yes.'

'Won't you sit down?' I said.

She sat down on the comfortable sofa and crossed her legs.

She was immensely pale with large dark eyes, dark nostrils, her face under a veil. There was absolutely no family resemblance I could see at all – only that unmistakable *allure*. My heart was beating fast.

'How did you know? You just arrived in this country?'

'From ... over there? Yes.' She made a motion. 'I found you through the regiment. After all, it was his.'

I said nothing for a while. Then – 'Did the agent look after everything properly for you, Miss Davidson?'

'Yes, thank you. You were his great friend, were you not?'

'His great friend.'

'I wanted to see someone who was, now that mother has died.'

'He saved up for you for years,' I said. 'An officer's pay in our army isn't very princely, I fear.'

'I'm quite all right. I just wanted to see someone who had been close to him.'

'I was close to him, Miss Davidson.' I shut my eyes a second. The room seemed to have darkened in some way. We spoke in undertones, furtive. 'I promised him to try to see you and to find out if everything was all right with you – in case anything happened to him.'

'I know he killed himself.'

'He was entirely innocent. The tribunal acquitted us both completely.'

'He was a remarkable man.' She was looking at me steadily.

'I thought so.'

'You were with him some time then, in the desert?'

'Some time. We got to know each other well.'

'I have all his letters.'

'Probably a few didn't get through,' I said. 'Those mail trucks got strafed, too. To say nothing of the submarines.'

I tried to laugh.

'He died as he lived,' she said then, intensely immobile.

'Thank God you said that.' I bent forward and took her hand and kissed it. 'Oh I am so glad you said that. Up here there's so little I can do for you, but when I get out ...'

'Yes, yes, I'd like to see you then. Do you have anything ... personal of his?'

'Yes, of course.' I took the necklace of *kombolai* out of my pocket and handed it to her. 'String's none too clean, I fear, but you know how it was out there.'

'Thank you.' She put it in her purse in a businesslike way. She stood up. I was glad she hadn't cried.

'The men,' I whispered then, 'all the soldiers, I mean, they had such respect for him. That man couldn't have made a mistake in a tank in the desert. Each one of his actions . . . well, that was his richness.'

Quite quietly, in that complete control of herself that her father had always had, and with that sureness of soul I had once seen in Clara, she said: 'What were his last words?'

'You wish to know?'

'Yes.'

'They may not make much sense.'

'To me I think they will.'

So instead of that old round I had dug out of his calf, and later found in his pants pocket, I took out of my battledress blouse that stained notebook I had taken off his body and I read out the last entry he had made before dying: '*The world divides into facts. Anyone can either be the case or not be the case, and everything else remain the same.*'

She listened, then nodded, as if at some familiar name, shook my hand and walked with sure steps towards the door.

But when she opened the door I flinched. I heard the roll of the gun limbers coming up, the men riding their cabs, and the first explosions of the minefields being cleared ahead . . . but of course it was only some civvie truck making a racket in the road below. All the same I did not go to the window, lest I might still hear them singing:

Look around the mountains, in the mud and rain –
You'll find the scattered crosses – there's some which have
  no name.
Heartbreak and toil and suffering gone,
The boys beneath them slumber on.
Those are the D-Day Dodgers who'll stay in Italee.

BETTER TIMES THAN THESE

BY WINSTON GROOM

The shattering classic novel of a dirty war

'Bravo' company, U.S. Seventh Cavalry. Raw recruits and ambitious commanders. Men with the tradition of General Custer and the Indian wars behind them. This is the story of another bloody chapter in American history: the battle of Ia Drang valley, and of the soldiers who fought there. But it is more than the story of those soldiers: it tells of the world – and the women – they left behind them, and of what happened when they came up against the horrors of combat. It shocks, horrifies, moves and enthralls – because it always tells the raw truth.

'A mirror of hell that leaves one awestruck'
NEW YORK TIMES

'A thoroughly realistic portrait of men at war . . . frightening . . . genuinely merits comparison with James Jones'
PUBLISHERS WEEKLY

WAR 0 7221 4100 9 £1.75

WAR STORY

BY GORDON McGILL

Berlin, April 1945.

The city – and Germany – is only hours away from final defeat. Deep in the underground passages of the burning city a four-man British unit is fighting a desperate battle against time. Its top-secret mission: to bring a German general back alive, whatever the cost. And to keep one step ahead of the advancing Russian army.

But why?

Find out in WAR STORY

IT'S THE WAR STORY TO END ALL WAR STORIES

WAR FICTION 0 7221 5901 3 £1.00

THE ELDORADO NETWORK

BY DEREK ROBINSON

1941. Hitler rampant. Spain neutral. Madrid the launching-pad for spies from each side.
One of the most audacious of these spies was codenamed 'Eldorado'. He had no right to survive, let alone succeed – he was far too young, inexperienced, and impetuous. Nevertheless he prospered and set up a network of agents whose information proved so valuable that it altered the course of the war. In the process, Eldorado made a lot of money. He also made a lot of very dangerous enemies. Soon the big question was: who would hit the target first? Would Eldorado turn himself into a millionaire before his enemies could turn him into a corpse?

THE ELDORADO NETWORK was inspired by the known facts about the daring and outrageous career of the 'Eldorado' who really existed.

'Spy thrillers usually leave me cold, but this one is plainly outstanding in its class'
GUARDIAN

FICTION/WAR 0 7221 7421 7 £1.50